APPRENTICE OF MAGIC

The Fairy Tale Enchantress Book 1

K. M. SHEA

APPRENTICE OF MAGIC

Cover Art by Deranged Doctor Design
Edited by Jeri Larsen

www.kmshea.com

ISBN: 978-1-950635-03-0

For all the Champions who stood by me, thank you.
We're finally here, and it's because of you.

MAP OF THE CONTINENT

CHAPTER 1

Angelique had magic, which normally meant she would be respected and honored. Unfortunately, she had too much of the *wrong* type of magic. At best, she was a liability. And at worst...

Angelique spared herself the pain of dwelling on the more unpleasant possibilities she presented and instead listlessly followed the two academy instructors who led her down a shadowy hallway.

A mage stood at the end of the passageway, guarding a giant door. The guard was a war mage—if the halberd she twirled with ease was any indication. She shifted her stance so she stood with the weapon extended in an attack position as they drew closer.

Maybe that's why they're so scared of me. They know the guards could never hurt me if I used my magic.

Angelique shoved the unwanted thought from her mind. If her teachers—never mind the Council—knew her dry musings, they'd seal her magic the moment she stepped through the door.

Madam Quarrellous ruffled her plum-purple cloak and peered at the guard. "I am Madam Quarrellous; this is my colleague

Master Gladio. We are here by the invitation of the Council to discuss a matter of grave importance."

The war mage peered past them, her eyes settling on Angelique. Her lower jaw dropped in a very unprofessional manner, so her mouth formed an O. "Angelique?" the guard asked.

My infamy has reached outside the academy, has it? Angelique pasted a lopsided grin on her face. "Unfortunately, yes."

Madam Quarrellous pinched her lips together until they were barely a thin line.

The war mage didn't seem to notice, for she offered Angelique a flicker of a smile before she leaned her halberd against the wall and started unlocking the charms that barred the door.

Master Gladio glanced back at Angelique long enough to raise a bushy gray eyebrow at her. "Behave," he warned her.

What do you think I'm going to do, engage in a sudden murder spree? Good thing you said something, because words *would definitely be enough to stop me.* Angelique wanted to scoff back at him, but he already eyed her warily as if she were a rabid wolf. She forced her smile to obediently straighten out. "Yes, Master Gladio."

When the door swung open, Madam Quarrellous swept inside, marching forward with—Angelique imagined—years of glee spurring her.

Today would likely mark the instructor's crowning achievement: she was finally booting Angelique from the Veneno Conclave—something she had heavily campaigned many years for. (Ever since the Academy had discovered how much magic Angelique possessed, really.)

Master Gladio stepped aside and motioned for Angelique to follow in Madam Quarrellous' wake. When she trailed after the female instructor, Master Gladio fell in step behind her, cutting off any escape route.

The Council—a committee of enchanters/enchantresses that represented the Veneno Conclave as a whole and made rulings, judgements, and laws on behalf of all magic users—met inside what was fondly called Hallowed Hall.

It was dark. The only light in the room fell in focused beams that haloed the three Lord Enchanters and three Lady Enchantresses who served on The Council. There was one extra ring of light that surrounded a raised platform hemmed in by wooden railings.

Madam Quarrellous made her way to that raised platform, the rich plum color of her cloak subdued under the onslaught of the bright light.

Angelique, several steps behind her, shivered in Hallowed Hall's chilly air. She squinted when she stepped into the bright light—which made it rather hard to see anything besides her instructors and the lit-up forms of the already-seated Council Members.

The chamber was stuffy in its silence—all noise seemingly muted by the power of the six Council Members seated at their raised desks. Angelique knew there was an audience in the darkness somewhere off to the left, but she couldn't hear more than the occasional shifting of a chair.

Master Gladio hesitated for a moment before snapping the wooden gate shut behind him, penning Angelique into the raised platform.

"Wise and venerated members of the Council." Madam Quarrellous curtsied and bowed her head. "I bring before you today a student of Luxi-Domus, Angelique, with the request that you would seal her, cutting her off from her dangerous magic—"

"Now, now, Madam Quarrellous," one enchanter called in a playful tone. "Let's not be hasty. Every type of magic could be considered 'dangerous' if one misuses it."

It took more squinting before Angelique could make out the large golden plaques placed before each enchanter and enchantress.

The Council Member who had spoken out was Lord

Enchanter Crest—the youngest of the Council Members. He appeared young, perhaps in his late thirties, but magic slowed the aging process and greatly lengthened the life expectancy of all enchanters and enchantresses. There was a chance he was old enough to be her grandfather, even though he had jet-black hair with a distinct blue haze to it.

Enchanter Crest leaned forward, his eyes lingering on Angelique. "You have war magic, do you not, Angelique?"

"Yes, Lord Enchanter," Angelique said, her voice huskier than usual. She blinked rapidly, afraid either the bright lights or the painful lump in her throat would soon make her cry.

When I first entered this school as a naïve child, I never thought I'd be going before the Council to be tried. Like a criminal. Defeat left a bitter taste in her mouth, but Angelique was so tired. Tired of all the suspicion she faced, tired of the whispers that dogged her every step no matter how she tried to prove she wouldn't hurt anyone, and tired of fighting what should have been a lie but was starting to feel like a truth.

"What strain of war magic is it?" Enchantress Primrose—a smiling enchantress with a round face and rosy cheeks—peered down at the papers strewn across her desk. "Was it...speed, or strength?"

"No, Lady Enchantress," Madam Quarrellous said distastefully. "Angelique has the ability to control anything with a sharp edge—arrows, swords, axes, every weapon you can think of."

"That's an uncommon strain of war magic to be sure, but we have several active mages with similar magic," Enchantress Primrose said.

"The problem does not only lie with the type of magic she has, but rather with the amount," Lady Enchantress Felicienne, a cold but elegant woman, spoke in an icy voice. "Angelique has more than enough magic to become an enchantress, does she not?"

"That is correct, Lady Enchantress," Madam Quarrellous said.

"The Veneno Conclave has never had an enchantress—or enchanter—with war magic," Enchanter Crest said as Lord Enchanter Tristisim passed him a packet of papers. "There has never been anyone with enough power to claim such a rank."

"Some might consider that a prodigious blessing," Enchantress Felicienne said unfeelingly. "War mages have their places in society—to guard and protect. A war enchantress..."

Enchantress Primrose tapped her chin. "Master Gladio, you instructed Angelique in some of her war magic classes, yes? What is your estimation of her power?"

Angelique turned with the Council Members to stare at her instructor. Any tiny spark of hope she had that he would speak favorably of her fizzled out when he avoided her gaze and stared at the railing.

"Angelique has gone through the base tests multiple times," he said. "Each time she passed the required levels of magic needed to be considered as an enchantress candidate...and every time she would also break the spell that did the measuring." He shifted his gaze to his hands. "We do not know for certain how deep her magic runs nor where her boundaries lie."

That caused a stir in the audience, creating ripples of hushed whispers.

Lord Enchanters and Lady Enchantresses were the top rank a magic user could achieve in the Veneno Conclave and were incredibly rare. Usually only one new magic user joined their ranks per generation. As such, normally Angelique's level of power would have given her unparalleled opportunity. But with her type of magic...

Yes, I'm practically a monster. But couldn't you have mentioned how reluctant I am to use my powers? Or that I have been a diligent student? Or even that I have good hygiene—anything *nice at all? I always tried so hard.*

Enchantress Felicienne's frown grew as she studied her papers. "It says in this report that due to the unusual amount of magic she possesses, it is estimated Angelique could destroy an army in a matter of minutes. Is that true, Master Gladio?"

Master Gladio bowed his head. "It is, Lady Enchantress."

"With the ability to manipulate weapons, the student's magic is truly only good for battle," Enchanter Tristisim said, his voice cracking like the shaking of thunder.

"But war magic is merely her core magic," Enchantress Primrose said. "As an enchantress, she would learn other spells."

"Which would all be powered by her ability to *kill*," Enchantress Felicienne said. "She is only eighteen, is she not? It seems unwise to leave such dangerous power in the hands of such a young girl."

Enchantress Galendra and Enchanter Lazare, the last two members of the Council, shifted their gazes between their fellows, following the conversation but keeping silent.

"Has Angelique undergone all ethics and integrity tests?" Enchanter Crest asked.

"She has, Lord Enchanter," Madam Quarrellous said.

"And?"

Madam Quarrellous glanced at Angelique, but Angelique was too defeated to care, and numbly stared at her feet.

"Though she has passed the tests, she has shown to have an alarming amount of willfulness. On numerous occasions, she has refused to participate in classroom magic exercises and complete assignments. Several examples of such refusals are recorded in the papers I gathered for you, but there are many more than I had time to list."

I refused because I didn't want to put anyone in danger! Angelique started to open her mouth to defend herself, to explain that she was reluctant to use her admittedly unsafe magic in a classroom full of other students whom she might accidentally harm. But why bother?

When Angelique first entered the academy, she had been a bright—*stupid*—young girl who didn't know any better and loved to show off the finesse with which she handled her magic. These days—though she was more learned and held back her magic with a stranglehold—her powers sometimes slipped her grasp when she wielded them. She was actually *worse* at casting magic now, as a student about to graduate, than she had been in her first year due to the potential inconsistency of her powers.

But explaining that will only further convince them I need to be sealed. And maybe they're right. If I really am a danger to those around me whenever I use my powers, could I ever be a force for good?

Angelique felt the cold, metallic sensation of her magic swirl around her arms. With a mental kick, she savagely shoved her magic away and barely kept a snarl off her face. *I hate my magic!*

Madam Quarrellous, unfortunately, had not yet finished. "Furthermore, she lacks friendships among her peers and is often alone. Given these habits, even if she passes ethics and integrity examinations today, that does not mean she will in a decade or two from now when she is a fully-fledged Lady Enchantress, able to kill armies in moments with no one to check her."

This accusation elicited another cloud of mutters from the invisible audience. Angelique only glanced in their direction, unable to see past the too-bright circle of light she stood in.

"It is the instructors' official recommendation to seal Angelique," Enchantress Felicienne said. "I believe we should follow their suggestion."

Enchanter Tristisim frowned in thought.

Enchantress Primrose cleared her throat. "Though her magic may be *dangerous*, I don't believe Angelique herself would willingly reject the oath of a magic user and harm anyone."

Angelique wanted to laugh. *What happened to not labeling my magic? Though I cannot blame her. I'm only good for destruction and devastation. My instructors taught me that much.*

Vaguely, she wondered if crying would help, but it was not likely. She was too...*stately* (to put it kindly) with her tall height, dark hair, and unforgiving silver eyes. (She'd heard her teachers describe her in whispers as appearing lethal, which, of course, did *wonders* to her confidence.)

Enchantress Felicienne did not look convinced, but Enchantress Galendra—who had been silent until now—cleared her throat. "That is certainly a kinder way to phrase it: it is not Angelique who is harmful, but her magic."

Her words sounded gentle, but Angelique flinched all the same. Her magic—however unwanted it was—was still part of her. Every accusation of her magic being dark was a reflection on *her*.

"Her magic has nothing to do with her rejection of instruction," Enchanter Tristisim said. "As both of you—Galendra and Primrose—are forced to admit, her magic is lethal and potentially hazardous."

"Or have you forgotten *our* oath to protect the people of the continent from magic?" Enchantress Felicienne asked.

Enchantress Primrose paused tellingly, and the unseen audience murmured once more.

It's over. Angelique could feel it in her bones. *The Veneno Conclave's first priority is to guard the people and keep them from harm. They can't risk leaving a monster like me unleashed. And I don't know that I disagree with them.*

Her shoulders slumped, and Angelique stared down at her hands, flexing them as hot tears of frustration pooled in her eyes.

Her blasted magic stirred at the emotion. Angelique clenched a hand, strangling the bit until it snuffed out like a candle.

Enchanter Crest drummed his fingers on his desk as Enchanter Tristisim scratched his thick gray beard.

"I make a motion to seal Angelique, containing her magic for her lifetime," Enchanter Tristisim said.

Enchanter Crest sighed. "I'm sorry, Angelique. I don't see how we can allow you to keep your magic. If there was someone who could teach you—who could assure us of your safety and those around you as you grew into your powers."

"Indeed," Enchantress Primrose appeared to wipe a tear from her eye. "But there are few equipped to handle one with your strength and..." She didn't have to finish. Angelique knew no one wanted to take her on as an apprentice, to train her in the ways of enchanters and enchantresses.

It was a heavy commitment—and not just because the average apprenticeship for enchanters and enchantresses lasted anywhere from ten to twenty years depending on the student. It was also because whatever damage she wrought in the future, her master would share the blame. And no one was willing to risk their career for someone like her.

"I am sorry, my dear," Enchantress Primrose continued. "I would train you myself if I could, but Council Members are forbidden from taking on apprentices."

Enchantress Felicienne folded her hands and placed them on the desk. "You are too kind, Primrose. I second Enchanter Tristisim's motion to seal the student. Call a vote."

Enchantress Primrose stood to record the vote, when a deep and melodic voice shattered the stuffy silence.

"Wait."

CHAPTER 2

The shifting of chairs and buzz of gossip thickened in the area where Angelique thought the audience was seated. She squinted, trying vainly to see through the light as the quiet tap of footsteps filled Hallowed Hall.

I didn't recognize that voice...but who would speak up for me if not Master Gladio—

Angelique's jaw dropped when her potential supporter effortlessly hopped over the wooden railing of the platform, joining her and her two instructors.

Though she had never met him before, she recognized him on sight. It was a Lord Enchanter who had stopped the proceeding, the famous Lord Enchanter Evariste of the Fire Gates, to be precise.

That explains the shock. Angelique stared dumbly at the Lord Enchanter as he joined her by the railing.

He winked at her, then raised his gaze to the Council. "I'll take Angelique on as my apprentice."

Enchantress Primrose gaped at him. "*Pardon?*" she squeaked.

"Both you and Enchanter Crest said you would consider leaving Angelique unsealed if a suitable enchanter could train her," Enchanter Evariste said. "I'm willing to take her on, and with my magic, I am more than capable of handling her training. Even if there are hiccups."

Primrose sat down, blinking rapidly.

Even Enchanter Crest seemed shocked. "Really?" he asked.

Evariste nodded.

"You will take responsibility for her future?" Enchantress Felicienne inquired, her voice dagger sharp. "Madam Quarrellous called her willful."

"In my experience, willfulness is not an indication of evil," Enchanter Evariste replied in his smooth, bright voice.

"That could change if she grows corrupted in the future," Enchanter Tristisim said.

Evariste slightly tilted his head. "The Council seemed to be unusually concerned about her actions in the future despite the fact that no instructor has ever reported even a *whiff* of corruption or evil magic around her. Besides, as recorded in the report, Angelique has been hauled to Verglas on numerous occasions. The Snow Queen's magic that guards Verglas' borders from any harmful magic did not stir at her presence."

"You acquired our council report?" Enchanter Crest asked.

"Lord Enchanter Evariste is of high enough rank to request any report submitted to the Council," Enchantress Felicienne said.

Enchanter Tristisim returned to scratching his beard. "Very well, so you believe the girl to be a bleeding lamb; that's fine. But I want you to explain what you will do *if* the worst should happen. No matter how innocent you think this student to be, we cannot allow you to teach her if you are ill prepared."

Evariste shrugged slightly, though his charming smile didn't dim. "Perhaps the Council has forgotten my particular magic? No matter where we are, I will be able to instantly transport myself and Angelique to other locations—whether they be remote ones to remove the possibility of harming others, or Verglas to seek out the Snow Queen's magic."

Which would kill me if I really did go rogue. Not that I have plans to. Or want to.

Hope started to move in her chest—almost painfully so. Angelique hadn't given herself the luxury of dreaming that she might come out of her trial with her magic intact. She had given up all hope of living as a magic user, but now...

The Council members leaned close together, murmuring quietly to one another and arguing in hissed whispers.

"Lord Enchanter Evariste." Madame Quarrellous started to reach for the enchanter, then seemed to think better of it and dropped her hand. "You are too kind; but I'm afraid you are on the cusp of making a monumental mistake!"

Evariste ignored the instructor and turned, slightly, to face Angelique. "I must apologize, Angelique: it was rather bold of me to suggest to the Council that I take you as my apprentice without asking you if you'd like me for a teacher."

Angelique felt her eyes bugging as she stared at Evariste. *Is he joking?* She studied him for another moment, but it seemed he was sincere.

Enchanter Evariste was an idol among magic users. Though he was only a little older than Angelique, he had been a Lord Enchanter for years. He earned the rank when he was still a child —*a little boy!*—making him the youngest Enchanter ever. He possessed incredibly rare magic and was renowned for the depth of his power.

Mages would fight for the honor to be Evariste's student, and here he was asking her—a potentially dangerous student whose own *instructors* didn't trust her—to become his apprentice.

Enchanter Evariste didn't seem to notice her hesitation and blithely continued, "You would be my first apprentice, which means I might bungle your teaching, so I'll have to request your patience before we even begin. But I believe we might get along splendidly—if you're willing to try, that is." He slightly tilted his head, making the hood of his cloak rustle against his face. "Are you?"

Though I hate my magic, I still love being a magic user. I want to work to uphold the oaths of the Veneno Conclave. It's all I ever wanted, though I thought I might be too dangerous to ever do that. But now! Angelique nodded eagerly. "Of course, Lord Enchanter."

"Excellent!" Enchanter Evariste smiled. "This will be *such* fun."

Angelique shifted slightly. "There's no guarantee they'll do as you ask, Lord Enchanter."

"Nonsense. Of course they will." Evariste's smile turned mischievous. "If they don't, they'll have to admit they're just scared of your power and potential—and won't *that* make them look bad?"

"The Council has come to an agreement," Enchanter Crest said, his expression unreadable as he stacked his papers. "Lord Enchanter Evariste will be given custody of Angelique and has permission to take her on as his apprentice."

"*However*," Enchantress Felicienne said, her voice loud and forceful. "There are several stipulations and agreements. Lord Enchanter Evariste must make frequent reports directly to the Council regarding Angelique's progress. We will send mages to test Angelique throughout her apprenticeship, and if we see any sign of wrongdoing, she will be sealed immediately."

The Council Members nodded their heads in affirmation.

"Additionally," Enchantress Primrose added, "we ask that as long as Angelique is an Enchantress-in-Training, she only use her war magic under Enchanter Evariste's direct supervision." The plump enchantress smiled warmly. "It's for your protection, dear," she said with all sincerity.

None of the requirements surprised Angelique, and she nodded—though she didn't miss the slight downturn of Evariste's mouth at Enchantress Primrose's stipulation. *What is he upset about? That is all perfectly reasonable given what I am.*

"I'll agree to your requests, but I think they should be revisited several years into my apprentice's training," Enchanter Evariste said. "Particularly the provision that she shouldn't use her core magic without me."

Angelique almost choked on her own spit. *THAT was the one you were most upset by? It's the one that makes the most sense! My magic is weaponized—I don't WANT to use it without supervision!*

Enchanter Crest nodded. "You may make your request at a later date—but you'll need proof and evidence for our consideration."

Enchanter Evariste slightly bowed his head. "Of course."

"If that's all, I believe we can declare this hearing over," Enchanter Tristisim said. He eyed Angelique and Enchanter Evariste with something akin to curiosity. "I assume you are aware of the new records and forms you'll need to fill out, Evariste, and the provisions you'll have to make?"

"Indeed," Evariste said in his musical voice. "Thank you, Council Members, for my brilliant new apprentice."

Enchantress Primrose's forehead puckered slightly—as if she didn't fully understand what he meant and was bothered by it—and Enchantress Felicienne looked icy, but Enchanter Crest nodded briskly.

"The Council will adjourn in preparation for the next ruling," Enchanter Crest announced.

The spotlights dimmed slightly, and Angelique let go of the breath she was holding.

It was done. She still had her magic, *and* she was now the apprentice of one of the most respected Lord Enchanters of their time. *The impossible has happened. Though I'm not certain I trust it.*

"Angelique," Madam Quarrellous said stiffly.

Angelique cringed slightly as she turned to face her Magical Integrity instructor. The older woman's lips were caught in a severe frown that she rarely wore—except when Angelique was around—and the longer she gazed at Angelique, the sharper that frown grew.

She opened her mouth—no doubt to remind Angelique that her core magic was based on bloodshed and that her great power was not a good indication of her soul—but before she could say anything, Lord Enchanter Evariste stepped smoothly between them.

"If you'll excuse us, Madam Quarrellous, Master Gladio. I fear my apprentice and I have much we need to accomplish and see to before we leave, and a very short time in which to do it." His voice was warm and sunny, and he placed a hand on Angelique's left elbow—making her jump at the unexpected contact. "Good day to you both!" He bid them farewell with a smile as he gently directed Angelique off the platform and out of the light.

Blinded by the sudden dimness, Angelique nearly tripped down the last step but righted herself in time to avoid falling on her face.

"We'll need to gather your belongings from your dorm room, and there are forms I'll need to pick up, but we needn't bother filling out any of it yet." Evariste's voice remained bright as he gently toted her along, making his way through the dim hall with no difficulties. "With my magic, it's an easy thing to trot the papers back to the Council. And they won't expect me to file anything for at least a week I'd say. Given all of that, I think we'll be able to leave the Conclave by evening, wouldn't you agree, Apprentice?" he asked as they strode through the door.

The war mage still stood guard, and at Enchanter Evariste's words, she nearly lost her grip on her halberd. She shifted her gaze to Angelique and offered her an excited smile. "You're going to become an enchantress?" she asked.

"I'm not sure," Angelique said honestly.

"She is." Enchanter Evariste grinned charmingly at the war mage.

The guard tightened her grip on her weapon and laughed. "We'll finally get an enchantress with war magic!"

Angelique felt her forehead furrow in surprise as she followed Enchanter Evariste. *She says that as though it's a good thing.*

"Good luck, Apprentice Angelique!" the guard called after them.

"Thank you," Angelique replied automatically.

"Why don't we divide and conquer," Enchanter Evariste suggested. "You pack up, and I'll grab the forms and necessary registration papers. We can meet at the kelpie fountain in the gold courtyard—I can perform magic there without stirring any wraths."

"Aren't there supplies that will be necessary to purchase?" Angelique asked tactfully. *He can't have been planning on taking me on. There will be books, linens, and necessary teaching supplies to buy.* The thought made the wrinkles on Angelique's forehead deepen. Traditionally, an Enchanter bought the supplies for his apprentice, with the thought that the apprentice would pay them back through their work.

But given their rather unusual and hasty arrangement, was that fair? On the other hand, Angelique had very little money. *I could maybe afford a book or two. But I can sleep on a bare mattress, and my school clothes will suit me. It always struck me as a bit prissy the way many mages demand the finer things of life, anyway.*

"Yes, supplies, but we needn't purchase them here. There's a larger variety in the marketplaces of Baris, Torrens, and Loire. And I already have much of what we'll need," Evariste said. When he glanced over at her, he laughed a little and tapped her forehead with a gloved finger. "And I can see what you are thinking, but worry not! I will spare no expense for my apprentice. You will not pay for a thing, Angelique."

I can't afford to make him feel too much pressure for taking me in, or he may regret it. With this thought ringing through her mind, she objected, "But surely I am an expense you were not expecting."

"You'd be surprised," Enchanter Evariste said evasively. "Besides, it is my right as your teacher. Now off with you—to your rooms. Remember, we'll meet at the kelpie fountain!" He instructed when they came to an intersection in the hallway.

Angelique bowed. "Yes, Enchanter Evariste."

Enchanter Evariste waved a hand in farewell before he strode off in the opposite direction, his hooded cloak sweeping behind him.

Angelique watched him for a moment. *Is this all a dream—or maybe a delusion—brought on by the sealing process?* She pinched herself on the forearm, relaxing a little when pain flared. *It's real. Thank the skies above, it's real.*

Angelique felt her cheeks lift in a smile—a real smile that started with a bubbly feeling in her chest—and she almost laughed.

It wasn't until her magic swirled around her—stirred by her good mood—that Angelique remembered herself. She ruthlessly shoved the magic deep into her soul, so she could barely feel a faint tickle of it, then hurried off to her dorm room.

I better be quick. I need him to fill out that paperwork before he changes his mind!

CHAPTER 3

Evariste was already waiting when Angelique arrived, toting four rucksacks that held her clothes, study materials, and the few trinkets she had salvaged from her ruined home before coming to the school.

He was studying the kelpie fountain with his hands tucked into the voluminous sleeves of his black cloak, but when Angelique shuffled across the courtyard, he pulled off his black gloves. "Are you ready to see your new home?" He reached out and tugged on the two rucksacks that dangled from Angelique's right fist. They were the heavier ones, filled with her scrolls of notes and the few books she had purchased.

"It's fine," she said.

"I insist," Evariste said. "This is going to be your first trip through a portal. I want you to enjoy it—because you'll be doing it quite often—and not worry about losing your things through the gate."

Angelique relinquished two of her sacks, which Evariste held with ease.

"This will be your first lesson as my apprentice," he said. "Or rather, your first demonstration of my core magic."

He turned to face an empty portion of the courtyard, murmured a few words under his breath, and extended his hand out in front of him. Blue magic rippled around his fist as his powers shifted under his direction.

A door of light bloomed before him. It started as a rectangle of pure golden light, but when his blue magic wrapped around it, it hardened at the edges. Wooden timbers decorated with swirls of blue paint and imbedded glass beads formed the frame of the door.

The inside blazed for a few moments longer, crackling like flames before it was consumed by blue fire. The light cleared and faded away, leaving a view of a bright, picturesque forest through the portal.

"This is a portal," Evariste explained. "I have an unusual type of magic that lets me make cuts through reality, so to speak, and temporarily stitch them together. It creates doorways that allow for instant travel."

Angelique listened avidly as she peered behind the door—which still had the wooden frame but was blocked off by the gold light that had previously faded away. She knew of Enchanter Evariste's rare magic—no one else alive had it—but she had never heard an explanation for how his magic *worked*.

"I can create portals to any place I have already visited—though the time it takes for me to accomplish this varies. Since we're going to my home, I can make it almost instantly. If we mean to travel to a place I have not often gone to, it takes more time."

Enchanter Evariste watched Angelique as she completed her circuit around the portal, and continued, "The way in which the portals manifest varies as well, but the biggest drawback to this magic is that it requires a safe environment to raise a portal in. This magic can be rather disruptive, so I have to be careful when and where I use it. Particularly, if an area is unsecured or in danger, it's not recommended that I create one as it *will* affect the door itself. It's part of the limitation of my magic." He paused for a moment. "You were taught about limitations and prices, yes?"

Just how poor of a student does he think I am? "Yes, all magic users —from mages to enchanters—have either a limit or a price they pay for using their magic," Angelique said, reciting the text-book explanation from memory. "Most mages have limitations on their magic—set rules and conventions they have to follow. Enchanters and enchantresses, however, usually have a price."

Evariste nodded in satisfaction. "Well said. I am in the minority in that my magic has a limitation, but it's not entirely unexpected given my type of magic. Those of us with rare strains of magic usually have limitations rather than prices. Do you know if you have a limitation or a price?"

Angelique shook her head. "I haven't used enough of my war magic to find out."

"I see. Well, that will be a project for another day. For now it is enough that we head to your new home!" Evariste gestured to the glowing portal. "All you must do is step through the door."

"That's all?" Angelique asked. "I don't need to say any magic words?"

"No," Enchanter Evariste chuckled. "Though the experience might be a strange sensation. Ready?"

Enchanter Evariste waited for her nod before he stepped through the door, leaving the Veneno Conclave behind for the cute forest.

Angelique nervously adjusted her grip on her remaining rucksacks, sucked in a deep breath, then stepped into the portal.

It was a strange, tingling sensation—a bit like walking through thickened water. She could feel Evariste's magic brushing against her skin and clothes, then it abruptly released her, popping her into the forest.

Angelique blinked as she stared up at the sky.

At the Conclave, the sky had been a moody gray, covered by

clouds. Here, the sun was high on the horizon—blocked only by tree branches.

The woods were a vivid green that almost made Angelique's eyes hurt. The trees ranged in height, but the majority of them were short and knobby, and there was very little underbrush besides the moss-covered rocks and boulders strewn everywhere.

She peered over her shoulder and watched as Enchanter Evariste collapsed the portal.

"Where are we?" she asked.

"Welcome to Wistful Thicket—a small woods located in Torrens."

Torrens? Angelique nearly dropped her bags in surprise. Torrens was on the other side of the continent from Mullberg—the location of the Veneno Conclave.

In a single step, she had traveled a journey that would normally take weeks!

Enchanter Evariste chuckled at her obvious shock and set out at a loping walk. "This way—to your new home."

Angelique hurried after him, though when they rounded a thick patch of trees, she stopped.

Enchanter Evariste's home was a mixture of comfortable elegance and wonders of magic.

It was a neat, cube-shaped building made of gray stone, outlined with golden timbers, and topped by a bright blue shingled roof.

The very center of the roof was deeply concaved. In the middle of the dip was a blazing ball of crackling blue magic, cradled by a wrought-iron crescent moon that saddled the roof.

The peaks of the house had circular glass windows, decorated with a window frame made of stars and moons. They and the smaller windows of the house—which were similarly decorated—were clearly of elvish design. In fact, between the ornate ironwork that bloomed around the doors and edges of the house, and the glowing blue globs of magic that seemed to be fastened to the corners of the roof, the house was a beautiful blend of magic and understated elven design.

But how did he manage that? Elves don't often venture far from their woods in Farset.

"Come along, Apprentice!" Enchanter Evariste called as he crossed the brick bridge that spanned a large pond which curled around the front half of the house.

A pair of white swans looked up at the enchanter as he passed by, and a few ducks quacked in greeting.

Angelique hurried after him, though her thoughts were still trying to catch up with her eyes.

It smells clearer here—the air doesn't have that stale aftertaste that the Academy has.

Angelique twisted around like an owl, scanning the edges of the forest. She saw a badger and two rabbits, and what looked like a deer farther in. None of the animals were bothered by her presence, and they didn't move even when Enchanter Evariste opened his door.

"Here we are." He led the way inside. "The salon, dining room, and library are in this front half of the house; the kitchens are in the back half. Upstairs are our rooms and washrooms."

Evariste motioned to the salon as they traipsed through it. Angelique noted with interest that it had windows that looked out over the pond and front yard, and windows on the back of the room that seemed to be windows into some very *different* locations—including a beautiful forest, a snowy mountain top, and what was likely to be the palace of Baris.

"The library is that way—it's warded against fire and magic, so we'll hold most of your lessons in my workshop."

Enchanter Evariste freely motioned to a slightly darkened room as they marched up the square staircase that snaked through the center of the house.

He stepped onto the landing for the second floor—which had a far lower ceiling than the first floor. With a motion up to the top floor, he continued, "Up top is the workshop—it's the attic, really, but I need space and a lot of it when using my magic, so it was necessary. We'll go up there if we have time before dinner. But only after you've settled in."

Another smile, and he was off, gliding towards a door, which he opened. "Your new quarters—though I'm afraid your washroom is not attached, but it is right next door."

Angelique bobbed her head in wordless thanks as she stepped into the room and paused, puzzled.

The room was tastefully decorated with gold and mauve shades of purple—it rather reminded her of a sunset.

The flooring was constructed with a golden wood that almost seemed to glow from within. The brocade wallpaper was a creamy white with dusty purple flourishes and swirls woven into its surface and was complemented by a thick purple rug and an armchair with purple damask cushions placed in front of the empty fireplace.

The wood frame of the gigantic poster bed—screened by gold curtains, though Angelique still caught sight of several purple pillows with gold tassels hanging over the side—was made of the same golden wood as the flooring, as was the chest placed at the end of the bed, the dressing table, and the wardrobe that was bigger than Angelique.

Thick towels were stacked on the dressing table, and a number of magical books—all ones a master would provide for his or her student—were arranged on top of the chest.

I was expecting a guest bedroom, but it seems like Evariste was planning for me? Or for an apprentice, at least? Perhaps he meant to have a different apprentice, but ended up taking me on out of pity?

Angelique shook herself from her stupor. "It is beautiful—thank you for lending me use of it."

Evariste leaned a forearm against the doorframe. "You don't have a desk for your work, but there's not really room for one, I'm afraid to say. I cleared away a space for you in the workshop instead."

Angelique set the first of her rucksacks down. "For me?" she carefully enquired.

Evariste ruefully grinned. "Yes, you, Angelique. I'd heard of you before, and I had an inkling of what was going to happen to you. There were rumors."

"You *wanted* me as an apprentice? You planned for this?" Angelique asked.

Evariste laughed. "I can't say I've been looking forward to having an apprentice—I was hoping to skate by another decade before the Council finally realized I haven't had one. But I couldn't let you slip through the system. You're a powerful mage, Angelique. The Veneno Conclave is lacking sense to seriously consider allowing someone with your amount of magic get sealed."

The concept that someone would *want* to see her become an enchantress was so foreign, it took Angelique a moment to mull it over. "But I have war magic."

"Yes, but if those instructors of yours actually examined our history instead of sticking to official Conclave records, they would remember Farrin—the Snow Queen's consort." Evariste stepped only far enough into the room to set Angelique's bags down, then retreated to the door again. "Farrin likely had enough power to be considered an enchanter. The term simply wasn't around until years after he died, and folk tend to forget about him as he mostly stood in the Snow Queen's shadow anyway."

"Farrin had that much power?" Angelique cocked her head. She was aware of the story of the Snow Queen—she was considered to be the founder of the Conclave, though the organization hadn't become official and created the ranks and oaths that magic users still followed today until long after she had passed on. She was aware, even, of Farrin's part in the tale. He was among the first recorded war mages, after all. But she had not heard much mentioned of the strength of his magic.

"As far as I can tell by my readings, Farrin could have snapped the Snow Queen in half if they fought one-on-one—though I am certain the thought never would have occurred to him," Evariste laughed.

"But...he's considered a hero," Angelique said. "To have war magic and that much power," she hesitated, unable to say more.

Enchanter Evariste smiled. "The kind and amount of magic a person has doesn't determine their actions, Apprentice. You have great potential to be a force for good. It will be my duty to help you realize that potential. And when you're made enchantress, it will be my honor to stand with you and poke fun of the Council when they realize how silly their concerns were."

His laugh was contagious, and Angelique found herself smiling slightly in response, even if she didn't quite believe him.

At least now I understand why he took me on: he's as mad as a loon, even if he is nice. Who could think there is the potential for good in the powers of bloodshed?

"Unpack your things, and freshen up as you like. I'm going to change and then head upstairs to my workshop. Come find me when you're finished—or when you get hungry."

Enchanter Evariste unfastened the throatlatch of his cloak and tugged off his hood, giving Angelique her first good look at her master.

Simply put, he was dazzling.

Enchanter Evariste's butter, almost platinum, blonde hair was slightly mussed from the hood, but it still looked silky and nice. His fine nose, high cheek bones, and full lips—which made his smiles extra generous—looked like they had been masterfully carved by a genius craftsman. He had different-colored eyes—the left was a forest green while the right was bright blue, which only added to the effect.

Angelique almost staggered under the full onslaught of his

smile, but she had steeled herself in advance. (Most magic users were good-looking, and the more magic they had, the more breath-taking they became as their magic made them almost magical in nature.)

Enchanter Evariste seemed oblivious to her observations as he carefully folded his cloak.

With the cloak off, Angelique could see that his shoulders were broader than she realized, and he was a hand taller than she was—a true accomplishment, as she was quite tall for a female.

Angelique mashed her eyes shut and cleared her throat. "Meet you in your workshop, I understand. Thank you, Enchanter Evariste."

Evariste nodded. "Welcome home, Apprentice."

"Thank you, sir." She watched as he strode across the floor landing, disappearing into a room on the other side of the house.

Slowly, Angelique shut her door and set her bags on the floor. Glancing around the room once more, she shook her head.

How can he be so positive about my magic when nearly every instructor and most magic users I've encountered have taught me otherwise? He can't really *be cracked in the head.*

But Evariste was a prodigy—or he had been. Now he was more of a legend. It seemed improbable that he would be ignorant of such matters.

Which means he must be fixing to put in a lot of work to keep me on the straight and narrow.

Angelique brushed against the bed curtains, marveling over the soft and shimmery cloth.

I don't want to be sealed. I don't care about my core magic—if I could change it, I would. But if I can become an enchantress, I can use my good-for-nothing core magic to learn other abilities.

The thought made Angelique stand taller. She had always been proud to be a mage—even if she despised her own core magic. It was a noble calling, one she had genuinely wanted to pursue.

I cannot let Enchanter Evariste ever regret taking me in or decide the Council may be right. If I mess up, I'll be sealed.

She had come to the conclusion before, but she had thought it mockingly. Now, for the first time in years, Angelique could feel her determination unfurl.

Long had her primary concern been being as harmless as possible and avoiding as much attention as possible in hopes of escaping the endless whispers, the dark looks, and the predictions told to her face that she was a monster for her magic and would one day kill because of it.

But Enchanter Evariste—to all appearances—seemed to believe the opposite. For now, anyway.

I'll do everything in my power to prove him right. No matter how I have to suffocate my own magic or how sugary I have to act. If my teachers thought my sarcasm and so-called willfulness were signs of my evil temper, fine. I'll hide it. I won't use my dangerous magic, and I will not stray or ever harm a soul.

I can't mess up this last chance.

CHAPTER 4

As it took Angelique longer than expected to unpack—not because she had much to put away, but because she spent some minutes in front of the mirror trying to practice less-guarded smiles that didn't make her look like a snarling wolf—Enchanter Evariste took her straight downstairs for dinner, so it wasn't until the following day that she got to see the workshop.

"The purpose of a workshop varies greatly from mage to mage," Enchanter Evariste explained as they climbed the staircase. "For instance, the Council Members predominantly use theirs for paperwork. But every high-ranked mage has one. When you make Enchantress, you'll get to settle your own home and make a workshop for yourself, as well."

"I understand," Angelique said, her voice as bright as she could make it.

Evariste paused long enough to twist around and raise an eyebrow at her, then took the last few stairs two at a time. He spun around with the grace of a swordsman and threw his arms wide. "Welcome to your new classroom."

There was a glittering globe, which was not a map of the continent and the countries beyond, but rather a representation of the night sky. Something glittered in the center—either magic or a candle—and light escaped through the little holes in the globe and dotted the workshop with the constellations of the night sky.

Stacked maps and charts and at least four different compasses and spyglasses were placed on a sturdy table. Above the table were two shelves of oddly shaped bottles that sparkled and glowed with different colors.

Drapes of crushed blue velvet were scooped to the side, letting the two giant circular windows that decorated the two peaks of the house filter light inside. There were several chairs in different sizes that were laden with blue silk and satin cushions.

But despite the finery, the workshop had hidden signs of wear.

There were a few spots on the walls where the white plaster had crumbled, letting patches of stone peek through.

Elaborate, standing candelabras were strategically placed to lighten the room—their metal frames flourished with little trees, deer, and occasionally a fox or rabbit. But underneath every stand were pools of dried wax in swirls of different colors, a testament to the hours Enchanter Evariste submerged himself in his work.

"I mostly use my workshop for experiments." Evariste meandered over to a massive table that was cluttered with papers and knickknacks. "I tinker with new spells and magic, but most of my work is calculating potential locations for portals—both temporary and permanent. We'll hold most of your lessons here. The rest we'll do in the library downstairs."

He grinned ruefully and continued. "When I was an apprentice, my master told me a magic user's workshop should not be near his library, lest a spell combusts and he lose his workshop *and* his books. But I keep most trinkets from my travels here."

Angelique nodded as she turned in a circle, spying an elven bow hanging from the rafters, a polished lyre that had to be from Torrens, a polished helm placed on the mantle of a giant fireplace, a tiny model ship, and a glass ball that swirled with snowflakes. "It's a very nice workshop," Angelique sincerely said.

"I'm glad you think so. Here, our desks are at this end." Evariste ducked into a sort of indoor gazebo. It was made of pillars of white rock veined with gold, though it had a plaster roof painted blue with gold stars. Two desks were arranged inside of it, and the same fancy velvet curtains that were pinned to the side of the windows were tied to the pillars and would provide a sort of privacy screen when tugged loose.

Angelique hesitantly approached the smaller of the two desks, assuming the handful of books, stacks of papers, and bottles of different-colored inks were for her.

Enchanter Evariste patted her desk. "We'll get started with your lessons this morning, but first we ought to take our oaths and seal our bond as master and apprentice."

Angelique could have shouted in glee. *Wonderful! Once we take our oaths, he'll have a much harder time getting rid of me!* Despite her delight, Angelique kept her smile controlled and her nod slight. "Of course. What do you need me to do?" she asked, her voice pleasant.

"Here, this is your part." Enchanter Evariste handed her a thick piece of parchment paper, emblazoned with a short speech written in blue ink. "Sign it first, then read it after me." He was already scratching his signature across the bottom of his paper with a peacock feather. Once he finished, he passed it to her and waited for her to finish before he started reading.

"I, Lord Enchanter Evariste of the Fire Gates, claim Angelique—student of Luxi-Domus—as my apprentice," he read. "I vow to teach her well, to school her in the ways of magic, and to show her the world and her place in it. I will protect and provide for her, and I will instruct her to the best of my abilities."

Angelique licked her lips and waited for him to nod to her before she began. "I, Angelique—student of magic and Luxi-Domus—hold Lord Enchanter Evariste of the Fire Gates as my instructor. I promise to listen to his wisdom, heed his words, and apply myself to my studies of magic and my role as an enchantress-in-training. I will watch, learn from, and work for my master to the best of my abilities."

The blue ink on Angelique's paper started to glow.

"Perfect, now summon a bit of your magic to your thumb, like this." Enchanter Evariste held up his right thumb, and blue magic flared at the pad.

Angelique hesitated. "But...my magic..."

"It'll be fine," he promised in a soothing tone. "This just seals the deal."

Angelique reluctantly held up a thumb, her forehead wrinkling in concentration as she allowed the tiniest trickle of magic to escape her hold. It took a few moments, but silvery magic gathered at the pad of her thumb.

"Sealed!" Evariste declared as he bumped the pad of his thumb against Angelique's, almost making her jump in place when their magic briefly meshed.

He laughed at her expression. "I'm just jesting with you, Apprentice. Press your thumb against your oath, and then mine."

Angelique had a hard time swallowing as she did as instructed, her magic leaving a silver circle behind on the papers each time she lifted her thumb.

The lettering glowed brighter, until the papers crackled and the light faded. The ink had turned emerald green, and the magical marks on the papers seemed to sparkle a little.

"Well done." Evariste opened a drawer of his desk. "I do have a little something for you." He scooped up an item from the drawer—a silver bracelet that held what looked like a glass bead tinted blue surrounded by a little cage of silver.

"This isn't part of the ceremony, but it's my gift to you." Evariste offered the bracelet to Angelique.

"Thank you." Angelique took the bracelet, even though her first instinct was to eye it warily. She could feel magic in the bracelet. And if she squinted, she could almost see it floating in the glass bead.

"I got a craftmage to spell it for me," he explained. "You can use it to alert me—just say my name while touching the bead. It has a bit of a tracking spell in it so I'll be able to find you, should you need aid."

Ahhhh. Angelique relaxed slightly as she slipped the bracelet over her wrist. *That's the real point of this: he doesn't want me wandering around without his knowledge. That's sensible—and reasonable, given what I am.* "Thank you, Enchanter Evariste," Angelique said.

He waggled a finger at her. "It's Master Evariste now. No more of this stiff formality. And I expect you won't have to wear it long. Once I teach you some defensive spells, you'll be safe enough to wander off on your own."

"I'm sure," Angelique lied through a sugary smile.

Evariste tilted his head as he studied her, his blonde hair glinting in the candlelight. "I'll have to get you some new clothes, too."

"No, my wardrobe is fine." Angelique smoothed the blue skirt of her simple gown.

"As your instructor, it is my duty to see you clothed and fed." Enchanter Evariste leaned back on his heels as he studied her.

Eager for the opportunity to launch her scheme to be as easy-to-maintain-as-possible, Angelique smiled. "I am comfortable with my clothes. Should I need repairs or replacements, I will ask."

"Hmm," Evariste said. "In any case, with the formalities finished, we can begin lessons!" He spun around and poked through the books piled on Angelique's desk. "We'll begin with illusions. I think that's a magic you'll adjust to nicely, and we can sweep through it with the intent of graduating into alteration magic—that's when you change something so it doesn't just *look* different, it becomes what you want it to be. As long as your magic is present to power it, that is. Here—this is the book you'll need."

He pulled a book with a cracked leather cover from the stack and passed it off to Angelique. "Take a seat, Apprentice."

Angelique slid into her chair, taking a moment to arrange the books on her desk so she had space to take notes. "Can you begin teaching me a new kind of magic so swiftly?" she asked. "I only know how to wield my core magic."

"You took all the required academy classes?" Evariste asked. "Besides Magical Integrity and Ethics, that is."

"Yes, I have a foundation in mathematics, magical history, environmental studies, the basic science courses, as well as the classes for war mages: weapon-based combat, archery, hand-to-hand combat, caring for weapons, and so on."

"Yes, you are more than ready to jump into illusions. But perhaps I should begin with a bit of magical theory." Evariste rubbed his jaw. "It has been explained to you that what divides enchantresses and enchanters from other mages is the level of magic they possess, yes?"

Angelique nodded. "The depth of their power allows them to use their core magic—that is the magic they are naturally gifted in—and use it for other varieties of magic that would normally be out of their reach."

"Exactly," Evariste nodded. "You'll never be as good as a weather mage at summoning a snow storm, and any enchantments we put on items can't hold a candle to a craft mage's work, but our ability to weave all these different types of magic together can be a very powerful tool."

"But how does one accomplish that?" Angelique asked.

Evariste held up a single finger. "Through a great deal of control."

"Oh," Angelique said, some of her joy dying a bit.

Control was something she lacked terribly. If she strangled her magic with enough force, she could let little bits of it ooze out and control that—as she had done with the oath. But that wasn't the type of control Enchanter Evariste meant.

"By control, you mean the ease with which one wields her magic, and the finesse she uses to manipulate it?" she asked.

"Exactly so," Evariste said.

Yeah, I don't have that at all. My magic is as subtle as a sledge hammer.

"Control lets you do delicate work on spells. It helps you gather the necessary amount of magic for the task you want to complete, and it means channeling your magic so it alters the very purpose of your powers into something entirely different."

"Entirely different?" Angelique asked.

"Yes—I'll demonstrate with an illusion since that's what your first magic will be." Evariste flexed his knuckles, and blue magic glittered at his fingertips. "This is my core magic in its raw form. But if I spin it and twist it, it powers an illusion and essentially becomes illusion magic."

The blue magic swirled in a little funnel, faded, and was replaced with a miniature dragon the size of Angelique's hand. The dragon circled Angelique and spat little puffs of fire. When Angelique poked the image, her finger passed straight through it.

"Some disciplines of magic require words or phrases—it varies greatly depending on the strength of the spell and the mage casting it." Evariste held out his hand, and the dragon seemed to land on top of it. "Being a good enchantress or enchanter isn't merely a test of power, but a testament to your mind. It takes a lot to not only remember all the different spells, charms, and powers you can funnel, but to also be able to react and adapt your magic, changing it as you wish."

"But you're really changing it?" Angelique asked, digging into the most important part—to her anyway. "It's not your magic anymore?"

"No, it is still mine—or I wouldn't be able to control this illusion as I do," Evariste said. "But it changes the magic and shapes it into something new, so though it is powered by your abilities, it lets you transform it into something different."

Angelique could have laughed; her relief hit her so hard, she was almost dizzy.

So my terrible magic—my devastating powers—can be changed if I cast something outside my war magic. It's no longer harmful.

She almost sagged back in her chair. *I'll stay on the straight and narrow. I won't hurt a single soul with my powers, and when I use magic, it won't* be *war magic.*

"How do I make an illusion?" she asked eagerly.

Evariste smiled and held out his hand. "Come join me, and we'll get started."

If Enchanter Evariste found it suspicious that his apprentice—who was previously labeled willful for refusing to do her homework—was a dedicated student at illusion magic, he said nothing about the matter.

Lured in by the promise of transforming her magic, Angelique threw herself into studying illusions.

After two weeks of careful book work and another week of painful practices, Angelique spun her first illusion: a white cat.

"Well done, Apprentice!" Evariste studied the feline with his arms folded across his chest.

The illusion-cat licked its paw and scrubbed at its face, ignoring Angelique, who was studying it with narrowed eyes.

"She's not like your illusions." Angelique circled the cat with a wrinkled brow. "Your little dragon looked *real*. My cat is...transparent." Angelique squinted and was able to see the stack of books piled behind the cat through the hazy image of its fur.

"My illusions look solid because of practice," Evariste said. "Yours will improve as you continue to learn more and grow more familiar with twisting and channeling your magic."

"Hm," Angelique said, still not quite satisfied.

Evariste set a warm hand on her shoulder, breaking her close scrutiny. "You should be proud, Angelique," he said. "Your first illusion was of an animal—they are far harder to create than something stationary and without life—like a book or even a lit candle."

The furrows in Angelique's brow shifted from critical to puzzled. "Why would someone want to make an illusion of a book or a candle?"

Evariste grinned. "You'd be surprised. If you do the unexpected, you'll often be able to get the better of your opponent."

Angelique stiffened and felt her spine tingle. *I don't know that I like the sound of that.* "Having an opponent implies fighting."

"It works well in fighting but also in things like conversation, meetings with royals, and so on. Our lives will be spent helping and aiding others. But as part of that, we must sometimes test people," Evariste explained.

Angelique slowly nodded. "I see." *Maybe. It still sounds like fighting.*

As if he could sense her thoughts, Enchanter Evariste chuckled. "You'll see what I mean when we start traveling."

Angelique blinked. *Traveling?*

Before she could inquire, Evariste knelt down next to the desk the cat had taken over. "You should attempt a book or something similar next, but for now, let's review your cat. You did a magnificent job with the fur and the cat's mannerisms—that's partially why animals are so tough to make illusions of: they each have different ways of moving."

"It'd be more life-like if it wasn't *transparent*," Angelique said.

"I imagine you'll have better luck with the book," Evariste said. "But if you see here, the right back paw is a little blurry. You need your illusions to be sharp and crisp, or they'll give themselves away straight off. Do you recall the spellwork for that?"

Angelique leaned over her desk and flipped a page in her text-book. "It means I twisted my magic wrong towards the end of the spell since it's the back foot. Right?"

"Correct. You want to get an even texture to your magic, and use more of it next time—that will help some with the transparency."

"Yes, Master Evariste."

A MONTH and a half into his new role as teacher, Evariste was forced to admit that Angelique was decidedly not what he expected.

I knew she was diligent and powerful, but she's learning illusions nearly as fast as I did. He sat on his desk as he watched his apprentice.

She was kneeling in front of the empty fireplace, her tongue sticking out slightly in concentration as she worked on creating an illusion of a toy ship *while* keeping three illusionary mugs of ale and an illusionary burning candle going.

Feeling like he ought to offer some sort of moral support or encouragement, Evariste let a smile ease over his lips. "Neatly done, Apprentice! The candle is an especially tidy piece of magic work."

Angelique smiled brightly and replied in a sugary tone. "Thank you, Master Evariste! It is only possible because of the lessons you have taught me."

Evariste chuckled. "Not at all. I only supply the know-how. Your dedication and the power of your magic is all your doing."

Angelique's smile didn't budge. "Thank you." Despite the shape of her lips, Evariste could still see it: the glittering light in her eyes.

Before, he thought it was just her intelligence. But now, having worked closer, he could recognize the signs of her determined personality—no matter how she tried to disguise it.

When he said nothing more, she returned to her work, her eyes narrowing in concentration.

Yes, not what I expected at all.

When Evariste had first heard news of the war mage with the power of an enchantress several years ago, he had looked in on her lessons with curiosity. (After all, to have that much power meant that at the very least she rivaled him—a thing he would eagerly welcome.)

At the time, she had been bright and happy. When Evariste finally thought to look in on her again in her last year of schooling, he was shocked to find her worn-down and wary.

It angered him to see how differently Angelique had been treated by Luxi-Domus, when—given her power—they should have welcomed her as warmly as they had him when he was a mere child.

Even before the Council made it clear they would seal her, Evariste had decided he would take her on as his apprentice—both to rescue her from such a possibility and because, selfishly, Evariste knew if he inserted himself into her life this way, he would always have a relationship with her.

It's surprisingly lonely being a legend. But with her power, she could become a legend in her own right.

Angelique hissed out a breath as she compared her small illusionary ship to a sketch in a book and went about fixing several small details that frankly no teacher would care about.

It was something Evariste had noticed about her, her drive for perfection.

He wasn't entirely certain what caused it, but it seemed that she had decided that perfection was the only way to keep from being sealed.

When he first decided to take her as his apprentice, Evariste worried she might look at him the same way everyone else did—with hearts in their eyes or a face alight with hero-worship.

It was everywhere he went. With the exception of his old

master, nearly everyone from fellow enchantresses and enchanters to mages to *royalty* looked at Evariste with expectation and admiration.

Angelique, however, watched him the way a wolf watches a herd of animals, seeking out the right one to pounce on.

(He knew she'd be horrified at the comparison, but he couldn't think of it any other way. Other mages looked at Evariste and saw his power. Angelique saw a teacher she believed she had to deceive, or at the very least, an oblivious man she had to keep in an ignorant state. There were no hearts in her eyes, only sharp cleverness that she tried to disguise with her smiles and sweetness.)

He started to chuckle but quickly cut it off with a cough. He busied himself looking at some papers on his desk while Angelique peeled her attention off her work long enough to suspiciously eye him.

Only when she again went back to her magic work—this time adjusting the colored flags hanging from the rigging of the ship, did he look back at her.

What is perhaps even stranger is that there is something endearing about it. And it is fun to tease her with it and use what she perceives as my obliviousness to say things I normally wouldn't dare.

Feeling a little devious, Evariste announced, "You have worked so hard today, Angel. We should take the afternoon off. If it weren't for the short notice, I should consider taking you to meet King Channing and Queen Lisheva of Torrens to show you off."

A muscle twitched in Angelique's cheek before she said in her overly sweet voice, "Master Evariste, I'm afraid you cannot show me off until I have enough magic skills to warrant such a thing." She ended with a sweet laugh, but Evariste suspected she was privately thinking he was half mad.

"I'm not convinced," Evariste said. "But as I said, it is too short of notice. There's a good chance the queen is riding abroad and hunting thieves or something similar. She'd be disappointed to hear she missed meeting you, so we will have to wait."

"How wise of a plan," Angelique 'marveled' with a smile. When she returned her gaze to her book, she scowled briefly.

Evariste held in a snort. *One day she'll realize the act isn't necessary and that she's safe with me. But in the meantime, this is rather enjoyable.*

CHAPTER 5

By the second month of her tutelage, Evariste started to introduce Angelique to some of the more unusual aspects of his magic: namely, his visitors.

"It's important to understand there is more to core magic—*all* core magic—than would first appear. Weather mages control the weather, which might seem obvious, but it also gives them some piece of power over crops, trade—as they can make the roads passable or a mess—sea navigation, and more."

"Yes, Master Evariste," Angelique said in a sing-song voice. *I really, really hope he does not mean for this to be a lecture about embracing my core magic. I'll prance stark naked through the Conclave before that happens.*

"My core magic is much the same way. In particular, the portals my magic forges have additional advantages," Evariste continued, taking a surprising veer in the conversation. "They can actually cut through to other realms in this world."

Angelique's eyes popped. "I beg your pardon?" she asked politely, even though she wanted to gape.

Evariste laughed and nodded. "That is correct, Apprentice.

There are other lands in our world besides our continent. The elves came from one, but theirs is not the only one."

I knew there were other lands, but I didn't know it was possible to reach them with magic. Travel between them was rare. I don't think we've had anyone from the other lands come to our continent in at least four or five decades.

"I don't open portals to those places often—and usually it is only at the behest of the Council," Evariste continued. "But because of the nature of my magic, I tend to attract...visitors."

Heaven save me. If he's constantly playing diplomat to foreign powers, I am going to get us accidentally killed, I just know it. Angelique had to stiffen her spine to keep from sucking her head into her shoulders.

"Like this fellow, for instance." Evariste stepped into the unlit fireplace, stuck his head up the empty chimney, and grabbed something.

When he emerged, not a speck of soot dirtied his blonde hair or his clothes, and he held out a beautiful crimson red bird that was approximately the size of a cabbage.

The bird arched its long, graceful neck. Its tail feathers seemed excessively long given its small stature, but it made a pretty crooning noise as it settled on Evariste's hand.

"Is that a-a *phoenix*?" Angelique stammered.

"Indeed, it is. A young one—that's why he is quite small for one of his kind." Evariste extended his arm so Angelique could get a better look.

Under her attention, the phoenix sang a little trill and half extended his wings, which burst into tiny flickering flames. The fire did not burn the bird, even as it crawled across his back and down his tail feathers.

"I'm not sure if they can smell the other realms on me or just sense it, but I usually have a few visitors in my house, and if there are any in the lands I travel through, they come find me," Evariste continued. "They're quite useful—they can give me power to boost a spell, among other things."

"That is quite a delightful side-effect," Angelique said, careful to keep her intonation pleasant.

She'd never be so greedy as to want Evariste's rare magic, but seeing this *did* feel a bit like a slug to her gut. *There's no positive or unexpected benefits to wielding weapons besides killing. If only I had* any other *type of magic!*

"Do you want to hold him?" Evariste asked after several moments of silence. "His flames won't burn you—not when they're this color, anyway."

"Yes, please!" Angelique almost wiggled in place with excitement.

"Hold out your hand."

Angelique did as instructed, keeping herself lax as Evariste used his free hand to adjust her hand so she held it in a manner similar to a falconer.

A tip of his arm, and the phoenix obligingly hopped onto Angelique's arm, greeting her with a little coo.

Evariste observed them for a moment, watching as the phoenix happily clicked his black beak at Angelique. "You're coming along quite well in your studies."

"Thank you, Master Evariste," Angelique smiled.

"I think at this point, we can run off on a fieldtrip." Evariste sat on the edge of his desk, plucking up a tiny jade statue of a wolf.

"Is there an assignment to complete from the Veneno Conclave?" Angelique asked, delicately rubbing the phoenix on the top of its head.

"No, but there's a close friend of mine I'd like to visit, and it will be a good experience for you," Evariste said.

"Where are we going?"

"Farset. To see the Alabaster Forest," he said nonchalantly.

Angelique almost dropped the phoenix in her shock.

"*Alabaster Forest*? Home to the elves?" she asked in a squeaky voice.

"Yes, the Elf King is my particular friend," Evariste said in the same tone he used to inform Angelique they were having scones with lunch.

Angelique was grateful when he briefly turned his back to her, so she could give him an appropriate expression of crazy. *The Elf King? He's friends with the Elf King—and he wants me to go to the elven forest?! That's it; I'm going to die. He'll ask me to do some magic, then my wretched war magic will slip, and I'll die with an elven arrow to the heart. Farewell, my brief time in this world—at least it will be a truly momentous way to pass on.*

"You didn't travel much as a student in Luxi-Domus, did you?" Evariste asked.

Angelique tried to clear her throat but found it difficult, as her mouth felt like it was stuffed with cotton. "No," she said. "I went to Verglas several times, but we didn't visit any cities, just camped on the border."

"That's what I thought," Evariste said. His tone was a bit darker than usual, and his lips briefly tightened in a miniscule frown before he flashed a smile at her. "Which is why I think you will enjoy this."

Angelique stared at the phoenix, which climbed off her hand and onto her wrist. "You don't think the elves will be upset?"

"Why would they be?"

"Because of my magic?" Angelique asked.

"No," Evariste said immediately. "The elves value a good warrior. And with their long lives, they have seen enough ages pass by to know folly when they see it. Your magic, my apprentice, is *fine*."

Angelique wasn't entirely certain she believed him, but she trusted him. Or rather, she trusted him enough to know he wouldn't take her into a land that was potentially dangerous.

"But you *will* need a new wardrobe," Evariste added.

When Angelique slowly lifted her gaze to his, he gave her his most charming and brilliant smile. "We will be spending the majority of our time with elven royalty, after all," he said.

Angelique stared at him, a thoughtful frown threatening to tug on her lips. *When he first took me on as his apprentice, I thought he was mad. But I was mistaken*, she mused. *He is not crazy—just incredibly crafty. He waited to talk about this until I had the phoenix on me, which means I cannot react with as much passion as I would like to or run off to end the argument.*

As if agreeing with her, the phoenix chirped and rustled its wings.

But his argument is not invalid. I can't really meet the Elf King in my school clothes—it would reflect poorly on Enchanter Evariste and the Veneno Conclave. "Perhaps one new dress," Angelique said reluctantly.

"Mmm," Evariste said, not committing.

"Or two," Angelique said as an olive branch.

Evariste smiled brightly. "We won't leave for a week, but I'll see to it that we're packed when the time comes. Now which would you rather do: break for lunch or practice your illusion technique?"

"Illusions!"

"That's what I thought. Pass me our little phoenix, and then try your hand at copying this wolf statue. Pay special attention to the way the light bounces on the stone—that will help with making it appear more solid."

"Yes, Master."

When Evariste mentioned a new dress...I pictured a sensible gown, not a piece of art. Angelique wondered if she dared to shift her weight as she waited for Evariste—who was fussing in bidding a small water dragon farewell as he closed up the house.

Her new "dress"—if it could be called that—featured enough layers of silk and satin to provide for at least three of her old school dresses.

It was snow white, though the top layer of fabric was a transparent layer of pinkish gauze that settled over her skirts and the short sleeves of her arms. The dress was *soft* and almost cloud-like in the comfy way it wrapped around her.

She wore her silver bracelet from Evariste, but he had also given her a silver necklace with a pink gem and elaborate, pink satin shoes.

A woven strand of flowers stretched across her forehead like a tiara, and Angelique tried to hide a scowl as a butterfly passed by her. *I feel ridiculous.*

In school, she had mostly dealt with spears, sabers, and arrows. Now she was wearing...*flowers*?

Granted, most enchanters and enchantresses were swell dressers. But Angelique had never seen an *apprentice* so well dressed before. Even just guessing at the cost made her feel ill. If she ever damaged it...

She pressed her lips together and brushed imaginary dirt off a sleeve.

I'm not sure if I'm more disgruntled about the cost of this getup or the fact that it actually feels comfortable despite the puffy skirts.

"Angelique." Evariste strode across the brick bridge and joined her in the front yard. "Judging by your expression, it seems that I failed to mention all of your new clothes are spelled for comfort. They also are resistant to tears and dirt."

Angelique brightened. "Really?"

Evariste chuckled slightly and adjusted her flower tiara. "Exactly so, my diligent student. I cast enchantments—or have a craft mage do so on my behalf—on all my clothes. With my propensity to attract little friends, I've found it's the sensible thing to do. Naturally, I will do the same to your clothes."

"Thank you, Master Evariste," Angelique said with real relief.

Evariste nodded. "Of course. Besides, as enchanters it is our duty to be among the people and help them. To worry about our clothes at such a time would be silly. Are you ready?"

"Yes. Can I hold your satchel for you?" Angelique asked.

Evariste shook his head. "It's no trouble. It only has our clothes, and it's spelled so it's not heavy at all."

Although Angelique nodded, she couldn't help the pesky feeling that her apprenticeship with Evariste was *very* different from what a usual enchanter or enchantress-in-training would encounter—and that wasn't just because most mages, enchanter or otherwise, did not call the Elf King of Alabaster Forest their friend.

"It will only take me a moment to create the portal," Evariste explained as he rolled up the sleeves of his snugly fitting jacket—a creation of dark blue cloth with decorative white feathers sewn on its sleeves. "I most often travel back and forth between my home and the Veneno Conclave, but the Alabaster Forest is the place I travel to most often after that, to see Emerys."

Evariste turned away from Angelique and—as he had for the portal he had made from the Conclave to his house—murmured a few words under his breath. This time, however, he made a beckoning motion, as if urging something to come closer.

As his blue magic swirled, thickening the air with his power, trees—saplings, really, that only looked a few years old—sprouted up from the ground, bearing fragrant white buds and dark green leaves.

The trees' lower branches intertwined, and white fire blazed between their trunks, shooting up to the branches.

Evariste's blue magic encircled the door, and the white fire flickered, then faded, leaving behind a portal that led to another forest—though even through the doorway Angelique could see how the trees stretched much higher and were far larger. Many of them seemed to sport leaves nearly the size of her head.

Evariste smiled as he held his arm out in front of him. "After you, Apprentice."

Angelique smiled shakily, then stepped into the portal. The strange sensation of thick water embraced her for a moment until she popped out on the other side.

There she felt a different sort of magic—a zingy, strong flavor of power that could only belong to the elves.

"Alabaster Forest," Evariste said as he joined her on the other side of the portal. "Out of respect, I never walk directly into their lands through a portal and instead set it up just outside the border of their woods. But it will only be a short walk to Sideralis—the city of the elves."

Evariste collapsed the portal with a meaningful nod in its direction, then strode through the trees. "Come, Apprentice," he called over his shoulder. "If we hurry, we'll make it for lunch."

Angelique started after him, then paused when the feeling of elf magic thickened. "Is it really all right to go walking in?" She dug a slipper into a bit of moss. "I thought they required escorts for any humans entering Alabaster Forest."

Evariste stopped and leaned against a tree that had a trunk so thick he wouldn't be able to wrap his arms around it. "They do. Unless," he grinned cheekily, "you're an elf-friend. Then you have free run of the place."

"You're an elf-friend?" Angelique asked as she took another step into the forest.

"I am. And they won't mind that you're with me."

Angelique buried her hands into the soft cloud of her skirts and took a breath.

The forest smelled different from the one that surrounded Evariste's. The air had almost a minty scent to it, and elf magic seemed to tap Angelique on the end of her nose. When her own powers rose up in response, Angelique grimaced. She squashed it back down—as deep as she could in her soul—then trundled after Evariste, determined to ignore her magic.

Evariste pushed off his tree and ambled deeper into the forest, walking shoulder-to-shoulder with her. "When we're in Sideralis, watch the elves," he said. "Pay close attention to their magic. They're more like us enchanters—able to use their magic in multiple ways—though they do have individual strengths and weaknesses."

"Do they cast magic the same way we do?"

Evariste shook his head. "They're a different people, so though it appears similar, there are different mechanics behind it. But they're more similar to us than you might think, so with your bright mind, you'll be able to learn a thing or two."

Angelique nodded but straightened her head when she heard the muffled sound of hooves pounding the ground. "It seems we might soon have some visitors."

"Ahh, yes. That's likely Emerys."

CHAPTER 6

The thundering grew closer until a large unicorn with a coat as black as coal emerged from the shadows. The unicorn was quite large—far more muscled than the average unicorn for certain—and it had glowing red eyes, a pearly black horn, and hindquarters covered by what looked like gray swirls of elvish script.

Mounted on the ferocious unicorn's back was an elf, who could easily give Enchanter Evariste competition in degrees of handsomeness.

His eyes swirled between a dark and pale blue, and his long silky black hair was pulled back in a high ponytail that made him appear a tad cocky. A black moon and star were tattooed across his brow, adding to the elegance of his straight, chiseled facial features.

He grinned—a smile that was surprisingly wolfish—when he saw Evariste and slid off his mount's back with ease. "Evar—you ingrate. You're back finally, are you—and with company?" He arched an eyebrow at the enchanter as he flicked his eyes back and forth between him and Angelique.

"Angelique, allow me to introduce you to King Themerysaldi

of Alabaster Forest—it's a dubious honor to meet him," Evariste laughed. "Emerys, this is my new apprentice, Angelique."

"Apprentice?" the Elf King snorted. "They trusted you with an apprentice? Are you even a legal adult?"

Evariste gestured for Angelique to come closer and smiled warmly. "He thinks he's funny. It's polite to laugh, but don't feel that you have to."

"That's rich coming from you, boy-o." The king paused, and his gaze rested solely upon Angelique.

Angelique kept a slight smile on her lips and tried to make her gaze as innocent and artless as possible as she felt the Elf King's magic brush her.

"Did you choose her?" the Elf King asked. "Because she seems a bit empty-headed—OW!" He broke off with a yelp when Evariste ground the heel of his boot into the elf's foot.

"Angelique has war magic as her core." Evariste gave no indication of irritation as his voice was as sunny and smooth as ever. "And since she is my dear apprentice, I expect you to welcome her."

"Fine—I got it." Emerys sniffed then offered Angelique a brief but attractive smile. "Welcome to Alabaster Forest, Apprentice Angelique."

Angelique used the fanciest curtsey she knew. "It is my honor to be here, Your Majesty."

"I'm sure," Emerys said. "Come, let's head for Sideralis. Some of my men and I were heading home from a hunt when I sensed you and made a detour. I want to eat!"

He patted his unicorn on the neck but didn't remount it, and instead sashayed past. "Pookie, follow me."

The unicorn fell in line behind him, as did Evariste and Angelique.

"I assume you're here for a reason, not just because you missed my pretty face?" King Themerysaldi asked.

"I thought it would be a good experience for Angelique, and I was hoping for a rematch of our last card game," Evariste said.

"I see how it is—hide your real purpose with a claim of education, nicely done." King Themerysaldi laughed—a deep, throaty sound. "You mean for her to learn about elven culture? I can set Alastryn after her. She'd be *delighted* to tutor your little apprentice."

"I was hoping Lady Alastryn could be convinced to teach Angelique about elven tea, and perhaps show her a few demonstrations of elf magic," Evariste said.

Angelique only half listened to Enchanter Evariste's request—she was busy gawking at the famed white trees of Alabaster. Lights that morphed from an apple red to a crimson orange floated around the trees, which oozed raw magic.

The trunks were a pure white—like lamb's fleece—and their leaves seemed to glitter like stars or rippling water.

A longing pierced Angelique's heart as she felt the untainted magic of the trees. It seemed to almost caress her, but before she could get a real feel for it, it was gone, sliding away from her.

"How perfect," the Elf King said, breaking Angelique's reverie. "While my cousin is occupied with your apprentice, we can settle that score in our card game," he said with another wolfish smile. "Step lively now; my fellow huntsmen have finally caught up."

If Angelique strained her ears, she could just *barely* make out the pounding of horse hooves. The noise changed from a low throb to a light tap—likely as the riders slowed their horses—and four mounted elf warriors appeared among the trees.

Like King Themerysaldi, they were almost other-worldly in their elegance and good looks, though they seemed more refined than their king as they bowed their heads gravely, first to Enchanter Evariste, then to Angelique. (Their horses were distinctly less...threatening, but still held a whiff of magic to them as they tossed their elegant heads.)

"My brethren, please join me in welcoming Lord Enchanter

Evariste and his new apprentice, Angelique, to Sideralis," the Elf King said, his voice becoming markedly more formal.

"Welcome, elf-friend Evariste and Angelique," the front-most elf greeted. "May you enjoy your time with us as you stay in our fine city."

"Thank you," Enchanter Evariste said. "I'm certain we will."

It took several minutes of walking to reach Sideralis, and Angelique spent the whole time pinching herself.

I'm with the elves. In Alabaster Forest. Going to their city, Sideralis. This is amazing! Angelique pressed her lips together to keep her bubble of laughter trapped in her chest. She glanced at Enchanter Evariste, who was chatting pleasantly with one of the mounted elves.

But is this another one of his secretly crafty plans? Or is he really this easy going and just wanted to visit an old friend and show me elven culture?

"Angelique, look." Evariste pointed in front of them as the trail took an abrupt curve. "You'll see your first glimpse of Sideralis."

Sideralis was a tribute to nature, as the homes and buildings were built intermingled with unimaginably *enormous* trees. The dwellings—though most were built tall and narrow with glittering glass windows and spires topping most of the peaks—were each built out of different kinds of wood.

As they drew closer, Angelique could see they were stained and coated with a protective resin, so they glimmered in colors ranging from an earthy brown to a sunny gold.

The tallest building in the city—which was also the closest—was built out of white wood that glowed like the white trees had.

A river flowed down the center of the city, cheerfully gurgling as it passed under ornate bridges and spat frothy flecks of water at a small basin at the foot of the city.

Angelique's first impression was that the city reminded her of a statelier—and perhaps less cozy—version of Enchanter

Evariste's home. She could see it in the moons and stars that topped the spires on the buildings, fountains, statues, and gates that lined the river.

"There's Alastryn," the Elf King nodded at a tall elven lady who was gliding in their direction with smooth steps and admirable speed.

The lady curtsied with the grace of a swan. "Welcome home, Your Majesty."

"Alastryn, I've brought some guests. You know my elf-friend, Evariste? He's got an apprentice now—a syrupy girl."

Though the elf lady—Alastryn—did not let her soft smile slip from her face, she narrowed her eyes at her kinsman with an expression that would have made Angelique nervous. "*Your Majesty*," she said in a tone that was respectful but held a commendable amount of ire. "Your manners appear to be lacking at the moment."

Evariste laughed. "Hello, Lady Alastryn. Please allow me to introduce you to my bright apprentice, Angelique."

"Greetings, Lady Alastryn." Angelique curtsied, but she felt like an ungainly calf before the elegant elf aristocrat.

Alastryn's smile softened considerably. "Greetings to you, child of magic," she said.

"Lady Alastryn, I was hoping I could impose upon you and ask you to show Angelique around Sideralis," Enchanter Evariste continued.

"Yes, that's a *marvelous* idea," King Themerysaldi said. "Evariste and I can bum around in the Four Moons Pub. We have important affairs to catch up on."

The sharp look was back in Lady Alastryn's eyes. "But, cousin of mine, I was searching you out, for you have important matters to see to in the palace."

"I'll get to them later," the Elf King promised.

"Please, Alastryn," Enchanter Evariste asked. "I would

consider this as a particular favor to me—and I do believe Angelique will enjoy it."

When the elf lady glanced in her direction, Angelique nodded. "I would," she said—truthfully. "I have not traveled much in my life, and I am astounded by the beauty of your city."

The Elf King whistled sharply. "I apologize, Evariste, and take back my previous judgement. She's not stupid—she's cunning with her words."

The observation made Angelique flinch. *That's the exact sort of description I want to avoid! I'd rather if I was thought to be empty-headed.*

Alastryn slightly tipped her chin up and studied Angelique carefully. She smiled, and whatever she was pondering she must have made up her mind. "Very well, child. This way, to the palace. *We* can partake of our luncheon in a civilized manner inside the castle."

Angelique took a step towards her, then hesitated and looked back at her teacher. "Master Evariste, is it really a good idea for me to go alone?"

Enchanter Evariste smiled. "You're in fine hands, Apprentice. Alastryn is a wonderful hostess; I imagine you'll enjoy your meal."

"Doubtful," King Themerysaldi coughed. "Unless you enjoy being bored to tears."

Angelique paused another moment. *Master Evariste seems to trust that I'll be fine. So I will have to be.* She kept her eyes downcast as she discreetly checked her magic—making sure she had shoved it deep enough that it wouldn't unexpectedly stir—then curtsied. "Good day, Your Majesty, Master Evariste."

Enchanter Evariste waved merrily, and the Elf King yawned.

"Right, Alastryn is distracted. Let's go have some fun," King Themerysaldi said.

"Actually, before we see to our game, I was hoping you could help me with something," Enchanter Evariste said, right before he fell out of Angelique's hearing range. "I'm wondering if you know of any troubled youths..."

Angelique took a deep breath and fixed her practiced smile on her face as she followed after Alastryn, taking in everything she could.

As I need to be a model enchantress to keep suspicion off me, I couldn't do better than to pattern myself off the refined and polished manners of the elves. Yes, I'll be fine. And hopefully I'll learn a great deal besides what Master Evariste had planned.

TWO DAYS LATER, a slightly confused Angelique found herself tramping through the forest with Enchanter Evariste.

They had left the boundaries of Alabaster Forest nearly half an hour ago, but they traveled parallel with it and often trekked away from it only to come right back.

Are we lost? Angelique wondered.

Ahead of her, Enchanter Evariste glanced at the map once again, then set off away from the border of the elven woods, heading west.

No, she scolded herself. *Enchanter Evariste wouldn't get* lost. *He has portal magic—he must know exactly where we are going.*

"Tell me, Apprentice, what is the duty of a magic user?" Evariste asked. He started down what looked like a deer trail that wound around the edges of a giant rock the size of a small cottage.

"To protect people from the misuse of magic," Angelique recited as she had a thousand times during her time as a student.

"Correct," Evariste agreed. "But it's more than just that."

Angelique almost tripped on a tree root but caught herself by slapping a hand on the big rock. "Is that so, Master Evariste?" she asked politely.

"Yes. I know as a general rule the Veneno Conclave teaches us to be reactive—to act only when magic or foul magical creatures are interfering with the lives of folk. But mages with as much power as we do have a duty to *help* the weak as well."

"Help?" Angelique furrowed her forehead as she tested the word. "In what way?"

"However we can." A fallen tree blocked the path, so Evariste turned and started traveling south again. "It means something different for every situation—though of course you must not act against your morals, and many times you'll find that helping a person does *not* mean giving them what they most desire."

Evariste looked around the woods for a moment, then continued. "It might, however, mean bringing rain to a village experiencing a drought or helping a child lost in the woods. It can be more difficult if a royal is involved—anything political tends to make our honorable leaders skittish, but understandably. They don't want any mage mucking around with politics, believing they can force change."

"That's something we're told to ward *against*," Angelique added.

"Yes, and it is an important principle to uphold. But a family on the brink of starving, or a poor town plagued by wolves: *that* is something we can help that won't change the continent politically, but will change the world for a few people," Evariste said as they started to drift back to the Alabaster woods.

"So you think—whenever we can—we ought to help the common people as well?" Angelique asked.

Evariste nodded as he studied the map. "Yes—as long as it does not impose on your morals, as I said earlier. Of course, sometimes that aid goes beyond the physical."

"Beyond the...pardon?" Angelique repeated, confused.

"Sometimes we must act as teachers and help a soul reach an understanding of their actions," Evariste continued. "And that's what you're going to do today. If we can ever find the village of Boyne, that is."

"We're lost?" Angelique asked in surprise.

"Not exactly, I just can't seem to get us where I want us to be." Enchanter Evariste glanced at her, his eyes full of mirth. "Would you like to give it a try?" He held out the map—which was a fairly detailed image of the human woods that surrounded Alabaster Forest.

Angelique reluctantly took it and brushed the slightly faded ink that recorded the area. "Where did you mean for us to go?"

"This village down here, Boyne." Evariste pointed to a small village squatting in a brief gap in the trees. "It's a town built around forest industry—they have many carvers, carpenters, loggers, and the like. But they have some livestock and agriculture to support the village."

Angelique nodded. She glanced up at the sky—barely able to make out the position of the sun between the thick branches that stretched high over her head—and used the zing of elf magic that radiated from Alabaster Forest to help place herself before she turned around and led them northwest.

They fell into companionable silence as Angelique rotated between glancing down at the map and carefully studying the forest terrain.

"What did you mean?" Angelique asked.

"Pardon?" Enchanter Evariste pushed his hood off his head. Even in the muted light of the forest, his blonde hair seemed shiny.

Not that I'm jealous. "You said that sometimes we have to help people reach an understanding of their actions. What did you mean by that?"

"Ahh, yes. Sometimes folk become misguided. They act in ways that will bring harm to those around them—and eventually themselves. Occasionally—not often mind you—it is our duty to help a soul reach enlightenment."

"So...we have to lecture them into acting better?" Angelique asked.

Evariste laughed. "That's a rather frank way to put it, but yes. Most often, we'll be asked to teach or guide a child, but there have been a number of times I've had to talk with an adult—particularly if their selfishness or greed is affecting their entire village."

"But we wouldn't dare to do such a thing to rulers, yes?" Angelique found a break in the trees and took a moment to study her shadow, giving herself a better idea of what direction they were traveling in, before course-correcting a bit.

"No, even attempting to teach a monarch a harmless lesson would be meddling in the affairs of a country. That's something we cannot do as magic users," Evariste said.

"That's a bit odd, isn't it?" Angelique asked, only half thinking of her words as she finally found the big rock they had wound around before. At the rock, she turned sharply, setting them west.

"In what way?" Evariste asked.

"The Veneno Conclave considers the Snow Queen to be the founder of the modern mage, don't they?"

"Yes."

"And she rallied an army and fought a war to free Verglas from invasion. That seems to muck around in some pretty big politics." Angelique froze in the middle of her step when she realized what she had blurted out. "I mean..."

Evariste patted Angelique on the shoulder. "You're not wrong—though the enemy she saved her country from was an organization of evil—and misled—magic users, which is where the Conclave's oath to protect the continent from misused magic comes from."

Panic made Angelique's heart beat twice as fast as they started walking again. *You dolt! Those are the kinds of observations I need to avoid making if I want to ever make the rank of Lady Enchantress!* She cleared her throat and smiled widely. "Yes, of course!" She was careful to pitch her voice as happy and carefree. "It was just a silly observation."

"It wasn't silly," Enchanter Evariste said.

Angelique raised the map higher and snapped it as loudly as she could, desperately trying to change the topic. "We should be headed in the right direction. I don't think it will be much longer before we reach Boyne."

"Did they teach you how to read maps in your classes?" Evariste asked.

Angelique relaxed, overjoyed he was letting the previous conversation die. "I believe most people can read maps," Angelique said, "regardless of whether or not they have magic."

"Yes, but most mages can't read a terrain map as well as you are," Evariste said.

"Oh, well." Angelique glanced up at her instructor, who smiled kindly at her—seemingly expecting a longer reply. "My father taught me. He was a soldier and did a lot of forest scouting."

"A solider, you say?" Enchanter Evariste asked.

"Yes," Angelique paused, her mouth twisting slightly as her heart warred between bitterness and longing.

"He must be very proud of you," Enchanter Evariste said.

"I like to think he would be." Angelique stared at the map with more care than necessary.

Several long moments passed. When Evariste spoke again, his voice was soft and pained. "Angelique...is he still alive?"

She mashed her lips together in an effort to keep her face from crumpling. Even though it had been years since her parents had died, the loss still sometimes throbbed in Angelique's heart like a re-opened wound.

"No. He died in a goblin attack—saving a mother and child," Angelique said.

Another few moments of silence. "I'm sorry," he said.

Angelique shrugged. "He was proud to be a soldier, to save people."

"Didn't your magic first manifest during a goblin attack?" Evariste asked.

Someone has been doing some research on his apprentice. Hopefully that's not a bad sign. "Yes," Angelique agreed. "It was that one." She hesitated, then added. "After both my parents were killed, my magic ripped free, and I finished off the goblins."

"Angelique..." Evariste's voice held a lot of feeling, but Angelique couldn't risk looking at him.

She had once been *so proud* of her magic. It felt like proof that she was her father's daughter, that she would carry on his legacy... until it became apparent she wasn't a budding hero, but a monster.

CHAPTER 7

The baa of a noisy goat rang through the air—sounding like the sweet tolls of salvation to Angelique. "I hear livestock; that must be Boyne!" She said with cheer that sounded hollow. She folded up the map and offered it to her master. "I believe I can confidently say it's through that line of trees."

Evariste took the map, then briefly held Angelique's hand and squeezed it. "Thank you for getting us here safely." His voice was a low rumble, and the light in his green and blue eyes was regretful.

"Yep," Angelique said stupidly, affected—against her will—by the look on his handsome face.

He squeezed her hand again before he released it and ambled in the direction the goat bleat had come from. "Let's see if we can find you a misguided youth to teach, Apprentice!"

Angelique obediently trailed after him, watching as he slipped the folded map into a pocket of his bright blue jacket.

I am surprised Enchanter Evariste isn't good at terrain maps. He gives off the feeling of competence—if not mastery—in all areas of life.

She thought of his library—which was incredibly impressive

given it housed only his private collection of books and maps he didn't want to risk in the workshop.

Angelique's eyes widened, and she halted, imitating a statue.

Wait a minute! He has portal magic and has said plainly that much of his work with magic involves studying the terrain and pin-pointing locations on maps. He's not just good with maps; he's an EXPERT!

Angelique's jaw threatened to unhinge as she studied Evariste's back with critical eyes.

This was one of his crafty moments—and that had to have been a test. I don't know what it was a test of, but I can only hope I passed it.

Angelique gulped.

"Are you coming, Apprentice?" Enchanter Evariste called in his charming voice.

"Yes, my apologies!" Angelique hurried after him, wondering what exactly she had agreed to when she became his apprentice.

ENCHANTER EVARISTE INSTRUCTED Angelique to wait in the trees while he entered the small village to check on something.

Angelique leaned against a tree and shut her eyes as she listened to the familiar bleats and snorts of livestock and the tolls of the bells that hung from leather collars on their necks.

"What excellent fortune!" Enchanter Evariste declared when he finally rejoined her. "I have found the perfect assignment for you. This way."

They skirted around the village until they were south of it, where a large meadow stretched between the buildings and the trees.

A little boy who couldn't have been older than ten walked among a flock of sheep. He yawned widely as he scratched his rib cage and called to a sheep when it started to wander towards the forest.

"Do you see that young boy?" Evariste asked.

Angelique nodded.

"He is tending to his uncle's flock of sheep. His job is to keep the herd together so no lambs wander off, and to call for help if a wolf or wild animal comes from the woods and attacks the livestock," Evariste explained.

"I see?" Angelique said. *Why is he telling me this? That's a fairly standard task for a shepherd boy.*

"It can be rather dull work, and unfortunately this boy, Wybert, has learned to get his entertainment by shouting to the other villagers that there is a wolf. The villagers rally to drive the wolf away, but find only the boy, laughing and mocking the villagers with no wolf to be seen."

"He is lying when he calls for help?" Angelique asked.

"Precisely. He's done it about half a dozen times now, and the villagers are growing resentful," Evariste explained. "They can't risk ignoring the cry—this is the only herd of sheep in the village, and it would be a grave financial loss if something were to happen—but they disrupt their own work to answer his false cries."

"They can't assign him to a different role?" Angelique asked.

"They could, but I think it would be best to curb his lying behaviors now. Besides, his father is a soldier in the Farset army and isn't home often. His mother needs the extra income he earns tending sheep for the family to survive, and there are no other roles suited for a boy his age that pay as well."

Angelique frowned slightly as she watched the boy try to poke a butterfly with his staff. "What do you plan to do?"

"I won't be doing anything," Evariste said, flashing her a grin. "It is *you*, Apprentice, who will be acting. Your task is to set this boy down the proper moral path."

"...you mean you want me to lecture him so he stops lying?"

"Yes."

Angelique squinted at her master and forced herself to snuff out the desire to ask what made Evariste think—based on their short acquaintance—that Angelique was suited to scold small children.

But if I refuse, the Council will find out about it in the reports—and who knows how they'll interpret it. I guess it's off to verbally harangue a child I go.

"Very well," Angelique grasped the skirts of her gown as she smiled wide enough to make her cheeks hurt. "I shall endeavor to make you proud, Master Evariste!" She put a spring in her step and held in the eye roll she wanted to execute as she traipsed across the meadow, making a beeline for the bratty boy.

The boy had busied himself with tugging on a twig stuck in the wool of a fuzzy sheep. When he caught sight of Angelique, however, he stopped pulling. His mouth dropped open and he stood, his eyes enlarging as she drew closer.

Angelique released her skirts and smiled as the white and gauzy pink material settled around her. *Maybe Master Evariste is onto something with the fancy clothes, because something tells me he would not be nearly as impressed if I waltzed out here in my dreary school gowns.*

"Wybert of Boyne," Angelique cooed in the syrupiest tone she could muster.

"H-how do you know my name?" the scruffy boy asked.

"I am a mage." Angelique gestured theatrically. "There is nothing that can be hidden from my kind."

The boy scratched the top of his head, making some of his hair stick straight up. "You look pretty young for a mage."

"That is a *charming* thing to say to a lady," Angelique said. "I suggest you keep that in mind when you're married and have children of your own."

"Huh?" Wybert asked.

Angelique slowly waved. "No matter. I have come today to speak to you of your actions."

The boy frowned at her. "What about 'em?"

Angelique artfully clasped her hands at her belly, buying herself a moment to think. "You are such a brave little boy to stand here and watch these sheep," she started. "It's a very important role. Your uncle *and* the villagers are counting on your courage and diligence to keep the sheep safe."

"Uh-huh," was the boy's ever-so-encouraging response.

"But I have heard that you have—on occasion—misled your fellow villagers." Angelique let dismay color her voice and placed a hand over her heart. "That you have called out to them, claiming a wolf is attacking when there is not one anywhere near the village *or* bothering your flock!"

Wybert shrugged. "So?" He didn't sound—or appear—at all repentant, sheepish, or guilty about the act. Instead, he planted his staff on the ground and leaned on it, eyeing Angelique as if she were a nagging schoolmarm.

The gall *of this child!* Angelique didn't let her irritation show and instead let her mouth droop slightly at the corners.

"You cannot do such a thing, Wybert," she said in an urgent tone. "If you continue to do so, not only will the villagers resent you, but no one will come to trust you. It is important to be honest and upright in all that you do!"

She paused, but Wybert didn't reply.

I should keep going...I suppose? I don't know how you're supposed to lecture a child so they'll listen!

"You must not lie or mislead others, Wybert," she said finally. "It might seem funny for a time, but you will encounter consequences for your actions. And I wish with all my heart that you would come to learn this before you encounter pain for your lies. Stop with the falsities."

Wybert squinted at her.

Angelique took a few steps closer to him and crouched slightly so she could look him in the eyes. "I'm serious, dear boy. You must stop. Do you promise to do so?"

The stick-like boy shrugged. "Sure."

I'm not sure I believe him. That seemed too easy, especially for a child bratty enough to lie in the first place.

Angelique forced a bright smile to her cheeks. "I am so happy to hear so." She patted him on the cheek, then stood straight. "Stay truthful, Wybert, and you will enjoy a life of esteem and respect from your fellow villagers. Stay vigilant!"

Wybert chewed a grass stem and did not reply.

Angelique nodded at him, then trekked back across the meadow, making her way to the smudge of blue among the shadows that marked out Enchanter Evariste's position.

"How did it go?" the enchanter asked when Angelique joined him in the forest. They walked a few paces deeper so they would not be visible to Wybert or his sheep.

He is an unrepentant brat, and I hope a sheep bites him.

"I'm not certain," Angelique said when she was able to speak without sarcasm. "I tried to be reasonable and explain to him why he should not do such a thing again, but it was rather tricky."

Enchanter Evariste nodded and flicked his blonde bangs from his eyes. "Morally guiding a person is often one of the trickiest tasks we can receive." He started the journey back to Alabaster Forest. "Often, the recipient does not want our guidance—even if those around him or her know better—and it is difficult to know how your words might affect them."

"How do you go about it?" Angelique asked. She faked dismay and put a hand to her mouth when she saw a fallen log ahead.

"The same way we improve at magic—practice." He offered her his hand, which made Angelique inwardly cringe.

I hadn't meant for my theatrics to move him—I just thought it was how a genteel lady might react. That goes to show me, I guess.

But Angelique took his hand and let him guide her around the log.

"Helping people requires patience and experience. The more you try, the more you learn about people—how they think, what moves them," Enchanter Evariste continued. "You will fail, and sometimes you might make things worse—whether through words or magic—but you must accept your mistakes and keep trying, Apprentice. That is *key*. Don't give up."

Angelique nodded slowly. "I suppose you are right—"

"*Wolf!*"

Angelique spun around and ran back the way they had come—hopping over the log with the ease of a coyote.

"*Wolf!*"

It was indisputably Wybert calling—Angelique recognized his reedy voice.

Her skirt snagged on a stick, and it took a moment to pull it free. Evariste passed her in that time, though he skidded to a stop not far ahead of her—just where the trees started to thin out.

Angelique jogged the short distance and scowled when she saw the meadow through the trees.

The villagers were pouring out of the tiny town, shaking pitchforks, carrying bows, and shouting.

Wybert was laughing so hard he bent over, almost kneeling on the ground, the sheep eating placidly around him, and not a wolf in sight.

"You should see your faces!" the little brat laughed. "All red-faced and splotchy—a bunch of carvers coming to chase off a wolf..." he trailed off, unable to speak over the belly gusts of laughter.

The villagers growled to each other in anger as they made their way back to their buildings with their makeshift weapons.

Angelique had barely enough time to make her ugly glare a slight frown of disappointment as Evariste turned to face her.

"It would seem the young boy did not heed your warning," he said.

"So it would seem," Angelique echoed. She flattened her lips as she watched Wybert fall on his rump due to his laughter.

What a thoughtless little troll—doesn't he see what his "fun" is doing?

Angelique took a step into the meadow, intending to go

deliver a few more words to the boy, but Enchanter Evariste placed a hand on her shoulder.

"Wait," he said. "You can try again tomorrow." His fingers brushed her arm as he released her, then turned to plunge back into the forest.

Angelique glared at the unrepentant boy for a moment. *He doesn't regret his actions at all. I might have even spurred him on with my lecture.* She reluctantly followed after her master. "Do you think I might have done more harm than good, Master Evariste?"

"No." Enchanter Evariste glanced over his shoulder at Angelique, then paused, waiting for her to catch up. "I think Wybert would have reacted so no matter who told him to stop."

Angelique gazed up at the trees and watched a fluffy tailed squirrel run from branch to branch. "Do you think it's merely because he's spoiled, or is it a cry for attention?"

Enchanter Evariste tilted his head as he thought. "Either is possible. Though I find it commendable you would consider it might be the result of a deeper conflict." He held back a branch, allowing Angelique to pass in front of him. "It is something you might want to consider speaking to him about tomorrow."

Angelique scratched her chin. "As you say, Master Evariste," she finally concluded. *Hopefully I can get through to the little beast. I'm not sure if there is any other approach to take.*

CHAPTER 8

The following day, Angelique was *prepared*. She had spent the late hours of the evening in her beautiful room in the elven palace planning out the words she would say to Wybert that would convince him to leave his lifestyle of a lying little shepherd behind and pursue a life of righteousness. (She could even say that, now, without snorting in laughter or wanting to swat his ear.)

"Are you ready for your second try, Apprentice?" Enchanter Evariste asked.

Angelique nodded. "Yes, Master Evariste. This time I'm much more prepared. Hopefully Wybert will find me more persuasive."

"I wish you all luck." Enchanter Evariste's smile was just a *tiny* bit cynical as he scratched his neck. "It seems you will need it."

Angelique nodded, then grabbed fistfuls of her skirt and again did her best to "float" across the meadow like an elf, when all she wanted to do was charge at the disreputable boy—snarling like an angry badger—and pounce on him.

Wybert saw her coming and smirked.

Angelique ignored him and wiped a fake tear from her eye. "Wybert, you bring sorrow to my mage soul with your lies. Why did you call for the villagers yesterday when there was no wolf?"

"Because it's funny!" Wybert thumped his staff on the ground for extra emphasis, upsetting the closest sheep.

Angelique sighed. "Are you certain? Because it seems to me that it is a cry for attention—a desire for love and companionship, perhaps?"

Wybert frowned at her. "What?"

"Perhaps you miss your father, or you resent the responsibilities that have been put upon you in your father's absence," Angelique suggested.

"Papa comes home every week," Wybert said.

There goes that defense. The little weasel! Angelique patted a sheep's wooly back. "Then I do not understand what drives you to act out in this way."

"I already said—it's because it's funny!" Wybert snorted. "The blacksmith's face always turns purple with anger, and most of the carvers and craftsmen get splotchy!" He laughed and slapped his thigh.

"But Wybert, in telling so many falsehoods, you will soon isolate yourself," Angelique said. "No one will believe you. How could they when you play practical jokes regarding a very serious matter?"

Wybert jerked his shoulders into a hunched shrug.

"Do you not see how *angry* your fellow villagers are?" Angelique persisted. "Wolves are a very real risk. By lying about them, you are creating a mockery of your role as shepherd."

Wybert shook his head and rubbed his nose on his shirt. "There's no harm. Wolves rarely come 'round here. I've never seen one."

"Don't be too sure about that," Angelique said. "And what if a threat doesn't come in the form of a wolf, but as thieves? A bear? A rogue mage?"

Wybert rolled his eyes and groaned.

"Consider it, Wybert." Angelique started to drift back to the forest. "If you don't change your ways, you'll forever tarnish their trust, and when you need help, there will be none who believe you."

Angelique did her best to float back to Evariste's hidden spot in the gloom, but it was a little tough when she stubbed her toe on a rock hidden by the thick grass and was reduced to little more than a hobble.

"Maybe that talk will stick longer than a few minutes." Angelique tried to sound cheerful, but the words came out hued with sarcasm.

"If he persists in lying, it is through no fault of yours, Apprentice," Evariste said.

Angelique yanked on a curl of her brown hair—which had escaped from her elaborate braid. "Perhaps, but isn't it my task to teach him a better path?"

"You can teach him, but it doesn't mean he'll choose that path." Evariste offered her a sad smile. "Which is something I am afraid you will become rather familiar with. There will be times when you will have every piece of evidence on your side, and still the man or woman you are trying to convince will disregard your words and will instead take a path of pain and regret."

Doesn't that sound cheery?

"But even so," Enchanter Evariste continued. "We must give them the choice. It is the right of every human to choose how they will live their life and reap the consequences that will come with it. What we cannot allow is the poor decisions made by others to harden our hearts and make us into cynics."

Is it too late for me? I feel like I am naturally a bit of a cynic. Or perhaps I'm lucky, and I'm just a jaded individual with a taste for sarcasm?

"Yes, Master Evariste," Angelique said. "I understand what you—"

"*Wolf!*"

Angelique grit her teeth and swung around to face Wybert, his flock, and the meadow.

Again, there was no wolf in sight. The young boy was turned eagerly in the direction of the village as he shouted again.

"*Wolf!*"

He turned around long enough to smirk at Angelique—flaunting his dishonesty.

That little RAT!

Angelique clasped her hands together—to keep herself from screaming like a banshee and tackling the little ingrate.

As she watched, Boyne once again stirred with life, the villagers rallying against a cry they likely guessed was not truthful.

Angelique mashed her eyes shut and scratched the back of her head.

"Don't take it to heart, Apprentice," Enchanter Evariste soothed. "Tomorrow, I will join you in speaking to Wybert."

Angelique nodded and sighed. "Thank you, Master Evariste." She was able to keep her disappointment out of her voice as together they watched the villagers charge out of Boyne, only to shout at Wybert—who was again laughing.

Angelique drooped as she watched the snickering boy.

I failed. I'm not taking responsibility for Wybert-the-rat's mean streak and lies, but this was my first real assignment. And I failed it. Terribly. He isn't any better—he calls wolf even more often now out of spite!

"Come, Apprentice. Let us make our way back to Sideralis," Enchanter Evariste called as he started edging his way through the trees.

Angelique bowed her head, then fell in step behind her master.

What will Master Evariste tell the Council in the reports...and what will the Council decide as a result? Will he tell them Wybert is beyond help and needs to get thrown into a vat of butter before being tossed to housecats—as I wish we could?

And even if he does, will the Council believe him? Or will they see this as more proof that I shouldn't be an Enchantress and that the Conclave has no place for me?

At dinner, Angelique was grateful for the loud-mouthed and boisterous Elf King as he and his equally raucous generals kept Enchanter Evariste entertained.

Though Enchanter Evariste occasionally patted her hand or nudged a dish at her plate, he didn't try to pull her into the conversation.

This suited Angelique just fine. Though the food was delicious—enough to make her salivate on her walk to the dining hall—her thoughts were occupied by the bratty Wybert.

How could I have done better with him?

She delicately picked at her food—quail served with figs and wild rice—as she tried to review the things she had said.

A warm hand touched Angelique's shoulder. "You seem thoughtful tonight, Apprentice."

Angelique straightened up and put on a pleasant expression so she could properly greet Alastryn.

The elven lady set a steaming clay cup of tea in front of Angelique's plate, then took a step back. "Is the food not to your liking?"

Angelique shook her head. "No—it is scrumptious! I fear Master Evariste may have to roll me home when we finally leave these beautiful woods."

"Then what troubles you?" Lady Alastryn asked.

"It is only..." Angelique hesitated, then blushed a little in embarrassment. "Master Evariste gave me an assignment as an enchantress-in-training, and I fear I have failed it rather terribly."

"I see." Alastryn pointedly looked at the male elf who sat on Angelique's other side. When he realized the king's cousin was staring at him, he shifted his attention to her.

Alastryn made a shooing gesture, which popped the elf out of his chair and had him edging around the table without exchanging a word.

Alastryn smiled as she sat in the abandoned chair, adjusting her wine-red skirts so they elegantly flowed over the seat. "And what assignment has your teacher given you?" she asked.

Under Alastryn's kind but expectant gaze, the entire tale spilled from Angelique's lips. She told her of Wybert and her frustration and inability to convince the boy to *stop lying*!

"He sounds like a weasel," Alastryn said when Angelique finished.

"I think *rat* might be a more apt description," Angelique sighed.

Alastryn laughed. "Perhaps! If he were an elf child, his mother likely would have thrown him to the wolves by now to teach him a lesson."

Angelique smiled at the thought and slightly shook her head.

"I couldn't help but notice, however, that you have limited yourself to speeches and pleas," Alastryn said.

Angelique took a sip of her tea and blinked to keep her expression straight, for she had *not* been expecting a warm drink spiked with what was very obviously hard liquor. She swallowed and had to wait a moment for the burning sensation to pass from her throat. "Yes."

"Perhaps you might think of trying a different method—like speaking to his mother?" Alastryn suggested. "Or have his uncle threaten to dock his wages."

"Those are very fine suggestions," Angelique said diplomatically. *They might temporarily patch the problem, but I don't believe it will fix Wybert's behavior. He was gleeful when he called the others. I don't know that withholding money would change that. And his mother already knows about the problem.*

"Regardless, I think you ought to try once more," Alastryn said. "You are the apprentice to Lord Enchanter Evariste—one of the most powerful enchanters on the continent. And he chose *you*," Alastryn said.

Angelique judged that this was not the time to explain Enchanter Evariste had acted only to save her from getting sealed.

"You are an intelligent and clever mage," Alastryn continued. "I think you will figure out a way to bring this shepherd boy to heel."

"Thank you for your kind words, Lady Alastryn," Angelique said.

"Of course," Alastryn's smile turned sly. "I wish my dear cousin shared some of your sense of decorum. Perhaps you and Evariste might teach him some."

Maybe refraining from serving spiked drinks would help? Though I expect if this is what they frequently consume, they must have high tolerance for it. "I don't know that I could ever teach the *Elf King* anything," she confessed.

"It's not so farfetched," Alastryn said. "As an Enchantress, you will share a similar lifespan with us, and you have a greater knowledge and understanding of the world—or you will. Give it some time, Lady Apprentice. You will find your place in the world."

Alastryn lovingly patted Angelique's cheek, then stood. "If you'll excuse me, I ought to check on the rest of the guests and the next course. Enjoy yourself, Apprentice."

"Thank you, Lady Alastryn," Angelique said. "I will." She bowed her head in respect as the elven lady drifted away.

A female servant whisked Angelique's quail away and set down in its place glazed turkey, which—judging by the smell—was baked in some sort of alcohol.

A very high tolerance indeed. Angelique smiled, but after a moment or two, her thoughtful frown returned. *Perhaps Alastryn is right. Maybe I should give Wybert another try.*

THE FOLLOWING DAY, Angelique made her way through the village of Boyne, alone.

She had managed to convince Enchanter Evariste to give her one last chance at helping Wybert fix his ways. Even better, she had convinced him to remain behind in Sideralis. (She didn't think she could stand him witnessing her failure a *third* time.)

If she couldn't get through to Wybert, they had agreed that Enchanter Evariste would come the following day, and Angelique would remain hidden in the woods to observe.

The scent of sawdust tickled Angelique's nose as she wandered past a woodcarver's store. She had been hoping something in the village might provide inspiration or give her a better idea of how to approach Wybert. Instead, as she neared the far side of Boyne, she found a mob of angry villagers re-entering the village, carrying bows, pitchforks, hammers, and the like.

She cleared her throat and tried to make her voice smooth yet elegant—like an elf's—when she approached a rather purple-faced man who seemed to be contemplating murder with his chisel. "Excuse me good sir," she started, "Could you tell me what has happened?"

"What?" the man rumbled. Angelique was afraid, for a moment, that he might jab her with his chisel. But his scowl faded when he got a look at her, and he made himself stand upright with his shoulders back. "Ahh, beggin' your pardon, you're the Lady Enchantress who travels with Lord Enchanter Evariste, yes?"

"I'm afraid I'm only an enchantress-in-training," Angelique smiled. "But has something happened? You appear troubled."

"Aye, I'm troubled," the man growled, a vein throbbing in his neck. "All of Boyne is troubled! It's that fool Wybert. He called us saying there was a wolf again."

Angelique tilted her head. "He called just now?"

The man nodded. "Used to be a rare joke he'd play, you know? But now he calls most every day—sometimes more than once."

Angelique felt her smile turn brittle. "Does he, now?"

"It's a nuisance, and his mother can't seem to make him mind himself." Another dark frown twisted the man's lips. "I thought Lord Enchanter Evariste might be able to talk some sense into him, but it seems I was mistaken."

Angelique's skin-deep veneer of sweetness and good cheer started to flake. *That little rat. It's not enough that he makes his whole village angry, now he's dirtying Enchanter Evariste's reputation? Enough. If he can't be reasoned with, I'll teach Wybert a lesson he won't soon forget.* "How unfortunate," she said, aware there was a hint of frost to her words. "I was sent here by Lord Enchanter Evariste to try to talk to the boy one last time. Perhaps I will finally succeed in making him see the errors of his ways."

The villager snorted but had the good manners to grimace guiltily afterwards. "Excuse me, lady; that was no judgement on you. It's just I don't know *what* would get through to Wybert now. Lord Enchanter Evariste can't."

CHAPTER 9

Angelique had to physically force her lips to remain in a smile. Even if she wasn't completely sold on Enchanter Evariste's motivation for helping her, he was a great enchanter whose reputation *should* have been unreproachable. "I am certain Master Evariste could, for it was I he charged with Wybert."

The man cleared his throat with a loud harrumph and scratched his beard. "If you say so."

"*I do*," Angelique said in a hardened tone. She cleared her throat and elegantly folded her hands together. "I shall make my last attempt, but as I do so—good sir—I must ask that if Wybert cries 'wolf' in the next hour, I want you and *all* the villagers to ignore it."

"Ignore it?" he echoed.

"Yes. Could you pass the word along of my request?" Angelique asked.

The man nodded. "Sure I can. I wish you luck in your ventures, Lady Enchantress."

Angelique grabbed fistfuls of her skirt, raising it slightly. "Thank you—and it's enchantress-in-training." She didn't wait around for his reply but marched through the village, exiting out the other side and bearing down on Wybert with the anger of a raging bull.

A plan was forming in her mind—one that skirted the edge of what would be an acceptable action from a mage, much less an enchantress. But Wybert had done enough damage, Angelique was willing to risk it if it meant finally getting through to him.

It's a good thing Enchanter Evariste will not be here to witness it, or I would not dare attempt this.

Angelique grit her teeth when she saw the shepherd boy, who was still snickering to himself over his last prank as he picked a clover leaf off his shirt. "Wybert!" she barked, the glitz and gloss gone from her voice.

The boy had the nerve to *smile* as Angelique stomped up to him. "Back to give me more lectures of piety, lady—ACK!"

Wybert coughed when Angelique grabbed the boy by his shirt and yanked him closer.

"Listen well, for this is the *last warning* you will receive. Stop calling wolf, and perhaps in the future you might be able to make things right," Angelique hissed.

"Let me go!" Wybert struggled.

"Liars aren't believed even when they speak the truth, Wybert," Angelique said. "You will soon learn this for yourself."

She abruptly released his shirt, making Wybert topple over. He scowled at her as he dusted his pants off.

I ought to give him the chance to agree—even though he won't—for this next bit might be a jolly good time for me, but as for Wybert...

"Do you understand?" Angelique asked, her voice hard.

"Sure," Wybert sneered.

Pompous little—

Angelique forced a smile on her face, but she was so angry, she was aware it looked more sinister than it should have. "We shall see..." She drifted off to the woods, not bothering to look back at the imp.

When she reached the trees, she continued for several

minutes until she couldn't see the miscreant shepherd, but the faint bleats of his sheep still reached her.

Angelique bit her lip for a moment in indecision, then took a deep breath and dredged up a glob of her core magic. It took her a moment to get the right amount before she mentally threw the locks back on her magic and shoved the rest down into her soul.

She grimaced as she handled it, but she kept her mind focused as she twisted the magic this way and that, gradually spinning it into an illusion.

The Council would be horrified if they learned of what I am about to do. But as much as I try to deny myself and act how they would like me to, I can't deny this method suits me much better. At the very least, it should fix Wybert—and no one *will doubt Master Evariste's abilities! Best yet—he won't even hear of it! Hopefully.*

Angelique smiled as the first wolf illusion took shape, its bronze eyes glowing in the shadows of the forest. Cream, tan, and gray fur appeared next, wrapping around the beast's wiry frame.

The wolf sniffed the ground as Angelique shaped a second one—this one with an all-black coat.

The ebony wolf gave an experimental yip as Angelique finished the puff of his tail. She narrowed her eyes as she watched the illusionary wolves sniff each other, then wag their tails and wiggle their butts.

I put too much dog in them. I'll have to adjust that before we head out, Angelique thought as she wove together a third, all white, wolf. By the time she started to create a fourth wolf, Angelique could feel her magic stretching.

I guess four is all I'm going to get. I don't fancy drawing more of my core magic, and this is about my limit of concentration anyway. She frowned as she poked a finger through the slightly transparent hindquarters of the final wolf—which was white and shale gray in color.

All of the wolves were ever-so-slightly transparent, but it was only noticeable if one was close enough and really *stared* at the canines and realized that some of the patterns in their fur wasn't due to color but the textures surrounding the animals.

It will have to do. Besides, if I can scare Wybert enough, I don't think he'll notice.

Angelique groaned as she finally stood up straight again.

Though Enchanter Evariste had promised the more she practiced, the faster she'd be able to work her magic, Angelique guessed her illusions had taken roughly a quarter of an hour to spin.

But I needed them to be my best, most convincing work, or this won't work. Frowning at the thought, Angelique made an extra twist to the magic in the illusion, so the white wolf's muzzle was flecked with blood.

She wiped the bit of sweat she had worked up off her brow and nodded at the wolves. "Let's go terrorize a deviant," she suggested.

The wolves very unwolfishly wagged their tails and barked.

Yes, far *too much dog.*

Angelique crept to the edge of the woods, staying down low to avoid detection.

Wybert stood, oblivious, in the middle of the meadow. His back was to her, as he used the butt of his staff to prod a grazing sheep.

Though Madam Quarrellous might argue it's a sign of my evil soul... I'm going to enjoy this.

Angelique dug her fingers into the wolves' transparent bodies as she adjusted and shaped her illusions, so the wolves stopped wagging their tails and instead growled and peeled back their lips —showing bone-white teeth.

Perfect!

Angelique grinned in satisfaction as she dropped to her knees and began to crawl her way towards Wybert. The grass and alfalfa only hid her somewhat, but as long as Wybert had his back to her, she was probably safe. He was—hopefully—going to be otherwise occupied when he finally *did* turn around.

She twisted uncomfortably to peer behind her. The wolves stayed in the shadows of the forest, as she had spelled them to. *Good.*

Angelique hoped the spells Evariste had placed on her clothes held strong as she crawled adjacent to Wybert.

Once satisfied with her position, Angelique crouched in the grass and tugged the strands of her illusion spell.

The four wolves slunk from the forest, guttural snarls leaking from their throats as they stalked across the meadow.

Wybert scratched his side as he slowly turned around to investigate the noise. When he saw the wolves, he emitted a choked yelp as he stumbled backwards.

"W-wolves!" he shouted. "*Wolves!*"

Angelique held her breath, hoping the carver had gotten around to everyone.

"Wolves—in the meadow!" Wybert yelled.

The village of Boyne was silent.

The wolves fanned out. They ignored the sheep—which scattered and ran for the village—and instead formed a half-circle around Wybert.

Wybert held his staff out in front of him. "Wolves! I mean it—wolves!" He shouted so loudly his voice cracked.

Nothing stirred in Boyne.

Wybert trembled as he started backing up.

The white wolf growled and lunged at him.

Wybert screamed. He tripped on his own feet and fell to the ground. As he scrambled to stand, Angelique crawled around behind him.

The wolves flattened their ears and licked their chops as they stared at Wybert, their white teeth flashing with every snarl.

"*Wolves*! Why...why is no one coming!" Wybert sobbed.

When Angelique was directly behind him, she stood up. She

drew as close to him as she dared, then whispered. "Because, Wybert, *no one believes a liar—even when he's telling the truth.*"

Wybert whirled around, his face scrunched in terror. "H-h-help me!" he begged.

"Stop lying, Wybert," Angelique advised. "For the consequences of lying are a far higher price than you are willing to pay."

Angelique stepped around the boy and walked towards the woods.

Her wolf illusions growled and circled the shepherd boy for a few extra moments before they turned and slowly stalked after her, occasionally pausing to snarl back at Wybert.

When Angelique reached the forest she stepped behind a tree. Her wolves loped past her, hopefully disappearing from the boy's sight. Cautiously, Angelique leaned around the trunk and peered back at the meadow.

Wybert had fallen to his knees and was visibly trembling.

Yep, that ought to fix the little runt.

At Angelique's inattention, the wolves had degenerated back to their more dog-like behavior.

One of them sniffed her skirts, while the black wolf and white wolf busied themselves with sniffing each other's hindquarters.

Angelique cringed at their behavior. *It's a good thing Wybert wasn't looking* too *closely. They are definitely more transparent than when I first made them.*

She smiled as she held out her hand to the inquisitive wolf. *But...I never dreamed I'd be able to make something like this with* my *magic.*

She watched Wybert take a shuddering breath, then stand on unsteady feet. He tottered after his wayward sheep, glancing back over his shoulder every few steps.

Angelique smirked and poked at her illusions. All four of the wolves raised their heads and howled soulfully to the sky.

Wybert turned ashen and fled, sprinting to Boyne.

Angelique chortled to herself. "Oh, that was fun," she said.

"Giving just desserts warms the cockles of my heart," she informed the wolves as they peered up at her. "Though I probably shouldn't tell anyone that. Regardless, thank you for the help."

A flick of her fingers, and the wolf illusions faded away, leaving Angelique alone. She checked on Wybert—he had made it safely to the edge of Boyne and was gathering up the sheep again.

Yep, he'll be fine, she concluded. *And I suspect this has fixed him for good—though Master Evariste should follow up with him tomorrow.* That thought made her pause. *Maybe I can convince him to speak to Wybert's mother, instead? I'd rather not let him know that I got through to the little troll by traumatizing him.*

Angelique trudged through the forest, enjoying the cheerful cheeps of song birds mixed with the occasional high-pitched screech from a hawk.

She was so gleeful, she nearly hummed under her breath as she clambered over a fallen tree trunk. *Master Evariste said we would stay in Sideralis for a few more days, but we'll have to go home soon, I expect. The Council will be expecting their monthly report on my progress.*

Angelique grimaced at the thought, which was unpleasant enough to make her walk faster, anxious to reach Alabaster Forest so she could tell her teacher the good news.

She wasn't far from the elven woods when she felt her magic stir within her.

Cautiously, Angelique slowed to a stop. She frowned as she shoved her magic down but looked around. *My magic—as terrible as it is—usually doesn't stir without a reason—or a strong emotional reaction from me. But I'm fine, so what caused it?*

She looked left and right, but saw nothing—just greenery and brush.

...Just greenery and brush? What about the birds and other forest creatures?

Angelique turned in a slow circle as she listened for any sound of animal life, but not even a crow cawed. The wind stirred the branches of the trees overhead, making their leaves snap in a thunderous applause.

Angelique held a hand out and brushed the branch of a pine tree as her magic shifted again.

Yep, time to get out of here. She hurried towards Alabaster Forest, almost jogging. *I don't know what's going on, but whatever it is, I don't want to be here.*

She heard branches moving and turned just in time to see the tree trunk tossed her way.

CHAPTER 10

Angelique dove to the ground, and the trunk whistled over her head, colliding with two oak trees in an explosion of splinters and bark.

Angelique held her hands over her head as woodchips struck her back. She waited for the debris to settle before she dared to peel her face from the ground.

A troll stomped in her direction, dragging a sapling stripped of its branches in one fist.

For a terrible moment, Angelique gaped. *What is a troll doing here?*

Trolls were cousins of a sort to ogres and spent most of their time in swampy wetlands or moldy forests rarely visited by mankind. They were smaller and less intelligent than ogres, but they were at least eight feet tall and strong enough to flatten a cottage with just a few swings of their meaty fists.

This troll had a large, bulbous nose, a craggy brow that sank low over its beady eyes, and thick strands of yellow drool dropped from its toothy jaws. Shaggy hair sprouted from all over its body, and the creature smelled of putrid swamp water and dead carcasses.

The troll bore down on her, purposefully raising its sapling—which Angelique could see it had sharpened at the base into a wooden spear of sorts.

It raised the small tree, and Angelique felt her magic slam against the tight wards of her control, struggling to get out.

She ignored its call and scrambled to her feet to sprint away, dodging through the trees.

The troll threw his sapling-spear, and Angelique's war magic surged through her body with such force it made her misstep and trip. The spear passed so narrowly at her side she heard it whistle; she had barely avoided being impaled.

"Evariste!" Angelique struggled to grab at the tracking bracelet Evariste had given her and regain her balance well enough for her to run. "*Evariste!*"

She took an abrupt left—running north for a few moments before she again veered back east.

I have to make it to Alabaster Forest. If I can, the elf magic guarding their borders will kill it!

The troll rumbled after her, smashing through small trees and saplings like they were made of paper. It snarled and flung a rock the size of a small apple, which pelted Angelique on her lower back and sent her sprawling.

Her back ached, and her magic railed at her—demanding release. Clenching her teeth, Angelique pushed herself to her knees. She tried to force herself to stand, but her back burned as though it were on fire.

The troll bounded closer. It grabbed two tree trunks with its hands and pushed off them, launching itself forward like a rock in a slingshot.

It landed close to Angelique as she finally managed to rise to her feet and take a few toddling steps behind a tree.

The monster snatched up a rock the size of Angelique's head. Just when it raised its arm, a bolt of fire struck it, engulfing the hairy creature.

"Angelique!"

Evariste popped out from behind the troll—which was bellowing in pain as the last few flickers of fire went out.

Angelique choked on the scent of singed flesh and hair but took a staggering step towards her teacher.

"Stay there," Evariste shouted to her. "We'll be able to fight it easier if its attention is split."

"Can't we run to the border of the forest?" Angelique pleaded.

He shook his head. "A troll isn't much trouble for someone with magic of our caliber."

A chill crawled up Angelique's spine, and she shook her head. *No, no, no. He better not be thinking about having me use my core magic.*

Evariste didn't see the sign of her refusal—his eyes were fixed on the troll.

The creature slammed a fist into a tree trunk, making it snap like a toothpick.

Angelique yelped and sprinted out of the way, hopping over another fallen tree.

Evariste's lips moved in words Angelique couldn't hear over the enraged snarls of the troll. The enchanter paused, then jabbed his fingers into his mouth and whistled.

The troll swung around to face him, and Evariste flicked his wrist.

A fist-sized rock hurtled through the air and hit the troll in the brow, as if it had been flung by a slingshot.

The monster once again roared in pain, making Angelique's ears ring. It shook its head, and she had to duck behind her trunk to avoid getting a face full of troll slobber.

"Angelique, try using your core magic on it," Evariste instructed.

"What?" Angelique shouted, unable to keep the fear from her voice.

"You'll be fine," he promised in a soothing tone shortly before taking an abrupt sidestep to avoid the troll's grasping fingers.

"There's a great number of sharp and jagged pieces of wood from this brute's propensity to snap trees."

"My magic is *dangerous*," Angelique argued.

Evariste wriggled his fingers, and a tree wrapped a willow-y branch around the troll's neck and reeled it backwards, yanking it off its feet.

The troll hit the ground with a thump that vibrated beneath Angelique's feet.

"Your magic is nothing of the sort," Evariste argued. "You need to use it so you see that!"

Angelique shook her head. "I don't have enough control over it. But I can distract the troll while you finish it off!"

"No." Evariste watched the troll struggle with the tree before it finally yanked the murderous branch straight off the trunk. "This is part of your lessons, Apprentice. You *need* to do this."

The troll lumbered to its feet, then charged Evariste.

The Lord Enchanter darted behind a tree, but the troll rammed into it and collapsed it.

Evariste kept running, weaving between the trees.

Angelique ran after them, scratching her arm on a thorny bush as she gave chase.

Evariste wove around a mud puddle, then stopped just past it. When the troll splashed through it, the mud sucked on its feet like quicksand, and it fell to its knees.

It started to crawl out of the mud but caught sight of Evariste again and tried to snatch him.

Enchanter Evariste lingered just out of the troll's reach, teasing it. "Now, Angelique," he said.

Maybe...maybe this will be okay? Her mouth was dry, and her heart pounded so loudly in her ears it was hard to think. *I've learned a lot. But, but...* She grimaced as she watched Evariste dodge the glop of mud the troll threw at him. *I don't have much of a choice. Not if I want to stay his apprentice.*

Angelique licked her lips and slowly loosened the ties on her magic.

Her hands shook as a silver cloud of her magic grew around her fingertips. She blinked as her magic stretched her awareness, and she searched for anything in the woods with a sharpened edge.

Splintered stakes of wood broken off from snapped trunks started to float in the air like dust motes, suspended by the power of her magic.

Though they didn't have the cutting power of a blade, the wood could still impale.

Don't use too much. Take as little as possible, Angelique reminded herself. She sifted through the chunks of wood, then rearranged them so they were pointed at the troll's back like wooden daggers.

The troll, unaware of the danger lurking behind it, finally boosted itself into a standing position.

"Good control, Apprentice," Evariste praised as he took a single step backwards.

The troll chomped its jaw, and more phlegmy drool fell from its mouth as it growled. It took a giant step towards Evariste, nearly blocking the enchanter from sight.

I need to strike now! Angelique hesitated a moment longer, then launched her attack, pelting the sharpened stakes of wood at the troll's back like a storm of arrows shot by an army of archers.

But as Angelique launched her attack, the troll lunged for Evariste, twisting the angle of his body.

While most of the stakes hit the intended target, two shot past the monster, on a straight path for Enchanter Evariste.

NO! As soon as Angelique saw their trajectory, she yanked back on her magic...too late.

One of the wooden stakes stabbed Evariste in the shoulder, the other grazed the side of his chest.

The enchanter grimaced in pain. And as the troll bellowed—laid flat by Angelique's attack—blood started to stain Evariste's fine jacket.

Something in Angelique broke.

She opened her mouth to scream—to call for help, to give voice to her horror, anything!—but not a single sound could claw its way from her throat.

I hurt Enchanter Evariste—I hurt my instructor! The man who has only shown me kindness I don't deserve!

Her magic started to boil with her terror, and Angelique ruthlessly shoved it deep—so deep she couldn't even *feel* it anymore.

I really am a monster.

Her legs gave out, and she couldn't *see*. Everything was darkening rapidly—though she was faintly aware of Enchanter Evariste shouting.

I'm a monster. A monster! The thought rammed her in tandem with the throb of her heart, and it was hard to breathe.

She heard sounds of a struggle—but they were muffled as if the encounter was far away.

The troll roared in pain, and there was a bone-vibrating thud that reverberated through the ground.

They were right about me. My instructors, the Council. I am a danger of the worst sort.

"Angel!" Warm hands grasped her shoulders and shook her.

Angelique blinked dazedly and slowly raised her head.

Evariste gazed worriedly at her, his eyebrows furrowing as his green and blue eyes traced her face. "I'm fine, Angel," he said. "You did well."

Behind him, the troll was collapsed on the ground—motionless and likely dead.

Angelique's eyes strayed from the defeated creature to Evariste's bleeding shoulder wound.

Before she could get a good look at it, Evariste yanked her against him so her face was mashed into his good shoulder. He encircled his arms around her in a rather forceful embrace.

"I'm fine, Apprentice," he said in his soothing, musical voice.

Angelique shook her head.

"I am," he insisted. "You were fantastic."

The metallic scent of blood assaulted Angelique's nose, and her stomach heaved.

Enough—I'm not the one hurt! We have to get Evariste back to Sideralis, or he might bleed out! I will have plenty of time to dwell on this later. "We have to get you help," she said, forcing her jaw to work again.

"It's nothing to worry about, Angel," Evariste said. "I felt you yank back on the trajectories right before they hit me—they barely nicked me."

The increasingly overwhelming scent of blood disagreed with his claim.

"We still need to seek aid for you," Angelique said. She tried to pull away, but Evariste kept her sandwiched against his chest as they sat in the dirt.

The enchanter didn't answer but patted her back.

Angelique wanted to scream at him. *What is he doing? Why is he trying to pacify me when he is bleeding from two wounds* I *gave him!*

She shifted her face slightly so she could see his wounded shoulder.

The stake was no longer there, but the bloodstain was growing rapidly.

Angelique succeeded in prying herself from his grasp. "Can you make a portal back to Sideralis?"

Evariste shook his head. "Emerys will arrive soon, I'm sure. He'll take us back."

Angelique snapped her head in a nod. "Is there any healing magic you can use on yourself?" She stood on shaky legs, ignoring the way her lungs felt crumpled and her thoughts screamed at her.

Now is not the time—as much as I deserve it.

"Angel," Evariste stood as well and gently cupped her right hand in his. "I'm fine," he repeated.

Angelique's eyes shifted to the still-growing bloodstain on his shoulder, and her stomach heaved.

She staggered to a bush and retched. Her throat and lips

burned, and a few tears escaped her control and rolled down her cheeks.

Stop it! Evariste needs help because of ME!

"Angelique?" Evariste rubbed her back and made a soothing noise.

Her stomach heaved again. This time she dropped to her knees.

How could I have hurt him? Just how black is my soul?

Her stomach finally settled, but the rancid taste in her mouth —and her heart—remained.

Wretched and miserable, she again staggered to her feet.

"We have to get to Sideralis," she croaked.

Evariste tilted his head as he listened. "Emerys will take us back," he said.

Angelique miserably rubbed her face and nodded, though she didn't understand what he was talking about.

A few moments later, King Themerysaldi—riding his war unicorn—shot into the area of ruined forest.

His unicorn picked its way through the wreckage and brandished its horn at the fallen troll.

The Elf King whistled. "A troll? In Farset's woods? That's unheard of—" he cut himself off when he spotted Evariste. "You're injured?"

"Just a scratch," Enchanter Evariste said.

Angelique emitted a gurgling sound of hysterical laughter, then slapped her hand over her mouth. With great effort, she made herself look the Elf King in the face and curtsied. "Lord Enchanter Evariste is in dire need of medical aid. Could you take him back to Sideralis?"

The Elf King furrowed his brow as he studied Angelique. "Certainly. One of my men will bring you back—here they come." He placed a hand on his unicorn's well-muscled hindquarters and twisted to peer behind him.

Elven warriors mounted on prancing horses stormed the area.

The horses snorted at the sight of the troll, but instead of shying away as most mounts would, they tried to charge the dead monster, and their riders had to fight to keep them calm.

"Sharych," King Themerysaldi started.

"Send at least two warriors with Angelique," Evariste said suddenly.

Angelique stared at the ground but was determined not to close her eyes in shame when she thoroughly deserved to be punished.

"And Abynth," the Elf King said as if he had not been interrupted, "escort Apprentice Angelique back to Sideralis. The rest of you, investigate this troll. I want to know what it was doing in Farset—and so close to Alabaster Woods."

The elves murmured to their king and dispersed.

Angelique watched King Themerysaldi slip off his unicorn and beckon to Enchanter Evariste. "Come, friend," he called. "Pookie will be extra gentle."

"I'm not an ailing old woman," Enchanter Evariste took Angelique's left hand and squeezed it. "We will talk about this later, Angel," he murmured to her. "What happened was *not* your fault." He squeezed her hand again, then released it and wandered towards the waiting Elf King.

"Not an old woman? You could have fooled me," King Themerysaldi snorted. "If you move at a pace faster than a turtle's waddle, I'll consider giving you a leg up."

"Unnecessary, you strapping young lad, but I appreciate the sentiment," the Lord Enchanter joked.

Two elves approached Angelique.

"You will ride my mount, Apprentice Angelique," the darker haired one of the pair said. "This way, please."

Angelique nodded and woodenly followed them.

She wanted to cry but stuffed the feeling down. When she felt the tiniest glimmer of her magic surface, she ruthlessly cut it off.

I'm never using my war magic again.

"This is entirely unnecessary, Emerys." Evariste said. He frowned up at his friend, who fussed with settling silken elven blankets around him on the bed.

"I know that, but I also want to know what happened," Emerys said. "And if you keep acting evasive, I'm going to strangle you with your own blanket."

Evariste shook his head. "I need to see Angelique."

"*Evariste*," Emerys said in his rare, Elf King voice that sounded like iron and left no room for argument. "*Explain.*"

Evariste sighed. "I made a miscalculation."

Emerys arched one black eyebrow.

"When the troll attacked, I told Angelique to attack it with her war magic. She's so *frightened* of herself, I wanted to give her the opportunity to see the good in her powers." Evariste stared at the gauzy canopy stretched over the top of his bed. It was accented with tiny, intricate leaves that looked like they required a ridiculously long amount of time to embroider.

"And?" Emerys prodded, his voice flat.

"She attacked, but the troll moved, and like an idiot, I was standing in range." Evariste groaned. "Part of her attack hit me."

Emerys nodded. "I see."

Evariste studied his friend. "You do?"

"With great clarity. You made two mistakes—both of them stupid," the Elf King declared with no hesitation. "First of all, you pushed your apprentice to use her magic far sooner than you should have."

"I did," Evariste admitted. "I thought the troll was a good opportunity—even if it was earlier than I liked. I got impatient."

"Impatient?" Emerys snorted. "You pushed a student—whom you have spent your *entire visit* rambling about, so even I know the very unwanted information of how shaky her relationship is with her own magic—to attack a *troll*—a large and potentially dangerous creature for a mage as unpracticed and paranoid as your apprentice."

Evariste winced at hearing his mess-up so ruthlessly and clearly voiced by his friend. "It was unwise of me," he agreed.

And unfortunately, Angelique is the one who will pay the price for my idiocy. Evariste could see it in her eyes after he killed off the troll.

She was never going to trust her magic again.

If he ever wanted her to master her war magic, it was going to take a great deal more effort...and a long, long time.

"Secondly," Emerys continued, ticking off Evariste's sins on his fingers. "Yes, you were an idiot for sitting by the troll like a target," Emerys said. "You should have known better than to stand in the strike zone of a green mage."

Evariste pinched the bridge of his nose. Both his shoulder and his side were down to the barest whispers of pain thanks to elven magic, but somewhat perversely he wished his wounds still hurt. It might make him feel a bit better.

"She is a student," Emerys continued. "That means you're supposed to guide her through this, not throw her in, and particularly *not* setting her up for disaster as you did."

"I know, *I know*," Evariste groaned. "I just...forgot."

The furrow in Emerys' brow became even more pronounced. "You forgot about your *apprentice*?"

"No—it's just..." Evariste sighed and shifted so he sat upright. "She's so clever. I don't think she realizes how fast she's been learning illusion weaving. Her power, it's *breathtaking*. And she has no idea! She could have stabbed me straight through, but I felt her react and yank back in a split second. No inexperienced student could do that—not even most veteran mages!"

Evariste stared at his bed's canopy again, unable to face Emerys.

"Really, it's not so much that you forgot her, but that you forgot she's not yet on your level," Emerys said. "You're hoping she's as strong in her magic as you were, which is why you let yourself be stupid."

"I don't know." Evariste tiredly ran a hand through his hair. *Why did I have to befriend an Elf King of all people?*

He knew the answer to that: it was because there was no one else.

Being a prodigy—and now, perhaps, legendary—made for a very lonely life. Regular mages were overly pleasant to him of course, but even other enchanters and enchantresses always beheld him with too much respect.

No one actually *liked* him—or at least no one wanted to befriend him.

Emerys was in a similar position.

He was the youngest Elf King in centuries, and he hadn't been prepared at all for his parents' death, which plopped him on the throne in a rather abrupt manner. He was more sarcastic and brash than an average elf—never mind the Elf Kings before him.

And so, their friendship was a bond forged out of shared experiences, and a desperation for a friend who would see them as they really were and wouldn't be afraid to speak their mind.

Though sometimes I do wish Emerys wouldn't speak his mind quite so bluntly.

"I need to tell Angelique that this was *my* mistake, not hers," Evariste said finally.

Emerys snorted. "Obviously. She's walking around like a kicked puppy."

"Can you talk to her about it, too?" Evariste asked.

Emerys tossed his head much like his pet unicorn. "*What? Why?*"

"Because she needs to hear it from someone else besides me, or she won't believe it," Evariste said.

"I don't want to deal with your sugary-sweet apprentice. She's going to cry," Emerys said plainly.

"She's *not* sugary-sweet, she's just acting like that," Evariste said. "I told you the night we arrived that she has war magic—she has bones of iron. But that's going to make it worse in this case because she's going to take this as a sign that she's evil."

Emerys rolled his eyes. "So, she's not just sugary-sweet, she's dramatic too. Charming. My answer is still no."

"Emerys..."

"Ask Alastryn. She actually *knows* the girl," Emerys complained.

"Yes, but you are my personal friend *and* the Elf King. She's less likely to think you are lying," Evariste countered.

Emerys groaned but finally conceded. "*Fine*. I'll talk to your dear apprentice," he growled. "But if she cries, I'm leaving without finishing."

"She won't cry," Evariste promised.

Emerys looked unconvinced. "Stay in bed. If you come tottering outside like a babe first learning to walk and your dear apprentice sees you, you're only going to make her feel worse."

Evariste nodded. "As you say." He waved farewell to his friend.

The dark-haired Elf King grunted once then strode off, looking as excited as a weasel caught in a trap. He ducked out of the palace's sick room, leaving Evariste alone.

Evariste scratched his forehead and leaned back against his bed's headboard.

It seems I won't be getting any awards for my skills as a teacher. He ruefully smiled and shook his head. *Particularly not if I forget that my student is on a different knowledge level than I am.*

To be fair, Emerys likely would have thought differently of Angelique if he had not witnessed how she dealt with the boy in Boyne.

Though Evariste agreed Angelique could approach Wybert one last time by herself, there was not even the slimmest chance he was going to let her go alone through the woods, no matter how safe Farset was.

Evariste instead followed her from a distance, then trekked

down to their usual spot south of the meadow as she walked through the village.

He couldn't help but smile when she gave free rein to her irritation and growled at Wybert, but he almost fell out of the tree he had climbed because he was laughing so hard when he saw her start to weave her wolf illusions.

She had pulled off her idea beautifully. The wolves were a solid piece of spellwork—even if she put less power into them than she should have. (It was, Evariste was coming to learn, her signature mistake.) Moreover, Evariste would bet his house that Wybert would never cry "wolf" again.

He was still snickering to himself, which is why he unfortunately lagged behind her in returning to Alabaster Woods.

Thankfully she had evaded the troll with relative ease, but still.

What was a troll doing in Farset?

Evariste shifted uncomfortably in his bed, itching with the desire to get up and go chat with Emerys' generals.

Though the continent had seen some shake-ups in the past fifty years or so, they were usually limited to specific areas. (Baris, for example, had seen some trouble.) But for the most part, the continent was enjoying unprecedented peace.

So why was a troll wandering around a populated human forest—and so close to elven territory?

He'd have to submit a report to the Council about it with his monthly progress report for Angelique.

We probably shouldn't travel home by portal gate, either.

Evariste eyed the door and wondered if he could safely disobey Emerys, or if one of the elves was lingering unseen, posted to stop him from getting up.

I hope he can get through to her—I hope I can make her see that her magic isn't evil. She's too clever to waste—and too powerful to lose.

CHAPTER 11

"So, you see, it's his fault. All his fault." King Themerysaldi scratched his elbow and looked as though he would rather be anywhere else. "He is your teacher. He should have known better. But sometimes he acts like a dunce—try not to hold it against him."

The sun shone brightly, casting warm beams on Sideralis through the branches of the giant trees that surrounded the city.

From their spot in a gazebo constructed of white wood that stood at the center of the palace gardens, Angelique could hear the neigh of horses and faint laughter and chatter of elves.

"Do you understand?" King Themerysaldi asked.

He had spent the last fifteen minutes telling her why she shouldn't feel guilty about injuring Evariste. ("He should have known better than to stand directly behind your target," and "he was an idiot for pushing you to use your magic without any guidance," were commonly repeated phrases throughout the talk.)

Angelique didn't doubt he believed his words—at least partially anyway.

But even so, Angelique could have accidentally killed Enchanter Evariste with her volatile magic. As it was, she had injured him—more badly than he let on given that he was *still* resting in bed under the attention of an elf doling out healing magic.

King Themerysaldi tapped his foot. "Do you understand?" he repeated.

Angelique nodded slowly—though she didn't agree with the Elf King's explanation. "Yes, Your Majesty. Thank you for taking the time to explain this to me."

The Elf King narrowed his eyes. "You don't believe me at all."

Angelique forced a smile. "You are a wise elf, Your Majesty. How could I—" Her false words of assurance were drowned out by King Themerysaldi's groan.

"Look. Evariste is one of my only friends, and he likes you quite a bit. Believe me for his sake—because then I can tell him, and maybe he'll finally stop sighing like a disappointed dog," he grouched.

Angelique curtsied. "I will take the time to ponder your words, Your Majesty, and contemplate on my actions."

The Elf King stared at her for a minute. "I really hope you turn out to be worth all the effort Evariste is going to put into you." He shook his head slightly, making his thick black hair dance. "And I sincerely hope one day you lose this syrupy edge of yours. Farewell!"

He hopped over the side of the gazebo rather than take the stairs and purposefully strode through his gardens.

Angelique slowly lowered herself onto an unornamented—but beautifully simple in its design—wooden bench.

What now? She wondered.

She had hurt another human being with her magic. Such a thing had always been her worst nightmare and something she strode to avoid.

And now I've gone and proven everyone's judgement about me right.

Angelique pressed her fingertips against her closed eyes.

I can't use my core magic. It's too dangerous, too dark. I'm selfish enough to admit I want to be an enchantress, badly. If I make enchantress, I can spin my wretched powers into something good. But I don't know that I deserve that sort of position.

I am too much of a liability—no—a danger to remain unsealed.

Angelique studied her shaking hands.

It seemed like Evariste intended to keep her on as an apprentice. He wouldn't have pointed the Elf King in her direction if he planned otherwise.

Angelique didn't think it was very wise of him, but she was too self-centered to suggest that or to willingly let herself be sealed.

Maybe that's just another way I'm a monster. But if I don't use my core magic, I won't be as much of a danger, right?

Angelique stood abruptly.

I'll get better at stifling my core magic and work even harder to improve in other areas. I'll study relentlessly.

The image of Enchanter Evariste—his jacket turning red with his own blood—assaulted Angelique's mind. She could almost smell the tangy, heave-inducing scent of blood again.

"Never," Angelique whispered, the word dropping from her lips like a weight. "I'll *never* let that happen again."

ANGELIQUE FELT like an imposter as she stood side-by-side with Evariste to bid King Themerysaldi and Lady Alastryn farewell.

"Thank you for your visit, Apprentice Angelique." Lady Alastryn smiled as she clasped Angelique's hands between hers. "I look forward to seeing you frequent our Sideralis. Lord Enchanter Evariste is a common guest; I am glad you will join him, and I eagerly await our next meeting."

Angelique did not miss that the lady elf had purposely phrased all extensions of another trip not as a request or hope, but rather a statement.

She offered her a smile. "Thank you for all you have taught me during my stay."

"It was my pleasure—you are such a pleasant student," Lady Alastryn said. "Unlike others." She glared briefly at her royal cousin.

King Themerysaldi ignored her. "Watch yourself, Evariste," he said with a lopsided smirk. "Come back when you can slip your duties and Conclave leash," he suggested. He glanced at Angelique and nodded. "That goes for you as well, Apprentice."

Angelique curtsied. "Thank you for your hospitality."

King Themerysaldi awkwardly scratched the back of his neck. "Yeah, sure. *Oof*—"

He coughed when Lady Alastryn smacked him in the ribs.

"I mean, our pleasure," he amended. He nodded again to Evariste. "You've decided against opening up a portal here because of the troll, right?"

Evariste nodded. "Yes. I'm going to risk summoning *him* instead."

"Good luck," the Elf King said doubtfully. "Please make sure he doesn't rampage through my kingdom, again, in his anger."

Evariste laughed. "I'll try," he said. He placed a hand on Angelique's elbow. "Come, Apprentice. This way."

Angelique followed obediently, trying to take inventory of his wounds.

The troll attack had taken place a mere two days prior, and Enchanter Evariste was already moving as if his wounds did not hurt him.

She suspected this was more a testament to elven healing arts than the gravity of the wounds, but she was thankful regardless.

Enchanter Evariste hadn't treated her any differently since the troll. Rather, he had repeated the entire talk she had with King Themerysaldi—albeit in a far nicer way. She believed him even less than she believed the Elf King, but she took it as a sign that he planned to keep her on as his apprentice.

For now.

"I'm going to summon Pegasus to carry us home," Evariste explained as they drew a little farther away from the elf party that was still waiting to send them off. "He is an *unusual* steed to say the least."

"In what way, Master Evariste?" Angelique asked.

"In the way that he is a strange mash of pure magic and animal," he said. "Technically, he's a star constellation. But he has magic and can take a bodily form as well."

A constellation? "Oh?" Angelique said since he seemed to expect a response.

"He's quite temperamental and doesn't care much for humans, but he owes me a favor, and in exchange lets me ride him whenever I call," Evariste explained. "But you have to be careful around him. He's wild and unpredictable—much like raw magic."

"And he can carry both of us?" Angelique asked.

Evariste nodded. "At the speed of a shooting star. He's *fast*. But I don't like summoning him too often, or he might one day decide no favor is worth this and choose to kick me." He laughed, but Angelique suspected he didn't mean it as a joke.

"I want you to take shelter behind this tree." Evariste gestured to an ancient oak tree that was thick enough Angelique would have been hard pressed to hug its trunk. "And come out when I call."

"Yes, Master Evariste." Angelique moved behind the tree and leaned against it, pressing her forehead into the rough bark as she waited.

Evariste smiled, then raised his hand and gazed at the sky. "Pegasus! It is I—Lord Enchanter Evariste of Fire Gates. I summon you from the skies to carry me across the lands. Come!" he shouted.

Something thundered overhead—like an explosion of magic. Evariste stared up expectantly at what bits of the bright blue sky were visible through the canopy of trees.

A black streak shot across the sky in a mixture of stars and wings. It hurtled towards them, flexing its wings when its front hooves struck the ground with a boom loud enough to force Angelique to her knees.

Carefully, as she scrambled to her feet, she peeked around the tree.

Pegasus, the living constellation was…indescribable.

His mane and tail were made of dark blue flames that flared and flickered as he tossed his head. His black body seemed insubstantial, because his coat was the night sky molded into the shape of a horse.

With every prancing step he took, thunder crashed and shook the ground. His black wings broke down into thousands of black feathers—like a log rapidly turning to ash—that spiraled away into the sky.

"Pegasus!" Evariste smiled as the heavenly equine approached him—his hoofbeats turning quieter until they were muffled thumps. "It is so good to see you again. I'd like a ride to my home in Wistful Thicket in Torrens, please."

Pegasus arched his neck, making his muscles pop.

"Wonderful, thank you. I have another passenger I'd like you to carry—she's my apprentice, actually. Please allow me to introduce you. Angelique!" Evariste's voice was all sunshine and joy, but Angelique could tell he was carefully measuring his words and interactions with the constellation.

How promising. Angelique grimaced, then lifted her chin and fixed a smile on her face as she left the protection of the large tree and joined Evariste.

"Pegasus, this is my apprentice, Angelique," Evariste said. "Angelique, make your greetings."

"Good day to you, Pegasus," she said in a pleasant tone. She was proud that her voice didn't falter, even when Pegasus gazed at her with eyes as black as the darkest parts of the night sky.

Pegasus snorted, and the red of his nostrils flared, glowing like coals. He tossed his head and swished his flaming tail.

Inspired by the mount's obvious rejection, Angelique threw in a curtsy for good measure.

The constellation briefly moved his muzzle closer to her—close enough that she could feel his hot breath fan her hair. Just as abruptly, he moved away, the flaming fringe of his mane sparking.

"How perfect: Pegasus approves!" Evariste said brightly.

"*That* is what his approval looks like?" Angelique asked, shocked.

"Oh, yes," Evariste nodded. "If he hadn't liked you, he probably would have broken one of your limbs."

The Lord Enchanter strode after Pegasus, leaving a shocked Angelique in his wake.

Perhaps it's a good thing I'm Master Evariste's first apprentice, she thought. *It's not a loss if I am injured, and maybe he will learn on me so as to keep his future students from being...impaled.*

"Come along, Apprentice. We're leaving!" Evariste called in his obstinately cheerful voice.

"Coming!" Angelique hurried after him, hovering awkwardly just behind his shoulder as Pegasus lowered himself to the ground.

"You'll get on first, and I'll slide on behind you," Evariste said.

"*What?*" Angelique squeaked.

Evariste motioned to the constellation's broad back. "You get on first." His eyebrows slanted with sympathy. "Or do you not know how to ride a horse?"

"I know how to ride a *horse*," Angelique had to work hard to keep the hiss out of her voice. "What I do not know is how to ride a *constellation*!"

"Everything all right?" King Themerysaldi called to them.

"Just fine, thank you, Your Majesty!" Angelique curtsied to him because it seemed like a good idea with all the powerful beings in the area.

"Riding Pegasus is just like riding a horse," Evariste told her confidently. "Except you don't steer at all; you can't ever use a saddle since he wouldn't stand for it, and you have to hang on a bit better. Believe me, you don't want to fall off at the speeds he runs."

Angelique stared at him for a moment. *He is my instructor and master*, she reminded herself. *Not to mention that I injured him—badly, I think. I have lost all right to question him, even over his admittedly dubious ideas.* "Very well," she said, finally.

Angelique felt a sweat break out on her back as she slowly approached Pegasus.

He watched Angelique with his uncomfortably dark eyes, and snorted again when she drew close enough that the skirts of her dress touched his side.

Angelique flinched but made herself slide onto his back, adjusting her gown so she could more easily sit astride.

He wasn't warm or solid like a usual horse. Instead, Angelique felt as if she sunk a bit into his coat, and he gave off a sort of frosty, *biting* heat.

Evariste slipped on behind her and snaked his arms around her waist so he could grab a thatch of Pegasus' flaming mane.

When Angelique cautiously copied him, she found Pegasus's mane was warm and made her fingers tingle, but did not burn her skin.

She had her jaw clenched shut in apprehension, but a squeak still escaped when Pegasus rocked into a standing position.

"Hold tight," Evariste advised. "He'll spend a moment getting his bearings, and then we'll be off."

Angelique nodded and adjusted her grip on the mount's mane.

Evariste disentangled one hand from Pegasus' hair long enough to pat Angelique on the arm. "You're doing great," he said. He twisted slightly—knocking one of his shoulders into Angelique's as he addressed the elves behind them. "Take care, Emerys. We'll come again soon," he called as the constellation walked in a tight circle.

"Safe travels," Emerys said. "And remember, don't be stup—" the Elf King's words were cut off when Pegasus bolted.

He galloped through the forest at a speed that made it hard to breathe—and impossible to see due to tears gathering in Angelique's eyes.

Somehow, the constellation didn't collide with any trees, and instead veered wildly as he charged through the forest.

Angelique clamped down on the animal's body, half frozen between fear and awe as the wind stung her face.

The world was a blur as Pegasus charged ahead.

Angelique started to laugh as she realized, *I think...I think this is how flying must feel!*

WITH PEGASUS AS THEIR MOUNT, a journey that normally would have taken Angelique and Enchanter Evariste almost two weeks—perhaps more—was finished in two days.

And, Angelique suspected, if they hadn't stopped for the night at an inn in Sole, they could have traveled through the night and made it home by morning.

"Thank you for your aid, Pegasus," Evariste said as he bowed to the horse.

"Thank you, Pegasus." Angelique, windblown and still mentally shaken by the impressive rides, parroted.

The constellation stared at them and wrinkled his nose—perhaps in distaste—before he turned his hindquarters to them and took a few sauntering steps.

His ebony wings reformed—building up feather by feather. He gave them an experimental flap, then leaped into the air.

Lighting struck in the meadow, making Angelique jump like a startled dog—though she managed to silence any yelp she would have ordinarily uttered.

When she could *hear* again and the stars from the white-hot light finally faded from her eyes, Pegasus was a dark smudge in the sky, rapidly disappearing.

Angelique licked her lips. "Pegasus is..."

"Yes," Evariste agreed. He strode for his home, casually drifting across the brick bridge that spanned the pond—as if riding constellations was a normal occurrence. "He's from another realm—technically."

Angelique tried to restore some sense of order to her wind-blown hair. (Evariste, she was curious to see, looked fine. Not a strand of hair out of place or a wrinkle in his robe. *Now* that *is a spell I want to learn!*) "Isn't he the Pegasus constellation in the sky?" she asked.

"Yes, but the sky is considered a realm of its own. The citizens there don't often interact with our continent." Evariste waited for her on the far side of the bridge.

"Why?" Angelique asked.

"I'm not entirely certain," Evariste admitted. "Even my little friends won't tell me, but I believe it has to do with some of the earliest mages, in a story older than the Snow Queen."

Angelique frowned at the thought and mindlessly trailed after Evariste's perfectly neat back.

Yep. Once I make myself certain that I can contain my magic well enough, I will ask him to show me what spell keeps him so tidy. I need it more than he does, anyway. Angelique grimaced. *Though maybe I shouldn't ask. I don't deserve to know.*

"What's this?" Evariste paused outside the door to his home.

A white, folded letter was pinned to the door by a thorny vine. Evariste tugged it loose, and the vine shriveled up and died in the span of a breath.

Peering around his shoulder, Angelique could make out the Veneno Conclave's crest—a stylized V and C set over a four-pointed star—set in the red wax that sealed the letter shut.

"It seems we had a magic visitor while we were out." Evariste winked at Angelique and tapped her on the forehead with the letter before he pushed the door open.

Evariste entered his home and veered into the salon by the entrance, plopping down on a settee as he opened the letter.

Angelique made her way to the stairs—intending to retire to her room. (For there was no better time to practice confining her magic than *always*.)

Evariste made a noise of surprise. "Oh," he said after several additional moments.

Angelique paused, her foot on the lowest stair. "What is it, Master Evariste?" she called.

"It seems we will soon have company," he said. "A mage representing the Council is coming in person to collect my monthly progress report next month."

Angelique's heart fell, plummeting straight through her feet as she slowly made her way back to the salon. "Oh." She contemplated leaning against the salon doorframe but forced herself to stand straight at the last moment.

Evariste refolded the letter "It will be fine, Apprentice. The representative will want to see you work some illusions and perhaps ask you a few questions about magic theory or magic history. But they won't ask anything too difficult this early into your training."

Angelique pressed her lips into a thin line. "Do you really think that is all they'll do after they find out I hurt you?"

He tossed the letter on the settee and sauntered over. "I was injured through my own folly, Angelique. You share no part of the blame."

Angelique stifled the desire to roll her eyes at the blatant lie.

"Which is why," he continued, "I'm not going to tell the Council about it."

Angelique gawked at him. "You're *what?*"

"If I did tell them, it would reflect poorly on my teaching skills.

They might decide I *am* too young to have an apprentice after all and dissolve our oaths." Evariste batted his thick eyelashes and held a hand to his heart. "And you wouldn't want *that*, would you?"

If he hadn't been born a magic prodigy, he could have become a roaring good conman. Angelique held her sarcasm in check and managed to produce a brittle smile. "Is it really wise to keep information from the Conclave? Ought they not be informed of the troll?"

"Oh, I will tell them all about the troll," Evariste promised. "I'll just leave out how we slayed it."

Angelique pursed her lips.

Evariste sighed. "Angel," he said, shortening her name as he had during the troll attack. "You need to agree with me on this. Please."

"Yes, Master Evariste," Angelique said immediately.

His smile was back. "I knew I could count on you." Another wink, and he was sauntering off to a different part of the house—the kitchen, guessing by the way he bypassed the staircase.

Angelique watched him go with a frown. *I'm not certain it is wise to leave out information in a report, but he is my instructor.*

She heaved a sigh, then headed up the stairs. *Now, it is time to practice. Because I need to be better at cutting off my magic by the time the representative comes, or my apprenticeship might get dissolved anyway.*

CHAPTER 12

One month later, Angelique stood in the front salon, wearing a new dress she was desperately trying not to brush with her sweaty palms.

I cannot get this dirty. Master Evariste bought it specifically for this occasion!

"My apprentice, how lovely you look!" Enchanter Evariste exclaimed as he swept into the room, a baby unicorn trailing behind him. "And I'm not just saying that because we match," he added with a grin.

Evariste had proposed that to illustrate their "solidarity" and close relationship, they wear matching clothes.

So, Angelique was dressed in a white gown with wide, drooping sleeves. The edges of the gown were splashed with blue silk stitched to look like waves, and pins topped with blue lapis lazuli hearts kept her dark, wayward hair back.

Evariste, however, was the opposite. His coat was blue with splashes of white drenching the arms and edges, and he sported a lapis lazuli earring.

"Breathe, Angel," he instructed. "You'll sail through this little formality with ease."

Angelique nodded, barely registering the use of her nickname. (Evariste had taken to it since their journey to Alabaster Forest and used it more often than her full name these days.) She wouldn't have even given it a second thought if she had not been thinking of the representative.

Wait, we ought to be on our best manners. Or at least I *ought to be. But still.* Angelique plumped a gold tasseled cushion on an armchair. "You won't call me Angel in front of the representative, yes?" she asked.

Evariste blinked. "Why wouldn't I?"

Because the representative might die of a burst heart! Angelique cleared her throat. "Some might find it inappropriate."

He made a noise of dissatisfaction. "It is a cute shortening of my cute apprentice's name. If the representative is displeased by it, it is likely because they are jealous *they* don't have such a name."

Angelique stared at her teacher. *He can't really be such a conman and still be this oblivious...can he? It must be an act.*

There was a firm knock on the door.

"That must be they!" Evariste meandered to the door—the unicorn filly trotting behind.

Angelique remained where she was, checking to make sure she held only the barest flickers of magic at her disposal and had dammed up the rest.

Assured she had her magic under control, she joined Evariste at the door just as he swung it open.

Angelique's smile threatened to fall when she saw the first woman, Madam Quarrellous. The teacher's mouth was already pulled down in a disapproving frown.

Surprisingly, however, a second woman accompanied the academy instructor: a squat woman with a bright smile, gold-wire-rimmed spectacles, plump cheeks, and shiny salt-and-pepper-colored hair.

"Welcome, Sybilla, Quarrellous! Come in!" He beckoned for the two ladies to enter the house.

Angelique lured the filly away from the door, letting the ladies enter in unhindered.

"Thank you, Enchanter Evariste. You said that so nicely, I'll forgive you for being the reason I've been yanked from my responsibilities to be here." The short woman stood on her tip toes and patted Evariste's cheek with a smile.

"Sybilla," Madam Quarrellous frowned. (It was unexpectedly pleasant to see her frowning at someone else for a change.)

"Don't pretend otherwise, Quarrellous," the other woman, Sybilla chided. "I'm a FAIRY Godmother—I should be out finding children with magical abilities, not checking on one who already has an apprenticeship!" Sybilla put her hands on her hips and appeared to be about five seconds away from wagging a finger in Madam Quarrellous' face.

"This is a serious matter, Sybilla, or the Council would not have asked you to come," Madam Quarrellous said.

Sybilla snorted. "Fiddlesticks. They didn't care if I put my dress on a bear and sent it in my place. You are the one who insisted on bringing me."

"Believe me, I did *not* request you. I'd rather have had anyone else." Madam Quarrellous scowled.

"I'm afraid it really *is* my fault that you are here, Sybilla," Evariste said. "When the Council sent word that a fairy godparent needed to attend as well, I requested you."

The baby unicorn nosed Angelique's hands before it sidled around Evariste and poked its head out from behind him in curiosity.

Sybilla reached out and tapped the filly on the tip of its horn. "Requested or not, I'm here. Now, let's meet the girl so I can get this over with and get back to my job!"

"Of course," Evariste said. "Angel?"

Angelique moved to stand side-by-side with Enchanter Evariste and dipped into a curtsy.

"You already know Quarrellous, but Angel, this is Sybilla. She's a fairy godmother."

"Aren't you a beautiful girl?" Sybilla glanced over at Angel, then did a double take and stared at her again, her eyes widening slightly.

Perhaps the matching clothes are a little too over-the-top?

The fairy godmother—or First Appraised Isolator Rank Yellow, which was a fancy title to say she ranked just below enchanters and enchantresses in terms of power and was charged with childcare and development—slapped a smile back on her face without a pause.

"And you have such lovely magic, too," Sybilla added.

Both Angelique and Quarrellous stared at Sybilla, as if she had just lost her mind.

But the cheerful lady didn't seem to notice. Instead, she bustled over to an armchair and plopped down, propping her feet up on a footstool. "And what a charming home—you've grown domestic on us, Evariste. I remember as if it were yesterday how the Council was forever begging you to pick up after yourself when you first made enchanter as a wee boy."

I am absolutely going to adore Sybilla. Angelique hid her interest behind a mask of attentiveness as she fetched a tea-tray that had been waiting on a sideboard and brought it over to the fairy godmother.

Quarrellous picked a stiff, wooden chair and waved Angelique off when she offered her tea.

Evariste laughed and caressed the baby unicorn's head. "If you keep recalling my boyhood, Sybilla, my apprentice is going to lose all respect for me."

Angelique grinned at her master as she poured a cup of lavender tea for Sybilla.

Quarrellous sniffed. "If she does, it will be to her detriment."

Evariste shrugged. "Perhaps we should begin?" he suggested.

"Yes, yes, let's get on with it—thank you, dear." Sybilla took the teacup and saucer—decorated with brightly painted sunflowers—and squinted at Madam Quarrellous over her steaming drink. "Quarrellous, ask your questions."

Madam Quarrellous took the papers Evariste handed her—the monthly report of Angelique's progress as a student. "You claim you have not had any difficulty in teaching Angelique illusion magic. Is that true?" she asked.

"Yes. Angelique has grown quite skilled at it and is ahead in her lessons." Enchanter Evariste smiled and took the teacup Angelique offered him with a wink as he sat down on the settee.

"Has she tried to use these illusions in any nefarious way?" Quarrellous asked.

Thinking of the wolves she had woven to frighten Wybert, Angelique froze, guilt making her stiffen.

"*Really*, Quarrellous. Nefarious? They're illusions! What do you think she's going to do with them?" Sybilla scolded.

"Angelique has shown great diligence and wisdom in *all* uses of her magic," Enchanter Evariste said. "Most often, she has done so for practice, but she also rather ingeniously used illusions when aiding a village this past month," Evariste said.

Angelique focused on keeping her hands steady as she poured a cup of tea for herself. *He knows about Wybert and the wolves? How? He never went back to Boyne—he was too injured and told me if I thought I had successfully schooled Wybert that he believed me!*

"Has she used her core magic?" Quarrellous asked.

Angelique seated herself on the settee next to Enchanter Evariste and tried not to rattle her teacup as her guilt deepened.

"Yes, once—under my direction when a troll attacked us," Enchanter Evariste said.

"A troll?" Sybilla asked. "Where were you poking around that a troll found you?"

"Farset—we were near Alabaster Forest at the time," he said.

Sybilla set her teacup down on an end table with a clack. "You were close to the elves, and you were *attacked*?"

Quarrellous's frown morphed from disapproval to concern. "That is very grave news indeed; I assume you included it in your report?"

"Yes—on the final page," Evariste said.

Quarrellous nodded absently as she flipped to the last page and briefly skimmed the information. "I'll see to it that the Council is informed." She slightly shook her head. "Trolls venturing so close to elven civilization, that cannot have been a random chance."

"Will the Council dispatch someone to investigate the area?" Sybilla asked.

"I should assume so," Madam Quarrellous said. "It is a serious matter."

"I am close friends with King Themerysaldi. He has led several bands of his warriors on several different tracking and hunting sessions outside their woods, but he said he was unable to find any evidence of additional trolls. I mentioned that in the report as well."

Madam Quarrellous nodded and gathered up the papers. "Thank you for your diligence and work, Lord Enchanter Evariste." She smiled, and a kind light—which Angelique had never witnessed before—warmed her eyes.

"There is no need to thank me," Enchanter Evariste said. "We all guard this continent together."

"Yes, but it is still very strange," Sybilla muttered.

"What other questions did you want to ask, Madam Quarrellous?" Evariste stopped the unicorn when it tried to climb into the open spot on the settee between him and Angelique.

"Ah, yes, I beg your pardon for the interruption." Madam Quarrellous settled back in her stiff chair, the frown making its triumphant return when she peered in Angelique's direction. "Has your apprentice refused to follow your instruction?"

"No," Evariste said. "She's been an eager student in all the subjects we have explored."

"She has not refused to use her magic when told?" Madam Quarrellous persisted.

Enchanter Evariste shook his head. "No."

Only because Master Evariste hasn't asked me to use my war magic since we got back from Farset, Angelique thought glumly. *If I refuse next time he asks, he might not be quite so pleased with me. Though if he can take a wooden stake to the shoulder and still consider me a "bright" and "good" student, perhaps it is safe to say he has a very broad definition of the term* good student*?*

"Has she improperly used her core magic? Or perhaps she played with it when you were not present?" Madam Quarrellous asked.

"No. The only time she has used her war magic was under my direct request and supervision," Evariste said.

Sybilla grunted. "I see what is happening here. You—Quarrellous—are on a sorceress hunt after this poor girl."

"The Council agrees that she is a potential liability," Madam Quarrellous primly slipped Enchanter Evariste's report into a leather satchel she carried.

"That was before Evariste took her on as his apprentice. The Council wouldn't have agreed to let him take her if they thought she was a real threat," Sybilla rolled her eyes. "It is beyond me why they let you waste time and resources on the unnecessary—particularly when *I* have a difficult time wheedling any money into the budget for us First Appraised Isolator Rank Yellow—and we're finding *students*! The future of the Veneno Conclave!"

Angelique smiled slightly. It was a familiar complaint. Master Narclay, the non-magic-possessing Luxi-Domus instructor who had taught her swordplay and always treated her well, had complained about the department budget. (When students were sloppy during practice, he threatened to sell them off for department funds.)

"The Council requested a demonstration of what she has learned," Quarrellous said, ignoring Sybilla.

"Of course. I think Angelique could whip something up for you," Evariste smiled guilelessly—as if he had *not* warned Angelique two weeks prior that she would likely be asked for a demonstration.

Angelique inhaled and nodded. Carefully, she pulled a few additional strands of magic from her stores. It wrapped around her fingers, dusting her nails with silver sparkles as the illusion grew.

I have to make this good.

The illusion shimmered to life much faster than the wolves she had woven for Wybert. Not because it was any less difficult—in fact, though the creature she was molding was smaller than a wolf's muzzle, the illusion was intricately more difficult—but because she had practiced so much, her magic twisted easily into the illusion.

Angelique licked her lips and added a final twist to her magic before releasing it.

The illusion—a ruby-throated hummingbird—buzzed into existence. Its tiny wings flapped so quickly they were blurs, and the miniscule feathers on its head and back glowed iridescent green.

The hummingbird shot forward and tapped Evariste on his brightly colored coat before zooming through the room.

Sybilla laughed. "How beautiful!"

"Well done, Angelique!" Evariste praised.

Quarrellous was silent as the hummingbird investigated Sybilla's tea cup.

Angelique beamed for one radiant moment. "Thank you." She watched the little bird land on Sybilla's finger.

The fairy godmother admired it. "Why, you can't even see through it—this is some solid work!"

"Angelique has done quite well with illusions," Enchanter

Evariste said. "I mean to start her on alteration magic next because of it."

"I'd say that's a good plan. Birds are notoriously difficult to capture with their feathers and ability to fly—an ability we don't have and would find hard to fathom," Sybilla said.

Angelique leaned into the cushioned back of the settee, and the sensation of walking on needles decreased slightly.

It's easy enough to keep the illusion going: the difficult part is creating it. But I was more concerned that Quarrellous might feel me access my magic stores and grow upset.

"It seems, Lord Enchanter Evariste, that you are as brilliant a teacher as you are a mage." Madam Quarrellous tapped her fingers on Enchanter Evariste's report.

"Not at all—my student makes me appear better than I am," Evariste laughed.

Quarrellous pursed her lips. "It seems Angelique continues to progress, particularly as you have not lodged notice of any sort of mishaps or troubles."

Angelique gulped but didn't dare look at her teacher.

"There is nothing to lodge," Evariste said with his easy, charming smile.

"That is good to hear," Madam Quarrellous said. "However, Apprentice Angelique, the Council charged me with reminding you that should you fail to listen to Enchanter Evariste—*or* use your core magic without his supervision—you will be exiled from the Veneno Conclave, and your magic will be sealed."

"Did the Council really tell you to remind her of that, or have you simply chosen to take advantage of the situation to preach your own beliefs?" Sybilla wryly asked.

Madam Quarrellous sniffed. "Do you wish to make a formal complaint against me?"

Sybilla shook her head. "Madam, use the head you were blessed with and recall that you are in *Lord Enchanter Evariste*'s home. You just finished lecturing *his* lovely student when she has done nothing to cause concern. And—in case you have forgotten—I am a fairy godmother, which means I greatly outrank you. And I say this meeting is over. Evariste, if you would be a dear and open a portal gate for me in the yard? I should like to be dropped off in Kozlovka."

Sybilla stood and smiled, looking much like a cheery grandmother.

Madam Quarrellous gaped at the fairy godmother.

Evariste rose from the settee. "Of course, Sybilla. I will construct a portal for you and a portal for Madam Quarrellous. But I'll need to do this outside."

Angelique hurriedly followed suit, dissipating the illusion so the hummingbird disappeared.

"Naturally." Sybilla sailed towards the door, leaving Quarrellous to hurry after the strong woman.

They trooped outside—shutting the door so the unicorn filly could not follow—then crossed the pond bridge.

"Madam Quarrellous, where would you like to go?" Enchanter Evariste asked.

"The Veneno Conclave, if you will," Quarrellous said. "I should spread the word of the troll as swiftly as possibly."

"Very well, I can manage that." Enchanter Evariste strode ahead and began to summon his magic.

Angelique watched him with longing as his blue magic rippled around him—she wished *she* could be so comfortable with letting her magic drift around, but that was something she could never do.

She nearly jumped out of her skin when Sybilla patted her on the shoulder. "Yes, ma'am?"

"Try not to mind Quarrellous," Sybilla said. "She means well, but even she can see you are a good girl." the fairy godmother paused. "It's not your war magic she's concerned about, I think. It's the sheer amount of magic you can channel."

Angelique could not help the wry edge to her smile. "Of

course. I've been told at my highest strength, I could kill an army."

"Or several," Sybilla cheerfully agreed. "You could mold nations for centuries to come with that kind of strength. Power often corrupts—as the ethics instructor, Quarrellous knows this. Unfortunately, it seems she does not see the nobility of your character that will keep you from that."

Thinking of the wolves and the way she had harmed Evariste, Angelique lowered her eyes. "Despite what Evariste has said, I don't know that I am really *good*."

Sybilla tugged her wire-framed spectacles down her nose and studied Angelique with the intensity of a wolf. "With all your teachers squawking and carrying on, they've made you doubt not just your magic, but your very self, haven't they?" Not waiting for an answer, she continued, "Dear, do you know how to tell if someone is evil—*truly* evil?"

Angelique shook her head.

"They *enjoy* the pain they create. They revel in the bloodstains of battle, in the hunger of the starved, and in the suffering they inflict. They are concerned only with themselves and would gladly see the world topple around them—or conquer it themselves. They thirst for power and are *never* satisfied, and they love to harm and bully the weak—the ones who cannot protect themselves. Now tell me, Angelique, does *any* of that sound like you?"

"No," Angelique slowly said.

Sybilla nodded in satisfaction. "That is what I think as well. Keep your chin up. With every monthly progress report, you prove yourself. And one day, people will see your vast power as a blessing."

Sybilla smiled, then marched up to Enchanter Evariste as Madam Quarrellous walked through the portal he had created for her.

Angelique adjusted one of her glittering hair pins and smiled when the older woman waved to her.

It's nice to know someone doesn't abhor me, however idealistic she may seem.

Everyone feared her magic—her ability to kill.

Although...no one treated me like a killer until it was revealed how much *magic I have. Is it really just the depth of my magic?*

Angelique shivered, remembering the numbing horror that had nearly stopped her heart when she had injured Enchanter Evariste.

No. It's everything. There isn't one good thing about my core magic. It cannot be redeemed.

CHAPTER 13

"Mirror," Angelique started. "Show me Wistful Thicket—top view, please."

Angelique watched the surface of the mirror ripple like a pond.

The please isn't really necessary, but it makes me feel better about making requests. Even if it is requests from a...thing. An image of scrubby treetops that were starting to turn orange and yellow with fall appeared in the mirror's surface. She could even make out the clearing in the woods, and the blue roof of Evariste's home.

That seems like a pretty accurate depiction. "Mirror, show me... Lady Alastryn's home in Sideralis, please," she finally settled on.

The mirror rippled and...did nothing. It returned to its regular reflective properties, making Angelique frown.

"Ah," Evariste stirred from the footstool behind her on which he was perched.

When Angelique turned around to face him, he had his long legs stretched out in front of him.

"You won't ever be able to see anything in Sideralis—or Alabaster Woods," Evariste explained. "The elves screen themselves from magical sight and prying. Most high-leveled mages do the same to their workshops and homes."

Angelique tipped her head. "Can individuals mask themselves from mirrors?"

He nodded. "Most enchanters and enchantresses do so. I'll teach you how once we have a chance to cover complex spellwork."

Satisfied, Angelique returned her attention to the mirror. "Mirror, show me...Boyne—in Farset. Please."

Slowly, an image of the village emerged. She studied it with narrowed eyes and gave the mirror a few more commands: she asked to see individuals in Boyne (checking in on the naughty shepherd), then a top view of the forest, then Fresler's Helm in Verglas, and so on.

After about twenty minutes of examining the magic mirror, Angelique turned back to Evariste. "It's genuine," she said. "A verified magic mirror."

Evariste unfolded his legs and stood. "King Rèmy will be glad to hear so. Magic mirrors are awfully rare." He brushed off his plain green shirt and black trousers before pulling on his elaborate cloak—a forest green cape that depicted a new embroidered forest scene every time you looked at it.

He opened the door of the tiny room in which the mirror had been placed and beckoned for Angelique to leave ahead of him.

"You seem eager for our departure," Angelique observed.

"I am." Evariste winked. "If the royal family finds out it wasn't just any Veneno Conclave representative who verified the mirror, but an enchanter and enchantress-in-training, they'll feel it is necessary to invite us to dinner, and we'll *never* escape. At least, not in time for our appointment with the tailor."

Angelique thought for a moment as they quietly made their way down the elaborate hall. The hall was leafed in gold with an arched ceiling decorated with gold swirls and a painted fresco. Crystal chandeliers dropped from the ceiling every few steps, and arched windows framed with gold molding flooded enough light into the room that it made the elaborate gold statues shine so brightly she had to squint to see.

Of course, Enchanter Evariste is worried about making our appointment. The only reason I'm not objecting is because he made an appointment with a tailor. *That means we are getting clothes for Evariste. Or it* should *mean so.* She glanced up speculatively at her teacher. *His tricky side is hard to predict, so it's possible he fully intends to use a tailor to make clothes for me just to put me off his scent.*

She shook her head slightly and followed Evariste when he made a turn down a different hallway—this one themed in silver. "If you are worried about our time, why did you agree to look in on the mirror when the Veneno Conclave posted the assignment?" Angelique asked. "I thought they only asked that someone in the area would verify the mirror—not you specifically."

"Yes, but it was a good experience for you. You'll need to be able to verify magical artifacts in the future, and since we happened to be in Noyers for the tailor, it was an opportunity we could not pass up," Evariste explained.

Noyers was the capital of Loire—the biggest and most powerful country on the continent.

"If we weren't on a schedule, I'd consider paying a social call to King Rèmy and Queen Nicole," Evariste said as they slipped out of the hall and into the equally ornate gardens. "But we can save that for another time, particularly as things are in a bit of a social uproar right now."

"Why?" Angelique asked, frowning slightly. She had been born and raised in Loire, but the Veneno Conclave tried to enforce impartiality of all countries in its mages to eliminate favoritism.

As such, she hadn't paid much attention to her homeland.

"King Rèmy—with the approval of his wife, Queen Nicole—has recently announced he is officially adopting his illegitimate son into the royal family. He won't be in line for the throne, but it seems they are steering him towards a military career." Evariste offered her a smile as they finally slipped free of the palace grounds, passing a line of uniformed soldiers on their way out.

"That certainly is unusual," Angelique finally commented.

"It is," Evariste said. "Which reminds me, I thought it was rather unusual you chose to verify the mirror's authenticity by using it. You could have loosened your hold on your magic and let it test the mirror instead."

Yes, because who doesn't love the feel of killer magic in the air? Rather than share her inner sarcasm, Angelique took a moment to craft a far more suitable response. "I do not want to become dependent on my magic, and I thought it was more logical to use the mirror to prove its own capabilities."

"It's true, magical dependence can be a problem," Evariste agreed. "It has occurred to me for some time that I ought to make sure you don't lose your physical prowess you trained for as a war mage as it's a skill most mages don't have. But in this case, using your magic would have been much faster."

Using my magic to make the verification would also mean dredging more of it up and using it in a raw form, without twisting it or channeling it into a different kind of magic—something I mean to avoid.

Angelique was silent as she walked with Evariste through the cheerful, bustling streets of Noyers.

"You'll need to loosen your hold on your magic eventually," Evariste said.

Surprised, Angelique glanced at her teacher. "What do you mean?"

"Most mages—no—*all* mages let their magic flow freely from their soul. I am aware you hold yours back—though perhaps it is more accurate to say you wall it off—and release as little as possible needed for whatever spell you are working on." Evariste fixed his green and blue eyes on Angelique, making her fidget with the seriousness of his expression. "You have to let go."

But do I really? Angelique smiled and lied. "Perhaps one day in the future—when I have more control."

Evariste lifted a brow. "You need not lie to me, Angel."

Angelique briefly lost control of her expression and gaped up at him, but mercifully, Evariste had raised his gaze to study the store signs.

"I understand that you keep your magic down because you believe it is dangerous," he continued. "Which is not true at all. But, I believe you will one day come to realize that. It is merely that, in the meantime, I wish to warn you that one day you will have to reckon with the stranglehold you have on your powers and release it. You need to explore your boundaries—and find out whether you have a price or a limitation on your magic, though personally I imagine you'll have a price."

"How can you tell?" Angelique blurted out. "That I'm holding back, I mean."

Evariste pulled his brow into a regretful expression. "I'm a little more sensitive to the magic in others than the average mage—though not nearly as discerning as a fairy godmother or godfather. But I'm good enough at sensing it to know that every mage leaks their magic, Angel. Every mage except for *you*."

Angelique licked her lips, unsure what would be a suitable response. *He seems convinced I'm going to change my mind—when I won't—and that it's a bad thing to stifle my magic—when it's not. But the smartest thing for me to do is continue what I'm doing and let him keep his naïve wishes. So how do I proceed?*

"Lord Enchanter Evariste?"

Angelique didn't even try to dim the smile that burst on her face as she turned with Evariste to face the speaker. *Saved! I am saved—thank you, kind soul, for taking pity on me!*

The "kind soul" was a woman with a magical beauty—which made her a mage at the very least. She had bright green eyes and perfectly coiffed red hair. The sapphires that hung from her earlobes sparkled, and the skirts of her minty blue dress were wide and poofed in Loire fashion.

Enchanter Evariste blinked. "Oh, hello, Enchantress Lovelana."

Angelique relaxed as she took a tiny step back so she did not stand shoulder-to-shoulder with Evariste, but just a little behind him. She then clasped her fingers together and settled into what she thought of as her "attentive-apprentice" pose.

"Enchanter Evariste, what a pleasant surprise it is to see you here!" Enchantress Lovelana said. Her voice was sweet like honey, and she took a step closer to Evariste as she smiled at him. "You are as handsome as ever."

"Thank you," Evariste laughed. "And you are just as beautiful as when I last saw you."

Enchantress Lovelana blushed handsomely. "You always have been a charmer," she took a step closer to Evariste so she could playfully tap his arm.

"What brings you to Noyers?" Evariste asked.

Enchantress Lovelana shrugged so her shoulder brushed his. "Oh, you know..."

Angelique was momentarily puzzled. *What is she trying to accomplish by continuously moving closer to him—oh.* She took another look at Lovelana while the enchantress giggled and smiled adoringly. *Yep, that is the face of a woman with a fancy for Evariste. She has high-caliber taste!*

Satisfied with the discovery, Angelique settled back into her attentive pose. *Good. This will distract Evariste plenty so he won't ask me anymore uncomfortable questions about magic. And at least she's not scowling at me.*

Lovelana giggled at something Evariste said, and Angelique stifled the desire to yawn.

Her difficult years as a student had stamped out all typical girlish cares—including romance. *Romance is for those who are carefree or have a lot of time on their hands,* she mulled. *I don't give two hoots what a man thinks of me, unless he is Evariste or a Council Member. Making it to enchantress is far,* far *more important!*

Privately, she scoffed. *Romance. So useless!* She speculatively glanced at Enchantress Lovelana. *Unless...could I leverage my position as Evariste's apprentice to befriend the women who adore him and thus improve my reputation?*

Dimly, Angelique was aware that one was *not* supposed to think of using another person's romances for personal gain, but it was likely Evariste wouldn't mind anyway.

"No, I'm afraid I must regretfully refuse the invitation to dine with you," Evariste said, bringing Angelique's focus back to the conversation. "I'm taking my apprentice shopping."

Angelique looked up just in time for Evariste to rest a hand on her shoulder and scoop her forward so she once again stood shoulder-to-shoulder with him.

"Oh," Enchantress Lovelana's peered at Angelique with markedly less enthusiasm.

"I don't think you've met her yet," Evariste continued. "Enchantress Lovelana, please allow me to introduce you to my prized student, Angelique."

Angelique slapped a smile on and did a quick curtsey. "Good day to you, Lady Enchantress."

"Good day," Enchantress Lovelana frowned thoughtfully at Angelique, as if she were an unexpected tangle found in a spool of thread.

"I'm taking Angel to a dress modiste," Evariste explained.

You said we were going to a tailor! Angelique kept her lips clamped in a smile that nearly cracked her teeth. *This sneaky man! That's it; I will ingratiate myself to his admirers without regret now!*

"Angel?" Enchantress Lovelana repeated.

"My pet name for her—because she is as sweet as an angel," Evariste said.

Both Lovelana and Angelique stared at Evariste for several long moments.

Who does he think is going to believe such a blatant lie?! Angelique clasped her hands so tightly her knuckles turned white. "Hah-hah," she said lamely.

"I see," Enchantress Lovelana said slowly. "Do you mean to stay long in Noyers, then?"

"No, I will make a portal to take us home this evening. Will you be here much longer?" Evariste asked.

They exchanged pleasantries for several minutes longer, until Evariste declared they would soon be late for their appointment and swept Angelique off.

Angelique glanced over her shoulder to look back at Enchantress Lovelana, who was fixing her hair.

"There might be some unusual aspects to being your apprentice I never counted on," Angelique said.

"Whatever do you mean?" Evariste asked with far too much innocence.

Angelique kept herself from rolling her eyes and instead answered in a sing-song voice. "Nothing! Now, Master Evariste, I fear you have mixed yourself up. You told Enchantress Lovelana we were going to see a dress modiste. What you really meant was tailor, was it not?"

"We're seeing the tailor first, and then dropping by the dress modiste after."

"*What?*"

CHAPTER 14

Roughly eight months since she had been made an apprentice, Angelique sat crouched in front of the crackling fireplace in the workshop, papers fanned behind her like the tail of a peacock.

Evariste sat on the edge of his desk as he sorted through the correspondences he had retrieved from the Veneno Conclave that morning. "I think you're just about ready to finish with weather magic and start on fire," he said as he opened a scroll, glanced over its contents, then added it to the stack of requests for aid.

"Fire magic?" Angelique studied the flickering flames for a moment. "When it behaves so erratically?"

"Which is exactly why we will start on it. You've mastered illusions and alteration magic, and you've done well with weather magic. But all three of those magics act within boundaries and rules. Fire is a little more difficult to control, which will make it a new kind of challenge for you."

"As you say, Master Evariste."

Evariste grinned as he set an envelope thick with papers on his desk. "It's because you're so talented, Angel," he chuckled. "Or I'd be forced to teach you something tamer."

Angelique highly doubted this but held her peace. Instead, she turned around to snatch up a fistful of her notes. "Are we going to continue with my magic theory lesson? Or should I put this all away?"

"We are nearly done," Evariste said. "We spoke of the different kinds of black magic, yes?"

Angelique peered at her notes. "Yes, Master Evariste. You last mentioned curses."

"Ah, curses are a week's worth of lessons in their own right, but we won't be covering them for a few more months. The last thing I wanted to cover today was countering a black mage."

Angelique nodded and scooted a little closer to the fire to warm her cold hands. The wind howled outside, making the window panes rattle, but the study was quite warm.

"Much of it depends on the type of magic the black mage uses," Evariste said, "but there are some common methods. You can subdue them using items charmed by a craftmage or other basic magics, but physically knocking them out is often the safer method until you can seal their magic—temporarily or permanently."

"How can you use magic to subdue another magic user?" Angelique asked. She froze when she realized the possible implications of her words. "That is to say, I don't plan to fight another magic user, just, it seems..."

"It's fine, Angel," Evariste chuckled. "I know they don't exactly teach you magic dueling in class. Most mages are never taught such a thing, but as the strongest magic users on the continent, it's important enchanters and enchantress are trained—so they may take down rogue mages if necessary."

Angelique relaxed slightly and nodded. "Yes, but how can we subdue them?"

"The limit is your imagination," Evariste said. "The Snow Queen was famous for imprisoning other magic users in cages of ice.

Enchanter Bizarre's core magic was illusions, and he once captured a dozen black mages at once by raising a maze of illusions around them. They wandered around for hours until more mages from the Conclave came and helped him officially arrest them. Enchantress Willow once captured a black mage by bringing a tree down on top of him. Mage Flare—a mage with fire magic as his core—held a sorceress for half an hour by surrounding her with fire."

Angelique thoughtfully studied her notes. "Are any of these magic users still alive?"

"No." Evariste shifted on his desk as he ripped open another envelope. "Black magic users are extremely rare. There seem to be times and periods in history where they show up more often, but for the most part, you will only see a few every century. Sorcerers and sorceresses are more common, but they are also more discreet and don't advertise their evil deeds like a black mage does."

"I see," Angelique said.

"Good, because when you make Enchantress, you'll probably be the one the Council will dispatch on behalf of the Veneno Conclave should a black mage appear." Evariste skimmed his letter.

Angelique sat ramrod straight and slapped her notes down on the floor. "I beg your pardon?" Practice kept her voice calm, even though she wanted to scream. (She was much better now at holding in words *and* her expression, though occasionally a sarcastic comment still made it through.)

"Hm? Oh. Well, with your core magic, you'd easily be able to kill the black mage," Evariste said.

"But you said earlier that to counter a black mage, one had to subdue them or knock them out," Angelique said.

"Yes," Evariste said gently. "Because for most people, killing isn't a possibility with their magic, and subduing is the only method available. Most mages aren't skilled at physical fights either—another area where you excel due to your war magic training."

"But to *kill* someone with my magic?" Angelique asked. "I'm aware it's only good for slaughter, but I never thought—I didn't..." She snapped her mouth shut before she could say something she would regret later when Evariste gave her that slight look of disappointment he occasionally gave her when she was reluctant to grab enough of her core magic to twist into something powerful and potent. (He thankfully had not yet asked her to wield her war magic since the troll. She wasn't certain if that was a good sign, for it meant she did not have to refuse him, or a poor one that did not imply good things about her magic.)

"There's a reason why the Veneno Conclave is far more proactive against a black mage than they are a sorcerer or a sorceress, Angel," Evariste said. "Black mages are deadly and can decimate an area with their ill-begat magic. It's not just that they have magic that can kill; it's that they *actively* kill and often do so to make themselves more powerful. When one is found, they need to be dealt with immediately to keep common folk from harm."

In other words, kill or subdue—do whichever one puts people in the least danger. Yes, I can see how they would think such a role would fit me perfectly. The idea made Angelique shiver and also delivered a dose of anger. *It seems even if I make it to Enchantress, I'll still be considered a mage of death and destruction—merely one that is useful.*

Angelique considered her notes with a great deal less eagerness.

"Regardless, that won't be an issue for some years. Though the traditional time for an enchanter apprenticeship is quite a bit longer, I think you might finish in a decade or so if you continue at this pace." At his desk, Evariste opened another letter. This time, he made a noise of interest when he skimmed its contents. "What perfect timing!"

Angelique started to gather up her sheaves of notes, stacking them in a tidy pile. "What is it, Master Evariste?"

"Princess Alessia of Sole has given birth to a baby girl, Princess Rosalinda Talia d'Avalas."

"Princess Alessia is the only child of King Giuseppe?" Angelique asked as her mind struggled to recall Sole's political structure.

(In addition to being knowledgeable of magic, all mages had to have a rudimentary grasp of the countries in the continent and the nearby island nations. As part of their vows, they could not favor any country above the other, so a general foundation of all countries' culture and government was necessary.)

"Yes. And we've been invited to attend the new princess's christening," Evariste said.

Angelique held her hands out to the fire. "Really?"

"Perhaps it is more accurate to say the Veneno Conclave selected us to attend, but it doesn't matter. It will be a good experience for you," Evariste said. He thoughtfully folded the letter, then scooted off his desk and strode past Angelique, grabbing a bottle clouded with fog that had bits of swirling snow in it. "You can put away your notes, by the way. I think that's enough of magic theory for today. You can begin practicing your blizzard technique. Today you'll add in sleet."

Angelique stood on legs that were prickling from the inactivity. She grimaced at a stone dog statue placed by the stairs—the thing seemed to be facing her no matter *where* she stood in the workshop, which always made her feel watched—then hurried over to her desk.

"As you might recall from your school days, when a royal family celebrates a new birth, they often send an invitation to the Veneno Conclave, inviting a representative to attend," Evariste said as he shook up the blizzard in a bottle he had made last week. "Usually only one or two representatives attend, but they always give the newborn some kind of blessing or gift. As a result, we're in high demand as guests, and it spreads good will about us mages. But it's more calculating than that."

Thus far, his explanation had been by the books, and that was as far as Angelique's Luxi-Domus classes had taught. *What does he mean by calculating? In what way?*

As Angelique rejoined him in front of the fireplace—the ever-watchful statue-dog staring at her back—she bit the inside of her lip as she considered how she could ask him such a delicate question.

"Can you see how it is calculating?" Evariste asked.

Thankful she didn't have to ask, Angelique shook her head. "No, Master Evariste."

He smiled and tugged slightly on the tip of the braid her hair was pulled back into. "Think about it for a moment," he suggested. "If the Veneno Conclave gives a gift to every child born to the royal family..."

Angelique puzzled through it for a long minute. She was acutely aware of Evariste casually studying the bottled blizzard, but she didn't want to give him a half-formed answer.

Though she trusted Evariste a great deal more now after spending nearly a year with him, she was still heavily aware that she needed him to believe in her if she wanted to make it to Enchantress.

"It establishes a relationship with them?" She finally guessed. "So we are active in the dealings of *every* royal family because who would not want their children blessed—Zancara withstanding of course."

"That's one half of the equation," Evariste admitted. "It's actually the more difficult half. Think something a little less shadowy and a little more obvious."

Angelique held in a grimace. *Shadowy, eh? I suppose it's always great to be reminded that I apparently have the magic* and *mind of a deviant. But what is more obvious and less suspicious, but still calculating? They invite us to a party, and we give their brats a magic gift. That seems pretty generous for a small return. But maybe that's it?* "It puts them in our debt?" she ventured.

"Exactly," Evariste rewarded her with a smile. "It's nothing large enough that they feel *beholden* to us, but it does make them more receptive to speaking with us."

"What gift will you give Princess Rosalinda?" Angelique asked.

Evariste popped the cork off the blizzard in a bottle but held his thumb over the opening. "I will adjust it based on what the other magical guest gifts her—if there is another magical guest. Though given that Princess Rosalinda will one day become Queen of Sole as she is a firstborn, I imagine there will be at least one other. But, we can discuss that closer to the time. Today we'll practice weather magic, then tomorrow we can review conduct between enchanters and royalty. It's tricky because we're neither below them nor above them precisely."

"I understand, Master Evariste."

"For now, though, get a feel for this blizzard, then change the snow to sleet." Evariste removed his thumb from the mouth of the bottle, and mist leaked from the bottle, forming a puffy white cloud the size of a mattress.

Angelique nodded as she funneled a tiny stream of magic from her stores, twisting it into the wet, spongy weather magic required for the task.

A Christening, hmm? It sounds fun. More fun, anyway, then contemplating my evident future of becoming the Veneno Conclave's assassin.

TWO WEEKS LATER, when Lord Enchanter Evariste and Angelique stepped through a portal that dropped them at the entrance of the Sole palace, the royal family was waiting.

King Giuseppe of Sole—tall and commanding, with an air of competent pride to him—slightly inclined his head. "Welcome to Sole, Lord Enchanter Evariste and Enchantress-in-Training Angelique."

Evariste gave the king a so-slight-it-was-barely-discernable-bow, but Angelique clenched the skirts of her gown as she performed a full curtsey.

"Thank you, Your Majesty," he said.

"Thank you, Your Majesty," Angelique murmured as well.

Princess Alessia and her husband Prince Consort Filipo gave a less majestic, but far warmer welcome as they beamed while they curtsied and bowed.

"Thank you for coming, Lord Enchanter Evariste." Princess Alessia fussed with the hood of her fur-lined cloak. "We are honored by your presence."

"And the presence of your apprentice, as well," Prince Consort Filipo added.

"We are glad we could attend such a happy occasion. Congratulations to both of you," Enchanter Evariste said.

"Please, come inside. The other Veneno Conclave representatives have arrived over the past two days. I believe they are waiting to extend their greetings as well." Princess Alessia took her husband's arm and let him guide her up the many stairs that led up to the imposing palace.

If Farset was a country of forests and wood, Sole was a country of chivalry and knights.

Famous for their Magic Knights—who were the only non-magic organization that could face down a sorcerer or black mage with ease due to their anti-magic equipment and elven-stock horses—Sole tended to be a more ornate country whose nobles kept careful separation from their tenants and citizens.

The palace reflected the majesty they commanded and expected.

Constructed of greenish stone and rectangular in shape, the palace was topped with a giant domed tower and marble statues of knights. It was excessive in its size—for it had two additional wings to the palace that stretched in front on either side—but was admittedly majestic and splendid, if not a tad ostentatious.

Angelique had always liked Sole—their Magic Knights impressed and intrigued her—but she had never visited the capital before and had never even seen a drawing of the palace before.

Though she wanted to gawk like the peasant yokel she was, Angelique kept a slight smile on her face as she followed Evariste up the stairs.

She shivered in the whipping wind that made the stinging cold air hard to breathe and nearly let out a sigh of relief when they stepped into the ornate palace.

The inside of the palace was just as awe-inspiring as the outside, and held with the Sole theme of knights. There were statues of knights, shields, armor, and weapons *everywhere*. But as she brushed snow from her hair, Angelique brightened when she saw who else had come to Princess Rosalinda's christening.

"Yoo-hoo!" Sybilla beamed as she marched across the entrance hall. "Enchanter Evariste, Apprentice Angelique!"

Evariste smiled so his eyes crinkled in delight. "Sybilla, what a pleasure to see you here!"

"I must say the pleasure is likewise!" Sybilla warmly patted Angelique on the hands. "How are your lessons, dear? It seems you have come *quite* far in your illusion abilities since we last met—your eyes look perfect! That is a neat bit of magic you have there." The older woman peered at Angelique's eyes, admiring the spellwork that changed Angelique's eyes from her natural—and unnerving—shade of silver to a bright blue.

(As soon as Angelique had mastered alteration magic and built up the stamina to keep a spell running for an extended period of time, it was the first spell she had tried.)

"Thank you." Angelique dipped in another curtsey.

"Quite neat," Sybilla repeated. "Although, it's a shame you've covered up your natural color."

Angelique barely kept from snorting and had to itch her nose to cover up the involuntary twitch that seized her face.

"There are four other representatives present from the Veneno Conclave," Sybilla continued. "You'll need to greet them."

"I see them—I'm surprised both you and Finnr were asked to come," Evariste said as he nodded at a tall, blank-faced man standing next to a marble support pillar.

"Yes, well, word has it Princess Rosalinda's delivery was a difficult one. It seems unlikely Princess Alessia will have another child, leaving Sole in a *precarious* situation as far as heirs go," Sybilla said. "Added to it that Sole is especially emphatic in the line of nobles—particularly of the royal d'Avalas family—and we've got a recipe for disaster if the little princess doesn't make it."

Angelique listened to the exchange with interest.

When Evariste made the arrangements for them to arrive on the day—via portal magic—of the Christening, he had found out that five other mages would be present at the ceremony—for the very reason Sybilla had just given.

Sole was famous for its pride in the d'Avalas family—particularly with the birth order. It would not bode well for the country if something happened to Princess Alessia or Princess Rosalinda, as a distant cousin would instead be put on the throne. In fact, it would almost certainly result in civil war.

And that is why we are here.

In addition to the tall man Evariste had called Finnr, there were three other mages—all female.

The shortest of the bunch was busy searching through the pockets of her gray robe, while the other two slowly drew closer to Evariste, Angelique, and Sybilla.

"I didn't know you were going to be here, Lord Enchanter Evariste," one of the mages said in a musical voice.

"Yes, mage...?" Evariste tilted his head as he studied the pair.

The musical one giggled. "I'm Melody—I have music magic. This is my friend Nimal—she's a shapeshifter."

The shapeshifter curtsied deeply when Evariste nodded at her.

"I am Enchanter Evariste—as you both seem to know—and this is my apprentice, Angelique."

"Good morning." Angelique smiled as broadly as possible, determined to appear friendly.

Melody's smile faded. "Yes, we heard you had taken on a student." She studied Angelique, and her mouth quirked in what could reasonably be called a slight frown while her shapeshifter friend merely quirked an eyebrow.

Ahh, yes. They don't approve. Angelique almost relaxed at their reaction—for Enchantress Lovelana had made a similar expression. *At least they are subdued about it, compared to the reactions my magic got in school, anyway.*

Evariste seemed unaware of the dampening of their spirits as he leaned closer to Angelique and rested a hand on her back. "Yes, I am quite proud of my apprentice."

"I see," Melody said after a few awkward moments.

This seems like the precursor to a smashing day, Angelique thought wryly.

"If you will forgive me for listening in on your conversation, I'd like to offer my greetings to you, Lord Enchanter Evariste—and to you, Apprentice Angelique," The short, pixie-thin mage smiled brightly as she joined them, her storm-cloud colored eyes bright with interest. "I'm Breeza—a weather mage."

"Hello, Breeza." Evariste gave the weather mage his full attention as he smiled at her.

"Hello," Angelique added.

"Sybilla was telling me about you, Angelique," Breeza continued. "Have you ever been to Sole before?"

"No," Angelique shook her head.

"We still have a few hours until the Christening. Come! We can show you around the palace," Sybilla declared.

The invitation surprised Angelique. She couldn't remember the last time another mage had invited her to an event for the sake of company—she was not exactly in high demand as a friend.

But this weather mage seems sincere. They usually give it away quickly if they find my magic...unsettling. Like Melody. She hesitated, "I'm not sure if I should."

"We'll have such fun! Yesterday Sybilla and I busted into the Magic Knight's administrative building." Breeza's grin seemed mischievous. "It's a shame, but they aren't holding practice right now. Still, it's fun to see their grounds."

"We'll have an enchantress with us. Maybe they'll let us see more," Sybilla pondered.

Melody's frown briefly deepened before she glanced at Evariste.

Concerned the legendary enchanter saw you scowling at his student, are you? Aloud, Angelique said, "In-training. I'm an enchantress-in-training."

"To non-magical folk, that's practically the same thing, Angelique." Sybilla patted her hand, dismissing the correction. "What do you say, Enchanter Evariste? Can we deny you the presence of your pupil for a few hours?"

"I don't see why not—though I shall miss my cute student while she's gone." He smiled playfully down at Angelique, who felt her eyebrows furrow painfully at his words.

He's lucky no one has misunderstood his meaning whenever he calls me Angel or his cute apprentice. Though if he got away with it during the interview with Madam Quarrellous without any repercussions, I guess that means he's fine.

"Thank you, Master Evariste," Angelique said.

Evariste briefly leaned closer to her. "If you change your mind, call me with the bracelet."

Angelique nodded, automatically raising her hand to feel the reassuring weight of the silver curled around the glass bead.

"Enjoy yourself, Angel," Evariste ordered. "I'll attempt to catch up with Finnr in the meantime."

"*That* will be a lonely conversation," Sybilla snorted.

"We will stay with you, Lord Enchanter Evariste," Melody brightly volunteered.

Enchanter Evariste offered Melody a courteous nod, then returned his attention to Sybilla. "He is a man of few words," Evariste agreed. "Take care of my apprentice."

"With pleasure," Breeza promised.

"Come, children," Sybilla beckoned as she started down the hallway. "We'll have to take a different route to the Magic Knights' grounds—I think they're watching for us after yesterday."

"I thought all you did was enter their administrative building?" Angelique asked as she kept pace with the two shorter magic users.

Breeza laughed. "We never said they *wanted* us in their administrative building."

CHAPTER 15

The christening of Princess Rosalinda Talia d'Avalas of Sole was held in the early afternoon, with plans for a splendid feast afterwards.

Angelique watched the cooing princess, who happily gurgled in a cradle gilded with gold and stuffed her fat little hand in her mouth. Princess Alessia and Prince Consort Filippo stood behind the cradle, beaming with joy.

Sybilla, the next one out of the six magic users who were to present magical gifts, approached the cradle. The plump woman smiled down at the adorable baby and patted her head. "She shall be liked by animals," Sybilla said. White magic fell from her fingertips, blanketing the baby like stardust.

Melody frowned, slightly. (Not the dark look she had given Angelique whenever Enchanter Evariste wasn't around—something more like disapproval.) "Liked by animals? That's a useless gift."

Angelique glanced at the princess and prince consort to see if they had heard, but the magic users, lined up beneath royal banners and standards at the side of the room and a distance away from the royal babe, were out of earshot as long as they spoke in lowered tones.

Breeza snorted. "It's certainly better than your choice. It is beyond me how you think blessing the princess with the 'voice of a nightingale' will aid her in the future."

Melody sputtered. "It is a perfectly reasonable gift—one that has often been granted to royal babes!"

"Indeed," Melody's friend, the shapeshifter, said. "It is much more customary, unlike your gift of *courage*!"

"Hear, hear," Melody sniffed. "Courage is not a proper characteristic for a princess to have!"

"Ladies," Lord Enchanter Evariste said. He hadn't pushed back the hood of his black cape, so even Angelique couldn't see the expression in his eyes, but the gentle downturned slope of his lips and the disappointed air to his silken voice expressed his opinion easily enough. "We have been gathered to celebrate the arrival of a future monarch, and each of us are to give her whatever gift we feel will help her the most. It is not our business to question one another's blessings."

"Yes, Lord Enchanter," the other magic users murmured.

Angelique, proud of her master's wisdom, removed her eyes from the gurgling princess long enough to sneak a peek at him.

Today Enchanter Evariste wore a black cloak—edged with blue—fastened at the shoulder with an elaborate wing-shaped pin. Underneath that, he wore black linen pants, a leather jerkin that buckled at the sides—dyed black and edged in blue to match his cloak—and white boots and gloves. As usual, he had provided a matching outfit for Angelique, though her colors were white and plum.

He glanced down at her and caught her staring. Embarrassed, Angelique shifted her gaze to the ground.

"Are you enjoying the christening, Angel?" Evariste asked.

She nodded. "It's very beautiful." She felt dwarfed by the immense hall in which they stood—a room encased with marble, fabulous tapestries, a red velvet carpet, and a vaulted ceiling painted with a sun motif.

Evariste nodded. "The royal family of Sole loves any excuse for a celebration."

Sybilla took her place on Evariste's other side. "It's your turn, Lord Enchanter. If I had your power, I would see if I could do something about her personality, or she'll be an absolute bore."

Evariste smiled—flashing his white teeth. "I've thought of something already."

"Have at it, then. I'm anxious to end this ceremony and get going. There is work to be done, and this celebration will drag on if we don't do something to end it." Sybilla winked at Angelique.

Angelique hesitated, then smiled at the fairy godmother.

"Don't you agree with me, Finnr?" Sybilla asked.

Finnr—whom Evariste had spent most of his morning with—grunted.

"I'll be only a moment, Angel." With another smile, Evariste swept off, his cape unfurling behind him like a pair of wings.

Evariste placed a hand on the princess's cradle and exchanged a few muted words with the proud parents. He removed his gloves and lowered his right hand into the cradle.

Princess Rosalinda wrapped her fat baby hands around his pointer finger and giggled.

"She will be clever," Evariste said. His blue magic flickered around him like ripples in a pond, brushing Princess Rosalinda's skin.

Princess Alessia and Prince Consort Filippo bowed in thanks, but beyond them King Giuseppe raised a thick eyebrow.

"Well done, Evariste. That was craftily worded," Sybilla praised when he rejoined them.

Angelique furrowed her eyebrows. *Craftily worded?* She didn't doubt it given it was Evariste making the gift, but what did the fairy godmother mean?

"Traditionally, Angel, beauty or intelligence is the last gift given to a princess—it depends on the country and family into which she has been born," Evariste explained.

"But Enchanter Evariste out-foxed some of the more dopey gifts our comrades granted the princess by giving not intelligence, but cleverness," Sybilla said.

"How?" Angelique asked.

"Intelligence is, at its bones, the ability to learn well," Evariste said. "But cleverness is the ability to apply intelligence. Understanding alone is no help if one does not apply it."

Angelique nodded. "I see. Cleverness will be a great boon to the princess in the future, then."

"Indeed," Sybilla said.

The princess and prince consort turned to King Giuseppe. The stately king inclined his head to the magic users—thanking them—then opened his mouth to address the crowd.

The sunlight that streamed in through stained-glass windows dulled as sudden thunderclouds covered the sky. The glittering candles of the chandeliers were blown out by an icy, damp wind, and a set of giant doors were thrown open with such force they were almost torn off their hinges.

A man stepped into the darkened room with a hint of a smirk on his lips. His skin was alabaster white, his hair a shiny black, and he wore costly robes embroidered in black and gray. While he was handsome, it was a skin-deep shallow mask, for his eyes were dark as an abyss, and a red mark—the brand of those exiled from the Veneno Conclave—was carved into the skin of his forehead.

Breeza gasped. "Carabosso."

The utterance sent a shiver down Angelique's spine, and she found it was suddenly hard to breathe. Carabosso had once been a promising magic user on the fast track to becoming a fairy godfather—perhaps even an enchanter. But after his schooling...he cracked.

He forsook all the vows he had made, all the promises to

abide by the laws and rules of the Veneno Conclave, and had lashed out with his magic and killed an innocent.

The Veneno Conclave had excommunicated him, thrown him from their ranks and turned him into an outcast. They had also sealed his magic, but—if that were the case—how had he made his entrance?

Carabosso chuckled. "I'm hurt. How did it come to be that I was not informed of this wonderful celebration?"

Evariste hadn't yet put his gloves back on, so Angelique could see his blue magic wrap around his fingers. "What are you doing here, Carabosso?" The usual gentleness and warmth that colored his voice was gone; instead it was as sharp as the blade of a sword.

"Isn't it obvious? I've come here so that I, too, might welcome little Princess Rosalinda to the world," Carabosso drawled. He sauntered across the hall, approaching the golden cradle.

Sybilla strode in his direction. "Don't you touch her—you fiend!"

"Sybilla, don't!" Breeza grabbed her by the arms and yanked her backwards. "Conclave law forbids the use of magic against him!"

Sybilla—despite her plump, motherly appearance—shook the weather mage off with ease. "Only if his powers are sealed."

Angelique's magic crept up her arms, and she found herself agreeing with Sybilla. As her cold, sharp magic tried to ooze around the death grip she held on it, she highly doubted Carabosso was entirely sealed.

"Leave, Carabosso," Evariste said. A blue ring of light flared to life beneath his feet.

Carabosso rolled his eyes. "You're such a spoil-sport, Evariste. Fine, I will leave. But first, since all of you have, I ought to give the princess a gift."

"No!" Prince Consort Filippo leaped in front of the cradle and unsheathed his sword.

Carabosso backhanded him, sending him flying. He hit a marble wall with an ominous crack.

Princess Alessia screamed. "Filippo!" She scrambled to pick up Princess Rosalinda, but Carabosso flicked his fingers at her and blew her backwards towards her husband.

"Magic Knights, assemble!" King Giuseppe shouted.

Carabosso tilted his head back, laughed, and folded his arms across his chest. "Oh, yes. Please do assemble your little protectors."

The Magic Knights grouped up and stalked towards Carabosso while Evariste threw his hands out in front of him and started murmuring, calling his magic to him so it pooled around his feet.

The act seemed to rob Carabosso of some of his nonchalance, for he leaned over the cradle and spoke very quickly. "All the gifts given to the princess shall indeed come true—she will be blessed with grace, a beautiful voice, great skill in dancing, and more. But! By her eighteenth birthday, she shall prick her finger on the spindle of a spinning wheel, and she shall *die*!"

During the pronouncement of the curse, Evariste shouted a word in the tongue of magic that crackled. Bolts of blue magic sizzled around Carabosso, but he was too late. A flicker of red magic had already dusted the tiny princess's cheek, sealing her fate.

Carabosso grimaced under Evariste's attack, but he still managed to laugh. He ran from the room—his robes streaming behind him and several Magic Knights of Sole chasing after him, shouting.

"Surround him!"

"Activate your shields!"

"Close off that gateway!"

Breeza and the shifter mage gave chase as well, brandishing their magic.

Sybilla scowled at the golden cradle, where Princess Rosalinda now cried. "So much for his magic being sealed."

"It, that, that's impossible," Melody stammered. Her blossom pink dress was wrinkled, and her eyes were pinched with fear. "He was publicly banned and sealed. No one is strong enough to undo such a binding!"

"It seems that someone is," Evariste said grimly.

"What do we do?" Melody asked.

Sybilla rolled up the sleeves of her powder-blue dress like a mother preparing to clean her cottage. "We undo the curse, that's what."

"But we can't!" Melody clenched her hands over her heart. "We're allowed to give only one gift each."

Princess Alessia stood shakily, her eyes wet with tears as she retrieved her beloved baby—her *only child*—from the cradle. "Please, you must do something!"

Prince Consort Filippo was at her side in an instant. "We'll give you whatever you want—but please, save her!"

King Giuseppe strode towards his daughter and son-in-law. "I want that creature captured and dragged back here!" His voice was quiet and low, but it sent more guards scrambling. He turned to address the magic users with the same quiet intensity. "Money, jewels, wealth—no expense will be spared for the one who removes the curse."

"But we can't help—six magic users are already far more than usually allowed. We'll upset the balance if we use such powerful magic to help. We'll have to call for another magic user from the Conclave," Melody said.

"Pish-posh." Sybilla rubbed her hands together. "We have taken vows to help those in need."

"But the other countries will say it is favoritism," Melody warned.

King Giuseppe frowned, making his angular face sharp and

stormy. "My granddaughter was just cursed in front of me by a rogue mage, and you claim you can do nothing to help?"

"We will send for help from the Conclave—Evariste can use his magic and open a gate for us!" Melody said.

"It will take him time to secure a safe enough space as long as Carabosso is roaming around, and we haven't hours to spare," Sybilla snapped. "We have to modify the curse now, while it is still fresh."

"But we have already given her gifts!"

"Both of you are correct," Evariste said.

Melody blinked. "We are?"

"Stop with your puzzling words, Evariste, and spit it out," Sybilla said.

"The curse must be modified as quickly as possible, but if we who have already given her a gift grant her another, it will have political repercussions. Unfortunately, it will also endanger the princess." Evariste turned to face Princess Alessia and Prince Consort Filippo, who cradled their crying daughter between them. "Did you hear the wording Carabosso used? He tied it to the blessings we gave her. If we try to give her another, it is likely that the curse, layered into our magic as it is, will kill her."

Princess Alessia turned white. "No!" she cried, caught halfway between hysterics and a swoon. "Rosalinda!"

The prince consort handed the baby off to the King of Sole—who rocked her with surprising expertise—then guided his wife away from the magic users. The king followed them.

"But," Evariste continued, his voice gentle once again as he spoke to the mages. "It doesn't matter, because there is one more magic user who can grant a gift."

Sybilla and Melody stared at Evariste.

Finnr moved, reminding everyone he was still there. "Who?" he asked.

Angelique scanned the crowd of nobles and gentry, looking for the mage Evariste had alluded to. She was shocked when he placed a hand on her shoulder and said, "Angel."

"*Me?*" she squeaked.

"You cannot be serious, Lord Enchanter!" Melody said. "She is green and untrained—not to mention *dangerous*. You cannot possibly think of letting her alter the curse."

"It is true that enchanters and enchantresses-in-training generally do not learn curse modification until they near the end of their apprenticeship, but Angel is a clever girl. She can handle it." Evariste smiled down at Angelique with gentle affection, but at that moment Angelique did not feel pleased. She was instead filled with the desire to grab him by his fancy cloak and shake him.

Why does it seem like whenever something dire happens, he takes leave of his sensibilities regarding my powers?!

"Um, Master, you may be, uh, over-estimating my abilities," she said.

"Nonsense. He's right—you're more than powerful enough, my dear," Sybilla said.

"Maybe so," Melody spat. "But she's an abomin—"

"Finish that word, and you'll regret it," Evariste said. The gentleness was gone again, and his voice was as icy and steely as it had been when he warned Carabosso.

Melody gulped.

Sybilla nodded in satisfaction.

Angelique, however, was a little surprised by the strong... defense. She glanced up at him, but all he did was smile again.

"Come, Angelique." He glided towards the king, princess, and her consort.

Angelique scrambled to keep pace with him. "Enchanter Evariste?"

"Yes?"

"I don't think I can do this."

Evariste stopped walking and tilted his head. "You don't believe you can do it, or you don't think you should do it?"

Angelique nervously swallowed. "What if I hurt her?" she whispered.

"Oh, Angel." He sighed with warm affection. "You would never hurt someone."

"But my magic—"

"Is strong. Which is exactly what is needed at this moment." Evariste placed a hand on her shoulder again. "You needlessly fear yourself because of your years at the academy. I wish I could take back all the hurt they inflicted upon you, but even I cannot undo the past. So you must be brave and look to the future. You *will* be an Enchantress one day, and, as magic users, it is our duty to aid the weak. Princess Rosalinda desperately needs your help, Angelique, or she will die."

It was difficult for Angelique to breathe. *I'm terrified I'll make another mistake. Even if I'm not directly using my war magic, I still have to twist it! But...I don't want to disappoint Master Evariste.* She glanced at Princess Alessia—whose shoulders heaved with sobs.

Angelique curled her hands into fists and nodded. *Evariste said we have a duty...and at least this is a lot less dangerous. Or it should be. Ugh, but I'm using my magic on a princess.* Though she felt like she might be sick from her nerves, Angelique forced herself to say, "I'll do it."

Evariste removed his warm hand from her shoulder and instead offered it out to her. "And I will help you."

Angelique hesitated, then placed her hand in his. Reassurance surged through her as he intertwined his fingers with hers, and they approached the royal family of Sole together.

A knight approached King Giuseppe, his face ashen. "We failed to capture Carabosso, Your Majesty. We thought we had him cornered in an outer courtyard, but he slipped through our shields."

King Giuseppe stared coldly at Evariste as they approached

him. "You should have stopped him. You are an enchanter—you have the power." He spared a glance down at his granddaughter when she gurgled.

Evariste responded calmly. "It is not quite as easy as that, I'm afraid. Fortunately, we have a chance to modify the curse. My apprentice, Angelique, is quite capable. She will give the princess a gift as well, and she will modify Carabosso's magic."

King Giuseppe swung his gaze from Evariste to Angelique. "An *apprentice?*"

Angelique barely noticed the king's sour question and instead stared at Princess Rosalinda. *Can I really do this, with less than a year's training?* Angelique felt her magic curl around her—eager to be used—and she ruthlessly kicked it away again.

Evariste stepped around King Giuseppe and tugged Angelique towards Princess Alessia. "Princess Alessia, Prince Consort Filippo, rest assured we will save your daughter. If you give my apprentice and me a few minutes to prepare, we will modify Princess Rosalinda's curse shortly."

It took all of Angelique's will to keep from shrieking. *Shortly*? Curse-modification was a complex and advanced art! *I wouldn't trust a genius mage to begin wielding difficult spells immediately after learning them, much less trust myself with something that puts a life at risk!*

Angelique eyed Evariste and wondered if she dared risking his disappointment. She hated to fail him, but this was too perilous!

Princess Alessia's lower lip trembled. "You can break the curse?"

"The curse will unfortunately remain, but Angelique can save her," Evariste said.

Princess Alessia turned her lovely blue eyes onto Angelique. "Thank you!" She started crying anew as her husband curled an arm around her back and kissed her on the forehead. "Please, save our little girl."

Perfectly aware Evariste had used Princess Alessia to manipulate her, Angelique smiled. "I will do my best," she said between clenched teeth.

"If you would spare us for a few moments, we will be ready to begin shortly," Evariste said.

"Of course." Princess Alessia nodded and dabbed at her eyes with a handkerchief.

Evariste—still holding Angelique's hand—tugged her away from the couple.

Feeling a little betrayed by the man she nearly idolized, she uttered a strangled, "Master?"

Evariste ignored her concern. "Listen to me, Angel. When dealing with curses, it is important to understand that they can't be broken by personal will or power," he said. "Curses find their power in black magic and black emotions—bitterness, hatred, and the like. To break them, you have to use something even more powerful: love and light. There are many different ways to break a curse with the power of love. There is sisterly love, parental love, the love found between friends, and so on. All of these kinds of love are powerful in different ways. The kind of modifier I am going to teach you today, however, will be based on romantic love," Evariste said.

"Good choice." Sybilla popped up behind Evariste and Angelique. Melody and Finnr trailed her.

Evariste continued, "Romantic love is the easiest to deal with because it is one of the few kinds of love that will have a defined beginning. Using romantic love to break a curse often means harnessing romantic love at its starting point, and using it to shatter the bonds the curse created."

Melody clapped her hands. "Like the kiss of a handsome prince!"

"First of all, citing that he must be handsome is small-minded and stupid," Sybilla said. "Secondly, Evariste said the modifier will be *romantic love,* not puppy-like infatuation."

Melody squawked her outrage, but Finnr snorted under his breath.

Angelique stared at Princess Rosalinda and wondered how on earth a baby was going to find romantic love. *Should I ask Master Evariste?*

"What are you thinking, Angel?" Evariste asked.

"Princess Rosalinda isn't even a year old yet. How can we arrange for romantic love to break the curse?" Angelique asked.

"We modify the curse with your gift," Evariste said. "Anything else?"

Angelique tilted her head. "Is romantic love really that strong?" she asked. "Wouldn't it be easier to use the love Princess Alessia or the prince consort has for her?"

Evariste squeezed her hand. "You would be surprised how powerful romantic love can be."

Angelique had to cough to cover up her scoff of disbelief. *Pft, how very doubtful!*

"And I'm afraid using parental love or even familial love is beyond my abilities to teach you right now, and we are on a deadline," Evariste continued. "Now, when you give your gift to Rosalinda, you must modify the curse—remove the side-effect of death and replace it with something else—and add a way to break it. The two ways I suggest to you are true love's first kiss, or that she would fall in love with a man, and that he would love her. You'll want to make your choice based on the side-effect you use to replace death."

"So it is only words?" Angelique asked hopefully.

"No. You must wield your magic to make your words stick to the curse and change it," Evariste said.

"Rats," Angelique muttered.

"You must channel your magic in this method." Evariste talked Angelique through the process—showing her with his own magic, and occasionally helping her with her own. In only a few short minutes, he declared her ready.

Feeling weighted down with the hopeful stares of the royal family, the few Magic Knights who were assembled, and all gentry—as well as the narrowed gazes of the other magic users—Angelique slowly approached the crib where the king had placed Princess Rosalinda.

She licked her lips and steeled her spine so she wouldn't shiver, even though a cold sweat swept across her. "By her eighteenth birthday, Princess Rosalinda will indeed prick her finger on the spindle of a spinning wheel, but she will not die." Angelique paused, her heart squeezing painfully when she felt her magic—agile and sharp—channel across her fingertips in a silvery haze that was deceivingly pretty. "Instead, she will fall into a deep sleep, and she will wake up only when her true love kisses her."

Angelique sucked air between her clenched teeth when her magic drifted down and brushed the sleeping princess like tufts of dandelion fluff. A droplet of sweat dripped down her temple as she forced her destructive magic to work with gentleness. She kept a tight grip on it as her powers settled delicately across the princess, flickering brighter when it brushed a red tendril of Carabosso's magic.

She grimaced as she used her magic to worm between the pieces of his oily powers. His magic resisted, and Angelique's silvery magic flared, cutting straight through it in spite of its resistance. Her heart stopped as she yanked on her magic, reeling it back under her control, but the princess blissfully slept on. Angelique could feel the change in the tiny princess's curse deep in her bones.

She exhaled and took a shaky step. It was over. She had successfully modified the curse without harming Rosalinda. She leaned against the cradle and wondered if hanging her head would reflect shamefully on Evariste.

"That's your solution—a deep sleep?" King Giuseppe rumbled.

"It was well done." Evariste knitted his hands together as he joined Angelique at the crib. "It will do the least harm to the princess, and it limits the risk that the curse could still kill her."

King Giuseppe frowned, but Princess Alessia was pink with relief. "Thank you! She can survive this; I know it."

Prince Consort Filippo took one of his wife's hands. "And we will do everything we can to see that the curse does not come true."

"I would not count too heavily on your own efforts, but it would be wise to make certain the princess does not have direct access to any spinning wheels," Evariste said.

Angelique rubbed her souring stomach and leaned more heavily on the crib to keep from tottering. When Evariste held her elbow to support her, she smiled up at him in thankfulness.

"Please keep us informed," Evariste said. "Princess Rosalinda is now tied to Angelique—and by extension, myself. She will be our responsibility."

Princess Alessia retrieved the baby from her crib. "Thank you, Lord Enchanter—and Lady Enchantress."

"Enchantress-in-training," Angelique said—though she almost swayed on her feet. The curse modification hadn't used much of her power considering, but it required a huge amount of control —something she still had a terribly short supply of.

"If you'll excuse our early departure, I believe my apprentice and I should return home. We'll be in touch." Evariste nodded to the royal family of Sole, then swept an arm—and his cloak—around Angelique, supporting her as they retreated from the hall.

Sybilla and Breeza waved to them, but the three other magic users watched without emotion as they left.

"The modification was quite smooth." Evariste said as they followed the red velvet carpet to the castle entrance. "It would have been beyond any other apprentice so early in their schooling. All of them would have fumbled it, and most would have reached the end of their magic. But you proved yourself worthy today."

As they left the castle and stepped out into the frigid winter air, Angelique wanted to snort. The only thing she had proved was that it was going to take *a lot* of concentration for her to do any kind of deep magic not related to her core powers without risking killing someone. *I feel sick. I want to sleep.* Though she felt awful, she held her tongue. She still had to act the part, after all.

"I can't open a gate—even if Carabosso left, it is still too risky. But I'll do the next best thing and whistle Pegasus down from the sky. He'll get us home in a flash," Evariste continued. He nudged her against his side with the arm that supported her as a few snowflakes twirled through the air. "You were wonderful, Angel."

And that is all I ever want. Satisfied, Angelique closed her eyes and waited for Evariste to summon Pegasus. At the back of her mind, though, worry stirred for Princess Rosalinda and her cloudy future. Though Angelique had managed to take the sting out of the curse, she highly doubted the princess was out of danger yet. If Carabosso had felt spiteful enough to curse her, it was unlikely he was going to let her off so easily.

I hope she's strong enough to survive whatever difficulties he brings down upon her...

CHAPTER 16

Almost two years after Evariste made Angelique his apprentice, they had their first disagreement.

"Step up, Angel!" Evariste instructed as he dragged a rather tattered—and burnt—straw-stuffed dummy from storage. He shoved its stake in the ground, then used alteration magic to temporarily fix the dummy—making it bigger and removing all the burn marks.

"Are we practicing combat with elemental magic, again?" Angelique asked as she mentally shifted through possible attacks.

Since altering Princess Rosalinda's curse, Angelique had reluctantly agreed that being able to use magic in combat situations might be helpful—with the exception of her war magic, of course. (Carabosso had effectively opened her eyes to that matter. Particularly because she realized she did *not* like using her war magic for delicate spells like curse modification. If she could subdue her opponent before he could cast a curse, all the better!)

So, once she had reasonably mastered wind, fire, water, and the like, she hadn't objected when Evariste set her to throwing fireballs at targets and dousing a dummy with water before snapping the temperature down and freezing it.

End with fire, she decided as she studied the dummy with a puckered brow. *That always destroys it the fastest. Maybe blow it down with a puff of wind first, then use water?*

"We are practicing combat today, yes." Evariste busied himself with the dummy, tugging its burlap head straight. "And partially with elemental magic."

Angelique froze. *Partially?* She cocked her head slightly as she studied Evariste's back.

Though he seems relaxed, he's fussing with that dummy a lot considering I'm just going to beat the stuffing out of it.

"Enchanter Evariste?" She asked tepidly.

When he finished with the dummy, Evariste offered her a bright smile as he trotted back to the house...returning with a sword and several daggers.

I don't like the look of this.

Angelique's smile twitched, but she forcibly kept it in place. "Are we practicing deflection? Or...?"

"Today I'm going to teach you how to meld two magics together—your war magic and elemental magic," Evariste said.

Angelique cocked her head. "But you've already taught me to meld two magics together—water, ice, and even weather magic."

"True," Evariste said. "But you haven't tried to do so with your war magic yet, which is much more complicated as it requires twisting and channeling some of your magic—for the elemental bit—while releasing your core magic."

No. Absolutely not.

Angelique bit her lip as she started sifting through possible excuses, trying to figure out which one would make the most sense and leave Evariste the least disappointed. "Are you sure this isn't too advanced for me, Master Evariste?" she tried. "If I make a mistake, my war magic won't fizzle out the way my practice blizzards and thunderstorms would."

"You'll be fine," he assured her.

No, I won't.

"You are an excellent student."

No, I'm not.

"You have amazing control!"

I definitely don't!

"Now," Evariste began. "First you'll need to pull enough of your magic that you can power both pieces of magic."

"No," Angelique said.

Evariste stopped and tilted his head. "No?"

"I'm not going to do this," she said.

Evariste hesitated. "Angelique, I am aware you find your war magic frightening, but if you use it—"

"Use it for what, to *kill* someone?" She was unable to totally dampen the fire of her words, but she was proud that she could speak despite the lump forming at the back of her throat.

Evariste carefully put the weapons down. "It's part of you," he said. "You have to learn to accept it."

"It is *not*—" Angelique cut herself off and cleared her throat so she could speak without growling. "It is not part of me." She managed to say at a much softer tone.

Evariste studied her for several long moments. "You really hate your core magic, don't you?"

Angelique looked away, *angry* with herself when tears burned her eyes. "I hate what it represents. And what it means about me."

In the time Angelique wasn't watching, something *changed* in Evariste. It was like an icy coolness seeped into the corners of his smile.

"Take the day off today, Angel," he said in a cold voice Angelique hadn't heard before.

Angelique dragged her eyes back to her teacher. "Um, Master Evariste?" she ventured.

"You've earned it." Though his words were reassuring, the frigid look in his eyes was anything but.

You've done it now, Angelique. You haven't just disappointed him, you made him angry. Possibly for the first time in the history of the world. Well done. Excelling at the unwanted, as usual.

"Um," Angelique said.

"I'm going to run an errand," he continued as his magic pooled around his feet. "I'll be back by dinner."

As Angelique watched, he made the familiar stone gate that served as the portal for the Veneno Conclave.

That he made one, instead of using the one he had recently constructed in the house, was telling.

Wherever he was going, he was in a hurry.

"Goodbye—and...well," Angelique finished lamely when he ducked through the portal. It closed seconds later, leaving Angelique alone.

"That went terribly," she said reflectively. "Maybe next time I should just add insult to injury and tell him I think he's a maniac for agreeing to take me on as an apprentice." She shook her head as she ambled back towards the house. "I made a mistake. Instead of trying to be the sweet sort of enchantress everyone seems to expect, I should have cursed myself and sealed my voice!"

EVARISTE STALKED through the halls of Luxi-Domus, his icy rage slipping through the cracks of his control.

She was scared to use her core magic.

Angelique, whose valor was bone deep, was terrified to let even a wisp of her war magic loose.

It was one thing to be reluctant after she had accidentally hurt Evariste when they fought the troll near Alabaster Forest. But that single incident could not make her hate her magic so passionately. That incident could not make her want to divorce something that was so deeply a part of her.

I knew she was handled roughly at the Academy. I did not know they did their best to ruin her!

Evariste found the office he was looking for and flung the door open. It hit something with an ominous crunch, but he ignored it and prowled inside.

Madam Quarrellous sat behind her desk. She blinked owlishly at his entrance. "Lord Enchanter Evariste," she said. "What a pleasant surprise—"

Evariste set his hands on her desk and leaned in. He let little sparks of his magic slip his control so they glittered around him—small reminders of how powerful he was. "*What* did you do to her?" he growled.

Quarrellous sank down in her seat. "I'm a-afraid I don't know what you're talking about," she said in a squeaky voice.

"Angelique." His smile was of ice and rage, and he was pleased when Quarrellous gulped. *Good. She should be afraid, after all she has done.* "You have made her terrified of her own magic—not reluctant to use it, not wary, but petrified and hating that part of herself."

"W-with her core magic, she *should* be reserved in using it," Quarrellous said.

"She is not reserved; she is panicked at the very *thought* of touching it!" Evariste shouted, his voice filling the tiny office, making the teacher cringe. "Why would you do that to her? Any idiot can see she's *never* going to go rogue. She might be sly, but she would die before she let her soul turn black."

Quarrellous swallowed. "Her power."

Evariste glared at her. *If I didn't think Angel would somehow get the blame, I would freeze Quarrellous in an ice block right now.* "Who *cares* if she's the first War Mage to make Enchantress ever? We should be in awe that she *exists*!"

"She's a danger!" Quarrellous insisted.

Evariste snarled and considered building a gate to Verglas so he could kick her through and watch her blunder about in the Snow Queen's domain for a bit.

The instructor must have realized that her argument was not

particularly convincing, for she added in a panicked voice, "The Headmaster told me himself! At first I was like you—intrigued by the girl and the depth of her powers. But after the results of her tests came back, and it was discovered she was capable of making enchantress, the Headmaster himself pulled me to his office and told me to be extra diligent with Angelique."

The Headmaster? Evariste's glare lessened to a frown as he recalled the headmaster—a portly, jolly fellow with a deep laugh and a penchant for books. *Why would the Headmaster say such a thing?*

"What else did he say?" Evariste asked.

"He and several other instructors said we had to be cautious because she might hurt someone. Because she would have power over life and death, and there would be very few who could stop her should she ever falter from the path of good," Quarrellous continued. "He asked that I keep a careful watch of her."

Evariste rubbed his eyes. "And none of you stopped to *think* what the constant disapproval might do to her?"

"The Headmaster had good intensions," Quarrellous argued.

"Yes, and now my apprentice is a stunted shadow of what she *should* be because of his 'good intentions,'" Evariste snarled.

Quarrellous' lower lip trembled, briefly.

Enough scaring her. She named the Headmaster, and it doesn't seem she would have done this without his instruction.

Evariste again leaned across the desk, making sure he loomed over her. "I never want to see you near my student again," he growled. "If the Council requests another in-person report, you had *better* make certain you are not sent. I don't want you talking to her again, and if you *ever* come to my home, I will escort you through a portal that will drop you in the middle of the Baris desert. Do you understand?"

"Yes," Quarrellous squeaked.

Evariste swept out of the room, recalibrating himself so he was on a path to the Headmaster's rooms.

While he wouldn't really carry through on his threat to dump Quarrellous in the desert—even if he dearly wanted to—he wanted her to be scared that he would. *It will keep her away from Angel, and if she ever does dare to face my wrath, she'll never accept a portal from me again. And there is a certain amount of pleasure I can derive from that. But wasting a few weeks of her time so she is forced to travel by foot everywhere won't bring back the years of pain she inflicted on Angel.*

The thought made Evariste growl.

He never thought the *Headmaster* would have started the campaign against Angelique.

He had seen the jolly man personally mentor a student whose magic was capable of creating waking daydreams and nightmares. So why would he object to Angelique?

Evariste turned a corner—he only had two more turns before he reached his next destination—when someone caught him by the shoulder and spun him around.

"Evariste—it's a little early in the morning to be starting a war, isn't it?" Evariste's old master, Lord Enchanter Clovicus, greeted him.

Enchanter Clovicus was older than Evariste—he appeared to be in his mid-40s. Silver hair dusted his temple, a stark contrast to his copper-colored hair. He had deep smile lines, but around Evariste, he seemed to perpetually arch an eyebrow—as he was right now.

Evariste stared at his old teacher. "I'm going to see the Headmaster."

"I know," Enchanter Clovicus said. "Just about everyone on this *floor* heard you yelling at poor Quarrellous."

Evariste snorted. "She is *not* to be pitied!"

"She is," Enchanter Clovicus disagreed. "She's an ethics teacher who let herself be led into acting against her dearest-held values. She is deserving of pity for so abandoning herself." He slung his arm over Evariste's shoulders and forcibly dragged him in the opposite direction of the Headmaster's study. "Unfortunately, hiring incompetent ethics teachers is *not* an excusable reason to go storming into the Headmaster's study with murder in your eyes."

Evariste rolled his eyes. "I am not *that* angry."

"You're well on your way to working yourself up to it," Enchanter Clovicus snorted as he pulled him through the corridor that marked the end of the Academy and the start of the Veneno Conclave's buildings.

He waited until they stormed a private salon for enchanters and enchantresses only, then nudged Evariste into a well-cushioned chair before he folded his arms across his broad chest. "Now, tell me what the problem is."

Evariste spilled out the tale—how Angelique hid her cleverness behind smiles and practiced naiveté, but not out of a ploy but *fear*. How she refused to use her war magic, even though Evariste had been very carefully navigating the topic for nearly two years. How she always pulled the minimum amount of magic—as if she were afraid that even something benign like an illusion could do physical damage. And, apparently, how all of this had started because the Headmaster had warned his instructors to be wary of her.

Enchanter Clovicus thoughtfully rubbed his precisely-trimmed goatee. "Sounds like a proper mess."

"*Yes*," Evariste said.

"Quarrellous must have been mistaken," Enchanter Clovicus continued. "The Headmaster dotes on his students. There's no way he would have singled Angelique out and told everyone to fear her. If anything, he likely meant to praise Angelique. Quarrellous must have misunderstood him."

Evariste finally let himself lean back in his chair. "That seems more likely," he agreed reluctantly. "But why, then, did he not correct her?"

Enchanter Clovicus eased himself into a straight-backed,

wooden chair. He leaned forward, propping his elbows up on his knees. "Who can say? Things have been a little odd the past few years."

Evariste arched an eyebrow—much like his teacher. "Odd?"

"It feels like the quiet before a storm," Enchanter Clovicus said. "Princess Rosalinda's curse was no random act of violence. Carabosso didn't just *happen* to get his magic back in time for the princess' birthday."

"What does it mean?" Evariste asked.

Enchanter Clovicus shrugged. "It means you better do your part to get your *dear* little apprentice trained up."

Hearing the wry tone to his teacher's voice, Evariste frowned. "You think it was a mistake to take her on." When the other enchanter did not respond, his frown deepened. "Because of her magic?"

Enchanter Clovicus snorted. "Bosh her magic!" He folded his arms behind his head and leaned back. "You're right, I think you're addled for taking on an apprentice—because you're so flaming young! You can't be much more than a decade older than her."

"Less than a decade."

"*Less*? White Shores, my lad. You're lucky she respects you at all—even with your reputation. No—perhaps it's the opposite. You're lucky she's not giving you cow eyes and carving your name into tree trunks."

Evariste laughed. "I don't think she would ever be the type to do such a thing. And she seems, in general, rather unimpressed with romantic love. I think she'd rather slug someone in the gut than make eyes at a man."

"With the school life you've described, I suppose it's not a surprise. But if she were any less cunning and even just a *little* dopey, she'd look at you as a hero, and not some poor sop she's trying to swindle into thinking she's good." Enchanter Clovicus said. "It *was* a risk to take her on. If you were so concerned for her, you should have come to me—I could have requested her as my apprentice. Why didn't you?"

Evariste was silent. He had no answer for that—at least none that he wanted to explore, particularly with his old teacher. *Any answer I have is purely selfish. And yet, I don't regret it. And by the end of her apprenticeship, I'll make certain Angelique is no longer afraid of her own shadow and has powerful allies to support her in whatever ventures she chooses to follow.*

"Regardless, she's your responsibility now—which means you can't go around doing *stupid* things like storming the Headmaster's office and shouting him down," Enchanter Clovicus said.

"Then what do I do?" Evariste asked, defeated. "How do I make her see her magic is a blessing, not a curse? That it's something she should embrace?"

Enchanter Clovicus was silent for several minutes, his brow furrowed as he stared at an elaborate woven rug of vines and flowers.

Evariste waited patiently. *He won't suggest anything lightly, and I trust his judgement in this matter. He managed to make me a decent enchanter, when I could have easily turned into an entitled brat with the wrong master.*

"Teach her with all the warmth you have. Spoil her, take her traveling, and show her that the world doesn't think she's a monster," the enchanter said finally. "Don't make her practice her core magic if she doesn't want to. Give her as many books as she'll read, and get her to try every kind of magic you can. If you can get her to love what she can *do* with her magic, it will eventually lead her to being grateful for having such strong core magic that lets her do all these wonderous things. *But*." Enchanter Clovicus held up a finger and shook it. "You have to walk a fine line, Evariste. If she falls in love with you, it will only make things worse. She needs to learn to depend on herself, first, or she'll stay stunted forever."

Evariste nodded slowly. "I've been trying to get her to warm up a bit, but you're right about playing on her love of knowledge. She has a thirst for learning. Given the right tools, she'll happily explore different magic-work."

"Then push for that with everything you've got," Enchanter Clovicus said.

Evariste stood, feeling better now that his icy anger had eased—and he had a goal to work towards. "Thank you, for everything. You've given me some great ideas—and some new errands to run."

Enchanter Clovicus chuckled. "Of course. You were *my* apprentice—I'll always watch out for you. Just be careful with her," he warned.

Evariste was at the salon door when he laughed. "Yes, yes, you got that point across clearly."

"And Evariste," Clovicus called after him. "Don't you go falling for her either."

Evariste laughed. "I've never had a problem with romance before, master."

"Maybe so," Clovicus called after him as he stepped through the door. "But you've never met a girl who is more taken with your knowledge than your magic, either!"

CHAPTER 17

Enchanter Evariste did not come home that night, or the night after.

By dawn of the third day, Angelique was starting to grow nervous.

Why would he be gone that long? He was angry, but not mad enough to abandon me like an unwanted puppy. At least, I think not? Would he leave me in his house if he intended to break our oaths?

She finally shook her head and sprinkled sand on her paper to soak up the extra ink of the words she had just written. "No, I must be mistaken," she dared to say aloud. "Unlike me, Enchanter Evariste is kind and righteous. Mostly. Though I need to be careful and do everything I can to impress him, I don't think he would end my tutelage so easily."

Angelique nodded, taking some relief in the thought, then studied her paper with a critical eye, looking for errors. (Because when Evariste finally *did* come home, she was going to make sure it was to spotless work!)

She felt a familiar wisp of magic and paused—her quill hovering over her paper. *Did he just get back? I thought I felt a portal open, but he's got them running all over the house, so it can be easy to mistake.*

The front door opened, and even all the way up in the workshop, Angelique heard a cheerful call. "Angel? I'm back!"

Angelique abandoned her work and rushed down the stairs, steeling herself as she tugged her gown—a work of blue silk layered to look like a gushing wave—straight.

"Welcome home, Master Evariste!" Angelique said in a singsong voice when she reached the second floor. She continued down the boxy staircase, a big smile forced on her lips.

Her smile turned sincere when she saw Evariste, standing near the base of the stairs, with several packages arranged around him. He was wearing his favorite cape—the black and dark blue one—but had tugged down his hood for the occasion.

"Thank you, it is good to *finally* be back." He beamed as he unfolded his arms and held them open.

Angelique paused halfway down the last flight of stairs. *What is he doing?*

Evariste's smile didn't fade, and he kept his arms open, though he wriggled his right fingers at her in a summoning gesture.

He can't really be inviting me...there? Angelique stared at Evariste's chest, her eyebrows knitting together. (It was easier to think of it as Evariste inviting her to relocate to a position in front of his chest than a hug. A hug seemed...potentially embarrassing.)

Previously, Evariste had rested a hand on her back and placed his arm on her shoulders, but a hu—no—relocation to stand in front of his chest? Why the sudden graduation in physical expressions?

Angelique sucked her neck into her shoulders. *Something happened. His relatively few addled actions are multiplying. I'll have to get back to the Veneno Conclave and subtly request for a healer—a* powerful *healer—to come visit.*

Evariste laughed. "Aren't you going to greet me, Apprentice?"

"I was unaware that...our greetings, that is to say, were supposed to involve...such close...quarters," Angelique finished lamely.

Evariste's smile turned sly. "Come, Angel, my arms are getting tired."

Once again, Angelique stared...*there.*

I'm going to die, she realized. *He is going to kill me one day with his bizarre...ideas.*

Angelique reluctantly skulked down the last few steps.

Don't want to, don't want to, don't want to.

Her shoulders stiff with...apprehension? Anxiety? Angelique slowly drew closer to Enchanter Evariste, stopping directly in front of him.

Evariste enfolded her in a very loose but terribly comforting embrace. "Thank you for welcoming me, dear Apprentice."

Angelique tried to say something, but she only managed to make some sort of high-pitched squeak.

"You are very likely the best student I could ask for," he continued blithely.

"Thank you?" Angelique finally managed to say—through clenched teeth. *Why is his hug so warm and inviting? He's already got the looks, magic, and charisma! It's unfair that the world has given him so many advantages.*

"Which is why we're celebrating your birthday a few weeks early! Normally I'd wait, but the exact gift I got you makes that impossible, and I had to buy it while it was available." Evariste swiveled slightly, releasing her with one arm and tucking her against his side with the other.

Thinking of the year prior, when he had given her several new —and *expensive*—dresses, Angelique started protesting. "No, Master Evariste, that's unnecessary."

"It *is* necessary," Evariste said, a whiff of fierceness swirling in his voice. "You are a wonderful student and a talented enchantress-in-training. We're celebrating your birthday. And here is the best of your gifts."

He crouched down next to a wicker box held shut with a small latch. With his right arm still folded around Angelique's back, he tugged her along, so she ended up crouching next to him.

This close to the box, Angelique thought she could hear something moving inside the woven container.

"Open it," Evariste urged.

Angelique reluctantly pushed the latch down and peeled back the lid.

Inside was a fuzzy kitten. It stood on wobbly white paws, and his little black tail was puffed up to resemble a fat fir tree.

"His name is Roland Archibald Whisperpaws the Fifth," Evariste said. "I'm sorry to say you can't change his name—the man I bought him from was adamant on that, something about a family name—but I think you'll like him."

The kitten was mostly white with a coat of black spread across his back and over the top of his head, and a splash of it covering his top right lip, resembling a half-mustache.

Angelique carefully scooped him up, her heart melting when the kitten released a tiny mewl.

She laughed a little as she held the kitten against her chest. "What a handsome, brave little fellow you are."

The little kitten puffed his chest up, then said in a squeaky voice, "I *am* handsome, aren't I?"

Angelique almost dropped the feline. "He *talks*?" She stared, wide-eyed at Evariste.

Talking animals were not entirely unheard of, but they were rare. Rarer than unicorns. To *buy* a talking animal—even a mere cat—would cost an exorbitant amount of money.

"Of course I talk!" The kitten protested, his voice muffled by the way he was enclosed within her hands.

"Master Evariste, this is too much!" Angelique babbled. "The dresses were within reason—perhaps, though the level of craftmanship you insisted upon was not necessary. But a talking cat?"

"I am magic, too!" the tiny voice ventured.

"M-magic, too?" Angelique stammered.

Evariste laughed and slightly ruffled her hair. "He's meant to be a bit of a companion and a reference for you. As he grows, he'll learn spells and charms and will be able to assist you and teach you unusual bits of magic. He can be an assistant, of sorts."

"Assistant?" the little kitten ventured.

Evariste used a pointer finger to rub the kitten on the top of his fuzzy head. "It means you'll help her with her work."

"But, you can't just—talking cats cost a lot!" Angelique babbled.

Evariste chuckled. "Not much for an enchanter."

When he noticed Angelique bulging her eyes at him, he was quick to add, "At least not one on my paygrade. Besides, this seems like the perfect time to tell you that I'm going to start outsourcing some of my easier work to you."

Evariste stood and started gathering up the rest of the packages. "You can open these later, on your birthday," he told her.

Angelique had to shake her head to stop dumbly staring at him. "*Your* work? Won't people get mad when they realize they aren't receiving your spells, but the charms of your apprentice?"

The kitten made a noise of distress, and Angelique cuddled it closer. Evariste watched her do so with a grin, and Angelique was filled with the sense that each moment she hugged the creature, she was losing her battle of complaining that he cost too much.

"They won't mind—you're *my* apprentice after all." Evariste started up the staircase, taking the steps two at a time as though the parcels he carried were light as feathers. "Which means you're legendary, too," he called over his shoulder.

"I am *not*," Angelique said emphatically. *And I don't ever wish to be! That would be the worst-case scenario—to be famous for my ugly magic!* She hurriedly started up the stairs after him, jostling the kitten.

"Galloping troll," the young feline complained.

"I haven't even been your apprentice for two years, Master Evariste. Isn't that too early to begin doing work for the general public?" she asked.

"Nonsense," Evariste said in a laughing tone as he reached the second floor of the house. "You've been able to keep the illusion on your eye color and add in one for your hair color for a good year now. If you can hold spells that long, you're more than ready."

Of course I can hold the illusion that covers my silver eyes. I'm doing everything in my power to blot out any sign of my war magic—but I won't have that kind of do-or-die encouragement for other spells! Safely out of the enchanter's sight, Angelique grimaced before she reached the top stop. "Might it be hoped you will give me the absolute *easiest* jobs?" she asked. When she realized how that sounded, she was quick to add—to help her image, "for I am surely not worthy of working on anything that might cast a shadow over your name."

"Yes, I have two jobs for you," Evariste set the packages down outside his door and fished in an inner pocket of his cloak. "It seems a mage's spell went awry in a little border town between Sole and Trieux."

"What sort of spell?" she asked suspiciously. When Roland mewled as she resettled him in her hands, she kissed him on the top of his head. (He protested, *loudly*.)

"The mage was trying to make a puppet move and perform for a crowd of children."

"And?"

"He bungled the spell and gave the puppet sentience, so now it's running around, bothering the villagers."

If Angelique had not been holding Roland against her chest, she would have dropped him. "A living puppet?"

"It sounds quite terrifying," Evariste agreed.

A living puppet—that's more than terrifying; that requires holy water! Not liking her options thus far, she shivered. "What's the second job?" she asked, hoping for something easier.

"Ahh, yes. A Loire duke is holding a birthday celebration and wants special clothes for the occasion. It will be a simple matter for you to use your alteration or illusion magic to whip something up for the night," Evariste smiled.

Angelique rapidly blinked as she tried to figure out if she had heard him correctly. "Creating an entire *outfit* out of magic is markedly more difficult than changing a person's eye color," she finally said.

"You'll do fine." Evariste winked.

Terrorist puppets and vain dukes, these were not the type of missions I ever thought I would have when I was first accepted into Luxi-Domus.

"I'll just put your gifts in my room for now, then we can review a few spells that might help with the puppet. Something with fire, perhaps?"

Angelique's mouth warred between frowning and smiling when Roland settled against her with a sigh. "Don't you think the puppet would shriek the whole time we burned him?"

"A solid point. We'll have to reconsider," Evariste said. "But first, your gift. Why don't you find your new assistant a cushion or something to sleep on, and we'll reconvene in the workshop?"

Angelique nodded and trotted off to her bedroom, intending to snag one of her tasseled pillows.

When he left for the Veneno Conclave, I thought he was furious with me. But he comes back, giving me an expensive cat and orders for magical missions? I don't know what to think anymore, but I hope I can survive his newest schemes.

When she ducked into her room, she released the sigh she'd been holding. *At least it seems he's given up on making me use my core magic, for now. All I can do is hope it stays that way.*

ANGELIQUE EXHALED WHITE PUFFS, and leaves crackled under her feet as she slowly prowled around a practice dummy. Fall was settling over the woods, and a brisk breeze made the thicket cooler than usual.

Angelique clenched her teeth as she felt her magic—sharp and cold—try to push against the walls she had placed around it. Carefully she pulled more magic, twisting it as she waited for Roland.

The black and white cat—who had left kittenhood behind him years ago and was now a large and handsome cat—sat on a stack of books, reading one Angelique had opened for him.

Over four years had passed since Evariste had brought the magic cat home. And as the enchanter had predicted, Roland had picked up on the workings of magic—and could even perform some charms and defensive spells himself. He was a great help to Angelique and was not afraid to challenge her more than Evariste would.

Roland cleared his throat. "I am prepared; we may begin. Your opponent approaches you with—"

Angelique blew a fireball at the dummy, encasing its head in flames.

Roland scowled at her. "You may be an enchantress-in-training, but you are an uncultured brute."

"Better to defeat a confirmed enemy before they attack than risk injuring bystanders," Angelique countered.

Roland's long black tail twitched back and forth, betraying his irritation with her. "Fine. You attacked with fire. Your opponent retaliates with a poison rope flicked at your head."

Angelique had started to sprint towards the dummy but dropped to her knees and leaned back, skidding the last few feet. She tapped the ground as she slid past the dummy. A crack opened up in the earth, and the dummy fell in up to its neck before the ground clamped shut around it.

"Well done," Roland sourly said. "You have just ruined a city street, costing the taxpayers a lot of money."

"You never said we were in a city," Angelique argued.

Roland sniffed, and his tail quirked into a question mark shape. "You never asked!"

Angelique rolled her eyes as she made the earth spit the dummy back up and settled him into a standing position.

Roland is a wonderful resource and a challenging tutor, yes, but he's also incredibly bossy and smug to go with it. The little tyrant!

Roland swatted at the book with a white paw. He twitched his whiskers and must have used a charm or one of the minor spells he was capable of casting, for a page turned in the book. "For this next match, use an opening attack that will *distract* your opponent—not instantly draw the attention of the entire street."

"Why?" Angelique asked.

"Because at times you might rely on *stealth* instead of banging around like an ogre loosened upon a castle!"

Angelique considered first the cat then the dummy. "Ready," she said.

Roland graciously bowed his head. "You may begin."

Angelique made a flicking motion with her finger, and the dummy was swallowed up by a monstrosity of a gown—pink with enough bows, ruffles, and skirts to choke the tackiest of dress-makers. As an afterthought, Angelique added a pink headdress, as well.

Roland narrowed his bronze eyes and scowled at Angelique. "And what is *that* supposed to accomplish?"

"You said to distract him. I assure you he's quite distracted now," Angelique said. "I put a hoop skirt in that dress. Those things are horrific."

Roland made an anguished groan and turned in a circle on his book. "I try! I try to make you fluent at channeling magic and taking on opponents, but you are content to play dressmaker—

with excruciatingly *terrible* taste in clothes, I might add, which only adds to the insult of your opening move!"

It is such *fun to pull his tail—proverbially speaking.*

Roland *hated* when Angelique did anything less-than-elegant. He thought it didn't suit the image of an enchantress-in-training. Naturally, this meant she took great pains to do unexpected—and silly—spells in between bouts of serious training. (And particularly when Evariste was not present.)

Angelique struggled to keep a smirk off her lips. "Fine, I'll do better this time," she promised. She narrowed her eyes in concentration as she felt for her magic. She was faster at taking what she needed now—all thanks to Roland and his numerous drills, which also kept her physical skills sharp—but what she was about to attempt would take no small amount of control.

Picture it first, she coached herself. *Recall the noises, and bring them all in at once...NOW*! In the span of a few short seconds, a flock of at least one hundred chickens surrounded the dummy.

The chickens clucked, and some of them scratched in the dirt. A few even wandered up to the dummy and pecked at it.

Roland groaned and collapsed. "That's it. You're hopeless. Even a brilliant teacher such as myself cannot aid you. You are beyond reach."

"They're a distraction." Angelique let herself grin at the cat's back. "And it would be hard for him to maneuver around all those chickens."

Roland whipped around and glared at her.

"Fine, fine, I'll try again." Angelique made the dress and illusion chickens disappear. She furrowed her brow as she sifted through possibilities, then selected one and struck, flinging mud at the dummy so it spattered it in the face.

Roland rolled onto his back. "That's it, you've made it clear. I am not training an enchantress-in-training, but a court jester!"

Angelique frowned. "Flinging mud is a perfectly viable technique," she said, a little peeved the cat didn't approve. (Mixing water and dirt and flinging it at such a speed was not child's play!)

"What?" the cat sat up. "Oh, you actually used a magic technique that would work in addition to humoring children. How rare."

"You hadn't even bothered to look before you accused me of being a court jester!" Angelique complained.

Roland stuck his nose in the air. "I wouldn't have assumed if you acted your age!"

Angelique huffed as she returned her gaze to the dummy. Deep in her soul, her war magic pushed, longing to break free—and likely impale the battered target.

Angelique was so practiced in the art of ignoring her core magic, she didn't even think as she shoved it down deep. "He's distracted. Does that mean I get to strike again?"

"Yes," Roland said. "This time your goal is to arrest him."

Angelique nodded. "Still in a city?"

The cat tilted his head in thought. "No. The countryside. In a meadow with livestock."

Angelique nodded, then started pulling her magic and simultaneously twisting it into the spell she wanted. She could draw and twist with markedly more finesse—and at a greater speed than she had even a year ago. As she worked, a wall of thorns sprouted out of the ground, encircling the dummy.

"An excellent choice," Roland praised as the wall grew from knee-high to waist-high. "A plant-based wall won't negatively impact the environment, and while it will effectively stop your target, there is no chance of killing him. However, it is possible he could cut or burn a path through them."

"It depends on the type of magic he has," Angelique agreed. "But I thought it was my safest bet. Particularly if I can get them to grow fast."

Intending to demonstrate, Angelique pushed more magic into the vines than she had available and twisted at the moment, creating a sort of inner magical vacuum that made her reel and her stomach roll.

She fell to her knees and gagged, then groaned. "I was doing so well!"

Roland hopped off his book mountain and padded up to her. "This is why we practice—so you don't make idiot mistakes like this in the field." Though his words were smug, he leaned into Angelique and purred in a comforting gesture. "If you allowed your magic freedom..." he trailed off, mercifully cutting off the old argument.

Roland, like Evariste, felt Angelique should let her magic flow *freely*, that she shouldn't wall it off. (As if *that* wouldn't be a safety hazard for everyone near her!) But neither he nor Evariste pushed her much on the matter, thankfully.

When the nausea passed, Angelique rearranged herself so she sat pretzel style. She plucked up Roland, who meowed in protest as she cradled him in her arms and proceeded to cuddle him.

"I'm so lucky to have a companion like you, aren't I?" she asked as she kissed his head.

"I am not a companion; I am an assistant!" Roland yowled.

"There you two are." Evariste crossed the front yard, pausing to study the rather beaten-up dummy.

He looked different than he had that morning.

To begin with, his short blonde hair was long, now—illusion or alteration magic—and gathered in a silky ponytail at the nape of his neck. Instead of robes, he had on black trousers and a sort of sleeveless, leather jerkin that was ornately etched with gold symbols with a stylized heart and wings emblazoned over the heart. Arm guards, knee-high boots, and the red sash tied round his waist all looked far more serviceable than his usual pricy clothes.

Angelique tilted her head. "Are we going somewhere?"

"Yes!" Evariste beamed as he crouched down in front of

Angelique and tapped the tip of her nose. "I was just coming to tell you: we leave for Baris tomorrow morning."

Angelique shifted so she was in a kneeling position rather than sprawled on the ground. "On Conclave business?"

"Yes—and I thought I'd have you practice granting boons while we were visiting." Evariste scratched Roland under the chin. "And your assistant is welcome to come, as well."

"Really? Roland can come with us?" Angelique asked.

"Yes, he's old enough now; I don't think we have to worry about someone attempting to steal him. He'd be able to outmaneuver them," Evariste said.

"Excuse me!" Roland scrambled out of Angelique's arms, then looked at his mussed fur with horror. He glared at Angelique, then sat down facing Evariste. "No one asked me if *I* would like to come to Baris!"

"Wouldn't you?" Angelique asked.

"No!" Roland yowled.

Angelique frowned. "Why not?"

"It's a desert country—do you know what sand would do to my beautiful fur?" Roland shivered in horror.

"There's only one desert in the country—it has a lot of coastal land, too," Evariste said.

Roland sniffed. "Regardless, I want to be *far away* if Angelique is taking on assignments again."

Angelique glared at the cat. "I fixed the marionette, eventually. I just happened to discover I am highly susceptible to puppets."

"What you mean to say is you are afraid of them," Roland snorted.

"You would have been too if you saw the puppet—it was troubling," Angelique said.

"Angel did well with the Duke's clothes," Evariste said.

Roland twitched his tail. "Both of you told me how she broke her concentration for a moment, and the duke found himself giving his birthday speech to his guests *in* his birthday suit!"

"I dropped it for just a few seconds," Angelique said, though she was not nearly as emphatic in her defense. (Mostly because she had done it on purpose. The duke, it turned out, was a greedy, unlikeable man who was used to abusing the power that came with his position. Angelique had judged—at the moment—that it was her *moral duty* to see the troll brought down a peg or two.)

"The duke never said anything to us about it," Evariste said. "And you recast the spell at lightning speed—I think even I would have been hard-pressed to weave it faster than you did." Evariste smiled proudly, as if Angelique leaving a duke stark naked except for his drawers—even for a short length of time—was only a small matter.

Angelique faked a wince. "However, I believe all the party guests noticed." *Which was the point, of course.*

"I was impressed," Evariste said, as unflappable as ever. "I thought you'd only manage to keep the outfit up for an hour or so. It was quite impressive you lasted the entire night—a true testament to your abilities, as most apprentices wouldn't have lasted even half that."

Angelique gaped at her master. *That little sneak! He set me up!*

Roland twitched his whiskers. "You gave her an assignment you believed she would fail?"

Angelique had to forcibly click her teeth shut from adding a hearty sound of agreement to the cat's question.

"Angelique needs to explore her boundaries." Evariste winked. "And I must give her a chance to grow—like a bird helping its chick fly."

Roland looked back and forth between Evariste and Angelique. "The both of you have an unhealthy obsession with poultry."

"Besides," Evariste continued, ignoring the cat's observation.

"She's completed a number of assignments since those two with a stunning success rate! Her reputation is blooming."

"Into a beautiful weed," Roland muttered.

Feeling the need to change the subject—she didn't need Evariste cooing to build up her confidence while Roland actively sharpened his claws in it—Angelique set an eager smile on her lips. "You said we leave for Baris tomorrow morning. Is there anything I need to do in preparation?"

"We'll review boon-granting tonight—after dinner. Besides that, pack a satchel, perhaps?" Evariste suggested. "And a pillow for your assistant, should he choose to come."

"I. Will. Not!" Roland carefully enunciated every word.

Evariste chuckled. "As you wish, Master Roland."

Angelique stood and dusted dirt off her practice clothes. "I will begin preparations as soon as possible." She swiped up Roland, making him squawk. "Thank you, Master Evariste."

"Of course!" Evariste waved them off as Angelique hurried for the pond bridge.

"Why the hurry?" Roland complained as Angelique jostled him in her arms. "You aren't leaving until tomorrow."

"Yes, but while I pack, I intend to dump you into the library with a few books on boons."

"Aiming to get an edge on your studies?"

"Yes."

"How intelligent of you. There may be hope for you yet! You'll never be as smart as a cat, of course, but at least you are proving you can learn."

Angelique purposely bounced a few steps, jostling him again. "Thank you, dear Roland," she said with real sincerity.

I am grateful for his help. Boons are tricky business, as they require imbedding a spell in a person. Baris is going to be difficult, and I'll need every trick I can learn to get me through this, or my magic might do more harm than good.

CHAPTER 18

The following morning, Angelique stepped out of the dreary autumn rains that drowned Torrens into the bright and warm sunshine of Baris.

She squinted and shielded her eyes as a gust of wind made her light-and-breezy gown puff. "Is that Fillia?" she asked, pointing to a giant city sprawled across the horizon.

Evariste closed the portal. "Yes, in all its beauty and splendor."

Angelique couldn't see much of the city itself—it was hidden behind protective stone walls. But the palace—a giant edifice that towered above everything else—was visible.

The palace was a giant cylinder, topped with a royal purple dome that possessed only a slight curve—like a sea turtle's shell. Gold shapes and swirls were painted across the dome, glittering in the sun, and three similarly shaped and decorated cylindrical buildings were arranged in front of it in a triangular formation.

The famous Aurum Desert was quite a bit south of Fillia, but even here the dirt had a fair amount of sand in it, and much of the countryside was scrubby grass, except for brilliant plumes of greenery that marked lakes and ponds. Giant statues nearly as tall as Evariste's house marked the winding path to the capital.

"But we aren't going to Fillia right away," Evariste said. "The King and his family aren't expecting us until tonight. Instead, we—or you, rather—are first going to practice boon-granting in this little village."

Evariste put his back to the capital and gestured to the smaller village built around the edge of a blue-green lake.

Palm trees and scrappy, leafed trees encircled the pond and defiantly sprouted up in the middle of village roads and lanes. Most of the houses and buildings were constructed out of plaster and stone and were square- or rectangular-shaped, with rooftops that were only barely pitched for water drainage. Pots of tilting plants and unlit braziers decorated the area, many of them serving as resting perches for birds.

Angelique watched a young lady lead a prancing white horse up to the lake to sample the water. "Is there a specific reason why you chose this village?" she asked.

"Mostly because it is a convenient distance from Fillia," Evariste admitted. "But also because while it is not a poor village, its people are not wealthy. Can you tell me why that matters?"

Angelique thought for a minute, watching a shepherd boy herd his goats up to the lake and another man wade through the bleating herd, leading a camel and a placid ox. "Because boon-granting is most often given to peasant folk?" she asked.

"Exactly. Gift-giving, like we granted Princess Rosalinda, is almost exclusively done for royals only." Evariste tilted his head as he studied the village, making his silky blond ponytail slip over his shoulder. "Explain the process, please, Angel."

Angelique shifted her gaze from the animals to the lake and struggled to focus. It wasn't that she was so taken by Baris—though the country was beautiful. It was the sensation of latent magic that pressed against her senses. *It's everywhere! I knew Baris has historically been the most magic-friendly country, but it even dusts the air!*

She shook her head to rattle the observations loose, then

focused on answering her teacher. "If a person acts out of particular goodness—whether it is kindness, courage, valor, or gentleness—we are allowed to use our magic to grant them a boon. Sometimes it can be a physical thing—like a magic animal; other times it can be something less substantial, like good luck or favor among their peers," she recited.

Evariste nodded and scratched his bare bicep. "It's also one of the only ways we can leverage our magic for regular citizens without any expectation of payment. It's a different situation if there has been a disaster or they are in need, of course, but boon-granting lets us reward citizens *and* keep politics out, so no other monarchies can object."

Angelique managed to hold her disgruntled snort in check. *Of course, we must* always *be concerned with politics.*

"Usually, only enchanters, enchantresses, or fairy godmothers and godfathers are powerful enough to grant boons," Evariste continued. "But often, they are granted in one of two ways. The magic user appears to a person in disguise—as an old man or woman—and asks for a small favor. When a person reacts with kindness, they are rewarded. Conversely, sometimes magic users choose to appear as beautiful princes or princesses. And occasionally the magic user chooses never to appear in front of the person themselves, but instead uses animals or magic to test them. I've only seen mages gifted with animal magic do such a thing, though, and only rarely."

Another gust of wind encircled Angelique, and she had to grab her skirts to hold them down. "I understand," she said, struggling to keep her voice cheerful as she battled with the wind.

"It is up to the discretion of the magic user for how they choose to appear—and in the gifts they choose to give. One must be careful in selecting what boon to grant, however, as you don't want to upset the balance or ruin a person's life. Which is why today you will be granting two *temporary* gifts." Evariste explained.

"It's much easier to learn on temporary gifts that only last a day than something that lasts the rest of a person's life."

Angelique nodded emphatically. "Temporary is an excellent start!" she said, not bothering to disguise her relief.

Evariste laughed. "I am glad you are so enthusiastic about this opportunity! I will aid you with the first boon—I will tell you how to appear and what gift to give. The second boon, however, will be entirely up to you."

Won't THAT be fun. Angelique winced slightly.

Evariste had noticed, for he laughed as he draped his arm across her shoulders. "Fear not, Apprentice. You modified a princess's curse—something that is *far* more advanced than boon-granting. You'll do a wonderful job!"

"You said that about the duke, too, when you thought I wouldn't last the night," Angelique reminded him.

"You still did a wonderful job," Evariste winked. "You also just happened to make it an unforgettable night for everyone involved! And perhaps left a new impression on everyone."

"I'll try to keep the streaking to a minimum for today," Angelique said dryly.

"Always a thoughtful goal! Now, come. We're going to stake out a water well."

ANGELIQUE CROUCHED in the bushes as she waited for a young girl or boy to visit the well. She mentally rehearsed the words she would say to grant the boon as she scratched her cheek.

I'm going to get this right—I have to! Evariste is watching, and I'm using his words to grant this boon.

She glanced down to make sure her illusion was staying in place. (Since Roland's arrival, she had grown remarkedly better at effortlessly holding illusions and alteration spells, but she didn't need to be accidentally dropping her disguise in the middle of testing someone.)

Her lovely, gauzy dress was transformed into a tattered gown made of burlap. An illusion aged her face and hands—giving her weathered skin, age spots, and deep smile wrinkles—and she had folded her hair into a braid before turning it snow white with illusion magic.

All in all, she looked like a proper mysterious old woman.

Now all I need is a willing victim. Come on—why hasn't anyone sent their child to retrieve water?

Angelique perked when she saw a young lady strolling through the scrubby grass, carrying a wooden bucket.

She hummed as she almost danced along, her white smile brightening her warm terracotta skin and dark hair. She appeared to be, perhaps, fifteen or so.

Yes. This one will do just fine!

Angelique waited until the young lady plopped her bucket in the well—which almost overflowed with water—before stepping out of the bushes.

"Excuse me, dear," Angelique said in a voice as squeaky as a creaky door. "Could you perhaps spare me some of your water? I haven't the strength to draw any with these old hands."

Angelique's victim—no—benefactee smiled. "Of course, grandmother. Sit here, and I will tip the bucket for you." She patted the stone edge of the well and patiently waited for Angelique to hobble closer.

Yes, this is the one! She deserves a boon. Hopefully she likes the one Evariste picked out.

Angelique plopped down on the lip of the well. She smiled gratefully when the girl fished a ladle from a pocket in her skirt and offered it to her, then held up the bucket.

Angelique took a scoopful and was surprised to find the water tasted sweet and was still cool despite the afternoon sun. *Must be magic-made.*

She held out the ladle, intending to hand it back to the girl, but the young lady shook her head.

"No, grandmother, keep drinking. I can hold the bucket steady for you," she insisted. "You must be thirsty."

"Well...I guess I am," Angelique said lamely. She took another ladleful and—under the girl's watchful eye—a third.

I am going to have to use a chamber pot as soon as this girl leaves!

"Thank you, dear," Angelique croaked when she could drink no more. The girl looked like she was going to protest, so Angelique plunked the ladle in the bucket. "Your kindness and good manners are very becoming. In fact, I cannot stop myself from giving you a gift."

Angelique cast off the illusion—and perhaps, she *may* have been guilty of using a bit of her magic to make her hair glow golden and her eyes swirl blue and purple.

The young lady dropped her bucket, spilling water on her skirts as she gaped at her. "You're a Lady Enchantress!"

In training, Angelique longed to correct her, but Evariste told her under no circumstances was she to let that fact drop.

"Oh, stars and skies!" The girl hurried to curtsy, almost tripping on her bucket in the process.

Angelique held a hand out to her and said soothingly, "Fret not, child. I mean to grant you a boon."

And here's the important bit!

Angelique cleared her throat and held her hands aloft like a composer as she twitched invisible strands of magic into place. "Today only, whenever you speak, not only will a word drop from your lips, but either a flower or a jewel as well. This boon shall last until the sun sets this evening."

She held her breath as she twisted the last bit of the spell and watched it settle around the young girl.

The young lady stared wide-eyed at Angelique. "What do you mean?" she asked.

Two lilies, a topaz, and a ruby fell from her mouth, plopping onto the tipped-over bucket.

Hah-hah! I did it right! I can't wait to tell Roland he missed this moment of triumph!

Angelique scooped up the flowers and jewels and placed them in the bucket. "Here, you might want to hold this for the rest of the day."

"Thank you, Lady Enchantress. You are very kind," the girl said. Four roses, two diamonds, and two orchids fell into the bucket.

Angelique smiled in satisfaction at a spell successfully placed, but she noticed something was off with the girl.

She was smiling—and still bobbing in a curtsey every few seconds—but she didn't have the overflowing joy Angelique was led to believe boons brought.

"Are you dissatisfied with your boon?" Angelique asked.

The girl's eyes widened, and she shook her head with obvious fright.

Angelique chuckled. "You have nothing to fear, dear," she said, imitating Sybilla's way of speaking. "But as an enchantress, it is my duty to grant boons folk actually *want*. I am merely curious..."

"I am very grateful," the girl said, spilling pearls into her bucket. "The flowers are very beautiful and the jewels..."

"The jewels?" Angelique asked.

The young lady's smile seemed a little strained.

Angelique folded her arms across her chest as she mused over the boon. When instructing her, Evariste had said the giving of jewels was a common boon, and she hadn't given it much thought. But now, as she thought back to *her* childhood as a soldier's daughter...

"They're going to be bothersome, aren't they?" she guessed. "If many people know you have a hoard of jewels, your home might get robbed, and selling them will be a pain." Angelique frowned slightly as she considered the conundrum.

"I can take them to Fillia, but it will be difficult to get a fair price for them—no one will believe how I came to possess them," the girl admitted as flowers and jewels spilled into her bucket.

"You could keep a few and...make a jewelry set, I guess?" Angelique ventured.

The girl grinned. "And wear it while I finish my chores for the day?" Her bucket clanked when a particularly big sapphire dropped.

"It *is* a thoroughly useless boon," Angelique agreed. "Perhaps coins would have been a better choice—small currency, in particular. Too large of currency, and everyone will be convinced it is forgery—and it might affect the economy, which is politics, and we can't have *that*." She tapped her chin as she thought. "Obviously, I'll have to put more thought into this for the future."

"It is still a lovely gift," the young lady said—as a small bouquet of hibiscus flowers dropped from her mouth.

Angelique grunted. "The point of a boon is that it *aids* you—not causes additional heartache." Under her breath, she grumbled, "Why has no one realized this?"

Probably because powerful mages are usually taken from their homes at a young age and haven't the faintest idea what life is like for an average person. The only reason I know is that I was taken to the school at a late age. But by the heavens above, you would assume they would have thought their boons through—particularly the traditional ones!

"At least it only lasts a day," Angelique said.

The girl laughed again. "Lady Enchantress, even if I do not get a proper market price, these jewels will feed my mother, sister, and me for a long time. Thank you."

Angelique smiled. "Of course. Never abandon your kind and gentle heart, and you will be prized..." Angelique paused as she tried to think of something suitably vague and unhelpful—Evariste had been clear she had to give some sort of verbal blessing as a parting. "...as the jewels are precious."

She wanted to grimace. *Who came up with all these rules? When you make enchanter or enchantress, do you suddenly have oodles of time on your hands so you can worry about useless things like saying sufficiently mystical partings?*

The girl curtsied a final time. "Thank you, Lady Enchantress. I am not worthy of the boon you have granted me," she said, with a rush of tulips, dahlias, and a few garnets.

"You are," Angelique said firmly, trying to mentally return to her role of beautiful enchantress. "Take care, young one, and may your future be blessed."

The girl nodded and hurried away—her bucket empty of water but full of gems and half-crushed flowers.

When she was no longer visible through the branches of a drooping palm tree, Angelique retreated to her bush. "How did I do, Master Evariste?" she called, not knowing quite where to look.

"You did everything perfectly." Evariste's voice came from above.

Angelique peered up through the foliage of a tree, espying her master sitting comfortably on a thick branch. "But?" she asked.

Evariste shook his head. "There is nothing to criticize, Angel. You performed perfectly."

Angelique relaxed minutely—relieved. "Good."

"However—"

I knew it!

"I have never before seen an enchantress commiserate in the inconsideration of a boon," Evariste chuckled.

Judging by the relaxed tone of his voice, it had been a safe—if not slightly strange—conversation to have with the young woman. It just wasn't done often. Or maybe ever.

What a surprise—I did something unusual again. Shocking. I wonder when that will stop happening?

Angelique cleared her throat. "If I am going to give boons, I would like for them to be something that actually eases the person's concerns and difficulties—not add to them."

Evariste leaned back against a second branch that stretched out behind him. "And that, Angel, is why you are going to be a wonderful enchantress."

Angelique twitched her shoulders in her desire to shrug, but she managed to stay still. "Will we go to a new well to grant the second boon, Master Evariste, or stay here?"

"We'll stay here," Evariste said. "Though this time, the guise you take on and the boon you grant will be your choice. Though I suggest you try to vary it for the sake of practice."

Angelique nodded, then started adjusting a new illusion spell that made her into a blonde, blue-eyed maiden. The illusion made her considerably shorter and gave her the wide eyes of a child. She adjusted her clothes to a bunad—a Verglas dress that consisted of a white blouse covered by a vest and skirt—and used magic to coil her hair into an elaborate braid. As an afterthought, she added a few gold necklaces, bracelets, and pins to her hair.

Now, what to do about a boon? I don't want to use gems, and while I think my coin idea has merit, I would like to discuss it at length with Evariste—I don't want any countries getting angry at me for affecting their currency. But what could I use as a stand-in for the meantime? Perhaps I ought to give the person a choice?

A good half of an hour passed before Angelique heard someone coming.

Angelique hurried out of the bushes, wearing the guise of a young—but obviously wealthy and foreign—little girl, and ran to the well so she could reach it first.

Another young lady—this one a little older than the first girl, seventeen, perhaps—strolled around the trees. This young lady appeared very different—she had wild red hair and mischievous green eyes—though she carried a wooden bucket as well.

When she saw Angelique, she smiled broadly. "Hello there," she greeted her.

Angelique sniffled and stared in the water.

"Is everything all right, young one?" the red-haired girl asked as she drew a bucket of water from the well.

"I'm thirsty, and I can't find my Mamma," Angelique whimpered convincingly.

The girl's face transformed from cheerful to full of worry. "Got separated from her, did you?" She drew water from the well with her bucket and set it on the edge of the well.

Angelique nodded.

"We can fix that. Here, take a drink, then we'll go look for your Mam. Where did you lose her?" She passed Angelique a familiar-looking ladle and soothingly patted Angelique's head.

"Around the lake," Angelique pointed in the direction of the oasis before she took the ladle and drank. Again.

At least I'll be well hydrated, I guess.

She drank the ladleful and went to place it back in the bucket.

"Drink some more, cherub," the red-haired girl urged. "You're hot and upset—it will make you feel better."

What is it with this village that has these overly-conscientious peasants worried about dehydration?

Angelique pretended to sip at the second ladleful as she studied the older girl—who folded her arms across her chest and squinted out at the lagoon. "We'll check the village square first—if your Mam realizes she's lost you, she's likely raising a cry there."

Angelique tried to return the ladle to the bucket again, but the girl shook her finger.

"No, no, little miss. You need to drink. We can't go running around and finding your mother just to collapse because you didn't drink enough water." She smiled.

Angelique stared at her, feeling the pinch of a gutful of water. *Okay, I can't drink any more. Time to blow my cover.* She smiled as she dumped the ladle of water and offered it back to the girl. "Because of your kindness and willingness to help those in need..."

She paused as she threw off the illusion of a child and let her true self (accented with magic that made her eyes a deep blue and her hair glimmer like starlight) shine through. "I will grant you a boon."

The red-haired girl gaped at her a moment, then straightened and smiled. "Oh—you must be the Lady Enchantress who granted a boon to my sister—thank you on her behalf as well as myself and my mother!" Her button nose scrunched with the wideness of her smile, and she bent over in a bow.

Angelique blinked. "Sister?"

The girl laughed. "Yes, we get that a lot. We're step-sisters, really. But my step-father—that is, her father—died, and now it's just the three of us."

Angelique almost whistled. *Now that's sheer luck, to give a boon to a family of two girls and a widow. They are the sort who deserve a bit of happiness. Though to give a second one to the second daughter is a bit much. Oh well! Evariste said I would need practice anyhow.*

"I see. Then you know the gift I gave your sister?" Angelique asked.

The red-haired girl nodded. "Indeed, I do!"

"Good. I'm going to modify this boon so it is something *you* find useful," Angelique said. "It will also be temporary—just as your sister's boon is." She tilted her head as she thought.

Perhaps I really ought to give her the opportunity to choose what she wants.

"Think of a thing—a *small* thing, no people, currency, horses, or the like—which you would like to receive a lot of," Angelique instructed.

The red-haired girl thought for a moment, then smiled. "I have it!"

Angelique started gathering her magic and twisting it like thread. "Very good. Then, whenever you speak, not only will a word drop from your lips, but an array of the thing you most desire. This boon shall last until the sun sets this evening."

Angelique watched this new boon with a greater amount of

attention. *Leaving it vague and open ended is a bit of a risk, but Evariste said I should experiment.* She smiled when the spell seamlessly settled onto the red-haired girl.

Did it work?

CHAPTER 19

"That's all you need to say?" the girl asked, eyes wide in admiration.

Unexpectedly, a frog fell from her mouth and plopped into the water-filled bucket.

The girl stared down at the frog.

Angelique stared down at the frog with her.

The frog swam in its newly claimed bucket.

And silence.

I messed up. Angelique decided. *Badly. Very badly.*

"It worked!" The girl laughed, and a second frog joined the first.

"It *worked?*" Angelique's words were liberally coated with shock.

"I wanted frogs, toads, snakes and the like—my garden has been overrun with bugs. They're going to eat all my plants—oh!" The girl caught a toad and a green garden snake before they fell into the bucket with the happy frogs.

Angelique's head hurt. "Your garden is getting eaten, so the thing you most wanted was *frogs?*"

The red-haired girl nodded. "We used to have frogs, toads, and little snakes all around the oasis, but about five years ago, a bunch of herons escaped the royal aviary and flew here and ate most of them. Our gardens have been plagued ever since then—and not just mine, but the whole village," she explained, dropping two more toads and another frog. "This will help everyone!" she brightly finished, with another garden snake.

"I see. That is very...practical of you," Angelique said, slowly warming to the idea. "It will have a longer-lasting effect, anyway."

"Exactly," the girl said as she set the toads and snakes loose on the ground, releasing them on the oasis. "If I had wished for fruit or food, it all would have rotted in a few weeks! But these little fellows should successfully repopulate the oasis for years to come and save the villagers' gardens!"

"Yes," Angelique agreed. "I am glad you are pleased with your boon." *I just hope vipers and cobras aren't included with your wish for snakes!*

The girl peered at her bucketful of frogs and laughed. "I'll have to come back with a different bucket—Mamma sent me, seeing as my sister couldn't draw any water with her jewel bucket, but I'm not sure she'd welcome me home with frog bathwater." She winked, not at all shaken when a giant frog splashed into the bucket, flinging water across her gown.

"Then...enjoy? And may the boon grant you great happiness." Angelique said, not quite certain how to draw the conversation to a close. *What am I supposed to say—live happily ever after with your frogs, dear child? Ridiculous!*

"I will!" she promised. "Thank you, Lady Enchantress."

Angelique waved bemusedly and watched the girl hurry back up the pathway that led to the village, dropping two toads as she went.

"That was unexpected." Evariste's voice came from directly behind Angelique, making her jump.

Is appearing quietly and mysteriously an advanced skill covered directly before I am made a full Lady Enchantress?

"That she wanted snakes?" Angelique asked.

"And toads and frogs, yes," Evariste agreed.

Angelique scuffed a slipper in the dust. "Did I make a mistake in granting the boon? I thought that by making it temporary, she wouldn't be able to come up with anything that would have large-scale repercussions—politically or environmentally."

"No, it was a very good boon *because* it is temporary," Evariste agreed. "Though next time, you should ask them what it is they want and have them verbalize it."

"It was too risky to leave it up to her without hearing anything about it, wasn't it?" Angelique sighed as a fat toad hopped past her foot.

"Given that she clearly had a kind heart, it was a relatively safe bet she wouldn't wish for anything malicious, but it was a bit risky, yes," Evariste said. "The real danger, however, was in the magic. Often times, leaving things vague in a spell makes the spellwork unstable. That you got it to stick—and stay balanced—is very telling of your power, Angel."

Angelique scoffed. "You give me too much credit, Master Evariste."

"It's quite the contrary," Evariste said. "I learned myself as an apprentice that it is best to clearly define the terms of your spell. I had a charm blow up on me once—singed my eyebrows off."

Angelique stared at her teacher, trying to picture him without eyebrows. "You're fibbing," she blurted out.

Evariste grinned as he shook his head. "The stories my old master—Enchanter Clovicus—could tell you. Regardless, it's always best to keep the terms of your magic defined—whether it's boons, breaking a curse, or other work."

"I will remember that for the future," Angelique said.

"I'm sure you will. Besides that, you did a wonderful job and were a true credit to my name." Evariste fondly squeezed her hand, which Angelique bore with markedly more joy than she did the hugs.

Bizarre ideas, Angelique summarized internally.

"With two rounds of practice done, I believe we can move onto Fillia." Evariste didn't release Angelique's hand. Instead, he tugged her along, maneuvering her so she didn't step on one of the boon-granted grass snakes. "King Solon requested an audience with me. I don't know if that means he wants to consult me on a matter or make a request, but we're going to find out. This will mark yet another king you've met, Angel!"

"How exciting," Angelique said, though she felt like she'd rather sit by the oasis and watch more toads and frogs materialize.

While she liked traveling and seeing different countries, fraternizing with royalty was not high on her list of "favorite things to do." Already Evariste had dragged her to meet the King and Queen of Torrens multiple times, and they had briefly fraternized with the Farset King and Queen on one of their visits to Alabaster Forest.

Evariste gave her a sly look. "You could stay behind. That might be for the best, in fact, as I planned to purchase you a few new outfits."

Angelique snapped to attention, her sweet smile and honied tones back. "Oh, Master Evariste, it is my duty as your apprentice to follow you so I might glean every piece of wisdom from you that I can."

And also, to make sure you don't waste more money on my wardrobe!

"In that case, we ought to stop by a horse breeder," Evariste said. "I intend to purchase a set of horses and a coach for you in the next year or two. You can tell me if you prefer the more hot-tempered Arabian horses or perhaps a flashy Andalusian."

"What would I need a coach for?" Angelique asked, bewildered.

"I keep horses and coaches all throughout the Continent," Evariste informed her. "You ought to do the same as we travel more and more. But come—for now we must prioritize our meeting with the King. To Fillia!"

WHEN EVARISTE and Angelique were presented to the King of Baris, even Evariste was a little taken aback by the manner in which they found him.

He was seated on a cushion inside the royal aviary—a giant glass building filled with lush greenery and deep blue springs. A little girl sat in front of him, her lips pursed in displeasure as he—the King of Baris—braided her *hair*.

"Papa, you are not braiding tightly enough," the little girl scolded. "My hair is going to come loose!"

King Solon laughed. "You can't see the back of your head. How can you know?"

"Because when Mama braids my hair, it feels like she is trying to tear it out of my head," the little girl reported dutifully.

"Then aren't you glad I have a gentle hand?" King Solon asked.

"No!" the little girl said mournfully. "Because I am to have dagger practice next, and my teacher said if my hair gets in my face again, I'll have to cut it off!"

King Solon glanced up, catching sight of Evariste and Angelique standing in the middle of a gravel walkway that wound through the aviary.

"Lord Enchanter Evariste, it is good to see you again. This young lady must be your apprentice?"

Evariste nodded as he set a hand on her shoulder. "Angelique, yes. How are you, Your Majesty?"

"Apparently, I am a poor braider," King Solon said nonchalantly.

"You *are*," the little girl said mutinously.

"I'm not sure how I shall carry on with my life," the King continued.

"Very shabbily, I would think," the little girl muttered.

King Solon grinned and tugged lightly on the little girl's braid before he tied it off with a ribbon. "Lord Enchanter Evariste,

Apprentice Angelique, this impertinent child is my sun and moon —my daughter, Princess Astra. Astra—make your greetings."

The little girl pushed herself to her feet and gave them a slightly wobbly curtsy. "Welcome to Fillia, esteemed guests," she said.

The young princess couldn't have been more than seven or eight, but her words and expression were serious as she looked from Evariste to Angelique.

Evariste squeezed Angelique's shoulder, propelling her into motion.

"Thank you for the warm welcome, Princess Astra," Angelique said. "It is our honor to be here."

Angelique—being in a lower position—curtsied to the princess and king, but Evariste merely bowed his head.

King Solon kissed the top of his daughter's head. "Off to your lessons, Astra."

"Yes, Papa!" The little girl picked up a dagger that was easily as big as her forearm, then dutifully trotted off, carefully holding the weapon by its scabbard.

"Baris royals are strongly encouraged to learn basic defense, so they might fight for themselves and their people should the need arise," King Solon said as he stared at the path his daughter had disappeared down. "Including all royal daughters."

Evariste grinned slyly. "I think women who have a way with weapons are to be admired."

Never before had Angelique more wanted to grind her heel on Evariste's foot.

King Solon's dark eyebrows crawled up his forehead. "Is that so?"

Evariste laughed. "My apprentice has war magic that deals specifically with weapons."

The King's look of confusion cleared, and he stood, brushing wrinkles out of his robe. "Ahh, yes. I had heard something of her abilities. I am glad to hear the rumors are true. I am greatly relieved to know that a Lady Enchantress with war magic as her core will be roaming the continent when my children take over."

Since that was generally the *opposite* of what she was often told, it was now Angelique's turn to be confused. "If you don't mind my asking, Your Majesty...why?"

King Solon shrugged. "As an enchantress, you are practically a paragon of virtue—one capable of stopping any *unpleasantries* that might occur."

"Is that why you called us here?" Enchanter Evariste asked. "Unpleasantries?"

The King of Baris grimaced. "I'm afraid so." He strode across the small clearing and selected a scroll placed by a silver lantern. "Two months ago, I heard rumors of dark magic—in *my* country. Supposedly, if one had enough money, one could purchase the service of a black mage. My men tracked the rumors here to Fillia."

"And?" Evariste asked.

King Solon gestured with the scroll. "It was true. It was a small operation—only two black mages were a part of it—and apparently it was doing quite poorly before my soldiers broke it up."

"Then the mages got away?" Angelique asked.

"I'm afraid so," the King said.

Evariste frowned until his forehead puckered. "What would drive them to offer such services here in Baris—where one can buy magical charms next to a fruit stand?"

"I do not know, but I intend to make it clear that black magic is *not* welcome here," King Solon growled. He shook his head, then offered Evariste the scroll. "Here is the information my men gathered."

"Thank you," Evariste said. "With your permission, Angel and I will look into the matter a little more, then send word to the Veneno Conclave."

The king nodded. "Of course. I'd be grateful if you share any additional information you uncover. Two black mages working together is not necessarily unusual but..." He paused, and his gaze hardened as he once more glanced at the path his daughter had taken. "I don't like it," he finished.

To not like it is a mild reaction. I don't get on well with Madam Quarrellous, but I couldn't agree more with her lectures of ethics and the evils of black magic! Angelique suppressed a shiver and kept her expression bland.

Evariste nodded as he briefly unrolled a bit of the scroll and glanced it over. "Was there anything else, Your Majesty?"

"No." King Solon swung his gaze back to Angelique and Evariste. "Though I would like to express my early congratulations to you, Apprentice Angelique, in becoming the first Enchantress with war magic. I look forward to seeing what kind of Enchantress you will become."

Angelique forced a smile and curtsied. "Thank you, Your Majesty," she murmured.

Evariste offered another bow of his head. "Take care, Your Majesty. We'll be in touch."

King Solon nodded, then ambled over to a stack of scrolls as Evariste and Angelique went back down the path they had come from.

"It seems you'll be getting an eyeful of Fillia, Angel," Evariste said in a happy tone, as if this was a welcome excursion and not dire news.

"Yes," Angelique agreed. "I hope we can find what we need."

EVARISTE RENTED rooms for them at The Sesame Seed Inn, but it wasn't until the following morning that Angelique got her first good look at Fillia and its famous marketplaces.

"According to the reports, they had a stall in Lampros Marketplace, which they used to re-route potential customers to a basement shop," Angelique reported—having carefully pored over the papers the night before.

"We'll head to Lampros Market, then," Evariste said. "But along the way, we'll conduct a bit of a cultural lesson—or review."

"Very well." Angelique handed the scroll off to Evariste, then fell into step with him when he started down a street.

"Baris is a mixing pot of sorts—with Fillia in particular serving as the epicenter," Evariste began. "Baris has its own unique culture, but it's one of the most open countries in our continent, so you'll see echoes of Ringsted, Torrens, every country on our Continent, really, *and* our island country neighbors, and perhaps even occasional glimpses of countries beyond. Its long coastline is partially responsible for the mixture."

Angelique nodded as she tried to process all the bright colors and foreign smells at once. Birds crowed, and goats baaed as they passed by a store that only sold olive oil—from the olive groves planted at the coast.

Evariste grinned at Angelique and said leadingly, "And towards magic...?"

"Baris has historically had the most welcoming attitude—until the Snow Queen founded the early predecessor of the Veneno Conclave in Verglas," Angelique dutifully recited. "Before the Snow Queen, it was the *only* country in which those with magic were not persecuted or disdained or sold as slaves."

"Precisely," Evariste agreed. "Though the Veneno Conclave is now the cradle of magic so to speak, you'll find lots of charms, artifacts, and books on magic for sale in Baris."

"Is that why I can feel magic?" Angelique asked.

Since they had stepped outside, she kept feeling faint brushes of magic. Sometimes it was cold and icy, other times warm and welcoming, and occasionally zingy and electrifying. But there were so many whiffs and hints of it, she couldn't track it to any single spot—particularly when combined with all the new sights and smells.

"Yes," Evariste agreed. "There is latent magic all over Baris—but *especially* in Fillia."

Angelique nodded. *I guess this is a hint that I should be working more on my magic sensitivity. I've always been rotten at it, but with so many magic sensations, it dampens my awareness and is a bit overwhelming.*

"Unfortunately, all that magic can make a perfect screen for black and rogue magic users. Their magic would stick out like a sore thumb in other countries, but they can hide their magical signature—so to speak—more easily in Baris," Evariste explained.

"Do you think that is why the black mages tried to set up shop here?"

Evariste smiled wryly. "I think they were mistaken in thinking they could. Though magic is embraced in Baris, only *good* magic is accepted. Anyone who uses magic for dark purposes in Baris would likely never be seen again."

"Well, that's...comforting?" Angelique said.

Evariste grinned and gently tugged Angelique out of the path of a prancing chestnut horse and its rider. "This way."

They threaded through an enclosed alleyway that was crammed with stalls. Its roof was arched and painted a mustard yellow with dark blue tiles and paints creating swirling patterns.

"Governmentally speaking, there isn't another country like Baris," Evariste continued as they passed a stall draped with paper lanterns. "King Solon is the ruler, but his brothers and sisters each rule over the largest cities in Baris—for the most part—and are considered sovereigns there, though they pledge their loyalty to Solon, who is considered the King of princes, so to speak."

They exited the alleyway, emerging by an aqua blue pool—one of the oases the city was built around.

Angelique admired the beautiful color of the water as Evariste frowned and looked behind him. "Is something wrong, Master Evariste?" she asked.

"I don't know." Evariste frowned slightly. "I thought I felt something. But it seems I was wrong."

He walked parallel with the water, and Angelique trailed behind him.

She lurched to a stop, however, when her magic abruptly roared to life. It almost slipped from her grasp, and in that moment, she felt a foreign magic slither past. Though Angelique could not pinpoint its location, she felt the foreign magic's deep thirst for blood.

"Evariste," Angelique ran to catch up to him. "There's something—"

Her breath caught in her lungs, and suddenly she couldn't exhale or inhale.

Magic. This is a spell.

CHAPTER 20

Her lungs burned, and a stabbing sensation knifed through her heart. It felt like someone was trying to rip her chest open.

I have to warn Evariste. Unable to breathe, Angelique fell to her knees, her face growing red as magic forcibly choked the life out of her.

"Angelique!" Evariste shouted.

She thought he moved around her, but the world was starting to grow dark, and it was hard to see. Her own power clawed at her hold, struggling against her to free itself.

No. I'm not letting go!

Angelique stubbornly shoved her powers back down even as she flopped over, her face scraping the gritty cobblestone road.

Evariste shouted something, and she felt his hand on her forehead before the spell evaporated.

She sucked in a deep breath of air. "Black mage," she wheezed.

"I'm trying to determine their location." Evariste's voice was low. His tense back was to her, but he clutched her hand, even as she struggled to stand while he held it.

Angelique greedily sucked in another breath of the sweetly

fragrant Fillia air, then maneuvered herself so she stood at Evariste's right side.

"There are two of them," Evariste murmured, barely moving his lips. "One in the shadows in a putrid orange cloak to the right, and then one on the roof of a building to the left."

Angelique eyed the bystanders who milled around the oasis, laughing and chatting, unaware of the silent standoff happening in their midst. "Your orders?"

"Attack the one on the ground," Evariste said. "Use bodily force as your primary attack, and magic if you have to. I don't want anyone getting caught up in the fight."

"Is a physical fight really the best option?" Angelique asked.

"For you? Undoubtedly," Evariste chuckled.

Angelique frowned, slightly, unsure if he meant that literally or if he was trying to allude to her powers.

"As you have kept up with your physical training from the Academy due to Roland's efforts, I imagine you'll find him an easy target," Evariste said. "Which is why I'll take the mage on the roof."

"Yes, Master," Angelique purposely kept her eyes off the mage —she could see him lingering at the mouth of an alleyway.

"And Angelique..."

She made a show of peering farther down the oasis, attempting to lull the black mage into a false sense of security. "Yes?"

"Use your core magic if you must."

He was gone before she could object.

Angelique grit her teeth and raised her chin, then started to amble towards the alleyway—though she took a slight detour to make it look like she was heading to a food stand just a little way down. *Nice try, Evariste. But it's not going to happen.*

She lingered by the food stand, until she saw the black mage take a step out of the ally.

No—I can't let him fight me out here. I've got to contain him.

Angelique dropped all pretenses of strolling and sprinted at the black mage.

He was tall and rail-thin with a beak-like nose that made him look like a vulture when he smirked. He extended his hand and opened his mouth to utter a spell.

A horse-length from him, Angelique dropped to her legs and skid the rest of the distance. The gritty ground bruised her legs, but she rammed her left foot into the mage's shin, and he dropped like a ragdoll.

He tried to wheeze out his spell, but with the air knocked out of him, he had no breath to speak.

Angelique rolled to her feet and slammed her heel into the mage's neck.

He gurgled, and his arms twitched like the legs of a bug.

Grabbing him by the collar of his hideous robes, she dragged him to his feet. She spun him around and slammed him face-first into the wall. The mage shrieked, then sagged in her grasp. When she peeled him off the wall, he would have fallen if not for her grip on his clothes, as he was unconscious, and his nose was now crooked.

Well. That was unexpectedly easy. At a loss of what to do, Angelique looked around the street, the unconscious black mage still dangling from her grasp. *I guess other magic users don't have the constitution or training we war mages get. Maybe our reliance on magic is detrimental? Because I think even a basket weaver would have put up more fight than that.*

She studied the fainted mage as she pressed her lips together. *Maybe I ought to tie him up...*

There was an explosion, and the ground beneath her feet shook.

Angelique dropped the mage—who limply hit the ground with a painful-sounding crunch—then dashed out into the street, squinting up at the roof.

Evariste and the other black mage, a scrappy-looking woman, were facing off on the top of a one story, flat-roofed building.

Web-like magic the color of bug guts leaked from the black mage's hands, and a smoky gray wall protected her from Evariste's attacks.

Why hasn't he crushed the mage? Angelique wondered. Her eyes were drawn to a shimmering mass of magic. The inner spell belonged to the black mage—even this far from it, Angelique could feel the slippery quality to it. But the spell was held back by Evariste's glittery blue magic.

While the mages struggled, the spells did as well—Evariste's was fighting to hold back whatever the black mage wanted to unleash on the oasis.

The bystanders were no longer oblivious but frantic. They fled the area, ramming into each other in their fear.

Angelique scrambled for the building, speeding up when she saw the staircase that led to the building next door. She snatched a small board of wood from a shop—shouting apologies to the owner, pounded up the steps, then slunk across the roof, hoping the black mage—with her back turned to her—was unaware of her presence.

When she reached the edge of the rooftop, she paused to unwind just enough of her magic to use for alteration spells.

Carefully, she twisted her magic as she set the edge of her small board of wood on the roof. The wood glowed silver and grew, turning into a plank wide and long enough to walk across.

Angelique had slid it into position when Evariste shouted.

The black mage had advanced on him—her yellow magic slithering around Evariste.

Evariste, however, was focusing on the war between the spells, and was funneling more power into his as the black magic tried to break free. His face was twisted in pain, but he ignored the spell surrounding him.

Angelique sprinted across her plank and rammed the black mage from behind, sending her sprawling.

"Angelique," Evariste shouted. "Crush that spell!" He pointed to the dark mage's spell that had almost completely shaken off Evariste's magic.

"How?" Angelique asked. She reached down to grab the mage by her cloak, but yellow magic snapped at her fingers, sending a searing pain up her arm.

"Don't touch the mage!" Evariste yelled, his voice harsh and angry.

"Yeah, I figured that out," Angelique sourly said as she skulked across the rooftop to join Evariste.

"She's a healer who has twisted her magic," Evariste explained. "She can do immeasurable damage to you. I'll handle her."

"That's fine with me, but you never said what to do with the spell." Angelique narrowed her eyes as she studied it, trying to pick apart exactly what Evariste was doing to prevent it from casting.

"Smother it with your magic," Evariste instructed.

"*What?*"

"Release your magic in a raw form and snuff it out—make sure you use *enough*," Evariste said in a warning voice.

"But if I—"

"That spell is set to start a massive, uncontrollable fire. If it goes off, hundreds of people will die. *Use enough magic*," he said in a tone that brokered no argument.

Angelique snapped her mouth shut as Evariste struck the black mage with a lightning strike.

The mage shrieked in pain but fired off a ghastly black ball of luminous magic.

Evariste blocked it with a blue-tinted shield, then glanced at Angelique. "You can do this, Angel—it will be even easier for you than me."

Angelique nodded and licked her lips before she extended her arm and pointed at the black spell.

Careful, careful, she told herself as she started channeling her magic. *I don't want to harm anyone.* She bit her lip, ignoring the pain that grew in her head as her magic raged in her, howling to be freed.

As quickly as she dared, she wove her magic around the spell, replacing Evariste's powers as he focused on the mage. She narrowed her eyes as she studied the spell, able to make out the glowing black strands of filth that made up the magic.

She shuddered in repulsion when the spell rammed against her magic, but her magic rebuffed it with ease, partially slicing into the attack.

Angelique watched as her silvery magic surrounded the spell in a hazy cloud that was growing so large and thick, she could barely see the water of the oasis. Still, the spell showed no signs of weakening. *There must be a way I can disassemble it, because if it needs much more, this is going to get dangerous.*

Somewhere behind her, fire roared, and black magic hissed.

"Angel, do you have the spell contained?" Evariste called to her.

"Almost." Angelique tilted her head as she studied a particular loop of the spell. *There. That's the command that keeps it moving forward toward its target. If I could just slice through that part.*

She bit her lip and carefully used the raw form of her magic to make a precise cut.

The loop broke, and the spell abruptly ballooned in size.

Angelique cursed under her breath and pressed her magic down on it, containing it. Holding it back now made her palms burn, and pain exploded in her temple.

The dark magic no longer pushed forward, but instead turned its ire onto Angelique. She wanted to scream with pain when her raw magic buckled. The smallest trace of it slipped through her control, reverting to its pure form: war magic.

The flicker of her magic sliced straight through the black mage's spell.

Angelique hurriedly threw more of her power at it, but to her surprise, the spell ricocheted back to the black mage, smashing into her and disappearing under her skin.

The mage's eyes bulged, and she screamed. She clawed at her own face as her skin started to glow the same eerie color as the spell had, then collapsed.

Angelique quickly reeled in her magic while Evariste approached the fallen mage, his fingers glowing blue.

"What happened?" Angelique asked, somewhat shaken.

"It seems you sent the spell back to her," Evariste said as he knelt next to the mage.

"Then she's...?"

"Dead," Evariste said after checking her pulse.

Angelique gulped. "I *killed* her?"

"No." Evariste turned the mage over and frowned at her face. "She was killed by her own spell."

"Because I sent it back to her," Angelique said, a little bit of hysteria welling up inside of her.

I killed someone. I ended a life. Because I couldn't handle my own magic.

"Angel," Evariste started as he stood and turned in her direction. Abruptly, his face paled.

"What—" Before Angelique could finish, Evariste extended his hand and shouted in the twisty language of magic.

Angelique's hair stirred when a bolt of Evariste's magic flashed past her.

Behind her, someone screamed and then cut off in a gurgle.

Angelique twisted around and took a staggering step backwards.

The orange-robed black mage she had left unconscious was collapsed behind her, his limbs twitching.

He stilled, and not even his chest moved.

Evariste had killed him.

"I think he's dead." Her eyes bugged, Angelique turned to stare at Evariste.

"He was going to hurt you." The steel in Evariste's voice was gone as he crossed the rooftop to stand with her.

"I'm a war mage. I can take pain," Angelique muttered.

"I may have let my emotions get the best of me," Evariste admitted. He stopped when he reached her, his eyes tracing over her. He gently reached out and brushed a strand of her hair from her face. "Are you hurt?"

Angelique shook her head. "No, but now we won't be able to collect any information from them," she said glumly.

"We'll search them and write up a report for both King Solon and the Veneno Conclave," Evariste said. "Black mages don't usually work together in large groups, so it is unlikely this was more than a small operation set up by this pair."

Angelique nodded, but her eyes strayed to the body of the female black mage she had killed.

"Angelique," Evariste said.

"Yes, Master Evariste?" Angelique reluctantly shifted her gaze back to him.

Evariste kept his hands on her shoulders. "As a Lord Enchanter, I champion mercy and believe bloodshed should only be a last resort. But when someone attacks you with the intent of killing you, I want you to fight with everything you have, even if it means ending the life of another. Self-defense is *never* to be condemned, nor is action on behalf of those who cannot protect themselves."

Evariste slid his hands down her arms and pulled her into a warm hug. "You saved everyone in the area by disarming that spell. The black mage was the one who chose to commit such a cruel act. You acted in heroism. Do you understand?"

Angelique pressed her head into his shoulder and said nothing.

On a base level, she understood. It was better that the black mage was dead than if she had survived and managed to cast the spell. But what spooked her most was how *effortless* it had been on her part.

The hardest bit was holding back her magic. It had so seamlessly slipped through the magic and clipped it...

Angelique released the haggard breath she had been holding in. "So, we search the mages next?" she said when she could talk in a voice that wasn't wooden or dreary.

"Yes," Evariste said. "And then we send word to King Solon."

"THEY *ATTACKED* YOU?" King Solon repeated, seemingly unsure of what he had heard.

"The mage with twisted healing magic cut off Angel's air supply, yes," Evariste confirmed. "I'm not sure if they were trying to reel us in or legitimately kill her."

"But what on earth would possess them to attack an enchanter and his apprentice?" King Solon shook his head as he leaned against a stall door. (Today, Angelique and Evariste had been led to the royal stables, where apparently King Solon had just finished a ride with his son.) "They had to have known it was a losing battle the moment they waged it," the King continued.

Angelique kept a pleasant smile on her face and her hands clasped in front of her. The familiar scent of horses and straw was soothing, but her gut still churned from the knowledge that she had *killed* a woman.

"It also begs the question of their location here," Evariste said.

"Indeed, my men and I thought we had run them from Fillia. Apparently that was not so," King Solon said grimly.

"Angel and I mean to stay in Fillia a couple of days to more thoroughly investigate the matter," Evariste said. "In addition to your information, we'll have to submit a report on the attack, now, as well."

"You won't leave through a portal?" King Solon asked.

Evariste shook his head. "I use my magic sparingly when there are dark mages around—it's too risky to act otherwise."

"If you intend to stay, then please allow me to offer you housing," King Solon said.

"That's not necessary," Evariste said. "I'd like to be closer to the city for the sake of our investigation. Though we appreciate the offer."

King Solon nodded. "Understandable. However, if you change your mind, do not hesitate to return. I will inform my servants and guards that you have an open invitation."

"Thank you, Your Majesty," Evariste said.

Angelique was a moment too slow in adding, "Yes, thank you, Your Majesty."

A horse poked its head out of its stall and nuzzled King Solon as he studied Angelique. "Study well, Apprentice," he said. "We may have need of your magic sooner than I thought."

A chill ran down Angelique's spine, and she lowered her gaze to keep from snarling at the King.

Evariste, however, smiled and patted Angelique on the back. "In this, I hope you are wrong, Your Majesty."

"I hope so, as well," King Solon grimly said.

Angelique curtsied when Evariste bowed his head, and she followed him so closely she almost stepped on his heels when they left the royal stables.

"Though it is rather early, we can retire to the inn for the day," Evariste said as they marched through a sunny courtyard. "It's been a trying day. The Sesame Seed Inn has public baths—separated by gender, of course—with baths the sizes of ponds. We can rest—"

"Excuse me, Lord Enchanter?"

Angelique and Evariste swung around in tandem, blinking in surprise at the short woman who nervously addressed them.

She wrung her hands and gulped under their gazes but continued bravely. "Might I ask for a bit of your time?"

"YOU'VE FOUND A CHILD WITH MAGIC?" Evariste asked, his voice colored with surprise.

The woodcarver—a giant hulk of a man—nodded. "A street urchin—he goes by the name of Pest."

"A street urchin, he's an orphan, then?" Angelique raised her hand to shield her eyes from the bright noon sun. They had relocated to the woodcarver's shop, but they stood outside as most of the space was crowded with different kinds of woods and half-finished projects.

Master Dimi sighed. "His parents died several years ago. He's managed to scratch out a living, but his magic is getting stronger. And I've heard reports..." He trailed off and sighed while his wife—the palace maid who had first stopped Evariste and Angelique—patted his arm.

"If it becomes known he has magic, his life may be in danger. Street children are easy targets for practitioners of black magic," Evariste said.

Angelique pressed her lips together.

When her magic had exploded from her during the goblin attack that had killed her parents, Angelique had been housed by her village until a fairy godmother had come for her. It was a scary time for her, having lost her parents and learning she had magic in the same day, but at least her parents' friends had supported her, and her friends' mothers had held her in warm embraces while she cried.

She couldn't imagine having to deal with that alone.

"He swipes things—small things," Master Dimi explained.

"Scraps of leather and wood, pieces of paper, things like that, then he makes them into simple little crafts that he sells, but they have charms in them."

"I bought a bow from him not a month ago," Master Dimi's wife explained. "He promised it would bring me compliments. I sewed it onto a bracelet, and darned if I don't receive compliments whenever I wear it."

Evariste glanced at Angelique. "What kind of magic would you say he has, Angel?"

"It would be craft magic, wouldn't it?" Angelique asked.

Evariste smiled warmly. "Yes. He must have pretty strong magic to be able to cast enchantments on such base materials."

"And strong craftmages are rare," Angelique added for the woodcarver's sake.

"Indeed. You were right to contact us, Master Dimi," Evariste smiled. "We will talk to the boy and see him settled in Luxi-Domus."

When Master Dimi and his wife looked from Evariste to her, Angelique nodded in affirmation. "It is our duty," she said with real happiness.

This will be nice*—especially after tangling with the black mages. Even if I didn't have the best experience in school, I am certain this boy will do far better than I did.*

CHAPTER 21

"I'm sorry, Angel," Evariste said as they reached the edge of the market. "I promised you a relaxing day after the trial we went through this morning, and instead we continue to work."

"I don't mind, Master Evariste," Angelique truthfully said. "I'd rather find this boy than sit around the inn." *Better to keep my mind off this morning.* And in all honesty, Angelique was looking forward to approaching the young craftmage.

For once it's a mission for a child that does not *involve me trying to teach him/her a moral lesson! No illusionary animals or shouting will be necessary!*

"Hopefully we'll be able to find him. Master Dimi said he doesn't necessarily show up every day," Evariste explained. "He should be around here..." He trailed off as he looked from stand to stand, obviously sensing magic.

Angelique obediently followed Evariste through the market, feeling a little useless. *I can't discern between the different magics, so I won't be able to help him find this "Pest."*

Angelique brushed some of her hair from her eyes.

Maybe I should ask Roland to help me improve my magic sensitivity.

Evariste stopped at the edge of a thin blanket, scattered with an assortment of items. A young boy crouched at the edge of the blanket, barefoot with ratty trousers and an ill-fitting shirt.

Is this him? She glanced at Evariste, but he seemed more interested in the boy's goods than the child himself. "Master Evariste?" she said, wondering if she should say anything to the boy.

The boy immediately stiffened with suspicion, a wary look settling into his remarkable eyes that were rings of sky blue and royal blue. A thatch of his black hair hung over his face.

Ah, yes, no saying anything it is, then.

Evariste smiled charmingly—though Angelique could have told him to save it; the boy was obviously too sly to fall for such a trick. "How much for the flower?" the Lord Enchanter asked.

"Two copper coins." The boy raised his shoulders nearly up to his ears as he eyed them.

Evariste picked up the paper rose and tossed a silver coin to Pest.

"I don't have change for this," the boy said loudly.

"Keep it," Evariste instructed.

The boy rolled his eyes and tucked the coin into his dirty shirt as Evariste turned to Angelique.

"For the best of all women." He handed the paper rose to Angelique.

Angelique stared at the flower for a moment. *This is more of his strangeness—I can feel it in my bones. I wish he would stop this unnecessary bribing. How does he expect me to react? Shy? Thankful?* Angelique settled on meek, so as she took the paper flower, she smiled. "I will keep it for Lady Enchantress Lovelana, then?"

Evariste chuckled and patted her shoulder. "No, Angel. It is for you."

Yep. More strangeness. Must come with being a child prodigy and a legend. Angelique tried to force a blush and uttered a quiet, "Oh."

The performance was unnecessary. Evariste was already turning back to the boy—who was most assuredly the street child they were looking for. "A shell for luck? That must have been tricky to—" Before he could say more, the boy rolled up his blanket with a practiced snap, scrambled to his feet, and took off running down the alleyway.

"Well," Evariste said as he watched him run. "It seems we found our magically-inclined child."

"You can feel his magic?" Angelique asked.

"Yes, he's a craftmage for certain." Evariste tapped the top of the paper flower. "Can you feel the slight enchantment on this?"

Angelique miserably shook her head. "I feel magic, but it's indecipherable. It's like all the different strains have been stirred into a soup."

Evariste gently patted her back. "Fret not. Baris, and Fillia in particular, is difficult to sift through if you are not especially sensitive to magic. There's so much of it here—and so many different kinds—it is understandable you would find it difficult to separate."

Angelique nodded but stubbornly glanced around the marketplace, trying to pinpoint the various magic essences she could detect.

"I don't think we'll see that boy again today." Evariste studied her long enough to make Angelique shift under his gaze. "So I think we ought to return to the inn for some food. And that bath."

Angelique nodded. "I could finish up some more spell work, too."

His eyebrows slanted slightly. "You need to rest. Do you want to talk about—"

"No," Angelique replied before he could even ask the question. *No, I don't want to talk about killing the rogue mage.* She took a breath and settled her shoulders. "At least not right now."

Evariste gave her an indecipherable look and briefly threaded his fingers through hers, rubbing his thumb on the top of her hand. "You need to talk about it...but it can wait for another day. Speaking of which, as long as we are in Fillia seeking out this boy, we ought to tour the royal aviary or menagerie. I'm certain King Solon won't mind."

Angelique blinked at the conversation shift but was grateful for it all the same. "That sounds like it would be fun." *And it would keep him occupied so he wouldn't drag me off to waste more money clothes shopping.*

As if he could hear her thoughts, Evariste gave her a sly smile as they turned in the direction of their inn. "Of course, we could always visit a tailor."

"I would very much enjoy seeing the menagerie or aviary," Angelique said firmly.

"Very well. We'll plan for the aviary tomorrow, in that case." He winked.

Angelique relaxed slightly at the declaration. *I'll have to tell Roland all about the birds. Maybe he'll be sad he missed it!*

THREE DAYS PASSED before Evariste was able to successfully track down the craftmage boy.

Once again, the child was in the market with a blanket of goods. This time he was stretched out next to it, looking a bit like an ally cat.

As they drew closer, Angelique could see he only had a few items left to sell—a paper fan, a string of stone beads, and what looked like a dog collar made of white leather.

Evariste stopped Angelique by squeezing her hand, then held a finger to his lips.

Angelique nodded, and together they crept up on the boy as he napped in the afternoon sunshine.

When they reached his blanket, he lazily opened one eye, then practically jumped out of his skin.

"The fan is for cool air, yes?" Evariste asked, his voice warm and soothing.

It had no effect on the boy, for he rolled away and sprinted down an alley, even faster than he had the first time.

Evariste watched him run with a puzzled look.

"I think he's just going to keep running, Master," Angelique volunteered.

"Yes, but I'm afraid I don't quite understand why." Evariste said.

"I don't imagine he has stayed alive this long by trusting easily and smiling at strangers," Angelique said.

Evariste tapped his chin. "You know...you are right. But perhaps we can use that wariness to our advantage."

Angelique cocked her head. "How?"

Evariste grinned. "By using someone he *is* familiar with—however distantly—to stop him."

IT TOOK a week before the boy emerged again.

By now, Angelique was inclined to think he wasn't worth the effort, and they should pack up and send Sybilla or another fairy godmother or godfather to snag the boy, but Evariste was insistent.

"He's strong, Angel," he said. "And with what we've experienced here already, I'm not eager to leave him behind. Someone might attack him."

Angelique was unable to argue with such logic. "Very well. We must hope, then, that the woodcarver is able to approach him."

She fidgeted, then grimaced when her arm brushed against Evariste's chest.

As soon as they had spotted the boy in the market, they retreated back up a road, and now stood in a doorway—out of the boy's eyesight. Unfortunately, their position did not make for a roomy encounter. In fact, Angelique was pressed close enough to

Evariste, she could smell the faint whiff of sandalwood wafting off him.

This brat better be thankful once he realizes what's going on, Angelique thought rather ungraciously.

"Whatever soap you are using smells wonderful," Evariste commented.

Angelique forced a smile as she peered past Evariste's shoulder and watched the woodcarver sidle up to the boy. "Thank you."

She bit her lip and fidgeted again, then grinned when the swarthy woodcarver clamped a hand on the boy's thin shoulder.

"He's got him," she announced, her voice thick with satisfaction.

"Then let's go give our greetings!" Evariste winked and backtracked to the market.

As they slipped through the crowds, the boy with craftmagic kicked at the woodcarver and tried to bite him, but the woodcarver held him by the collar of his shirt the way one holds a miscreant cat by the scruff of their neck. (Not that she ever had to do that with Roland—even as a kitten, he probably would have bitten off a finger if she had tried.)

"You shape up, street urchin," the woodcarver said in a great, booming voice. "None of that, or you'll make Lord Enchanter Evariste regret wasting his time."

"Thank you, Master Dimi," Evariste chuckled as he joined the woodcarver.

The boy's eyes bulged to the point where Angelique was concerned they might pop out of his head and roll away.

Ahhh, he hadn't realized Master Evariste was an Enchanter.

Angelique idly tugged on the wide, trailing sleeves of her white, robe-like dress. The fabric was warm, as if the flames embroidered on the sleeves were real.

"What is your name, boy?" Evariste asked the boy—who had retreated into petulance—as he hung from the woodcarver's meaty hands.

The boy said nothing.

The woodcarver lightly jostled the boy. "He asked you a question."

Evariste took a step back and rubbed his clean-shaven jawline. "This isn't effective. He is too frightened to talk to me. Would you hold him for a moment, Master Dimi?"

The woodcarver grunted and swatted the boy's hands away when he tried to scratch him. "Of course."

Evariste placed a hand on Angelique's elbow and tugged her a few feet away, stirring her curiosity.

What plan would we need to discuss in private?

Evariste glanced back at the boy before proverbially slugging Angelique in the gut. "Angel, you need to talk to him."

"*Me?*" Angelique gaped.

"Yes. It's me he's wary of. I don't think he'll react the same way with you," Evariste said.

Angelique shook her head and held her hands up to forestall him. "Master Evariste, I am not good with children. Trying to talk to the boy who cried wolf in Boyne very nearly had an ugly ending, and I traumatized a number of children when I 'fixed' the animated puppet. I am *not* the welcoming, motherly type of person who can easily sooth frightened children."

"But you are kind and sweet," Evariste said.

I don't know if I should be grateful he believes the persona I've been desperately trying to project or dumbfounded that he hasn't figured it out yet.

Evariste set his hands on her shoulders and squeezed. "You can do this, Angel. You've shown your brilliance in your magic, but I am just as confident in your charisma."

By charisma do you mean the ability to hold back sarcasm? Because with magic as deadly as mine, I'm about as charismatic as a guillotine.

But as Angelique met his oddly colored eyes, her shoulders drooped, and she nodded. "I will try, Master Evariste," she agreed, unable to refuse her teacher.

Evariste smiled. "Then success will be ours. Come, let's retrieve him from Master Dimi."

Angelique sighed once his back was turned, but she obediently slouched after him. She set her hands on her hips when they reached the woodcarver and street urchin and tried to smile benevolently. "Please set him down, Master Dimi," she said.

When the boy gaped at her, Angelique turned on all the fake charm she had as she set a hand on his arm. "Now, you wouldn't fight a woman, would you?" she asked with a sweet smile.

The boy mutely shook his head.

Okay. If I'm going to convince this boy, it's not going to be with sweetness and cooing praise, unlike Master Evariste seems to think. I'll have to press him into this so he realizes that this isn't just the best option, it's his only *option.* Angelique glanced over her shoulder. "If you would give me a moment, Master."

"Of course. Come, Master Dimi. We can safely leave this to Angelique," the Lord Enchanter said, beckoning to the craftsman.

"Are you certain? He's an unruly one," the woodcarver said, gently smacking the boy upside the head.

Evariste chuckled. "I'm well assured that Angelique can handle it." He winked before he slipped out of the market, the flickering flames of his tailcoat snapping in the breeze.

The woodcarver gave the boy and Angelique an appraising look before he, too, left.

Before the brat had a chance to twist out of her grip, Angelique set his back against a wall with *just* enough force that the boy would feel it but wouldn't be hurt.

Angelique kept her warm and practiced smile on her lips as she started to speak. "Based on your performance over the past few weeks, you have been invited to join the ranks of the magical and attend the renown and honored Luxi-Domus, the Veneno Conclave academia of magic. Congratulations!" She kept her voice pleasant—which was hopefully a slight reassurance to the boy given that she held him with an iron grip.

The boy tried to wriggle out of her hold. "Don't wanna, let me go."

He's still not listening. Angelique ignored the protest. "It's a great honor. You've been identified as possessing magic, specifically craft-related magic!"

The boy grunted. "Don't care, leggo." He finally succeeded in twisting enough that he got away from the wall and tried to kick her.

Fine, let's try a different tactic. Angelique slammed him back against the wall and leaned in, her patience snapping. "Listen, you snot-nosed brat," she hissed. "Master Evariste asked me to recruit you, and I am *NOT* going to let him down. You are going to become the best craftmage there is, and you will be an upright and outstanding citizen of magic! Do you understand?"

The boy quieted in her grasp and meekly nodded.

"Angel?" Evariste called somewhere behind them.

Angelique slapped a smile back on her face and slipped an arm around the boy's elbow. "He's agreed to come with us, Master Evariste."

Evariste ventured closer and beamed. "Excellent!" he said. "Welcome into the ranks of the magical, boy."

The boy merely shrugged until Angelique elbowed him. "Thank you, sir," he said.

Angelique relaxed marginally as she watched Evariste introduce himself to the boy.

Well. I guess that worked?

Angelique looked back at the market, frowning a little. She could have sworn she felt the faint shiver of *dark* magic.

Perhaps Master Evariste is right. Maybe it's a good thing we're taking this boy with us...

CHAPTER 22

Evariste spent more time than usual checking over his dapple-gray horses so he could fight the impulse to laugh.

Behind him stood a bewildered boy—Pest, as he still insisted on being called—standing in a fine silk tunic with sapphire buttons that Angelique had stuffed him into.

Angelique stood by the boy, muttering ominously at him as she kept one hand around his little wrist.

She obviously missed the way the boy looked up at her with admiration but had taken him under her wing with the forcefulness of a bossy older sibling.

Somewhere between dragging him back to the inn and throwing him in a sudsy tub, the boy had come to greatly esteem her. It was probably the only reason why he let her stuff him into his new clothes. And now he followed her around like a duckling, watching her with hero-worship even as she hauled him in her wake.

Evariste briefly rested his hand on the neck of one of the horses as he finally let himself study the pair.

I should have rescued an orphan months ago—she doesn't hesitate to correct him, nor does she bother with her front.

Despite his best efforts, Angelique was never as open with him as she was with this young boy.

As if on cue, Pest squinted at the horses and cart. "What's going on?"

"Stop fidgeting," Angelique flatly said.

Evariste allowed himself a smile of amusement as he strolled up to the unlikely pair. "Sorry, Angel. This is the best we could get at such notice. I would port us through, but I don't want to risk opening a gateway here."

He meaningfully glanced down at Pest, leaving the second half of the sentence unsaid. *Because I shouldn't use that sort of magic in a place where black mages have been found.*

Angelique, of course, caught on, and answered him in a singsong voice. "Of course, Master Evariste."

Evariste nodded. "Can you drive? I have received word from Mage Serenfa," he said, referring to a mage from the Conclave. "There is a spell she wants that I need to get started on."

"Absolutely. Pest and I can manage the cart. You just work, Master Evariste," Angelique assured him.

Evariste grinned. "Excellent. In that case, let's be off!" He winked at Pest—who was scratching his side—and vaulted into the back of the cart.

Angelique took her place in the front and inspired Pest to do the same with one imperious look. She then took up the reins and guided the matched team through Fillia's streets.

Evariste waited until they passed through the city gates and picked up the main road that wound through the scrubby grass and bushes before he got to work.

He tapped his magic, unspooling a good amount as he considered what was necessary for the spell. He traced the first few symbols of the spell, using his magic to leave a glowing blue trail.

A tiny water dragon arrived after that, and a phoenix showed up a few minutes later as he continued with his work.

Though he was absorbed with his work, he was aware of the

faint murmurs of conversation coming from the driver's bench. When he finished off another paragraph of the spell, he looked up, cracking his neck as he watched Angelique chat with Pest. His apprentice laughed at something the mouthy child said, then scolded him with the next breath. Pest gave her a glowing smile that she missed because her attention was taken by the horses.

This is good for her, he decided as he rubbed the water dragon's head. *War mages treat her with reverence, but no one has looked at her with hero-worship the way this boy does. Even if she doesn't wholly notice it, she must be aware he doesn't treat her with the fright that others from the Conclave do.*

Though, as humiliating as it was to admit, he was perhaps a little jealous of the boy. Despite the fact that they had been together for years, Angelique had never relaxed around him as much as she had this unknown child whom they'd known for hours.

Though perhaps some of that is my own doing, he grudgingly admitted, *with my games and teasing about hugs and affection. She barely tolerates it.*

Evariste's smile turned wicked as he remembered how it irritated her to stand so close to him the day prior while they waited for Master Dimi to grab Pest.

She was always beautiful, but there was something about the flickers of the fire she hid from him that would briefly flare to life when he teased her enough. It was...addictive.

He thought to his cheeky compliment when he had mentioned the smell of her soap, and the brief narrowing of her eyes before she covered it with a forced smile.

Even thinking of it made him want to laugh again.

Any other girl I complimented so closely would have started planning a wedding by now. But not Angel. She just gets irritated and gets that little muscle twitch in her cheek that tells me she thinks I'm half-cracked.

A part of him wished she'd get a little flustered or maybe

blush. *But that's a dangerous wish, especially given my position as her teacher. Still...sometimes...*

He glanced at her again, looking up just in time to see her snort.

"Is too," she said.

"Is not," Pest said.

"It is." Angelique flicked Pest with the ends of the reins. "Darkness and unruliness throws everything into chaos. Being calm and tranquil—free from turbulence—lets a person think and be strong of heart and mind."

"Hmm," Pest hummed.

"Think about it," Angelique said. "You'll see." She ended her promise with a brilliant smile, and something in Evariste's chest twisted.

She is so beautiful.

Angelique glanced back at him and noticed his attention. "I apologize, Master Evariste, were we disrupting you?"

Back to all politeness now that she's talking to me.

"Not at all!" Evariste said cheerfully. "But you have intrigued me. What were you two discussing with such passion?"

"Names," the boy said.

"I was just telling Pest that a name of peace is the strongest sort of name there is," Angelique said.

Evariste nodded slowly. "Peace is one of the greatest gifts humanity can give one another—second only to love."

Angelique shot the young boy a look. "I told you so!"

The phoenix crooned its agreement.

"Worry not, Pest," Evariste said. "You have time to choose a name. We have a long while before we reach Luxi-Domus."

A long while, he warned himself. *Long enough to remember it's not a good idea to make calf eyes at your student—even if she is only a few years younger than you.*

"There it is," Angelique pointed out a large building made of white and onyx-colored stone. "That's the school."

She smiled as she watched Pest's eyes bulge and recalled how awed she had been when she first set eyes on Luxi-Domus.

The school was mostly towers, each competing to poke the highest into the sky, although there was a massive main building that was four or five stories tall and was checkered with white and black marble like a chess board.

The gates of the school were pearl white and sparkled in the sunshine, and the landscaping was a wash of flowers and lush greenery despite the cool fall weather.

Evariste stepped out of the cart and tapped the trunk Angelique was perched on. "These gentlemen will take your trunks for you," he said.

"What 'gentlemen'—YIKES!" Pest shouted when two large, muscled butlers appeared behind the cart.

He shot past Evariste—who held out a hand to Angelique.

These notions of Evariste's, Angelique internally sighed as she let him guide her from the cart. *Perhaps I should talk to him about it. But wouldn't that seem rather prideful of me to think I could correct his manners? Even if I'm right?*

A quick glance at her white, airy dress that was studded with rubies (nothing less than the best for Evariste's "cute little Apprentice." *Ugh.*) revealed the dirt-warding spell was active.

She glanced at Evariste and performed another weary, mental shrug.

Evariste, of course, wore an outfit that matched hers—a white jacket and trousers with ruby accents—and today he had adjusted his hair length so it was once again short.

I haven't been able to work out if that's illusion magic or alteration magic.

Angelique turned her attention to Pest—who was gaping at the butlers that carried the trunks through the open gates. She stepped closer to him, intending to announce she would see him to his rooms while Evariste dropped off the spell, when she caught sight of the teachers waiting for Pest in the front courtyard.

It was custom for several teachers to greet new students, and Luxi-Domus had made no exception for Pest. Angelique recognized a craftmage, a non-magic-possessing instructor who taught continental history and culture, and...Madame Quarrellous.

Angelique froze.

She hadn't seen the instructor since she had come for the in-person report conducted in her first year of apprenticeship. *And I have no desire to change that.*

Angelique looked to Evariste, unable to speak the question that hovered on her lips. *What do I do?*

Evariste, his expression icy, stared at Quarrellous as he maneuvered himself so he stood between Angelique and the school, hiding her from sight.

He cupped a hand around her elbow and slowly slid his fingers down her forearm until he placed his palm against hers and squeezed.

Normally such a gesture would make Angelique want to take a branch to his head, but for once she was grateful for his warmth and support.

It was also a clear answer—she was going with him and not to the school.

Evariste broke her reverie by addressing Pest. "I wish you luck, young man." He placed a gentle hand on top of Pest's head in a fond pat. "You have plenty of talent. If you apply yourself, you will go far."

"Try to graduate quickly," Angelique advised as she glanced at the courtyard. "It's much more fun when you get to play with your magic." She grabbed Pest, reeling him in for a hug.

Pest leaned back to avoid her grasp. "Wait, aren't you two coming inside with me?"

Angelique flattened her lips and looked down until Lord

Enchanter Evariste rested a hand on her shoulder. "No," he said with a sorry smile. "Sadly, we must depart immediately. I have a spell to drop off, and then we will leave the Conclave fortress tonight. But the school is aware of your arrival; there is a guide waiting for you past the gates. They have already received all the necessary paperwork."

"Oh," Pest said in a small voice.

Angelique grabbed him, this time succeeding in embracing him. "You will do well. More than well, in fact—you will thrive," she said impulsively. Feeling a little awkward, she added, "I know you will enjoy learning about magic, just as I *know* you will not do anything to tarnish Master Evariste's name," she said, her voice holding a warning.

"Angel," Evariste thankfully laughed.

"You could at least see me situated," Pest said in a voice that nearly broke Angelique's heart.

She was tempted to storm the school, but even if Quarrellous hadn't been there...*Luxi-Domus is not a place I am really welcomed.*

"I can't," Angelique tightly said. "But I will write. I promise." She squeezed Pest tight before releasing him and backing away.

Pest rubbed his face, then squared his shoulders and looked to the school. "Hey, Angel."

Angelique felt a quirk of a smile settle on her lips. "That's *Angelique*, and what?"

Pest looked over his shoulder and grinned. "I think I know what I'm going to call myself." He took a few steps towards the gates.

"Oh? What?"

"Stil! No turbulence, but strength in the mind and heart!" Pest—now Stil—said. He pumped a fist over his head and ran to the school grounds, nearly colliding with the craftmage teacher.

Angelique watched with a fond smile.

Evariste draped an arm over her shoulders. "He'll be fine. He's bright, and he has magic that will be in high demand. He really will thrive."

Angelique nodded. "You're right, of course." She watched him brightly greet the other teachers. "It's just it was so different…" *for me*. She trailed off before she could finish, of course.

But even though she hadn't finished, Evariste must have known what she meant, for he nodded.

They watched another minute as the instructors led Pest inside the school. Just before Angelique started to ease herself out from underneath Evariste's arm, he pensively stared at the school.

"I wonder if this is how non-magical parents feel when they send their child off on their own path," he said.

Angelique wrinkled her brow. "*What?*" She barely recovered in time. "That is to say, I don't understand what you mean."

Evariste grinned and winked at Angelique. "Don't you feel like we are proud parents cheering on our son?"

"No," Angelique said emphatically. "Not at *all*!"

Evariste laughed as she pulled away from him.

"That was not a funny joke," Angelique informed him.

"I didn't mean it to be a joke," Evariste said with his most charming smile.

It took all of Angelique's control to keep from narrowing her eyes at him. "Don't you have a spell to drop off?" she asked with a poisonous amount of sweetness to her voice.

"You are right—as always. Come, Angel. Let's be off!"

CHAPTER 23

Unfortunately, the trouble with black magic was not limited to Baris.

After returning home from dropping Stil off at Luxi-Domus, Angelique received word that Princess Rosalinda of Sole—the royal baby whose curse she had modified—was still in danger.

While the princess was a mere babe often times adults would find spinning needles in her cradle, among other suspicious circumstances. As a result, her grandfather— King Giuseppe—had her sent from her palace home to live in secret. She'd be raised as a normal girl, unaware of her heritage, but those around her would know. That had occurred before she could even walk, but years had passed since then. Now the young princess could talk and was old enough to venture far from her yard, opening her to more dangers.

Which was why King Giuseppe sent Angelique a request for aid.

"Is it really enough to send mages in my stead?" Angelique asked as she measured out tea leaves for two different teapots.

"You're an enchantress-in-training, Angelique. You cannot stay at the princess's side—you are too important and that is *far* too political a place for an enchantress to be," Evariste said.

"I'm still an apprentice," Angelique reminded him.

"It doesn't change my point.

"Yes, but it feels cowardly—to send someone else to protect the princess," Angelique sighed.

"But that is why King Giuseppe asked you instead of directly approaching the Veneno Conclave." Evariste added another teacup and saucer to the tray. "Since you are more deeply involved, you will do a better job of selecting the mages who will guard the princess than, say, someone merely reviewing the paperwork at the Conclave."

Angelique snorted. "I'm sure you being my teacher had *nothing* to do with the King's decision to contact me."

Evariste laughed. "Perhaps, but in the end you were the one who selected Mage Firra and Mage Donaigh when we were reviewing the candidates."

Firra and Donaigh were a pair of young mages—a fire mage and a war mage—who were just barely out of their apprenticeships.

Angelique had liked them because of their magic. Some of the other candidates the Conclave had suggested when the paperwork first began were less...helpful. (Music mages, storytellers, a mage with animal magic, and the like.)

All suggested candidates were excellent mages of course, but given the threat the young Princess Rosalinda faced, Angelique wanted the mages who stood with the princess to be capable of protecting her from physical violence.

Evariste had approved of her choice, though for an entirely different reason. He claimed Firra and Donaigh were close friends, and that the temptation of a long-term assignment together would make them more likely to accept when usually mages of their caliber would be given more choice—but separate—assignments.

A knock on the door shattered Angelique's thoughts.

She took a deep gulp of air. "That must be them."

Evariste set a hand on her shoulder and squeezed. "I'll go greet them. Join us when you finish." He started to leave the kitchen, but turned around at the last minute. "And Angelique?"

"Hmm?" Angelique poured hot water in the teapots, then sniffed the velvety drinking chocolate she had prepared in the last pot.

"You might find the war mage has a...different reaction to you," he said.

Angelique wrinkled her forehead. "Do I need to be worried?"

Evariste laughed. "Not at all. It is more that I don't think you are aware of just how popular you are with war mages."

Angelique pressed her lips together. "Whoever your source of information is, they're starting to lose their touch."

"You're going to be the first war enchantress *ever*," Evariste said gently. "They are a group of mages who have long lacked high level representation. That makes you a hero to them."

Angelique waited until he was down the hallway before she scoffed. *A hero? HAH! I'm closer to a villain!*

"You ought to use your popularity with the war mages," Roland advised. There was a pop, and he appeared at her feet, shaking off the invisibility charm he had recently mastered—and taken to using whenever possible to preen over his success. "If you had more mages at your back I imagine those in the Conclave wouldn't pick on you quite so much."

"Yes, because organizing a bunch of war mages to personally support me doesn't at all sound like the maneuverings of a budding tyrant," Angelique said flatly. She cocked her head as she finished preparing the tea tray, listening to Evariste greet the mages.

Roland sniffed. "You haven't the backbone to be a tyrant."

"That's a *good* thing," Angelique said.

"I suppose," Roland said with obvious reluctance.

"Thank you for coming today, Mage Donaigh and Mage Firra," Evariste's muffled voice meandered down the hallway. "Welcome to my home. Please, join us in the salon."

Evariste and the mages were quiet for a moment as the sound of footsteps prevailed.

"You have a beautiful home," a warm, feminine voice said.

That must be Firra, Angelique thought as she set the last teapot on the tray. She took a breath to set her shoulders, then picked up the tray and started down the hallway.

"Thank you!" Evariste said. "I'm rather fond of it myself, though I find I enjoy it more now that I'm not the only one rattling about it."

"This house has never rattled," Angelique said from the hallway.

"Indeed, or I shouldn't be willing to stay in it!" Roland complained as he sauntered after her.

Cat! We need to be putting our best foot forward! We have to convince them to take this assignment! "Roland, *do* mind your manners." Angelique grimaced at him before she swept into the sitting room, the tea tray in hand.

Evariste beamed at her. "Ah, I don't recall if either of you have had the pleasure of meeting my lovely apprentice, Enchantress Angelique. Angel, this is Fire Mage Firra and War Mage Donaigh."

Donaigh, the war mage, was a tall, stick-like man. His unruly blond hair was topped by a straw hat, which only added to the relaxed aura he gave off with his half smile. However, Angelique didn't miss the sharpness in his gaze, or the callouses on his hands that attested to long hours of weapon practice.

The fire mage, Firra, was drastically different. Her olive complexion gave her a warmer aura, but both her sleek black hair and her dark eyes held hidden flickers of blue—like the hottest of flames.

Angelique wore her smile like a shield, so she wasn't tempted to retreat and take a few steps backwards under the mages' intense gazes. Instead she fixed her grip on the tea tray so she could curtsey without dropping it. "Greetings. I am honored to meet you."

Firra and Donaigh were seated together on the blue settee, though Donaigh leaped off his cushion and bowed deeply. "The honor is all ours." When he straightened up, he offered Angelique a bright smile, his eyes eagerly studying her.

Angelique tried not to stare. *Oh my. Evariste might be right about war mages.*

"*Ahem*," Roland coughed.

"Oh, yes," Evariste said with his trademark easy smile. "May I also present to you Angel's pet cat, Roland."

Angelique glanced down at her snobby companion, already anticipating his acidic reply.

"I, rude sir, am not a *pet*!" Roland sneered. "I am a *magic* cat—I serve as a guide and reference for Lady Enchantress Angelique."

Evariste took the tea tray from Angelique and set it on a low end table. "He does that, too," he acknowledged as he seated himself in a straight-backed, wooden chair accented with clawed feet.

"I see," Firra said. The fire mage furrowed her brow as she watched Roland jump onto a cushioned footstool and fixate his unblinking eyes on her and her companion.

"He's a very handsome fellow," Donaigh said.

Roland broke the staring match and preened. "It is encouraging to see at least one of you has some semblance of intelligence."

"Roland!" Angelique hissed.

The magic cat licked one of his paws and scrubbed at his face.

Angelique briefly narrowed her eyes. *I should have tossed him outside before this started. Running from the mean swans would have kept him occupied. Oh well.* Angelique renewed her smile as she turned her attention to the visiting mages. "I hope your trip was pleasant?"

"It was, thank you," Firra said.

"Excellent. What would you like to drink?" Angelique gestured to the three small teapots that were settled on the tea tray. "We have black tea, drinking chocolate, strawberry tea, and —should you like it—we have several bottles of Sole and Loire wines."

"Drinking chocolate, please." Firra said. "To remind me of home."

Angelique started to pour some of the drink out for the mage, but Evariste tilted his head. "I had nearly forgotten. You are from Sole, if I recall correctly—yes?"

Angelique held in her snort.

When Evariste helped her sort through possible candidates, he mentioned Firra would be ideal *because* she was from Sole and would be more likely to watch the princess with extra diligence. *When I was a first year at Luxi-Domus I never dreamed I'd come to admire my teacher's ability to use his charisma like a legendary conman. He's a prodigy alright—in magic* and *mischief.*

"Bred and born of Sole," Firra said, her voice had an obvious note of pride to it. "Donaigh is from Ringsted."

"The shipping giant—though it surprises me it isn't better known for its striking shores and green lands," Evariste commented.

Donaigh nodded, but he didn't reply—though he had a slight smile on his lips as he watched Angelique.

Feeling more than a little awkward—because there wasn't anything special about her, she couldn't even trick a person half as well as Evariste—Angelique cleared her throat and babbled. "We were just in Ringsted not two weeks ago. It is a beautiful country." She handed Firra the drinking chocolate and made herself meet Donaigh's gaze. "And what would you like to drink, Mage Donaigh?"

"Black tea, please."

"With cream and sugar?"

"Yes, please."

Angelique set about preparing Mage Donaigh's tea—and filling a plate of sweets for him. She glanced at Evariste, wondering when he was going to bring the request up, but he seemed perfectly content with his lot and instead gave her one of his bright smiles before reaching out to tuck a strand of her brunette hair that had slipped free from the pearl netting she had her hair pinned up in.

Evariste briefly leaned closer to her so he could murmur. "Your hair looks lovely today, Angel."

Angelique pressed her lips into a thin line. *We're trying to negotiate for mage-guards to keep a royal princess safe, but yes, please do notice my hair right now.*

Thankfully, Firra spoke up before Evariste could continue. "If you'll excuse my bluntness, sir, but why did you invite us here?" the fire mage asked.

"I am hoping you will take on an assignment. Thank you, Angel." Evariste said when she passed him his teacup. (She didn't need to ask him his choice of drinks, she knew from daily life that he also preferred black tea.)

Donaigh tilted his head as he asked, "What kind of assignment?"

"A long-term one, I'm afraid," Evariste sipped his tea, then put it aside. "Have you heard of the plight of Princess Rosalinda—granddaughter of King Giuseppe of Sole?"

Angelique nonchalantly poured herself a cup of strawberry tea, but studied the mages, trying to gauge their reactions.

The pair glanced at each other, but surprisingly it was Donaigh who replied.

"I think every magic user on the continent has," he said.

"It is fortunate Lady Enchantress Angelique was able to modify her curse," Firra added, lifting her chin in approval.

Angelique poured cream into a saucer and absently set it in front of Roland. She was vaguely aware that he sniffed it and scrunched up his nose, but thankfully held his peace.

Though her throat felt constricted, Angelique still managed a smile. *I really want them to take this assignment. The princess needs someone trustworthy to guard her. I think they're our best choice, and since Evariste agrees they* must *be.* "I wish another enchanter or enchantress had been there to better modify the curse, but I did the best I could at the time." When she sat down, Roland leaped from his stool and meandered over to her. He sat on the hem of her skirts and twitched his tail back and forth—his non-verbal version of encouragement.

"Based on what I have heard, you pulled off a brilliant bit of magic," Firra said. "It was a sound modification—one that Carabosso won't be able to change."

Donaigh nodded and chimed in, "So what is the problem?"

The smile eased off Evariste's lips. "There have been...complications. Not with the curse—Mage Firra was right. Angel did a wonderful job."

"I should say so!" Roland said.

Angelique reached down to tickle her companion's chin. In reflex, Roland started to purr and arch his back before he remembered the mages and forcibly regained his grave composure.

"The issue is with the princess herself," Angelique said. "Her parents kept finding spindles in her bed and among her toys. The Magic Knights of Sole guarded her, but there were several close calls...so Princess Rosalinda was taken into hiding."

Donaigh fussed with the brim of his straw hat. "I believe I recall hearing that. Didn't your mother mention it in a letter to you, Firra?"

Firra nodded. "Rumor has it she was spirited off to Verglas so Carabosso and his minions couldn't reach her, but Mother said she had also been told the princess was taken down to Ringsted. That was at least two or three years ago."

"Yes. False rumors were planted so no one would know where she really went," Evariste said. "The princess has been safe, but the king is worried. It was easy to guarantee her safety when she was nothing more than a toddler and went no farther than her backyard. But she is growing up, and her cover story will be suspicious if she's not allowed out of eyesight of her home—not to mention she would eventually strain under such rules, I imagine."

Angelique glanced from the mages to her master, and slowly said. "She needs to be guarded—discreetly."

Evariste pressed his fingertips together, creating a steeple. "Exactly so." He shifted his gaze to Firra and Donaigh. "I was hoping you two would take the assignment."

The mages were understandably surprised by the request.

Firra sat back in her chair and blinked rapidly.

Donaigh whistled. "If I may be so bold—when you said long-term, you weren't kidding."

"Indeed," Evariste said. "If all goes well, you would be a part of the princess's life and guard her until she turns eighteen. That is over a decade from now."

Donaigh scratched his chin and glanced at Firra. Firra rubbed her thumb and the tip of her pointer finger and slightly pursed her lips.

Several long moments passed as the fire mage and war mage seemed to exchange words with meaningful looks.

"Why us?" Firra asked, breaking the silence. "We're untried fledgling mages."

"Yes, but that's exactly why the pair of you came to mind." Evariste leaned back in his chair, a smile back on his lips.

He picked up on something, he thinks they're going to say yes.

"The princess needs to be guarded, but the possibility of threats at this moment is quite low," Evariste continued. "I imagine it will ramp up as the years pass, giving you two plenty of time to learn, improve, and gather experience."

Donaigh leaned forward and rested his forearms on his knees.

"But why are *you* giving out this assignment...sir? Shouldn't it be the Veneno Conclave's job? It is for issues such as this one that it exists, after all."

"I'm afraid that's my fault." Angelique wanted to yank a lock of hair, but she suspected it would look unprofessional, so she settled for picking Roland up instead.

"Stop this mistreatment—put me down!" he complained.

Angelique ignored his protests and petted him. "As I was the magic user who modified the curse, the managing of the issue would naturally fall to me. However, I'm afraid I lack the experience and expertise required, and this is an issue with which one cannot be too careful."

Evariste tapped his fingers on the arm of his chair. "The Veneno Conclave offered to handle the matter—I believe several mages were being considered for it—but Angel was so concerned, I decided we should handle it."

Angelique smiled at her teacher as she hugged Roland closer to her chest. (The cat protested and tried to wiggle out of her grasp without luck.) "The Conclave resisted a little, but Princess Alessia and Prince Consort Filippo both said they would prefer Master Evariste and I be involved," she explained. "And King Giuseppe made a direct request as well."

"And so here we are," Evariste said. "If you like, I can give you two time to think it over, but I'm afraid we can't spare you more than a day or two. If you aren't interested, we need to find other suitable candidates."

Firra and Donaigh traded gazes. It was interesting, watching them communicate without words. But Angelique was convinced they had exchanged an entire conversation by the time they nodded together.

"There's no need. We'll guard Princess Rosalinda," Firra said.

Angelique almost sagged with relief. *Thank goodness—I wasn't sure they were going to agree for a moment there.* She let a real smile leak through as she also released Roland from her rather forceful hug. "Thank you! It is heartening to know that such competent mages are watching her."

Donaigh scratched the back of his neck and—interestingly—blushed a little. "I don't know that we're competent—Firra did say we're just out of our apprenticeships."

Angelique shook her head. "Master Evariste told me that you are accomplished mages. I'm glad it will be the two of you watching the princess."

Donaigh's blush deepened as he smiled sweetly at her.

Huh. I don't think I've ever had someone react to me like this. Maybe I need to meet more war mages—this is fun!

"As am I," Evariste said intruding on Angelique's thoughts. A frown tugged on the edges of his fine lips. "We worried over whom to choose—for it will be a tricky assignment as the princess must stay hidden and safe. Those with *gray* morals might seek to take advantage of the situation, but I know the two of you are true."

"Where is the princess?" Firra asked.

Angelique couldn't help her smirk. "Why, Sole, of course."

Firra half bolted out of her chair, but turned the movement into adjusting her clothes at the last second. "She's still in *Sole*?"

Evariste laughed. "Yes, that was a fine bit of trickery pulled off by King Giuseppe and the Magic Knights. He decided to keep her in Sole, for it would be the last place Carabosso would look for her. The rumors were spread so searching for her would be a wild goose-chase for anyone unscrupulous."

Donaigh laughed and slapped his knee. "It was nicely played. Very well, Lord Enchanter, when do we receive the details of our assignment?"

Evariste stood. "Now—if you'll pardon me for a moment, I will retrieve the papers."

"I'll get them," Angelique offered in what she hoped sounded courteous. (Really, she was dying to leave the room so she could do a victory dance in the library.) "Come, Roland. I saw you poking about Master Evariste's desk in the library earlier. If you moved anything, I'll need your help."

"I do not *poke about*," Roland declared. He twitched his tail back and forth, but followed after her. "I inspect with the greatest elegance."

"Thank you, Angel," Evariste called out after her. "I'm quite glad you agreed to the assignment," he repeated, still within Angelique's hearing range as she made for the library. "The candidates the conclave chose were..."

"Do you suspect foul play?" Donaigh asked.

Angelique lost the rest of the conversation when she sashayed into the library.

"You seem pleased," Roland commented. He sat down in front of the empty fireplace and curled his black tail around his white paws.

"I am." Angelique studied the papers mounded on the desk and plucked up the ones with the royal Sole seal. "This entire thing is more political than I like to be."

"I hardly think Sole requesting help is political—they're rightfully worried about the princess," Roland scoffed.

Angelique strode across the room, but paused in the doorframe. "I wasn't thinking of Sole. It's the Conclave. Selecting Firra and Donaigh was a matter of balancing all the right requirements and politics and still finding someone who would judiciously guard the princess."

Roland sniffed. "If you so disdain politics you could adopt the lifestyle of a hero and wander from village to village saving ignorant peasants and unthankful livestock."

Angelique laughed. "Yes, that's a lifestyle *certain* to win me points with the Veneno Conclave. Come, let's go back."

Angelique glanced through the papers as she made her way back to the sitting room, scrunching up her nose when she realized one of the necessary documents was missing.

Evariste saw her pause at the threshold of the salon and smiled. "Right then. Here are your orders."

"Actually, this isn't all the paperwork," Angelique confessed. "I missed one of the official forms from the Conclave. I'll go get it."

"No need!" Evariste stood and cheerfully smiled. "I'll fetch it. I need to get writing materials so they can sign the documents anyway."

Angelique glanced over her shoulder. "Oh, but I would be happy to—"

"No need," Evariste repeated more firmly. His smile briefly turned sly, and he wrapped the loose lock of her hair around his pointer finger, then winked as he leaned in so close their foreheads almost touched. "You can divvy out the paperwork."

Angelique gulped at the close quarters, but he was gone with a chuckle before she could react.

That man. Angelique would have shaken the papers at his retreating back if she had been alone. Instead she forced herself to smile at Firra and Donaigh—both of whom were smirking at her.

Just perfect. That hadn't caused some severe misunderstandings.

Angelique shook her head and cleared her throat. "Here are the papers," she said as she set about giving each mage the required forms.

Internally, she was not so dutiful. *I had thought the increase in his...ideas would wane. It's been years, and they haven't gotten better. I can only hope he mellows with age.*

CHAPTER 24

He didn't.

That is to say, Evariste did not decrease the amount of affection he bestowed upon her or stop saying things that really *shouldn't* have been uttered. He might have, in fact, grown worse.

In the spring of Angelique's eighth year of her apprenticeship, they stopped to visit the elves in Alabaster Forest.

"Lady Alastryn, it is so good to see you." Angelique curtsied, inwardly crowing with glee that her years of attempting to copy the elegance of the elven lady were finally paying off.

"I am glad to see you brighten the halls of our ancestors once again, Lord Enchanter Evariste and Enchantress-in-training Angelique." Alastryn smiled warmly. "I know King Themerysaldi will be particularly heartened to hear of your visit, Enchanter Evariste. He has been positively *sulking* since you have not come here for many months."

Evariste laughed and threaded his hand through Angelique's. "Hopefully he will forgive me, but while I have missed the glory of Alabaster Forest, I do not regret our absence. I have been showing Angel the continent."

"Yes," Angelique meekly agreed, until she realized Evariste

was raising her hand up, seemingly with the intention of setting it over his heart.

Why is he—his master utterly FAILED to teach him proper conduct! Angelique was forced to fake a sneeze to get him to relinquish her hand before he could achieve his end goal.

Lady Alastryn merely raised an eyebrow. "This way, if you will. I shall show you to a parlor for refreshments."

HIS BEHAVIOR CONTINUED, even when Stil—who was no longer a street urchin but a proper young man who had taken the rather puzzling mage name of Rumpelstiltskin—graduated.

"Any news from Stil?" Evariste asked as he joined Angelique in the library.

Angelique—who sat in an armchair in front of the fire with a dozing Roland on her lap—looked up from her letter. "Yes, in fact. He's graduating early from Luxi-Domus—he'll be finished in two months. He already has an apprenticeship lined up with a craftmage."

She frowned thoughtfully at the letter. *I need to get him a gift, but what would he find useful?*

"That's impressive; he's only been a student for four or five years, hasn't he?" Evariste leaned against her chair.

Angelique adjusted the way she held the letter so he could see it for himself. "Indeed."

Evariste whistled. "I wouldn't be surprised if he snags himself the title of Master Craftmage by the time he's finished with his apprenticeship."

Angelique nodded slowly at the thought. "He is exceedingly bright."

Evariste shook his head. "I know time moves slower for us enchanters and enchantresses as we age more like elves, but it still seems shocking."

"Yes," Angelique blithely agreed.

"Our little son, all grown up!" Evariste exclaimed.

"*What?*" Angelique asked.

Evariste was out the door before she could say anything more. "Ahh, but such is the life of parents," he said as he disappeared into the hallway.

"Rumpelstiltskin is not our son," Angelique tried to say as elegantly—and loudly—as she could.

On her lap, Roland stirred. "Shout that a bit louder," he grumbled as he stretched his white front legs. "I don't think the griffin roosting on the roof heard you."

YET, possibly the worst moment was in the summer of her twelfth year as Evariste's apprentice.

"You're doing well," Evariste remarked.

"Thank you, Master Evariste," Angelique said as she stood up from the crouch she was tucked in and wiped sweat from her forehead. Behind her, the scarecrow dummy sagged at the base of the stick it was attached to.

"I suppose she is *acceptable*," Roland sniffed.

Evariste thoughtfully rubbed his jaw as he considered the fallen dummy. "You're more than skilled enough that I should teach you a few advanced attacks."

"What do you mean by advanced?" Angelique asked.

"Sometimes, in dire need, the easiest way to face your foe is to hit them with magic in an unfiltered, pure form," Evariste explained. "It's a maneuver that will only work for you or me."

"You mean enchantresses and enchanters?" Angelique asked.

"No," Evariste said. "People with extraordinary amounts of power."

Angelique scratched her forehead and frowned a little. "What do you mean—" Before she could further inquire, an explosion shuddered behind her, making the ground shiver and filling the air with pelting pebbles and clods of dirt.

Instinctively, Angelique hopped closer to Evariste and whirled around.

The dummy was *gone*. Incinerated by Evariste's power.

All that was left behind was a crater, and Evariste's magic—which flickered like tongues of fire and enclosed a cottage-sized sphere.

Angelique felt her eyes bulge.

She hadn't seen Evariste display such devastation before—she hadn't even thought him *capable* of something like this!

I guess there is more to him than I know or understand. Angelique stared at the display of his power.

At her feet, Roland arched his back, his tail puffed up as he tried to keep from hissing.

Evariste stared dispassionately at the example of his power. "Using techniques like this, you can swiftly stop a person. It's not safe to use in populated areas, though, and it can be risky to use around other magic users."

"Why?" Roland asked.

"It's rather unstable," Evariste said.

His magic flickered, and another explosion went off, rocking the ground with enough force to make Angelique stagger.

She fell into Evariste, who slipped his arms around her back as he steadied her.

"Perfectly exemplified." Evariste coughed in the stirring of the dust and pressed Angelique's head into his shoulder so she escaped the worst of it.

"Entirely lacking finesse," Roland complained.

"Maybe, but it gets the job done," Evariste said.

The ground finally settled again, and when Angelique peered over her shoulder, she saw the sphere of magic was gone.

"This is something I should never attempt," Angelique

decided. She tried to take a step back, but Evariste still held her secure.

"You have the necessary control, Angel. It would be fine."

Angelique forced a smile to her face as she turned, intending to correct her good-intentioned teacher but gulped when she realized just how small the space was between them.

Evariste did not wear his usual smile. Instead, his lips were unusually set as he stared at her, his green and blue eyes boring into her.

I feel like an animal caught in a trap.

She swallowed unevenly as Evariste continued to study her.

What's going on? she mentally screamed, feeling excessively awkward and befuddled. Something in her stomach shivered, making her feel crabby. *No, we will not melt over...this!*

She lost the battle for mental fortitude when Evariste leaned close enough that his breath stirred her hair.

RETREAT! NOW! WHATEVER THIS IS, IT IS A LOSING BATTLE. RETREAT!

"Uhh," Angelique said with vast and unspeakable intelligence. "Thank you for the demonstration." She patted him on the chest—perhaps with a little more force than necessary given her desperation. This, unfortunately, only made her more aware of how warm and solid his chest was.

Evariste blinked, and his serious expression was gone, swapped for his usual smile. "Aren't you encouraged, Angel?"

"Incredibly so," Angelique falsely agreed. "I am now steady, though. Could you release me?"

"You want to end our sweet embrace?" Evariste asked teasingly.

YES! Angelique kept her internal howl shut up and instead increased the size of her smile. "Yes, please, Master Evariste."

"Very well," Evariste sighed.

Angelique nearly leaped away from him when his arms fell

aside. She busied herself with brushing off her clothes and sucked in a deep breath.

When she felt she had finally gotten herself back under control, she risked a glance at Evariste.

His smile was more playful now—and *suspiciously* close to a smirk.

Angelique cleared her voice. "Did you need something, Master Evariste?"

"Not just yet." He winked at her, then strolled away.

Angelique furrowed her forehead. "Did you understand any part of what just happened?" she asked Roland.

The black and white cat licked his front paw and used it to scrub at his face. "What I understood is that overly enthusiastic teacher of yours has made me *filthy* in his ill-timed demonstration!"

"I guess," Angelique said lamely. "I had better go get another dummy so we can continue with practice."

"Unless you mean to throw yourself at invisible foes, *obviously*," Roland grumbled.

Angelique grinned and purposely pet the cat the wrong way, mussing the hair on his back. She laughed when he tried to bat at her as she hurried off.

Once safely out of sight, Angelique tossed her head like a wild horse. *I have come to accept Evariste's oddities, but I wish I could control myself enough so he wouldn't fluster me so. It's disappointing to realize I can lose all my carefully practiced tranquility with a mere hug!*

"YOU REALLY OUGHT to study the art of breaking curses at a deeper level," Roland said.

Angelique looked up from her notes and studied her companion.

The cat sat on top of a stack of books, his black tail curled around his white paws. When he realized he had her gaze, he lowered himself into a lounging position and tapped the second-from-the-top book in his stack. "This particular tome has some very helpful information on curses and dark magic."

"I'll give it a look-over," Angelique agreed, "But right now Evariste is still covering magic sensitivity and advanced spellwork."

"What do you mean by advanced spellwork?" Roland twitched his tail.

"I'm not sure what else you would call it," Angelique sighed. "He's teaching me how to *see* spells and the way magic is shaped to create them, and then adjust them to my own liking."

"Isn't that work for a first- or second-year student?" Roland asked. "You've been apprenticed to Evariste for nearly fourteen years."

"Yes, and I've done this sort of thing with my own spells, but previously I didn't have the control necessary to be able to adjust another person's spell. The closest I came to it was modifying the curse on Princess Rosalinda of Sole, and that was under dire circumstances." Angelique frowned and tapped the leather-bound book that held her carefully copied notes. "It's a fairly advanced subject. I've gotten good at being able to read another mage's work, but I find modifying to still be tricky."

"Why?" Roland pointed his pink and black nose to the ceiling. "With your kind of magic, it should be an easy thing to slice through the spellwork and add your own modifications."

Angelique grimaced. "Perhaps, but if I cut the wrong thing, the spell will collapse—or possibly implode."

"An encouragement to keep you from growing sloppy and lazy," Roland decreed. "You should follow my example. I read this *entire* stack of books while you were gone wrestling with that robber-child."

"I did not *wrestle* with Goldilocks," Angelique sighed.

"Then how did you get her to stop breaking into peoples' homes?" Roland asked.

Angelique kept her eyes on her notes. "An illusion with bears might have been involved."

"*Bears?*" Roland scoffed. "You enjoy inflicting wild animals upon children, don't you?"

Angelique opened her mouth to reply when she felt a shiver of foreign magic.

Curious, Angelique shuffled to the staircase—absently patting the visiting, arm-sized dragon that was curled up in front of the workshop fireplace as she passed by.

There. Another shiver of magic. It took Angelique longer than it ought to, but she eventually felt it radiating from just outside the front entrance.

"Angel, could you get the door?" Evariste shouted from the library. "It feels like a messenger is outside."

"Yes, Master!" Angelique scooped up Roland when he nearly tripped her, then hurried down the stairs.

"Must you run with the elegance of a baby cow?" Roland complained.

Angelique patted his back. "You are such an encouraging pet."

"*Assistant*!"

Angelique chuckled as she hopped off the last step. She put Roland down and raced him to the front door, nearly wiping out on a new, thick floral rug Evariste had received as a gift from the King of Torrens.

She took a moment to tug her clothes straight—even though they were home, she and Evariste wore matching shirts and trousers that were tree-themed today—then yanked the door open.

Outside, there was a mass of glowing insects.

"Fireflies?" Angelique ventured as she watched the light emitting from the bugs' abdomen.

"Such *rare* skills of observation," Roland said. He couldn't seem to help himself when he stretched one paw out and tried to bat at a wayward bug.

The fireflies began to move, re-organizing themselves until they were arranged together so their light made letters.

Lord Enchanter Evariste?

"Keep an eye on the bugs, Roland," Angelique ordered before she retreated farther into the house. "Master Evariste?" She leaned against the open library door, peering in to see her teacher on the ground, surrounded by precariously stacked piles of books. "I think it's a message for you."

"Ah, yes. Very well, give me a moment to extract myself, and we can see what all the hubbub is about." Evariste smiled.

Angelique inched inside the room and helped Evariste push a stack of books out of the way, then followed him back to the front door.

"Fireflies?" he said when they rejoined Roland. "Must be from the Council."

The bugs jumbled together, bumping into one another as they moved into a new set of letters.

Pre-Evaluation for Apprentice Angelique to be given at the testing grounds on the next full moon.

"Pre-evaluation?" Angelique blinked.

"That seems on schedule," Evariste confirmed. "You likely only have a year, perhaps two, of your apprenticeship left. Now is about time for you to undergo the practice evaluation, and for us to review what will happen." To the bugs, he said, "Very well, we agree. Is there anything more to the message?"

The fireflies scattered, smearing the message, and returned to flying in a jumbled mass.

"I'm going to say that is a no. Thank you for delivering the news." Evariste pulled the door shut, nearly smacking Angelique —still in shock—in the face.

"But, but my apprenticeship can't be nearly over!" she protested. "I still have so much to learn!"

"I must agree," Roland muttered under his breath. "For starters, you could learn how to be *gracious*."

Evariste chuckled. "Only you, my cute apprentice, would feel unprepared after so many years of preparation. The truth of the matter is you are quite ready. You have mastered most basic forms of magic and have been working on advanced techniques for months. You've already studied boon-granting and advanced spellwork. We need to cover curse modification and a few other topics, but with a few months of practice, you will be ready."

"Except there is one gaping hole of a subject that hasn't been addressed," Angelique blurted out.

Evariste frowned slightly and tilted his head as if puzzled. "What subject is that?"

"My war magic!"

The words felt cold and ugly as they tore out of Angelique's mouth, but as much as she wished she could take them back, she knew she couldn't. Eventually, they would have to discuss her unwanted and dangerous core magic.

"Ah, yes." Evariste pressed his palms together, then tapped his chin with his outstretched fingers. "You are right. You will need to practice with your war magic. Specifically, you need to loosen your hold on it and let it move freely instead of walling it up, as you do so like to do."

Angelique tossed her head like a wild horse and prepared to lay a solid refusal on him.

"*But!*" Evariste interrupted her tirade before it could begin. "The majority of your test relies not upon the use of your war magic but on your ability to control and twist it into other magic —something you have, frankly, mastered."

The enchanter turned away and started for the library.

Angelique glanced down at Roland—hoping he might have words of wisdom to say, or at least back her up with the protest that she wasn't ready.

The cat was studiously licking his white chest. "What do you want?" he asked when she caught his eye.

Angelique sighed and hurried after Evariste. "May I ask how many parts there are to the test?"

"Just two," Evariste said as he re-entered the library. "The power evaluation—which is why you are being summoned to practice—and the general knowledge exam. The general knowledge exam involves a panel of enchanters and enchantresses who ask for demonstrations of the various types of magic you've learned, with a few dozen magical theory and instruction questions thrown in. That's the bulk of what most enchanters- and enchantresses-in-training study for, as it relies on their personal knowledge. The power evaluation requires very little preparation, however, as it is a means of measuring exactly how much magic you have."

Angelique frowned slightly. "Why is that necessary?"

"Officially, it gives you a visible representation of the amount of magic you possess, so you may understand your limits. Unofficially, it lets the Veneno Conclave classify your strength," Evariste explained.

He sat down in a velvet cushioned chair and smiled at her. "The power evaluation can be tricky, but you need not fear prejudice there. The test is carried out by magic itself. No one can alter your results or falsify them. As for the general knowledge exam, it is little more than a formality. The bulk of your test depends upon my personal recommendation."

Angelique's frown grew, and she clasped her hands together to keep from fidgeting.

Evariste rolled his eyes. "Angel, you're going to pass. I promise you. Once you become a Lady Enchantress, you will have to face your war magic—and those who have poisoned it for you—but I have a few ideas about that. And my master Enchanter Clovicus will help."

He sounded confident, but Angelique was not entirely certain.

They barely let Master Evariste take me on as his apprentice and have continued to send warnings throughout my apprenticeship. I don't think it will be quite as easy as he seems to believe it is.

Still, the idea of doing *anything* with her war magic made Angelique's stomach sour. *If I can control it enough to use it for other purposes, isn't that enough?*

She thought of the hopeful war mages she had met over the years and wanted to curse. Didn't they understand? They were gifted with things like speed, invisibility, or deflection. But Angelique... *I'm only good for killing.*

She shivered. *But I can control it. I can stifle it until my magic loses its edge, and I can spin it into something good.*

"Is everything all right, Angel?" Evariste asked.

"Hm? Yes. Thank you, Master Evariste."

He nodded. "Finish up whatever project you and Roland were working on. Tonight, I'll explain to you how the power evaluation works and what you need to do to pass it."

"Thank you, Master Evariste," Angelique repeated. She started to go but hesitated in the doorway. "Master Evariste, if it's not forbidden, can you tell me *where* this power evaluation takes place?"

"Of course." Evariste grinned. "On the edge of Baris' Aurum Desert."

CHAPTER 25

Angelique's stomach churned. She would have scuffed her foot in the grass, but as she was wearing leather boots, it would have ruined Evariste's lawn.

"Are you sure you don't want to come, Roland?" Angelique asked hopefully.

"How can I make my refusal any clearer?" Roland asked. "Must I go kill a rodent and present its carcass to you to show you just how little I would like to come?"

But it's my practice evaluation... The words died in her throat, and she could only manage a strangled smile.

The black and white cat sighed and sat on the toe of one of her boots. "Cheer up. You are going to an evaluation—Evariste isn't sending you to your death."

"But there are supposed to be enchanters or enchantresses there to observe," Angelique said.

"So?" Roland demanded. "You've rubbed elbows with plenty of other magic users over the past decade, and this is merely for practice. Stop worrying!"

"Sorry, Angel!" Evariste called as he jogged across the pond bridge, a satchel thumping against his side. "All set, now." He grinned as he halted next to her and placed a warm hand on the spot between her shoulder blades. "Don't we look sharp, Master Roland?"

In a move that Angelique was *certain* had political undertones to it, Evariste and Angelique wore matching trousers and dovetail jackets. The jackets sported wing designs on their shoulder blades and feathers at the hems and cuffs, but where Angelique's was white with blue embroidery, Evariste's was white with red.

He uses clothing as a weapon. It had taken Angelique most of her apprenticeship to realize this, but she was grateful for the subtle act that showed how he clearly supported her as her master and teacher.

Roland sniffed. "Good luck, Angelique," he said, ignoring Evariste's question. "I await news of your success." The cat then turned around and presented them with his butt, his tail high as he trotted back to the house.

"Are you ready?" Evariste asked as he motioned to the already-open portal—a structure of white marble pillars and baked golden light.

Angelique pressed her lips together but nodded.

Evariste cradled her face, his thumbs lightly dusting her temples. "You'll do fine, Angel." He bent over until his forehead rested against hers. "Breathe. This isn't a test; it's an evaluation of your power. They can't keep you from shining, even if they want to."

His closeness made it a bit hard to swallow, and she had to fight the urge to leap backwards, but his ever-constant warmth that he radiated broke through the icy clamp terror held on her heart, and despite herself, she relaxed a little. She exhaled, and her eyes briefly slid shut.

"That's my Angel," Evariste chuckled. "Come on, this is going to be *fun*," he promised. His grin showed more teeth than usual as he pulled back and motioned for Angelique to step through the portal first.

Angelique barely thought about it as she did, swapping the cool spring air and the smell of wet soil for the hot, arid winds that blasted her when she stepped into Baris.

The portal did not dump Angelique out at an oasis budding with life or near the hustle and bustle of Fillia, but on a large, red plateau that overlooked the golden dunes of Aurum Desert and sat huddled at the foot of the Arkane Mountains that separated Baris from Erlauf.

A jagged gorge split through the center of the plateau, creating a black gaping mouth in the otherwise flat and lonesome plateau.

The area rather reminded Angelique of a warm sunset—from the golden hues of the desert to the red rock of the plateau that shifted up into the browns of the parched mountains. (On this side, at least. Angelique knew from experience that the mountains on Erlauf's side of the range were covered with green trees and topped with white snow.)

"Ahem," someone said, yanking Angelique's attention from the landscape. Three people—the beautiful Lady Enchantress Lovelana, a lord enchanter who looked like he was in his early forties, and a bent, elderly man who had a thick monocle and the expression of a sour pickle—stood in a cluster, gazing expectantly at Angelique.

Evariste bumped her when he came through behind her and closed his portal with a casual gesture. "Enchantress Lovelana, Enchanter Lazare, thank you for coming," he said.

Enchanter Lazare—of the Veneno Conclave Council—pointed his cane at the other man, who wore a splendid green cloak. "What's *he* doing here?" he grunted.

"Enchanter Clovicus came at my request." Evariste offered his hand to the other man, who raised an eyebrow at him but shook his hand.

Evariste's old master is here? Why?

Enchanter Lazare smacked the end of his cane on the unforgiving plateau rock. "If I had known another Enchanter was coming, I would have refused to come, but no, you had to be impudent and keep it a secret." He squinted in the bright sunlight, his mouth screwed up in a scowl. "Rude of the Council to send me as it is! I'm a frail old man—why should I have to bake in the sunlight? And I'm half blind—I won't even be able to see the girl's magic. Foolishness!"

Enchantress Lovelana unfurled a silk fan. "Lord Enchanter Lazare, I cannot believe anything you say. You are a valued member of the Council—they likely elected you due to your experience."

"Hogwash!" Lazare limped closer to Angelique, his back bent so he was shorter than he should have been. "They elected me because I fell asleep when they were voting on the matter!" He leaned close to Angelique and peered up at her face. "Who are you?"

"Angelique, Lord Enchanter," she said. "Apprentice to Lord Enchanter Evariste."

Enchanter Lazare screwed up his face so it resembled a wrinkled prune.

"I appeared before the Council with Madam Quarrellous," Angelique said.

Enchanter Lazare grunted. "Must have been asleep for that, too. What are we waiting for? I'm going to fry in this heat—get a move on, girl!" He limped away, heading for the mountains.

"Enchanter Lazare, we have to explain to her how this works," Enchantress Lovelana called after him.

"You do it!" the old enchanter ordered. "Speaking to people ruins my good mood!"

"I was unaware he was in high spirits," Enchanter Clovicus said, a quirk of a smile playing at his lips.

Enchantress Lovelana sighed, then drew herself up, a regal smile placed on her lips. "Welcome, Apprentice Angelique, to your pre-evaluation. This is not an examination, but a chance for you to experience the magic of this area, so you will be comfortable with it when you complete it as the final step before you are made Lady Enchantress. Do you understand?"

"Yes, Enchantress Lovelana," Angelique said.

The enchantress nodded once, then gestured to the black gorge that yawned open behind her. "As your master has likely told you, your task is to release your magic in its rawest form and fill the gorge. The lowest amount of power an enchanter or enchantress can have and pass the evaluation is to fill the gorge to the rim. Most, however, spill over. For example, Lord Enchanter Evariste's magic streaked out past the village of Izmar you can see at the oasis."

Enchantress Lovelana pointed out a tiny village huddled around an aqua-blue pool located several leagues east of the plateau.

"He almost reached Fillia," she added.

"That's hardly impressive," Enchanter Evariste said. "Several enchanters and enchantresses have passed Fillia before."

Enchantress Lovelana shook her head. "All of those with such power have long since passed on. You are too modest, Evariste." She placed a hand on Evariste's arm.

Behind her, Enchanter Clovicus rolled his eyes and slightly shook his head.

Evariste chuckled at Enchantress Lovelana's obvious praise. "You are too kind."

Lovelana smiled. "Not at all," she murmured. Her cheeks blushed fetchingly as she kept her hand on Evariste's arm.

While Lovelana flirted with Evariste, Clovicus edged closer to Angelique.

"How can you stomach listening to others fawn over him?" he asked.

Angelique blinked, slightly confused. "I'm not certain what you mean."

Clovicus nodded at Lovelana. "Isn't it irritating to witness this?" he asked.

Angelique briefly considered the matter before shaking her head. "Not at all. It's quite pleasant."

"*Pleasant*?"

The incredulous tone to Clovicus voice made Angelique hastily add, "If they focus on Master Evariste, they are less likely to notice me—or speak to me."

"And that would be *unpleasant*?"

Drat it. I wish I hadn't opened my mouth and just smiled like a good little Apprentice! Angelique cleared her throat. "Usually."

Clovicus' furrowed eyebrows drooped until he looked at her with something akin to pity.

At least Angelique *thought* it was pity, until Clovicus sighed and said, "Evariste is a stupid git."

Angelique's jaw dropped. "I beg your pardon?"

Before Clovicus could say anything more, Evariste was there, placing his hand on Angelique's lower back to direct her towards the gorge. "Come, Angelique. I'll show you where to stand."

"But—um." Angelique twisted slightly to look over her shoulder.

Lovelana raised her hands to her blushing cheeks and shook her head slightly before she twitched her shoulders back and regained her elegant demeanor. Clovicus scratched his stubbled jaw and watched her—or Evariste?—with narrowed eyes.

"You remember how I taught you to release your raw magic?" Evariste asked.

"Yes," Angelique confirmed. She mentally cursed when she stubbed her toe on a rock she didn't see thanks to her unnecessary gawking. *Stop staring like an idiot—this evaluation is important!*

"Good. This next part is important, Angel: this is not just an evaluation of the amount of magic you have but of your ability to control it," Evariste explained. "Specifically, the test is searching to confirm you can control a certain ratio of your magic. The more magic you have, the higher amount it expects you to be able to control at any given moment."

This is going to be as fun as rolling in glass. Aloud, Angelique said, woodenly, "That's understandable."

They neared the edge of the gorge, but Evariste herded her along the rim of it, obviously aiming for a peninsula that jutted almost all the way to the center of the canyon.

The canyon reminded Angelique of a snake, the way the walls curved in and out and slithered through the formation of the flat plateau.

"You see those crystals?" Evariste pointed out a giant jade crystal easily taller than he was.

Angelique nodded. The crystals—scattered around the top of the plateau and the shadows of the ravine—glittered in the blistering sunlight.

"They're magic," Evariste explained. "Or rather, they *have* magic. The magic found in these stones is multi-purposeful, but what you mostly need to be aware of is that they are highly attuned to the ratio of strength and control that is required to be made an Enchanter or Enchantress."

Rocks with magic—nothing strange about that at all. "I see," Angelique said.

Evariste moved his hand from her lower back to her shoulder. "Angelique, if you don't pour out your raw magic fast enough to fulfill the required ratio, the crystals will yank it out of you to do it for you."

Fantastic! Rocks with magic that also call judgements! Angelique clamped her jaw shut so tightly she wondered if her teeth might crack. "And how am I supposed to know if I'm pouring enough out?"

"The stones will sing," Evariste said.

Even better! Judgmental magic rocks that sing! "Oh?" She asked weakly.

Evariste squeezed her shoulder. "It's more scientific than one would think: when the rate at which you pour out your magic matches the necessary speed-to-power ratio, your magic resonates with the magic in the stones. It's the resonation of two magics that creates the sound."

"These seem like very unusual crystals."

Evariste stopped by one of the rocks—which stood about as tall as if Angelique sat on Evariste's shoulders. "They are older than you or I, and their magic is mentioned in records that predate the Snow Queen by centuries," he said.

"They're also why this area is left alone," Clovicus added from directly behind them.

Both Evariste and Angelique jumped and spun around.

"They have a powerful spell on them that disorients anyone who enters this area that doesn't have power equal to at least a fairy godmother or godfather," Clovicus said.

Evariste raised both of his eyebrows. "Is there a reason why you followed us?"

"Yes," Clovicus promised. "You need to hurry up. Old man Lazare is going to get half-way to the mountains before you catch up with him and make a portal for us."

Angelique frowned. "Portal?"

Clovicus raised an eyebrow. "You haven't told her yet?"

Evariste's lips briefly turned down. "I was getting to it, before you interrupted us."

Enchanter Clovicus shrugged. "Carry on, then."

Evariste nodded, then motioned for Angelique to step out on the thin peninsula she had noticed before.

The walkway was narrow—she could not have walked shoulder-to-shoulder with Evariste—and she had the dizzying feeling that if she looked down into the craggy depths of the canyon, she might lose her balance. The gorge wasn't terribly deep—it seemed like it was only a little deeper than the tallest peak of Evariste's house—but she'd likely still die from the drop.

"You'll stand in the circle at the end of this path," Evariste explained. He walked behind her—closer than necessary. (And closer than Angelique wanted. The last thing she needed was to trip and fall and take him over the side with her!) "But the other enchanters and I will be seated at a viewing area on the closest mountain."

Angelique almost swung around to face him with that unexpected revelation. "On the *mountain*?" Her voice warbled with worry.

"Yes."

"Is it that *unsafe*?"

"No, no," Evariste said in the same soothing tone he used on young animals and crying children. "Rather, it is to give us a better view. Given the amount of magic you possess, we need to see just how far it goes."

"It's also unsafe, isn't it?" Angelique asked flatly.

When she finally reached the end of the peninsula—which opened up into a circle she could have safely skipped across—she turned around to face her instructor, watching his reaction with a critical eye.

Evariste hesitated. "There are a few records of evaluations that resulted in injury—but there are less than a dozen cases of this happening over the past two centuries."

Angelique shook her head. "I shouldn't do this. It's too risky."

"Not at all," Evariste promised. "If a candidate fumbles and loses control of their magic, the magic in the rocks have safeguards in place. You'll be unharmed."

Angelique pressed her fingers against her eyes. "It's not me I'm worried about!"

"Angel." Evariste took her hands and tugged on them for emphasis. "You can do this. I know you are capable of it. And this is only the practice round—it's held to *give* you the opportunity to make a mistake and learn how to properly channel your magic for the real evaluation. The other enchanters and I are on hand in case something goes wrong, *but it won't*. Raw magic is not directed at anything or channeled into a spell. It's harmless."

Angelique sucked in a deep breath of air and glanced at the shadowy gorge.

The sides of the canyons were the same jagged red rock of the plateau, though it was painted a purple hue from the shadows. She could see more of the jade crystals sprouting from the walls like sharp flowers.

I have to do this. If I ever want to become an enchantress—if I ever want to prove that I can take my bloody magic and spin it into something good—I have to do this.

Slowly, reluctantly, Angelique nodded. "Very well, Master Evariste." She barely managed to croak the words, and her fear was so potent it made her lungs shrink in her chest. *However little I like this test, I'll try to do it with dignity so I don't shame Evariste.*

Evariste's blue and green eyes were lit with an inner warmth as he released her hands. "You'll know when to start—the magic circle etched in the ground will light up. Don't doubt yourself, and please let your magic flow freely for once. *Breathe.*" He gave her another smile then turned around and sauntered back across the peninsula to Enchanter Clovicus, who was waiting with his arms folded across his chest and his foot tapping the ground.

Angelique watched the two men set out at a jog, hurrying to meet up with Enchantress Lovelana—who had given chase after the Enchanter Lazare. (Though the elderly Council member seemed to be ignoring her.)

She rolled her neck and idly swung her arms, trying to loosen up her shoulders, then settled down to wait.

"THANK YOU FOR COMING," Evariste said. Though he and Clovicus were walking so fast it was almost a jog, he managed to speak without sounding winded.

"Of course," Clovicus said. "I thought you might be overreacting, but that a Council Member was sent to watch her practice test? Even if it is ol' Lazare, it's a courtesy they've never paid any candidate *I've* heard of."

Evariste nodded. "Once I get her made into an Enchantress, I don't think the day-to-day outcry will be as bad—the war mages will rise up to back her then."

"Yes, but the key is she still has to make Enchantress," Clovicus said. "And I have to add, I am most displeased with you. I told you not to fall in love with her, but whether you're just stubborn or you love to be impudent, you went and did the very thing I told you *not* to do!"

Evariste laughed at his old master's sour tone. "I don't love her," he said.

"Really? You might want to think about those words again before you accost your apprentice in front of *an open portal*!" Clovicus snarled. "You're lucky Lazare is as blind as a bat, and Lovelana was preoccupied with testing the crystals' magic!"

"I'm more affectionate with her than I should be," Evariste said. "But with everything she's gone through, she deserves it. Yes, she's quite important to me. But it's not love."

Clovicus snorted and elbowed him.

"Or at the very least, I'm not going to act on it for a while," Evariste admitted.

Really, he wasn't entirely sure how he felt about Angelique, but he knew he wanted more, just as he was aware that it wasn't the proper time. *She's also not ready, which is the true wall in this...relationship.*

"There's the honest admission," Clovicus grunted. "And good—you'd be a *dog* if you wooed this girl while she is under your tutelage, no matter how small the age difference is between you two."

"She needs time to come into her own power," Evariste said.

"Luckily, as I am an enchanter and she an enchantress, we'll have centuries."

Clovicus grunted. "You take it for granted she'll love you back?"

Evariste raised an eyebrow at his teacher. "You doubt *my* ability to woo her?"

"Yes," Clovicus said. "Because she seems as interested in romance as a cactus is."

Evariste slowed from the almost-jog to a walk, so he could look back at Angelique.

His student stood in the middle of the circle, her arms clasped behind her back as she peered into the gorge.

"She may be," Evariste admitted. "But that's a problem for after she makes Enchantress."

"Sure," Clovicus said. "But you had best get moving again. Lovelana stopped Lazare, but if we don't catch up, he'll start walking again. And you can bet if his heart gives out and he croaks, someone will find a way to paint it as a bad omen."

Evariste rolled his eyes. "He's not going to die," he said. All the same, he resumed jogging and slowly sped up.

We need to get this evaluation going—before Angelique is given too much time to ponder it.

ANGELIQUE WAS FAINTLY aware of the twinge of magic that registered when Evariste opened a portal.

She glanced up the nearest mountain and scanned its rocky slopes.

There.

Faintly—halfway up the mountain—Angelique could see the blue glow of the portal where Evariste and the other enchanters would exit.

Angelique closed her eyes as the portal was snuffed out—

closed by Evariste. She tried to calm her frantically beating heart and ignored the siren call of her magic.

Her magic had surfaced from the deep recesses she shoved it in. Whether it was the crystals or her wild emotions that brought it up, Angelique was not thrilled to feel the cold and sharp sensation it brought as it wound around her.

(Of course, if Evariste was with her, he'd be telling her this is how it was *supposed* to be all the time!)

She clenched her teeth, and her fists shook as she kept herself from shoving it back down. *I'm better off not wasting my energy when I'll have to let it out shortly.*

Abruptly, the rock beneath Angelique's feet began to glow green.

It took her a moment to realize that the green light—the same shade as the jade rocks—traced out a crest. She had expected it to be that of the Veneno Conclave, but instead it was the image of two dragons fighting with the sun between them.

I guess even this testing practice must predate the Conclave.

Angelique swallowed, squared her shoulders, then reluctantly extended her hand to her magic.

It slammed into her with enough enthusiasm to make her grimace. Nervous, she eased off on the amount she channeled from deep within her. Once she was happy with the speed and amount, she let her power flow through her and start to fill the gorge with streams of raw, silver-colored magic.

She fought the urge to wince. As it twined around her, her powers scraped her magical senses raw.

Just another reason to hate it.

She glanced down into the gorge—which was easier to see now as it was illuminated by the silver glow of her magic. Her magic made the jade crystals—previously blocked from the sun—glitter.

But there's no singing—or any sound at all. I'm not going fast enough.

Reluctantly, Angelique loosened her hold on her magic, letting a fraction more rush through.

Her magic beat against her hold, unsatisfied, but Angelique refused to let anymore through. *I have to be careful.*

Sweat beaded across her forehead and a drop or two trickled down her temple as her shoulders burned from the physical and mental strain.

She glanced at the crystals, which were still silent.

Horse apples, Angelique mentally groaned. *Why couldn't I have less magic? That would make this task easier.*

Again, she painstakingly released another channel in her magic, to the point where silver churned at her fingertips like a frothy river, and the gorge was almost a fourth full.

She thought she heard a crackling sound.

Immediately, her eyes went to the stones. They were glowing now—not silver from her power or golden from the sun, but a minty green that swirled with the magic trapped within the crystalline depths.

Angelique held her breath and listened to the rocks.

She thought she heard a high-pitched noise—which was really more of a ringing sound than singing. *It doesn't matter. The rocks are singing—who am I to criticize their sense of music?*

Angelique let herself relax slightly, pleased she had reached the proper speed. *I can do this. I'm shocked it's working, but I can do this!*

That was when all hell broke loose.

CHAPTER 26

Evariste held a spyglass to his blue eye, watching Angelique as she channeled her magic into the darkened gorge. After a moment, he removed the contraption, letting him view the gorge as a whole—which now glowed silver and looked almost heavenly.

Enchanter Lazare grunted and wiped off the end of his hand-held telescope on his robe. "Can't see a danged thing," he said.

Clovicus joined Evariste at the edge of the viewing lounge—which was little more than a flat section cut into the mountain-side spotted with dried logs for seating. "She's releasing magic at a rate that is about on par with the lowest level of enchanters and enchantresses. It's no surprise she's not going fast enough."

Evariste shut his green eye as he once again peered down the spyglass. "She sped up." He was aware his voice was tight as he watched her magic speed up, but he couldn't help the worry that made him ill at ease.

It's not enough. I don't know the limits of her power, but I know she's got to go faster—much *faster—than this.*

Clovicus grunted. "Looks like that's about average."

"What are the rocks doing?" Lazare asked as he used his

spyglass to scratch the top of his head, having, apparently, given up on watching.

"Nothing," Enchantress Lovelana said. "She has not yet achieved the necessary ratio."

"Oh—there she goes, another increase in pace," Clovicus announced. "This pace puts her above average in terms of power."

Evariste clenched his jaw as he adjusted his spyglass to focus on one of the rocks. Nothing. Until he saw the sign he was dreading—the stones started to glow minty green, and even this far up the mountain he could heard the faint, keening noise they made.

"What's happening?" Lazare demanded.

Lovelana almost dropped her spyglass. "The crystals are preparing to yank more of her magic out—she *still* isn't going fast enough!" She wrinkled her brow and sounded bewildered as she gaped at the gorge. "Evariste, just how much power does she have?"

Evariste didn't respond. He focused his spyglass on Angelique, internally cursing when he saw her relax.

She thought she was going at an acceptable pace. *Speed up*! He wanted to shout, but he knew he'd be too late.

THE RINGING NOISE emitting from the rocks increased in strength, and Angelique winced in pain. The sound seemed to build up pressure in her head and made her ears ache.

What is—

Savagely, *something* ripped Angelique's magic from her.

She lost all control as her magic gushed from her like white water rapids.

"No! Stop!" Angelique struggled to regain control over her wild magic, but something—the wretched stones most likely—

ruthlessly yanked on her magic with enough force to make her physically stumble.

Her entire body ached, and her skin stung from the sheer volume of magic she was being forced to channel.

"Stop it!" Angelique shouted. A cry caught in her throat, and her hands blessedly turned numb as her magic swirled around her, rapidly filling the gorge.

The hateful crystals were now glowing a deep emerald color as they relentlessly dragged more magic from the depths of her soul where she had hidden it.

It was a struggle to stand. The pressure of magic escaping her grasp almost forced Angelique to her knees.

She was aware her magic was spilling over the sides of the gorge and flowing out in a circle, but she found no joy at the sign.

I would have preferred to have been able to just barely fill it!

Tired, Angelique stopped fighting the unyielding pull on her magic and focused instead on trying to *survive* the great volume of magic being flushed from her.

Already, her silver magic had reached the base of the nearest mountain and was starting to crawl up it. On the eastern side, it surged across the desert, wild and untamable in its raw form.

She watched it, almost resentful as it rolled over golden dunes and made the area so bright she had to squint to see anything.

I've seen my magic before, obviously, but this is the first time I'm seeing this much of it. She curled her hands into fists. *I hate it. It might look beautiful, but that's just a facade. There's no way you can dress up killing in any kind of package to make it acceptable. My magic will never be anything but ugly.*

She scanned the golden desert as her magic *still* rushed forth —making her uneasy. A headache roared in her temples, and the ache was back in her hands, but Angelique turned numb when she saw where her magic was headed.

The desert village clustered around the oasis was in the path of her rampaging magic.

Based on the force from which it still was flowing, her power wasn't going to stop anytime soon.

Her magic, in its rawest, unfiltered form, was going to hit the village.

It will kill everyone.

EVARISTE COULD SEE the moment Angelique saw the village of Izmar. She stiffened, and her entire body went still despite the obvious discomfort she was experiencing thanks to the stones.

Whatever you are thinking—don't.

Evariste had promised her that her magic, in this form, couldn't hurt anyone, but obviously she didn't believe him.

"She'll have to get better at control," Clovicus said, oblivious to the danger Evariste's stupid apprentice was about to put herself in. "To pass the evaluation, she needs to be able to do this herself. But at least now she'll get to see her limits, even if it will be uncomfortable to experience."

"Her magic is going to pass Izmar village," Enchantress Lovelana nervously said. "Is it safe for it to flood the village?"

"Of course." Clovicus didn't bother to hide the scoff in his voice.

"You sure about that?" Enchanter Lazare asked.

Evariste collapsed his spyglass and eyed the older enchanter. "What do you mean?" He snarled.

"That's *a lot* of magic that's about to pound into a tiny village," Enchanter Lazare tapped a rock with his cane. "Can you really say it won't do any harm at all?"

"What is she doing?" Enchantress Lovelana asked.

Evariste bit back a growl as he fixed his spyglass and searched out Angelique again.

She had her back turned to them, but Evariste would be able to recognize what her stance meant if he was half blind.

She was going to fight it.

"Angelique—DON'T!"

ANGELIQUE TRIED to regain control of her magic, but it overpowered her like a tsunami wave. It was all she could do to stand as the stones wrenched more and more of her magic from her. She scrabbled for a hold on it, but it mercilessly ripped through her control, overwhelming her with sheer strength.

Her limbs felt heavy, and she would have screamed if she could get her throat to work correctly.

"S-stop it!" Angelique cried.

The stones were mercilessly silent and glowed an eerie emerald green color.

Angelique grit her teeth as she watched her magic surge, rushing closer and closer to the village. She knew Evariste had told her it would be fine, but she could feel it in her heart. If her magic rammed into that village, it would raze it to the ground.

I have to stop it!

Desperation gave her new strength, and she once again grasped her magic. This time, when the avalanche of power slammed into her, Angelique dug her heels in.

She held her ground as she expanded her control, cutting off the flow of her magic.

It *burned.* Her magic rammed into her, trying to break through her hold. She was battered and *frightened* as the vast ocean of her magic curled around her, threatening to drown her.

"ENOUGH!" Angelique forced her magic back, pushing it back where it belonged—in the deepest recesses of her soul. It hurt. Every muscle in her body felt like it was on fire as she used everything she had to push it back, to fight against the compulsion to release it.

It took an enormous effort, especially as the jade crystals glowed stronger, and she felt *their* magic try to crack her control.

Battered between two powerful forces, Angelique looked out and saw that though her magic had stopped its outpour, it still surged on, streaking up the sides of the mountain and deeper into the desert.

Her magic was still going to plow over the village and wreck it.

Tears of pain blurred Angelique's vision as she reached for her rampant magic, while struggling to keep holding her powers back.

She grabbed her loose magic, then yanked it back.

It ignored her and poured mindlessly on, uncaring of the destruction it left in its wake.

Angelique felt the magic in the crystals flare.

She roared as she fought against the ancient stones, grappling for control of her own magic. Blood dripped from her nose, and the ringing noise pierced her skull like a nail, but Angelique clenched her jaw and again yanked on her magic.

It wasn't enough. She knew it in her desperation and wild fear.

Strangely—*unnaturally*—she felt something snap, and her magic's surging progression abruptly stopped. All was quiet for a moment, before her magic at the same pace it had advanced, rushed back to her.

Angelique took a breath and wondered if her heart was going to burst as she watched her ruthless, callous magic retreat.

When it reached the gorge, she smashed her eyes shut and gave her magic one last yank.

It crashed into her, knifing through her skin to return to her inner being.

An inhuman scream ripped from Angelique.

Her entire body flared with pain.

Her magic raced through her veins with a blistering, burning sensation. Even the tears that fell from her eyes lit her skin on fire as if they were glowing hot coals.

She had never felt such awful pain, and never before had she wanted to die so badly.

It was more than she could bear.

All around her, silvery magic clashed with green, colliding in an explosive conflict that shot magic into the sky and eclipsed the sun as the entire plateau shook.

Something cracked, offering Angelique a trickle of relief as she collapsed face-first on the unforgiving rock.

Her body spasmed with pain as the last of her magic returned, seeping under her nails and skin, leaving only awful, unending pain.

Her ocean of magic roared, but it sounded distant and muffled. All Angelique was aware of was searing pain that made her limbs twitch and her entire body shudder.

Just as the mist of magic started to clear and the first few rays of sunlight pierced the fog, it was too much for Angelique to bear, and she fell unconscious.

CHAPTER 27

Evariste opened a portal and lunged through it without waiting for the others. Fear flooded his mind. *She can't be dead—she had to have made it through...that.* He groaned, the hopelessness of the situation assaulting him.

"*Angelique!*" He staggered when he landed in the new location, moving carefully as he blindly crossed the peninsula.

The haze left by Angelique's silvery magic and the crystal's green powers permeated the air like smoke, but Evariste could at least see his feet and the path directly in front of him.

Why did she do this? Didn't she know what it would do to her? He cursed under his breath when the nagging voice at the back of his mind reminded him that she wouldn't care. Angelique was reckless in her blind and unnecessary desire to protect others from herself.

Everything smelled sulfuric and perhaps a bit metallic. He squinted, moving faster when the peninsula opened up into the circular testing area.

The dragon crest was starting to fade, but it glowed enough that Evariste could make out the one unlit area, smudged out by Angelique's body.

His heart stopped, and for one horrifying moment, his world collapsed.

"Evariste?" Clovicus called from somewhere behind him.

Evariste threw himself to his knees next to Angelique and carefully rolled her on to her side.

She looked terrible. Blood dripped from her nose, her skin was unnaturally flushed, and her forehead was crusted with dried sweat. But she was breathing.

She's alive!

He almost sagged with relief.

Her magic had done a number on her when she had wrestled it free. More correctly, fighting with the ancient—*untamable*—magic in the green crystals had nearly killed her. But her breath was strong, and her heartbeat steady.

His hand shook as he swiftly channeled and twisted his magic, forging a powerful healing spell. He applied it to Angelique the second he could, trying to provide relief to her shocked and wounded body.

The magic in the air continued to settle, but the sun was able to reach deeper, making it easier to see.

Clovicus staggered into the testing circle. "Did she make it?"

"Yes." Evariste winced when he shifted Angelique slightly and saw a rock dig into her cheek. Keeping the healing spell applied with his right hand, he carefully maneuvered Angelique, scooping her off the ground and tilting her so she leaned against his chest.

You little idiot, he thought as he clutched her, pushing as much as he dared to into the healing magic. *I am going to wallop you with an ethics book when you wake up!*

He felt her magic brighten slightly—with...*curiosity*, perhaps? But it settled back into place as quickly as it had appeared.

"What happened?" Enchantress Lovelana asked as she joined them in the circle, a hand pressed to her chest and her eyes wide with shock.

"It seems Evariste's apprentice wrestled her magic free of the stones and stopped the test," Clovicus said as he peered up at the sky as the last haze of magic cleared.

"But that shouldn't be possible," Enchantress Lovelana stammered. "The testing circle runs off ancient magic—she shouldn't have been able to interfere!"

"It seems she has," Clovicus said.

Evariste slightly shifted Angelique, wincing at the way she bonelessly leaned against him. (Any other day, she'd be giving him that pinched expression she gave when she thought he wasn't looking and would look like she'd rather suck lemons than hug him. He'd give anything to see her make that expression right now.)

"But these are sacred grounds!" Lovelana said. "No one can influence them or bend them to their will—that's the reason we hold evaluations here!"

Enchanter Lazare was the last to join them. He squinted at Evariste and Angelique but ambled past them to stand at the edge of the testing circle.

"She can't have actually wrested her magic free!" Lovelana continued.

"She hurt herself badly in the process; it's not like she did it without any consequences," Clovicus said dryly.

Lovelana shook her head and stared unseeingly at the gorge. "She shouldn't be able to do it at all! Centuries of tradition can't be broken so suddenly and swiftly like this!"

"She's going to be one to watch," Lazare said, breaking Lovelana's baffled tirade. He nodded and tapped his cane on the giant green crystal that thrust out of the plateau at the very edge of the peninsula. "One to watch, indeed," he muttered before limping back across the peninsula.

It took Clovicus nudging Evariste with his foot, then nodding at the crystal for Evariste to look closer.

From his position on the ground, holding Angelique, Evariste could make out the jagged crack in the rock that hadn't been there before.

Impossible.

Generations of magic users had used these testing grounds, and never had anyone been able to fight back as Angelique had.

Clovicus crouched down next to Evariste, his expression thoughtful. "It does raise the question...just how powerful is your apprentice, Evariste?"

Evariste could only shake his head in shock. "I don't know."

EVERYTHING HURT.

The world was no longer on fire; instead, it felt like every bone in her body had been rattled and bruised.

Even her eyelids felt pained as she struggled to open her eyes.

When she finally managed to peel back her eyelids, all she saw was Evariste's neck. "Master?" she croaked, her voice rusty and painful.

"Sleep, Angel," Evariste said, his voice deep and cool. She felt his arms move around her, and something soothing pressed against her back.

A healing spell, she belatedly realized.

"Rest. I'll take you home," Evariste promised.

"'kay," Angelique murmured as she relaxed again.

She was on the cusp of unconsciousness when she felt her magic.

A whisper of it had escaped her iron grasp, but she could feel it cower like a kicked dog. As she relaxed, she felt it relax as well and drift back into the dark recesses where she usually forced it.

What was that? She wondered before sleep finally took her, and she exhaled and sank more deeply into the pseudo-embrace Evariste held her in.

CHAPTER 28

"You shouldn't have done it, Angel."

Angel wanted to fold her arms across her chest and glare at her teacher, but she *still* had to keep up her cheery front, so instead she tapped her chin with her finger. "My magic was going to destroy Izmar village, Master Evariste."

"It was not." Evariste sat across from her, an eyebrow raised.

They were home—in the front salon, to be correct.

Two weeks had passed since Angelique had so poorly blown her pre-evaluation. Only three days ago had Evariste finally allowed her out of bed.

"The village was never in any danger," Evariste said. "Raw magic is unharmful."

"In the notes on my pre-evaluation results, it says Lord Enchanter Lazare felt the sheer power of my magic would perhaps be too overwhelming for the village," Angelique said.

Evariste, who seemed to be just barely holding onto his usual good cheer, frowned. "Who gave you the notes for your results?"

"Enchanter Clovicus did when he visited yesterday," Angelique said.

Evariste smiled—but it was rather toothy and forced. "I see."

Angelique avoided his gaze and instead pet Roland—who was sitting on her lap. She slightly smushed the hair on the top of his head, but the cat must have been feeling sorry for her, for he didn't complain and only flicked his tail in irritation once.

It's not a good sign if Roland *pities me.*

Evariste sighed. "Angel, even if your magic was dangerous—which it was *not*—there's a reason why other enchanters and enchantresses observe the evaluation. We could have protected the village if necessary."

Angelique scratched an itch on her arm and didn't dare look up at her teacher. *If I meet his sad eyes one more time, I'm going to bawl.* Her body still ached. Thankfully it was only a dull pain right now, but the way Evariste explained it, she had nearly fried her mind and her entire body by forcing it to reel back in magic that had already been expelled.

It was, as Enchantress Lovelana had said in her report, *Simply not done.* At least, not on ancient testing grounds where stupid rocks had the power to mold your magic however they wished.

Angelique scooped Roland up so she could cuddle him to her chin.

"Mind the fur," he fussed, but he didn't even threaten to bite her when she kissed one of his black ears.

"Angel, your magic can be used to cause harm, but that doesn't make it inherently dangerous," Evariste said.

I can't repeat this. Not again. Angelique let her forced smile drop. "We've had this conversation a thousand times."

"Because you don't listen!"

"No, because you refuse to see the reality of my magic," Angelique argued. "My core magic is only good for pain and suffering! I'm grateful that you have taught me how to twist and change it so I can do other things with it. I'm so happy that now I *can* use it for something besides pain. But despite what you believe, it is not a good thing."

"Angel, I can help you," Evariste promised in his musical voice.

"Once you unleash your magic as it is supposed to be, I'll walk with you in this."

For a moment, Angelique wanted to believe him, but then she shook her head. "Every time you tell me to use my war magic, it has ended in bloodshed. I don't need you to defend me or pretend it is beautiful. I don't need anything from you! You just have to understand that I will not use it!"

Evariste jolted back, as if her words were a personal attack. His easy smile fell from his lips, and for a moment he stared at Angelique with *hurt* bright in his eyes. The moment passed, and he shook his head. "You will have to in order to pass the evaluation."

Angelique stood, Roland dangling from her arms. "All I have to do is show off enough magic that I can make enchantress."

"Angelique, you *cannot* restrict your magic! The crystals won't allow it."

"We'll see." Angelique felt a muscle jump in her cheek, still angry about the rocks and the way they had torn her control from her.

"No, we won't!" Evariste spat, surprising Angelique with the fury in his voice. "Do you not understand? You nearly killed yourself when you stopped your magic. We don't even know how you survived! You cannot do that again." His green and blue eyes glowed with barely controlled rage.

Angelique stared at him, surprised by his anger. *Why has this upset him so much?*

Roland cleared his throat but did not struggle despite his precarious dangling position. "If I might interject..."

"Regardless of how you feel, you *must* learn to live with your war magic—and free it!" Evariste said.

The order made Angelique snort. "Over my dead body!"

"To make Enchantress, you *have* to," Evariste said, his voice a mask of stone.

"Maybe, then, I *won't* make Enchantress!" Angelique said.

"They'll seal your magic."

"That's *fine* with me!" Angelique shouted. "It's not like my core magic is anything good!"

Roland twitched his tail. "This situation is rather—"

"You're being dramatic," Evariste said.

Roland groaned. "You should not have said that," he told the enchanter.

In her heart, Angelique knew Evariste was right. More than anything, she wanted to be an enchantress. Even now she didn't want to give up on that dream.

But the situation struck her as being incredibly unfair.

He has rare and valuable portal magic. I can control weapons. How dare *he try to lecture me about my powers!*

"Perhaps I am," Angelique said. "Maybe Madame Quarrellous was right about me all along."

Evariste narrowed his eyes. "There is no way you believe those lies about yourself."

"The *only one* who thinks they're lies is *you*!" Angelique shouted.

"Perhaps we should adjourn this meeting," Roland suggested.

"Fine," Evariste said.

"Good," Roland said.

"Maybe you shouldn't be an enchantress after all," Evariste said.

"Why do you keep talking?" Roland growled. "You're going to *bungle* this beyond repair!"

Angelique ignored her cat and instead glared at her teacher. "What are you talking about?"

"You have great power and great strength, Angelique." Evariste took a prowling step towards her, looking fiercer than she had ever believed him capable of being. "But you are too frightened by what others think to free it and too cowardly to see exactly what your war magic could mean. So, fine. Run away and *hide*."

The words hurt enough to bring tears to Angelique's eyes.

Evariste, however, didn't see it. He stalked out of the salon, threw the front door of the house open and prowled outside.

Angelique watched in her peripheral vision as he stalked across the porch. He shouted something and made a twisting gesture, and a portal blazed into existence. He was through it and shut it behind him before she had a chance to see where he had gone.

The accusation hurt, likely more than Evariste meant for it to. Tears stung Angelique's eyes, and she took a shuddering breath.

Roland struggled in her arms until he was higher and could place his front paws on her shoulder.

"I *hate* him," Angelique whispered.

"You might right now but not forever." Roland purred deeply and didn't complain when Angelique pressed her face into his soft fur.

"Do you think...did I just ruin everything?" she asked.

"No," he said in the same self-assured voice he always used. "You are frightened, and he is hurt. You both blindly struck out. Give him space."

Angelique nodded and wandered in the direction of the kitchen, intending to make some tea. But the cat's words confused her. *Evariste is hurt? About what?*

I DON'T NEED *anything from you!*

The words struck Evariste with the force of a sword in the prime of its swing.

Remembering her narrowed eyes and the fire in her gaze only increased his pain.

Knowingly or not, Angelique had uttered the very words he never wanted to hear. She was rejecting him. She didn't want him and obviously did not see him as anything...*more*.

He groaned as he sank to his knees, barely taking in his surroundings.

Without thinking, he had opened a portal to Farset, near Emerys' Alabaster Forest.

He rubbed his eyes and wished he could take the last hour back.

Angelique had hurt him, yes, but he knew he was lashing out unfairly when he accused her of cowardice. He was her teacher—he was supposed to be above such tactics.

As much as Angelique's words hurt, there was nothing inherently wrong with them. He was her master—a close companion but certainly nothing more than that.

Clovicus was right. Angelique was incapable—at the moment—of falling in love. She was stunted.

The pain and accusations she had lived through had left her warped. Or perhaps it was better to compare her to an animal that had been abused and was now a little slower to trust. And instead of waiting patiently for her to come to him, Evariste had tried to tip Angelique's hand.

He didn't *have* to recommend she become an enchantress yet. She could remain his apprentice for easily another three or four years before most would expect her to take her evaluation. And while she was a bright student, there were other subjects they could dig deeper into in the interim. (They never had really studied curses, and she could use more practice with her healing magic.)

But no. Evariste selfishly wanted to walk with her, not as her teacher but as something more. He had pushed for her test when she clearly was not yet ready to face her war magic.

I hurt her because she acted exactly as Clovicus predicted she would. He sighed. *It's not her fault I feel this way for her and she does not reciprocate—or even see it. I am the one at fault for rushing her for personal reasons instead of thinking firstly of her.*

The snow (that was on the cusp of slush thanks to the warmer temperatures as winter eased off) seeped through Evariste's pants in an unwelcome and icy reminder of where he was.

I hurt her. "I have to bury my feelings deeper. I have to do better," he grimly said. "If I don't shape up, she might break all ties with me."

I don't need anything from you!

Evariste groaned as the words hammered at him again, only proving his point.

Angelique was not nearly as attached to him as he was to her. And if he tried to push her too far, their relationship would never recover.

That was an outcome he couldn't live with. *I'd rather have her friendship than nothing at all.*

He sighed. "How can I face her again?" he wondered. "How can I restore us to the way we were? Is it even possible?" He sank his fists into the slushy snow. "I need...time."

But as Evariste stared at the snow-dusted trees, he knew one thing in his heart: he was *never again* going to do anything to jeopardize his relationship with Angelique because of his feelings for her.

CHAPTER 29

A week passed, followed by a second. Snow made a ruthless return, and the yard outside Evariste's home was white, but the sun was stronger during the daytime.

Spring was fighting to poke through the last gasps of winter.

And yet Evariste and I...

Angelique trailed off, not entirely certain where they stood. He didn't seem *angry* at her per se, but they had never spoken of their shouting match—never addressed it.

Mainly, because Evariste wasn't *around*. He left notes—claiming he was running errands or visiting a fellow enchanter—and instructions for her lessons.

But Angelique hadn't done more than pass him by chance in the hallway since their disagreement.

He smiled at her when he saw her, but it seemed to lack its usual warmth and depth.

Which, annoyingly, made Angelique question her decision to abstain from using her core magic more than she'd care to admit.

He's brilliant—no—he's a legend. How can he be so stubbornly misguided when it comes to my magic?

Angelique sighed and turned a page in the book she was reading, then studied the collar she had made as part of her assignment. It was made of black leather and was encrusted with an aqua-colored jewel the size of her thumbnail.

Roland, in the process of cleaning his chest, snorted. "I didn't know reviewing alteration magic could cause such melancholy in you."

"I am merely tired," Angelique fibbed as she consulted the book's instructions and compared them to the collar—which was supposed to silence the words and magic of whoever wore it. Frankly, Angelique didn't see much of a use for it and thought it was a stupid exercise, until it occurred to her Lady Alastryn of Alabaster Forest might want a batch of them for her *dear* King Themerysaldi. "And I've been reviewing the basics of magic now for two weeks. I'd like to get back to something more challenging."

Roland sauntered across Evariste's desk, not caring when he tipped over a stack of papers and almost broke a glass bottle that contained a blizzard. "As I recall, Enchanter Evariste's first note to you mentioned you needed to use *less* of your magic for a few weeks out of worry from the after-effects of your practice evaluation."

"That's what he wrote." Angelique scowled at the book.

Roland yawned and hopped onto Evariste's velvet padded chair where he kneaded his claws for a few moments. "You could make a case for yourself—tell him you're fine," he offered. "He's downstairs right now. If you can make a solid defense, I dare say he'll give in."

"Maybe," Angelique said. *But that would mean talking with him. And things are still so...strained.*

"You'll have to face him eventually," Roland said. "Preferably with teary eyes and looking far sorrier than sour—as you do now."

Angelique rolled her eyes—she had heard at least five variations of this lecture now. "Roland."

"You're lucky I have the patience to deal with such fidgety, *unintelligent* creatures as you two. If you fight, at least have the good sense to meet up afterward to either apologize or continue insulting each other."

"Roland, I can't just go waltzing up to Evariste and tell him I'm sorry."

"Of *course* you can," the cat said, his voice scornful. "That is the very definition of apologizing!"

"But I'm *not* sorry! He was the one who wouldn't listen!" Angelique said.

"He was acting bossy, yes, but you are more stubborn than a donkey," Roland said.

Angelique groaned and pinched her eyes shut. "Roland, please. I don't want to talk about this right now."

The cat ignored her. "As long as you two act like bratty children, nothing will be resolved. And *no*, using creature illusions will not help you teach Evariste a lesson."

"I only did that twice." Angelique turned the collar over, inspecting the spell woven into it as she gave up stopping Roland.

"If you settled down like *sensible* creatures—instead of all this unnecessary drama—your little disagreement would be resolved already!" Roland continued.

"Uh-huh," Angelique said as she slightly tweaked the spellwork. *That should do it. But I'll need to test it to make sure.*

"Besides, it's painfully *obvious* why he reacted as he did. Any other yokel with two thoughts to illuminate his mind would be able to see it. It is disappointing you haven't noticed—unhand me!" Roland complained as Angelique scooped him up.

"If you're so keen to help me, you can start by testing out this collar," Angelique said. It took some wrestling, but she eventually buckled the collar into place. "How is it?" she asked, setting Roland down on her desk. "Can you talk or use one of your handy charms? Hmmm, though this particular spell might be meant for humans only."

Angelique reached for her book.

Roland narrowed his eyes in a look of cat-scorn, opened his mouth, and meowed.

Angelique stared at Roland, and Roland's eyes widened as he meowed again, and again, and again.

Angelique slapped a hand over her mouth to keep from bursting into laughter.

Roland hissed and growled.

"I didn't laugh!" Angelique defended herself.

Roland growled and stretched his neck as he flicked his black tail back and forth, obviously demanding she take off the collar.

"I guess it worked after all," Angelique chuckled. She reached for him, intending to loosen the collar—and restore Roland's voice and magic, knowing he would thoroughly lecture her, now, for an entirely new reason.

She paused when she felt a shiver of foreign magic brush her. Frowning, she turned away from her desk and stared unseeingly across the cheerfully lit workshop.

The magic was faint and muffled—as if it was hidden. In fact, the more she tried to pinpoint its location, the more it slipped from her grasp. Regardless, it certainly wasn't Evariste's or hers.

Her frown deepening, Angelique started down the stairs, her brow furrowed.

Behind her, Roland growled deep in his throat.

"I'll be right back," Angelique promised.

Roland flicked his tail and narrowed his bronze-colored eyes. She was halfway down the top flight of stairs when she heard the tell-tale thump of the cat landing on the ground, likely with the intent of following her.

But the foreign magic tugged on Angelique's senses, and she passed through the middle floor and clattered down to the main level.

Deep inside of her, she felt her magic quiver. Angelique paused with her hand on the front door and tipped her head. Her magic tried to surge out of her control, but Angelique caught it with the ease of practice and stuffed it back down.

"What is going on?" she muttered as she pulled the door open.

A dozen people stood outside in the front yard. They wore dark gray cloaks, and when a few of them turned to look at her, she didn't recognize any of them.

Angelique opened her mouth to call out to them when her magic roared deep within her.

Blood. These mages have spilled blood with their magic.

She didn't know how she could tell, but she knew it with every fiber of her being.

Angelique slammed the door shut. "*Evariste!*" she screamed.

"Angel?" Evariste's voice came from the library.

Angelique ran, pausing just long enough to scoop Roland up—who was standing on the bottom stair with his back arched and tail puffed. "There's something—"

The front door was blown off the hinges with enough force that it skidded down the hallway, smacking into Angelique and Roland.

Angelique yelped but managed to turn so she sheltered Roland as she was nearly flattened to the ground. She gritted her teeth—her left side, which bore the brunt of impact—was numb with pain. *Hopefully I didn't break anything*, she thought as Roland slipped from her arms.

Evariste shouted words of magic that should have made the cottage's defenses flare to life.

Instead, the gray-robed mages (they *had* to be magic users of some sort) started to file through the door.

Angelique shouldered the broken door so it fell off her back and forced herself to stand. Muttering under her breath, she pulled on and twisted her magic, a white-hot fireball forming at her fingertips. She flung it at the mage sauntering in through the busted doorframe. It made him pause and take a staggering step backwards before he was able to dispel it.

In that time, Angelique shot off two more fireballs, effectively halting the intruders' progress inside.

But the four who had already made it into the house streaked towards her like insubstantial shadows.

A female mage grabbed her by the wrists, but regretted it immensely when Angelique yanked her arms into her gut then smashed her head into the enemy mage's nose.

The mage yelped and nearly fell on one of her companions.

Angelique struck, kicking her in the gut, this time successfully knocking over the broken-nosed mage and the male directly behind her.

Yep, these are mages. They're terrible at physical fights.

Angelique flicked her fingers at the fallen mages, raining needle-sharp icicles on them while she struck one of the standing mages in the throat with the flat of her palm, making him fall with a choke.

She turned on the final mage, who spat some dark, vile sounding words and pointed at Angelique.

Pain assaulted Angelique in a wave that felt like heated needles being pushed through her skull. Her head hurt so badly she couldn't see. Her ears rang, and a scream tore from her throat.

Evariste roared, and there was the crackle of magic and lightning before the pain ceased.

Angelique groaned and had to blink several times before her blurred vision cleared enough that she could make out shapes.

Evariste stood in the hallway, his magic glittering around him like a miniature galaxy. Lightning dashed up and down the hallway, striking the rogue mages with absolute precision.

"Angel!" Evariste held out his hand and created a screen of lightning over the gaping front door without even looking.

Despite her body's protests, Angelique ran to Evariste's side, peering around, looking for Roland.

She didn't see the black and white cat anywhere as Evariste pulled her into the front salon.

The outer windows cracked, then shattered, and more of the gray-robed mages wiggled past shards of jagged glass and jumped into the salon.

Angelique kicked a coffee table and used a tiny bit of strength magic to make the furniture piece slam into two mages, toppling them like wooden blocks.

Evariste used another round of his lightning magic as he backed up against the wall. The room danced with lightning—which hit about eight of the ten mages attempting to advance on them.

When he stopped, he slapped his hand against the wall—which made the glass-framed window to Verglas glow.

Angelique stepped closer, hurriedly building a wall of ice that upset the furniture and made the room icy cold. Her breath came in white puffs as she added layers to the icy wall, thickening it.

"We're leaving?" she asked.

"Yes," Evariste said.

"But Roland—"

Roland yowled angrily as he landed on the top of the ice wall, then jumped over to their side.

"As soon as the full portal opens, go," Evariste ordered as his magic crawled down the wall, lengthening the Verglas window.

"Okay—" Angelique clenched her jaw shut when her wall shattered, battering her with jagged pieces of ice.

She slapped her hands together and copied Evariste's previous attack, creating jagged spikes of lightning that shot out from her in a fan-like formation.

Her attack was not quite as precise, but with Roland leaning against her leg and Evariste behind her, it didn't matter if some of the furniture was taken as collateral damage.

Most of the mages tumbled down—though three were able to raise protective spells that blocked the lightning.

Angelique took a breath and started to weave another spell

when her war magic flooded her so abruptly with a heavy and desperate weight, she almost fell to her knees.

She heard low chanting and lifted her gaze.

Two of the gray-cloaked mages had remained outside—a man with a jagged scar that slashed diagonally across his face and a woman with eyes covered with a white film. They chanted together, and vermillion red magic sank from their fingers and flowed across the yard, crawling in through the biggest broken window.

Angelique frowned. "Master, what is—"

The vermillion magic sprang, lunging at Angelique with the speed and deadly intent of a wolf.

The spell radiated a blistering heat as it lunged closer. Her magic raged in her, howling to be let out, but as Angelique tried to spin it into a defensive spell, she realized it wasn't coming fast enough. She tried to move but found her feet were stuck.

"*Angel!*"

Evariste yanked her back by the collar of her dress and shoved her through the portal. The magic transported her so quickly that for a moment she couldn't tell the sky from the ground, until she fell backwards and landed in a pile of snow.

She sat upright just in time to see the end of the battle.

CHAPTER 30

Evariste started to step through the portal, but the red magic grazed his back, and he fell to his knees, his face lined with pain.

He looked up, and his eyes met Angelique's.

"No," Angelique said. She tried to scramble to her feet and flung herself at the portal, but she was too slow.

Evariste said something, and the portal started dismantling.

Vermillion magic exploded behind him, and the doorway shut.

"*No!*" Angelique screamed as she reached out a moment too slow. The portal was gone, leaving her on the rounded top of Fresler's Helm, a snow-covered mountain in northern Verglas...on the opposite pole of the continent.

"That idiot!" She cried—tears of fear and frustration. "Why didn't he go through first?"

The wind shrieked and yanked on Angelique's clothes. It wasn't until her teeth started chattering that she thought to make a quick heat charm and use magic to slightly nudge the weather pattern to make it a little more bearable.

She shook her hand, making the bracelet Evariste had given her years ago jangle. "*Evariste!*" she shouted. "*Evariste!*"

Nothing responded.

I have to get back. Evariste made it—he must have! But after he fights them off, he might be hurt, or injured...

Angelique shut the thought off and gazed across the snowy landscape that surrounded her, orientating herself in the craggy mountains that surrounded Verglas.

Ice cold magic—remnants of the Snow Queen's ancient power—brushed against Angelique. Angelique held her breath for a moment—even if she didn't *mean* to be evil, there was a part of her that would always fear—but the magic prodded her like a dog looking for a belly scratch.

Angelique brushed it off and took in a deep breath as she tried to combat shock and stay focused.

The capital, Ostfold, it's east. I'll go there first—Evariste has a few horses kept there. Hopefully he'll have a sleigh, as well.

Her muscles ached and her temples throbbed, but Angelique started picking her way down the precarious mountainside, trying to rein in her fear and the worry that Evariste had just sacrificed himself for her.

USING magic and traveling at a merciless speed, it took Angelique over three weeks to travel south, through Loire, a corner of Erlauf, and finally reach Torrens. During the entire journey, she tried to call Evariste with her tracking bracelet.

He never came.

By the time she rode into the house clearing on a fresh mare borrowed from a nearby inn, her body shook with exhaustion. She had ridden through the night and stopped at the inn only long enough to swap horses.

As Angelique stared at her home—Evariste's home—she mentally berated herself for taking so long.

"Evariste? Roland?" Angelique slid off the mare's back, staggering when she hit the ground.

The house was still.

Angelique ran across the yard, almost wiping out in a slushy pile of melted snow. The salon windows were still broken, and the front door was missing, but when Angelique staggered across the house's threshold, the lights burst to life.

They have to be here. They MUST be here!

"Master Evariste? Roland?" Her throat cracked with grief, but she merely cleared her throat and shouted again, her persistent panic making her louder. "*Evariste! Roland!*"

She stumbled into the salon, her eyes flickering to the portals/windows mounted on the wall.

The glass frame that usually held a portal to Verglas was empty, but the wooden frame that faced the very edge of the Alabaster Forest and the white stone frame that overlooked Fillia still sparked with magic.

Some of Angelique's fears decreased at the sight of the portals.

If Evariste was killed, they wouldn't still be working—or operational. In theory, anyway. Evariste is legendary, so I guess there's a chance his magic could survive death, but no. He must still be alive!

Angelique glanced around the salon—which was a burnt husk of its previous splendor. There was some blood, but no bodies or bones. All the furniture was shattered beyond repair, and the walls were singed and dusted with ash.

"Evariste, Roland!" Angelique ducked out of the salon and made a meticulous search through the house—going floor by floor.

She hoped to find Roland—it seemed unlikely the mages would take a cat—particularly if his collar was still on and they didn't know he was magical. But she couldn't find him *anywhere*!

By the time the sun had risen above the trees that surrounded Evariste's home, Angelique's fears had matured into dread.

I need help! She glanced upstairs, where Evariste's room was.

She knew he had a portal straight to his office in the Veneno Conclave fortress, but she wasn't certain the Conclave was the most powerful option she had.

She bit her lip as her eyes strayed to the ruined salon. *But I'm not certain I can reach* them. *I might not fit.* She narrowed her eyes. *I'll have to.*

Angelique reentered the salon, making her way towards the portal-window that looked into Farset.

Evariste had once told her that technically the windows could operate as portals—though they weren't meant to, so the trip would be uncomfortable and perhaps a bit painful.

That doesn't matter. Evariste is missing! Angelique pushed a half-burnt stool to the base of the window, then started to crawl through.

It *was* a little painful and discombobulating—not because the magic was any different, but because Angelique was stuck in limbo—her upper body in Farset and her legs in Torrens—while she tried to maneuver her hips through the narrow window.

The magic made her body tingle, and the confusing limbo made her feel more than a little nauseated. When she finally managed to hoist herself through, she fell into Farset with a splat, landing in a pile of icy cold slush.

Shivering, Angelique automatically cast a heat charm on herself, then staggered up to the tree line that marked the beginning of Alabaster Forest.

She almost barged across the forest boundary before remembering that as she was not with Evariste, she couldn't freely enter the elves' territory. Only elf-friends could do that, and despite her many visits with Evariste, she had never received the title.

She cringed, but cleared her throat and shouted, "King Themerysaldi! Lady Alastryn! I need to speak with you!"

She waited for a minute—aware it might take a bit of time for elf scouts to hear her and trot her message back to the Elf King—

then shouted again. "King Themerysaldi, Lady Alastryn! It's me—Apprentice Angelique!"

She licked her dried lips and glanced behind her, relieved she could still see the window into Evariste's study—hidden in a tree trunk and spelled against prying eyes. She rubbed her hands together, then hopped in place. "King Themerysaldi? Lady Alastryn? It's about Evariste!"

Minutes passed, then hours.

No one came.

Angelique paced up and down the border of Alabaster Forest, shouting until she was hoarse, yelling until her voice was entirely gone, then shooting up plumes of fire and bolts of thunder.

The Elf King never showed, nor did any of his subjects.

The sun set, leaving the forest frigid and lonely, and Angelique was forced to admit that she wasn't going to find any help in Farset.

Almost blind with exhaustion and hunger, she found the tiny window back to Evariste's broken parlor.

Getting back through was a near thing. Even though she had her heat charm to warm her *and* used some strength magic to help her climb the tree trunk, her grasp on her magic was shaky. She precariously climbed through the window and struggled to get her hips through before abruptly falling. She hit her head on her stupid stool and sat in the salon for a moment, dazed and numb.

Get up! You have to get help! Slowly, painfully, Angelique climbed to her feet and dragged herself down the hall. Climbing the stairs was torturous, but she forced herself up each step.

Get help. Get help. Get help!

She banged into Evariste's room, not at all shy about entering his personal quarters—she was beyond all causal cares and regards by now.

The portal to the Veneno Conclave glowed, framed by goldwork and foreign scripts. Angelique staggered through it—grateful this method of traveling did not make her stomach churn

—and walked out of Evariste's bedroom and straight into his solid wooden desk in his office, painfully banging her shins.

"Enchanter Clovicus!" Angelique shouted. Her voice was so hoarse and crackling, she sounded more like a wounded animal than a human.

She threw the door open and blinked as she tried to place her location, but her thoughts slipped through her grasp like water. "*Enchanter Clovicus*!"

"Angelique?"

Angelique turned around and had to blink a few times before she could make out Clovicus' features.

"You look terrible," he paused and furrowed his brow. "Is Evariste hurt?"

Angelique's legs collapsed under her, and she slumped down, tears leaking out of her eyes. "I don't know," she whispered.

CHAPTER 31

After telling Clovicus everything she could, the Lord Enchanter guided Angelique to his office and left her in a comfortable chair, ordering her to rest.

She awoke when rays of sunshine pierced through the glass windows, and Enchanter Clovicus set a breakfast tray on his desk.

"Did you find Evariste?" Angelique groggily asked.

"Eat, Angelique." Enchanter Clovicus beckoned her to a wooden chair pulled in front of his desk and nudged the tray.

He didn't say "yes." That can't be a good sign. Angelique stood stiffly, her body protesting every move she made. She hunched her shoulders up and down a few times in an effort to loosen them up, then sat down in the chair.

The tray was piled with rye bread rolls, little pots of strawberry and cherry jelly, smoked fish, cheese, and boiled eggs.

Angelique's traitorous stomach growled, and it felt like a creature clawed inside her belly, but Angelique forced herself to meet Enchanter Clovicus' gaze. "Did you find Evariste?" she repeated.

"No." Enchanter Clovicus sighed and sat on the edge of his desk, reminding Angelique of Evariste. "But I'm not going to say anything more until you start eating," he said.

Woodenly, Angelique selected a roll and started nibbling on it. Though she couldn't attest to the taste, by the time she had finished it, she felt marginally better. The pounding in her head was far more subdued, and her entire body seemed to ease.

She hesitated, then picked up a boiled egg. "I'm eating," she reminded the Lord Enchanter.

Clovicus nodded and slammed his hands on his thighs. "Right." He hesitated, then began. "After I raised the alarm last night, a squadron of mages was sent to your home using the portal in Evariste's office. They searched the house and grounds and can say with almost certainty that Evariste was forcefully removed from the premise."

So, he's not dead. The assurance eased more of the pressure pounding in Angelique's temple.

"But," Clovicus continued, "They couldn't decipher where Evariste was taken or even what was done to disable him. Between your testimony and the damage done to the home, the leader of the squadron said Evariste was likely taken captive by a very *powerful* group of black magic users."

"How do they know?" Angelique asked.

"The spell you described that hit him as he shoved you through the portal." Clovicus sighed and pinched the bridge of his nose. "It's a known spell of black magic. It debilitates the target so they are no longer in control of themselves, and it requires a lot of magical ability to cast. Perhaps even the same amount of power as an enchanter."

Angelique set the last bit of her boiled egg down as a metallic taste coated her mouth. "What does that mean?"

"That it's going to be wretched hard to get Evariste back," Clovicus said bluntly. "The defense spells and precautions Evariste cast on the house were disabled—not many have the power to do such a thing. Moreover, they left no magical trail. It's possible they may have forced Evariste to use his magic and then ported out, but we have no way of knowing for certain."

Angelique ran a hand through her tangled hair. "How could this have happened? The Veneno Conclave exists to *protect* us from things like this! There are supposed to be safeguards in place! Isn't that why everyone watches me with a suspicious eye?"

"I am just as shocked as you are, Angelique," Enchanter Clovicus said in a firm but kind voice. "Fairy godmothers and godfathers search the continent for children with magic to eliminate the possibility of anyone using them for dark purposes, and while there has been an increase in mages who have been sealed from their magic and exiled from the Conclave, there are none capable of this."

I know all of this! Angelique longed to scream, but she kept her mouth shut and stared blankly at the tray of food.

"As part of the investigation, I was informed of some confidential information," he continued. "It seems likely that the twelve magic users you saw are the only perpetrators. They are a small sect of black mages. Though the Conclave has been trying to track and capture them for a decade or two, it was never thought they were capable of something like this."

Obviously, the Conclave thought wrong! Angelique curled her hands into tight fists.

"The Council is in the process of making a declaration that will raise awareness, but the investigation squad believes it is unlikely the black mages will be able to catch another mage or enchanter like this."

"Isn't that the kind of thinking that led to Evariste getting captured?" Angelique bitterly asked.

"The Council has seen sects of black mages rise and fall, Angelique. Throughout history, there have been tragedies such as this one, but it depends upon us to pull through, recover Evariste, and secure a brighter future."

Unbidden, the King of Baris' words returned to Angelique. *"Two black mages working together is not necessarily unusual, but..."*

Angelique frowned as she considered the situation. *I have*

never heard of a magic user getting kidnapped besides in legends and stories. How could this happen?

"I don't fully agree with the Council, but they are in a difficult position." Clovicus hesitated. "But I wanted to ask you more about the attack. You said Evariste pulled you out of the way of the vermillion magic and shoved you through the portal, then closed it?"

"Yes." Angelique mechanically ate a piece of cheese, not tasting it, but chewing because her stomach was starting to feel better, and she *knew* she needed to eat.

"Did the spell spring at you because you were closer or because it was aimed at you?" Clovicus asked.

"I don't really know," Angelique said. "I have no idea what the spell actually did—though it must cause some kind of pain. Evariste looked..." She trailed off and stared at her hands as she recalled the grimace of Evariste's features as he shut the portal.

He's gone. Because he saved me.

"This is important, Angelique." Clovicus set his hand on her arm, making her look up. "*Think*. Was the spell meant for you specifically?"

"Does it matter?" Angelique asked.

"Yes." Clovicus folded his arms across his chest. "Because it goes from being an attack on a powerful magic user for unknown purposes to a specific attack that targets *you*."

"They might have targeted me because they thought I'd be the easier target as an apprentice."

"Not necessarily. You are close to making Lady Enchantress, and you pose a far greater threat to them—both with your magic type and your physical abilities." When Angelique frowned at him, Clovicus shrugged. "*I* certainly wouldn't have thought to headbutt any attackers as you described to me last night."

Angelique shifted uncomfortably in her chair.

"But can you think of anything that would indicate they were specifically after you?" Clovicus asked.

Angelique leaned back in her chair and took another roll. She passed it back and forth between her hands as she thought. "They converged on me, but I was the one who answered the door. And while they didn't leave the front hall to track down Evariste, I was doing a fairly good job of keeping them occupied. As for the spell, I can't say for certain. Evariste stepped between it and me and took the spell aimed at me. That's all I could tell."

Enchanter Clovicus scratched his jaw. "*You* don't think they were after you?"

"Not specifically, no."

He nodded, but the wrinkles on his forehead multiplied. "It still seems odd. Out of all magic users, why attack the Lord Enchanter with portal magic and his apprentice who could have stopped them with—"

He cut himself off before he could finish, but Angelique knew what he was thinking. It had occurred to her as well.

I could have killed them where they stood if I had used my core magic.

She hated her magic. She *never* wanted to use it. But Evariste, the only enchanter who had fought for her, was gone—because she was too slow at channeling and twisting her magic, because she refused to use her core abilities.

"Angelique, you did well," Clovicus said, shattering her thoughts. "You fought beside Evariste and held them off when other apprentices wouldn't have stood a chance. You also made it back from Verglas at an unforgiving speed. You cannot berate yourself over this."

"But I—"

"No," he interrupted her. "Evariste has been a full-fledged Lord Enchanter for years. If he couldn't overpower them, it is unreasonable to berate yourself. He wouldn't want that."

No. As angry and upset with me as he was, he didn't ask me to use my war magic.

"The investigation will continue. Other mages with varying specialties have been called in and will likely go through the house." Clovicus stood, only to meaningfully tap the breakfast tray. "I can make arrangements for you to stay here in the Veneno Conclave. Or—"

"I'd like to go home," Angelique said.

Clovicus raised his brows. "Back to the place where you were attacked?"

"I might be able to find something, and Roland..." Angelique swallowed thickly.

"Ahh, yes, your cat. I'm afraid the squadron saw no sign of him, either." Clovicus drummed his fingers on the table. "You are free to take the portal back to the house, but I want you to check in with me daily until we get this sorted out. I expect the Council will make a statement on it within a week or so. Do you agree?"

Angelique nodded. "Yes, Lord Enchanter."

Clovicus sighed and mashed his thumbs into his eyelids. "I'll send word to Sybilla. You can likely expect to see her soon. But before you go anywhere, I want you to finish eating."

Angelique considered objecting, but her stomach still growled, and she had a feeling that if she said anything, Clovicus would reconsider letting her go home.

I need to care for myself—which means making sure I don't collapse—or they'll never let me stay there.

Angelique sucked a breath of air in and eyed the tray before she bit into her slightly smushed rye roll.

And I need to be ready. When they figure out who took Evariste, I will go with the mages they send out to recover him—whether they want me to or not!

TRUE TO HIS WORD, Clovicus let Angelique return home after she finished eating.

When she stepped through the portal, mages still swarmed the house.

They had replaced the windows in the front salon and the front door and repaired the damage inflicted on the walls—though the furniture was still trashed.

While the mages performed spells and searched the woods surrounding the house, Angelique searched the house—*again*—this time looking for Roland.

After crawling through every room, she was forced to admit that the talking cat was nowhere to be found.

Why did I put that collar on him? He can't even call for help! Angelique groaned as she sat down in front of the fireplace in the workshop.

"Apprentice Angelique?"

"Yes?" Angelique twisted in time to see Lady Enchantress Lovelana clear the top step.

The beautiful enchantress carried a large wooden box, but she glanced curiously around the workshop. "Have you noticed anything missing—any materials or possessions that may have been stolen when Evariste was taken?"

"Besides my cat? No."

Enchantress Lovelana sighed. "I see." She glanced down at Angelique, who was sprawled out on the floor in front of the fireplace. She cleared her throat and asked a little awkwardly, "Are you all right?"

Angelique met her gaze. "Evariste is gone."

Enchantress Lovelana winced. "Yes. Well. I'll have more questions to ask you. I'm here to consult the mages investigating this matter. The Council wants to see if I—as an Enchantress—will notice something they missed."

"Oh," Angelique blinked in surprise.

Lovelana's core magic is healing. I would think someone like Clovicus would be a better choice for this.

"The squadron is still searching, but they came across this when they went through Evariste's room." The Lady Enchantress handed Angelique the wooden box.

"Thank you," Angelique dully said. She took the box and set it on the ground next to her.

"It's for you," Enchantress Lovelana added, "from Evariste."

Great. Now I want to look at it even less. It's probably from before our fight.

Enchantress Lovelana cleared her throat. "I read Enchanter Clovicus' report. You were very brave."

Angelique snorted.

"You were."

The sincerity in the other woman's voice made Angelique look up at her.

Enchantress Lovelana offered her a slightly stilted smile, but the set of her shoulders said she meant it. When she met Angelique's gaze, she awkwardly patted her on the shoulder. "We'll find him, Apprentice."

Angelique nodded miserably. "Thank you, Lady Enchantress."

Enchantress Lovelana nodded and looked away, then shifted slightly toward the steps.

Taking pity on her, Angelique added, "I'll go over the study and workshop—to confirm nothing has been stolen."

"Thank you, that would be a help. If you think of anything, please inform one of the mages, and they will call me." Enchantress Lovelana looked around the workshop, her eyes lingering on Evariste's and Angelique's desks—which, despite their argument—were pushed against one another. She nodded once, then swept down the stairs as softly as she had arrived.

Angelique sighed and glanced at the wooden box. *How did she know it was for me?*

Angelique folded her legs in front of her and reluctantly picked up the wooden box, sliding the cover off.

Inside the box was carefully folded cloth, with a letter placed on top.

Angelique furrowed her brow as she snagged the note and studied Evariste's familiar handwriting.

Angelique,
You will make a wonderful Lady Enchantress.
I'm proud to stand by your side and honored I was allowed to teach you magic.
You'll pass both examinations; I know it.

The letter brought tears to Angelique's eyes—not because of the contents, but because it proved just how kind Evariste was. And the last time they had really spoken, she had shouted and railed at him like a spoiled child.

Angelique groaned. "Why didn't I apologize like Roland told me to? Why did I let our disagreement drag on? Even if I didn't understand what made him so upset, I should have asked! Or done something—anything!"

She shut her eyes and shifted, pulling her legs up to her chest so she could rest her forehead on her knees. *I'm so hopeless.*

She felt a faint spark of magic—like a flickering flame. It took her a moment to realize it had come from the cloth still sitting in the box.

She rubbed her nose before rising to her feet and unfolding the fabric from the box.

It was a gown—possibly the most beautiful one she had ever seen. It was fitted through the waist and arms but had soft, beautiful skirts that fell in frothy layers. The off-shoulder neckline was embroidered with tiny, sparkling opals, as were the cuffs, which extended across the top of the hand in a V shape and had a loop to push over her middle finger.

But what was most spectacular about the dress, was the fabric—or perhaps the charms *placed* upon the fabric.

Even just feeling the sleeves, Angelique could tell it was charmed against heat, cold, dirt, and tears, and was spelled for durability. But as she gazed at it, the dress changed colors. It was a beautiful creamy white that was gradually turning a golden, champagne hue. From gold, it faded into a pale yellow, and then shifted to a faint pink.

It was a dress fit for an adored and renown Lady Enchantress. Not Angelique.

More than ever, Angelique felt like a fraud. Her teacher had held her in such esteem, and she hadn't valued it enough. And while she still hated her magic and couldn't imagine using it, a part of her knew. If she had just used it...or rather, if she had been better at turning it into *useful* magic...

She hung her head and slowly refolded the gown, carefully replacing it in the box. *I'm sorry, Evariste. So sorry.*

CHAPTER 32

Angelique shifted impatiently. It took a great deal of effort to keep from tapping her foot on the ground as she waited for the Council to give their official statement on Evariste.

Sybilla kindly patted her hand and offered her a smile. "It won't be long, dear," she promised.

"Don't make promises you have no control over," Clovicus said dryly. He sat on Angelique's other side, his arms folded across his broad chest and his eyes narrowed.

Sybilla shot him a look, then adjusted her glasses. "Ignore the grump," she advised. "He's still young and petulant."

Given how enchanters lived such long lives—and that Clovicus already appeared to be in his early forties—Angelique imagined not many would dare call him "young."

Clovicus seemed to agree, for he barked a chord of laughter.

Angelique smiled faintly, but her eyes were focused on the Council Members, who were taking their seats.

I never thought I would so eagerly return to Hallowed Hall. But at least now I'm just part of the audience.

The seating area meant for observers was *packed*. Even though the only lights in the room were pointed at the Council Members and the mages who stood before them—the investigation team that had crawled around Wistful Thicket for two weeks before finally reporting back to the Conclave—it was still hot from the sheer number of magic users packed in the hall.

Angelique imagined the crowd was mostly due to Evariste's popularity, but she saw several concerned faces—like Mage Finnr and one of Stil's old craft magic instructors. They had likely come out of concern for the community as a whole, not just because they knew Evariste.

When the Council Members were all seated, Enchanter Crest—the youngest of them—cleared his throat.

The hushed whispers and murmurs of the audience quieted down, and Angelique clutched the sides of her wooden chair.

"Today we, the members of the Council, who provide guidance and serve as leaders in the Veneno Conclave, are to give our ruling over the attack and kidnapping of Lord Enchanter Evariste of the Fire Gates," Lord Enchanter Crest began.

Angelique swallowed thickly and leaned forward, waiting with bated breath.

"Unfortunately, a thorough investigation has not revealed much or given us any hope." Enchantress Felicienne's brows were slanted with sincere pain as she looked from her fellow Council Members to the investigating mages. "We have been unable to uncover much beyond affirming the testimony of Apprentice Angelique, enchantress-in-training."

"Lord Enchanter Evariste was taken from his home by a group of powerful renegade magic users," Enchanter Tristisim rumbled. "They used illegal black magic, presumedly binding his powers."

"We have no information—besides Apprentice Angelique's word and the magical remnants of their spells—that gives us any idea of their capabilities or number," Enchantress Galendra said.

Enchantress Primrose's lower lip trembled with feeling, and

her eyes were glazed with tears. "While the disappearance of Lord Enchanter Evariste of the Fire Gates is a terrible thing, we unfortunately must foremost focus on the capture of those who kidnapped him—before they strike again."

Angelique clenched her jaw but held her peace. *I had expected as much—those black mages pose a rather dark threat. They need to be dealt with—but when they are caught, we'll find Evariste.*

"With the matter as grave as it is, we have decided to set up a committee," Enchanter Crest announced. "The committee will be responsible for researching the spells we believe were used on Evariste, discussing our options in tracking the black mages, and authorizing mages to investigate leads and facts."

"They will also create and circulate reports on their findings," Enchanter Galendra said, "to keep all members of the Veneno Conclave updated and to issue warnings of potential dangers."

"To aid them in their goal, the committee will be granted priority access to all Conclave library materials, manpower, and needed magical charms," Enchantress Primrose added.

Angelique frowned slightly as she listened. *This sounds very good and all, but where is the action? Don't things need to move more quickly? It's already been weeks, and if we give these black mages enough time to regroup, what else will they do?*

Enchanter Lazare waggled his cane back and forth as he squinted at the investigative team. "The Committee will begin their responsibilities by investigating several reports of black mage activities—including one uncovered by Lord Enchanter Evariste himself in the city of Fillia."

WHAT? Angelique stiffened. *We took care of the black mages in Fillia years ago! They can't honestly think they'll find any new leads there!*

"We will announce all members of the committee at a future date, but Enchantress Lovelana—who consulted for the investigation—has agreed to be involved, which is a great boon considering her power and position."

"Evariste's capture was a terrible tragedy." Enchantress Primrose wiped a tear from her eye as she spoke. "We failed to protect him. And while we shall continue the search for him, we will do our best to see to the safety of all mages."

The other Council Members bowed their heads, then stood.

"That's it?" Angelique asked. She looked from Sybilla to Enchanter Clovicus. "That's all they plan to do?"

Sybilla scowled, but Enchanter Clovicus furrowed his brow. "Angelique," he started.

Angelique stood so fast, she toppled her chair. She wove through the audience members, then ran when she exited the seating area. "Wait!" she shouted.

The Council Members paused, tilting their heads as Angelique sprinted into the light, almost flattening one of the mages on the investigation team. "That's all you're going to do?" she asked.

Felicienne's gaze hardened, but Primrose shook her head at the other Enchantress, then smiled sadly at Angelique. "This is a massive undertaking, Angelique. While I am confident we will be able to free Evariste, we must use all due diligence and stamp out the black mages responsible for this."

"But Evariste and I encountered black mages in Fillia *years* ago —and those mages are *dead*! Going there won't improve any understanding of the situation!"

"Quite the contrary, Apprentice," Enchanter Tristisim rumbled. "The attack on you and your Master was the first act of violence from a black mage on an enchanter in decades. The matter must be thoroughly investigated, as it might reveal a wealth of information about the black mages and their goal."

But it won't, because both of those mages are DEAD and wouldn't have been able to help kidnap Evariste! And if it was so important, why didn't you do it YEARS ago!?

Enchantress Felicienne must have sensed some of Angelique's rage, for she frowned and narrowed her eyes. "I understand you are disappointed that you will not be able to take your examination and evaluation to be made into an Enchantress until Evariste is recovered—"

WHAT? Angelique gaped at the enchantress, horrified and shocked. *That's what they think I'm upset about? Just how terrible is her opinion of me?*

"But," the enchantress continued, "we must prioritize catching and containing the black mages first."

"I don't care about my test!" Angelique shouted. "I'm more concerned about what will happen to Evariste while the committee deliberates which lead should get the greatest amount of manpower! Can't you send a team to search for and free him while another focuses on the black mages?"

"Angelique," Enchantress Primrose said, her voice soft and sad. "I understand your feelings, but I'm sorry. We must also consider the safety of *all* magic users."

Angelique shook her head. *I can't believe this—he's a Lord Enchanter!* "But—"

"Enough," Enchanter Tristisim said. "If you have any complaints, take them to the committee."

Angelique looked from Enchanter Tristisim to Enchanter Crest, Enchantress Primrose, Enchantress Galendra, Enchantress Felicienne, and ended with Enchanter Lazare.

The ancient enchanter tapped his cane on the floor and said nothing.

Angelique glared and lifted her chin, but before she could open her mouth, Enchanter Clovicus was at her side.

"Steady, Apprentice," he murmured. "Lest you say something that gets you in trouble."

"I assume that is all," Enchanter Tristisim said. "Good day, Apprentice."

Angelique shivered with fury as the Council Members left Hallowed Hall, leaving the murmurs of the observers behind them.

"How?" Angelique asked. "How can they do this?"

Sybilla joined her with a sigh. "It's a tricky path all leaders walk. And attempting to get any plan moving swiftly with an organization as large as the Veneno Conclave is difficult. *However*, I agree with you. That they are sinking all efforts into stamping out the black mages and plan to do nothing for Evariste is a poor choice."

"His portal magic would be a help in sniffing down mages," Clovicus agreed. He scratched his jaw as he watched Enchantress Lovelana pick her way through the investigative team.

"Lord Enchanter Clovicus, Fairy Godmother Sybilla, Apprentice Angelique," Lovelana said.

Angelique—being of lower rank—forced herself to curtsey. "Lady Enchantress," she muttered.

"I will do my best to look for Evariste," Lovelana said. Though she addressed Clovicus and Sybilla, she glanced briefly at Angelique, including her in the vow. "He is my dear friend. I will not rest until I find him."

"What will you do?" Sybilla asked.

"My role will primarily keep me here in the Conclave, so I can receive reports and continue the research on the spells we believe the black mages may have used." Lovelana slightly pursed her lips. "In fact, I plan to ransack the Conclave library next."

That's great. But none of this is going to find Evariste! Angelique wanted to scream.

"You cannot be more...proactive?" Clovicus asked.

Lovelana blushed slightly and demurely looked down. "Unfortunately, my core magic is not conducive to fieldwork that may include combat. But if we find any black mages, I can be a bigger help."

Only if they're brought in alive.

Sybilla adjusted her glasses. "I'm sure you'll do your best."

Clovicus merely shrugged, but Lovelana didn't seem to notice their reaction as she nodded to herself. "If any of you hear any news of the black mages, please let me know."

Unable to stand it any longer, Angelique curtsied. "If you'll excuse me," she muttered before she stormed from Hallowed Hall as quickly as she could.

If I stay here a moment longer, I'm going to scream!

"Angelique!"

Though she heard Clovicus call after her, Angelique kept marching.

Within a few moments, the older enchanter caught up with her, easily matching her pace. "You're going back home?"

Angelique glanced up at him. "What else is there for me to do? As there is no search party for Evariste, I cannot offer aid. The Council Members might have a heart palpitation if I asked to be included in the *committee*." She was unable to keep the frustration out of her voice as she navigated the hallways, making her way to Evariste's office.

Clovicus ignored the challenge. "I want you to know you can come to me—despite whatever you do in the future—and I will help you."

Angelique squinted as she tried to puzzle through his offer. "What do you mean?"

"It's just a hunch," Clovicus said, failing to offer any more information.

Angelique forced her expression to clear and put on a mask of calmness. "Thank you for the generous offer, Lord Enchanter. I am honored you would think to help me."

"I suspect, Angelique, it will actually be the opposite. Nonetheless, you are my student's apprentice. I'll do whatever I can to support you, understood?"

Despite her confusion brought on by the enchanter's words, Angelique nodded. "Thank you, Enchanter Clovicus," she repeated.

Clovicus nodded, but he stopped when they reached a T-intersection in the hallway, and Angelique turned right. "Good luck, Apprentice," he called.

"Thank you, Enchanter Clovicus," Angelique called.

She could have *sworn* she heard him say, "It seems we shall see if Evariste was right about you." But when she turned around, Clovicus was strolling in the opposite direction, too far away to be within her hearing range.

CHAPTER 33

Three days passed, leaving Angelique utterly alone in Evariste's house.

With the damage now completely repaired, the attack almost seemed like a bad dream...except Evariste wasn't there.

Angelique stared at the salon wall. While the windows to Farset and Baris flickered with magic, she stared at the bare spot on the wall where the Verglas window had once been. "Where are you, Evariste?" she whispered.

His absence left a hole in the house.

No magical animals had showed up since he had been taken. And previously, the place always held the faint twinkle of his magic. Now it was still and lonely.

Angelique sighed and scratched her neck. "They'll find him," she told herself.

If only she believed it.

While the Veneno Conclave's actions were perhaps logical, it painted a grim picture of Evariste's future.

He's a legend, and no one is looking for him.

Angelique sighed and made her way upstairs. The unnatural

stillness of a house that had always previously brimmed with magic and comings and goings felt eerie.

When she entered her bedroom, the sight of the spelled gown mocked her.

Unable to leave it in the box but unwilling to put it on, Angelique had hung it up on the door of her armoire.

She curled her hands into fists and wanted to growl.

He believed in me, and I failed him. Because of me, he was taken. I might never have a chance to apologize for our fight or to thank him for all he has done.

Angelique wanted to scream or shout.

Evariste had rescued her from being sealed and had given her the chance to become an enchantress. Yes, he infuriated her with his insistence that her war magic was wonderful, but he was also the first magic user to extend a hand to her since the depth and horror of her powers had been revealed, and the first to really teach her how to use her magic.

Her eyes strayed back to the dress.

Evariste gave me a new life...and then shielded me with his.

He was a legend. And in the hour he most needed help, the Conclave was abandoning him.

Deep in her soul, Angelique felt her magic shift, and the last chain of her patience snapped.

"I'm not waiting for a *committee* to save him," she whispered, her voice a hardened vow. "I'll find him myself."

A lopsided smile—one she never dared show because it made her look all too dark for most magic users' sensibilities—lingered on her lips. She stalked to her armoire, removing her usual traveling cloak—the white and purple one edged with coins that matched Evariste's.

With its charmed pockets, it was an easy thing to slip several different purses of coins into her cloak.

I don't need clothes—I can always magic up some simple ones. I have enough money I should be able to pay for food and passage. But what do I need...papers. I need to be able to prove my position.

She left her room and rushed upstairs to the workshop, struggling to form plans and organize her thoughts at the same time.

She reached the workshop and started digging through the chests around Evariste's desk. "Where do I begin my search for him?" she wondered as she flipped open a chest, shutting it again when she saw it only held glittering jewels.

Both the Council and the Investigative team confirmed there were no leads here, but aren't there magical means of finding people?

She paused, her hand on another chest, when the thought struck her. "Loire. They have the magic mirror Evariste and I authenticated years ago."

There were other magic mirrors, of course—Evariste himself had told her as much. But those that she knew of were all owned by other magic users, who likely would *not* support her self-appointed task.

"Loire it is. And here we go!" Angelique smiled when she flipped open a spelled chest that held important papers, including several documents that cited Angelique as Evariste's apprentice.

Her smile dimmed when she saw the flourish of his signature.

I'm just a lowly apprentice...how can I even try this when he deserves so much more?

She looked at his desk, remembering the afternoons he had spent patiently tutoring her, the monster no one else wanted.

Lowly or not, I have to try.

Angelique started for the stairs but paused halfway across the room. Again, she turned around and stared back at his desk.

"There," Angelique started, stopping when she realized the soft timidity in her voice was the only thing breaking the stillness of the house. She swallowed and licked her lips. "There is one thing I could do...that might make this a bit more fair."

The reason why she had failed Evariste was because she hadn't unwound and twisted her magic fast enough. She could fix that...if she released it.

It was too dangerous to use in its raw form, but if she let it flow through her like most mages did, instead of keeping it locked up and strangled...

Slowly, she walked back to her desk and set the needed papers on the wooden surface. She started to sit down in her chair before changing her mind.

No, I might damage something. She moved away and instead sat down on the plush carpet in front of the fireplace.

"No one is here," Angelique told herself, "not a living creature besides myself. I can't hurt anybody."

Her hands shook, and she couldn't hear anything besides the throbbing of her heart. *This is insane. I can't do this. It's too dangerous.* She almost stood up and walked away, but she glanced at the desks and remembered.

Angelique took several deep breaths and felt for her magic.

It was pushed down deep inside of her, so she could barely feel the faintest hints of it. Trying to find it was like looking into the yawning black hole of a cavern and knowing a beast lurked in the shadows.

She felt the mental chains she had put on her magic, and something in her trembled.

I'm not letting it go, she told herself. *And I'm certainly not going to use it. But never again will I let someone sacrifice their life for mine. Never again will I let darkness take a person I care about.*

Angelique exhaled and released the bindings.

Instantly, her magic flooded the area with such force it rocked the house. Papers were tossed into the air, and all the magical spells Evariste had placed on the house roared to life. Flashes of silver filled her vision, and the flooring rattled as the candelabras shook.

She shut her eyes tight as magic coursed through her veins, filling her with the intoxicating promise of power. The pressure her magic brought made it hard to breathe. She felt like she was gasping for breath as it pushed against her in a simultaneously sharp and cold sensation.

Instead of strangling it and shoving it back like she usually did, Angelique held on, praying it would settle and that it wouldn't bring the house down on her, hoping that this terrible power of hers would be good for *something*.

For a strange, disconcerting moment, Angelique felt her magic settle inside her, stretching in its newfound freedom.

Carefully, Angelique opened her eyes. The world felt *different* with her magic swirling freely around her—brighter, in a way.

She stood and carefully gathered her letter from the new mess, then hurried down the stairs. She flicked up the hood of her cloak as she stalked down the hallway, banging out the front door. She shut the door behind her, briefly pressing her palm into the wood, which made a magical symbol flare, locking the house tight.

Angelique jogged across the bridge.

First, I'll need to purchase a horse. There's a village not a far walk from here; I'll get there before dark. And from there, to Loire.

At the edge of the yard, Angelique glanced back at the house and staggered in surprise.

The bright orb of magic that hovered at the apex of the roof was no longer colored blue, but silver.

"I'll find him," Angelique promised. "I won't stop until he's freed. No matter what I have to do. I may only be an enchantress-in-training, but I *won't* give up. I will not cease searching—a war mage never forgets."

Her cloak snapped in the fresh breeze. Her gaze steely, Angelique raised her chin. "Wherever you are, Evariste, I *promise*. I'll find you."

"You were supposed to get the GIRL!"

Evariste groaned. Every muscle in his body ached. His head sagged on his neck, but most worrisome was the gaping hole that was his magic.

It wasn't that his magic was blocked, but rather that he couldn't feel it at all. It was a numbness in his soul.

But even though he couldn't feel it, he was aware of something eating away at him, leeching on the magic his soul radiated.

Dimly, he was aware of the argument taking place nearby.

"We tried; he shoved her through a portal and closed it behind her. What else could we have done?"

"You could have gone after her, you nitwit!"

"He put her in Verglas—we would have died if we chased her there!"

"Don't you realize you've ruined everything?"

"We did not. We already cursed the elves. With the legendary Evariste as our power source, we won't have a problem carrying out the rest of the attacks."

"No—instead you've let the only magic user who may be capable of stopping our army run *loose*!"

Angelique, Evariste realized. *They're talking about Angelique.*

THE END

For free Apprentice of Magic extras and short stories, visit kmshea.com!

THE DUKE'S NEW CLOTHES

Angelique shifted in her side saddle and worked to keep a genteel smile on her face. Her horse—a buckskin gelding—plodded steadily after Evariste and his gray mount.

For the sake of the event they were attending, Evariste had nudged Angelique into one of her fancier dresses—a white gown with wine red lace and heart shaped embroidery. Her horse was dressed to match—the blanket beneath her side saddle as well as the animal's barding were white with matching red embroidery.

But Angelique had the pesky feeling they were overdressed, particularly given the state of the land they passed through.

She narrowed her eyes as she looked out at fields of stunted crops that were quite obviously wilting. On the other side of the pothole-riddled road was a fenced pasture that held a herd of five bony horses. The grass was chewed to the dirt. The wooden fence posts were half rotted, and the stable just beyond it fared little better.

This is not a prosperous land.

It was surprising, considering they were riding through a dukedom in Loire—the most powerful country on the continent.

Angelique pressed her lips together and glanced at Evariste's back, wondering if she dared to ask him about the state of the fields.

Her horse snorted and shook his head, ridding himself of a fly.

"We have almost arrived," Evariste called over his shoulder. "The duke's chateau should be visible after we pass that thicket of trees." He pointed to a small woods ahead of them and twisted in the saddle so he could smile at her.

Angelique blinked owlishly. Between the sunlight, Evariste's brilliant smile, and his white clothes, it was a little hard to hold his gaze. (He wore white trousers and a fancy jacket, which of course had red embroidery to match Angelique's—though his hearts were more of a dark burgundy color.)

"Is everything alright?" he asked when she didn't respond.

"It's fine!" Angelique said with a sunny voice. "It is merely... you said it is a *duke* we are here for, yes?"

Evariste nodded. "He's throwing a rather extravagant party for his birthday."

How extravagant can it be when his lands are in shambles? Aloud, she asked, "Isn't attending his birthday party a little too close to a political move?"

"It toes the line," Evariste admitted. "If it weren't for you, I would never have accepted the job, but as you need experience our presence will not be viewed with the same scrutiny. The Veneno Conclave understands this."

But do they really?

Angelique kept her skepticism to herself, and instead made a noise of approval. She glanced back to the countryside and frowned, watching a farmer attempt to hack at a patch of dry, hardened dirt with a chipped hoe.

"Officially, the job is for you to create a set of illusionary clothes for the duke to wear tonight for the entirety of his celebration," Evariste said.

The way he phrased the directions made Angelique sit up. "Officially? Is there unofficial business I am expected to conduct?"

Evariste held his horse back for a moment or two so he could ride shoulder to shoulder with her.

He smiled again—but it wasn't his charming or brilliant grin. Instead, it was dangerously close to a smirk. "There is no unofficial business, but at all times we should be aware of our duties as magic users."

"We are to guard the continent from magic, and aid those in need," Angelique recited. The temperature cooled as the road meandered between the trees, shading them from the sun.

Evariste nodded. "Yes, and?"

Recalling the brat-who-cried-wolf from Boyne, Angelique added, "At times we might find it necessary to teach folk moral lessons."

"Exactly," Evariste said with great satisfaction. His smile turned warm again. "As long as you remember that, you will do splendidly."

Angelique was not so convinced, but she managed to hide it behind a false smile. It dropped from her lips, however, a few moments later when they emerged from the small forest, revealing the duke's home.

It was built more like a small castle than a proper chateau as it was three floors of sparkling white stone with a red tiled roof, four towers that Angelique could see, and a lush green yard with bushes trimmed to resemble animals.

A giant fountain with an obnoxious gold sculpture of a man—the duke, most likely—was plopped in the middle of the road—which switched from dirt to cobblestone the moment they crossed the green lawn.

His vast lands struggle to survive, and this *is how his home looks?*

She glanced at Evariste.

For once he wasn't smiling, but was surveying the chateau. His unusual colored eyes were half shut and his expressive lips were straight. "Yes," Evariste said. "This evening will be an excellent experience for you...and the duke, too."

THE DUKE—OR, His Grace, Duc Hubert of Aube—was in his wardrobe room when Evariste and Angelique arrived, and it was there he stayed as his valet escorted Angelique and Evariste to him.

"Thierry," Duke Hubert called to his valet in a voice of exaggerated sadness. "Thierry, you have failed me. I have nothing to wear, I shall be forced to meet magical greatness in a *robe*."

His voice became more audible when the valet led Angelique and Evariste inside the "wardrobe."

The room was easily the size of the workshop back at Evariste's house, and clothes hung from rods fastened to the walls, from wires hung from the ceiling, and were tossed in great mounds that so cluttered the floor it was difficult to navigate.

Angelique lifted her skirts to step over a shoe ornamented with a large blue bow and ducked to avoid getting an apple green cape in her face.

"Your Grace, Lord Enchanter Evariste and his apprentice, enchantress-in-training Angelique, have arrived," the valet announced.

"Come in!" Duke Hubert called. "Come in—and you can see why I so badly need your help!"

Angelique and Evariste stepped around the last pile of clothes and found the duke dressed in a brocade robe and perched on a spindly footstool.

Duke Hubert was a short, skinny man who vaguely reminded Angelique of a drenched cat. His eyes bulged a little—from emotion—and his wispy goatee made his already pointed chin appear downright angular. (And he shook. With disdain, likely, but still. Angelique suspected she could have broken the man in half—*without* using her magic.)

The duke flung his arms up and motioned to the piles of cloth that surrounded him. "It's terrible, simply *terrible*! I am a fashion setter. All Loire nobles are *green* with envy over my brilliant taste and beautiful clothes. But alas, I have *nothing* that can contain my glorious self!" He sighed with great melancholy.

Angelique had to smile. If she opened her mouth, she'd give him a tongue lashing. *How can he complain about his lavish clothes while his lands are on the brink of starvation? Or did he push them to this stage as a result of his thirst for luxuries?*

"We read as much in the letter you attached to the work details," Evariste said, his voice melodious and smooth.

Angelique didn't know how he managed to be polite—she wanted to squeeze the duke for his excess until his eyes popped more than they already did.

"Then you will help me!" The duke imperiously stated.

"Angelique will provide you with the magic you require this evening." Evariste took her hand and bowed over it like a knight honoring his lady. "I am here for her support."

Angelique curtsied when the duke peered at her—though she was distracted when Evariste raised her hand towards his lips and spent most of her attention on discreetly yanking her appendage free. "It will be my...duty, Duke Hubert," she said, lacking any better description. (Because it *certainly* wasn't her honor!)

Duke Hubert stood and tried to look down his nose at her, but she was so much taller than him, he instead had to crank his neck to meet her eyes.

"I expect *magnificent* clothes," he said. "Made of cloth from the likes of which no one has seen!"

Angelique dipped her head. "Understood, however, I must remind you the clothes will be an illusion. It is not an outfit you will be able to keep."

Duke Hubert scoffed. "Of course—that is why I sought to hire a *mage*! I must have an outfit so *glorious*, no one will have anything like it, nor will they be able to reproduce it. I shall wear sheer *power* this evening!"

His propensity to emphasize words was starting to grate on Angelique's nerves, but she kept smiling.

Duke Hubert rubbed his scraggy facial hair and studied her. "It will be even *more* valuable given that an enchantress-in-training is performing the spell. Though I should like it more if you were an *official* Lady Enchantress." He swung around to face Evariste. "Can you not be convinced, Lord Enchanter, to do the spell in place of your pupil?"

"I must reject your request, Duke Hubert." Evariste's polite smile didn't so much as flicker.

"I'll double the price," the duke offered.

The Lord Enchanter shook his head. "Angelique needs the practice, and to do such a thing would forsake my vow of impartiality when it comes to politics."

The duke rolled his eyes and planted his fists on his hips. "Magic is *wasted* on you upper mages. None of you seek to use you powers in a *useful* way—you could make peasants bow before you! But never mind, the work of an apprentice shall be good enough for tonight—as long as she makes a good show! Now, as for what I wish to wear..."

This is not just greed, but a power move, Angelique realized as she listened to the man rail on. *He means to inflate his ego and show off his grandeur—that he has the money to hire an enchantress-in-training to weave a spell for him for a single night.*

Her smile twitched for a moment as she recalled the broken duchy she had ridden through. *His vanity and pride spring from a source that will only bring ruin.*

She watched as he yammered on while he picked up a dark blue cape and pointed to the fancy jewel buttons before thoughtlessly tossing it on the ground. He stepped on it as he yanked a waistcoat from a hook on the wall.

Unfortunately, it will be his lands that suffer. He needs to be taught better. But who...

"It should sparkle in the candle-light, perhaps in this shade of plum—"

"If you'll forgive the interruption," Angelique smoothly cut in. "But if you truly wish for a magnificent outfit, as the magic user responsible for the spell I must insist on being given full creative rein."

Duke Hubert frowned. "Why?"

Angelique's lips curled up in a smile that had a predatory gleam she couldn't quite hide. "No one knows my abilities as a mage better than I—and I know the spells available to me as well. I can create clothes beyond your wildest imagination. And tonight, I will do *just that*."

"Oh." The duke blinked, then grudgingly nodded. "I suppose that's true. But if I am not satisfied, you shall have to improve upon them!"

"Worry not, Duke Hubert," Angelique promised. "I will make you the clothes you so dearly deserve."

"THE TIME HAS *ARRIVED*!" Duke Hubert swept out of his bathroom and scuttled across his dressing room, wearing a new robe—this one made of crimson velvet. "The guests have been greeted, I have washed, you must now *dress* me!"

Angelique had been busy staring at the mounds of clothes cluttering up the room, but turned to face the bossy noble.

She watched as he started to throw the robe off his skinny shoulders before Evariste placed a hand over her eyes.

"Um?" she said.

"*Duke Hubert*," Evariste's normally cheerful voice was smoky with anger. "Though she is fulfilling a job, my pupil is a *lady*. You will act and treat her according to her station, and will not sully her eyes. Put. On. A. Shirt."

"My apologies," Duke Hubert gulped.

Evariste must look quite fierce to get that sort of response.

But Angelique was not surprised to see that, after he removed his hand from her eyes, his sunny smile was back in place.

Figures.

She glanced at the duke, who was studiously avoiding eye contact with her as he stood in black stockings and a white dressing shirt that was several sizes too big.

Evariste patted her on the shoulder. "Good luck, Apprentice." He smiled, then edged backwards, joining Duke Hubert's valet in standing by the entrance. There he slightly tipped his head as he watched her.

How perfectly splendid—and not at all worrisome! Angelique eyed the duke, attempting to disguise her dislike of the man. *But I had better perform well—or I'll hear from the Conclave, I'm sure, when Evariste's monthly report goes out.*

Angelique set her shoulders and put a smile on her lips. "It will take just a moment so I can get a proper measure of you." She strolled in a circle around the knobby-kneed duke.

"Of course!" Duke Hubert puffed up his chest, straining to stand as tall as possible.

As Angelique walked, she reached deep within herself and released the tiniest stream of magic. She carefully unwound it, measuring out only what she thought she would need before corking up the trickle and shoving her magic down again.

Her silvery magic splashed across her fingers as she twisted it, transforming it from the sharp, icy feel of her core magic into a delicate illusion spell.

Her magic wrapped around the duke, and though she had changed it, its core state must have still poked through, for Duke Hubert shivered and hunched his shoulders when it brushed him.

Angelique furrowed her brow in concentration as she directed her magic, building the base of the outfit. Ruffled cuffs and collar appeared, before a stiff red doublet reinforced with boning enfolded his torso.

Silk breeches the same red as the doublet puffed around his thighs and gathered at the knees. An elaborately embroidered slashed leather jerkin slipped over the top of his doublet, and Angelique finished the look with a wide-brimmed black cap.

Though the clothes appeared solid, Angelique continued with the illusion, adding sparkles and fancy swirls to the doublet and jerkin, and a fancy feather to the cap.

It's a shame this is only an illusion, and not alteration magic. She thought as she added a thick, jeweled necklace of rubies. *An illusion only looks real, alteration changes something—for as long as I pour magic into it anyway. If I merely altered some of his clothes I could have made them itchy and too small. For he certainly deserves some discomfort for his terrible management of his duchy.*

"Thierry! A mirror," the duke demanded.

His valet carefully carried a full-length mirror, setting it down in front of him. He bowed before he scuttled off, but the duke took no notice as he admired himself in the mirror.

"Very fine." Duke Hubert again puffed up his chest. "I look *magnificent*, indeed! Clothes *worthy* of me and of this very fortunate evening—they display my excellent taste and station!"

Angelique bit her cheek to keep from glaring at the man.

She blinked as she watched him, carefully keeping her expression even. *And now, time for the second part of this job—the self-appointed part, rather.*

She glanced at Evariste, but he was involved in a conversation with the valet, and wasn't even looking her way anymore.

Angelique smirked as she drifted closer to the duke. *It's entirely my duty,* she thought. *After all, Evariste has frequently reminded me our position might require us to deal out moral lessons.*

"You do cut a fine figure," Angelique said in a sing-song tone. "But I think I can do something more for you. You intend to give a speech to your esteemed guests, do you not?"

"Indeed, I shall!" The duke declared.

"How perfect," Angelique said. "At the height of your speech I will perform a *special* piece of magic, one that will perfectly reveal how worthy you are of your station, a spell that only the most intelligent of folk will be able to see."

"*Truly?*" the duke asked.

"Yes," Angelique promised. "And when they see it, the eyes of your people shall be opened."

Hopefully it won't forever mentally scar them.

"Excellent, I approve of this artistic direction, mage...mage," he repeated, apparently having already forgot her name.

Angelique's smile turned true. "It will be my pleasure."

ANGELIQUE BIT HER LOWER LIP, fighting back the impulse to yawn. *Why is it that whenever someone thinks highly of themselves, they talk incessantly and are great bores?*

The Duke stood on a stone staircase that abutted the back side of his chateau, delivering his rambling speech to a group of barely-listening nobles, dressed in bright and glittering clothes.

The party was starting outside, where candles lined stone walking paths and blooming hedges walled in the courtyard area that was to serve as the first location for the evening's merry making.

(The party would, Angelique had been told, move indoors for dinner and end the night in the ballroom.)

Servants skulked around the edges of the courtyard, adding more candles and silently presenting guests with refreshments.

Angelique stood with Enchanter Evariste and Thierry—Duke Hubert's valet—off to the side of the courtyard, visible but apart from the rest of the party attendees.

She busied herself with brushing off the skirts of her white and red gown as she listened to the duke prattle on.

"Thank you all for attending this celebration of *me*—the Duc of Aube. It is my greatest delight to host this birthday celebration, to welcome friends and family alike to view the *splendor* of my duchy and join me in merry making and joy."

Angelique pursed her lips, caught between anger and worry. *If I go through with this...am I overstepping my boundaries as a magic user? Teaching Duke Puffed-Up a lesson* could *be interpreted as a political move after all.*

Her gaze was momentarily drawn to Thierry. The lanky young man had a bright smile, but the angles of his face were enunciated, and he appeared leaner than a man of his age should.

The rest of the servants ghosting around the edges of the party were of a similar state—skinny and tired-looking.

But the nail in the coffin was the so-called "splendid duchy."

That afternoon—while Duke Hubert had greeted his guests—Thierry had taken Evariste and Angelique on a mini tour of the best lands in the duchy. All of the greenest places—the only fields that had *not* been over grazed, and the lushest forests filled with any sort of wild game—were for the duke's exclusive use. (He had taken the best field and turned it into a circuit for horse races, and an archery range for his guests.)

Duke Hubert had a lot of money—it was undeniable—but it was obvious he had earned so much in a short amount of time by neglecting his lands and failing to invest any back into his property and staff.

It's a quick path to ruin that he's on, and he'll drag his duchy down with him. No, political or not, I've got to do something. Particularly since I can use the excuse of a lowly apprentice mishandling a spell. Evariste might be a bit disappointed, but I don't think the Conclave could exile me over an 'accident.' At least one that involves illusion magic, and not my core magic.

Her mind made up, Angelique straightened and listened to the duke's speech with the intensity of a wolf listening for prey.

She tuned in at the perfect time, for he glanced in her direction, giving her a significant look.

That's my cue.

Angelique released a tendril of her magic, and prepared to change her illusion spell.

"To showcase my remarkable taste, I have arranged an evening of luxuries of the like you have never seen before," Duke Hubert boasted. "May it prove to you—and reflect—the superior taste of the Duchy of Aube, the worthiness of *my* character, and the nobility of my family!"

He threw his arms wide and Angelique gestured, using her magic...to cut the illusion spell the duke wore, shattering it so his fine clothes were gone, leaving the duke in his undershirt and black stockings.

At first, the duke didn't appear to notice. He was gloating, his smile so big it was almost a grimace.

His noble peers however, certainly saw.

A number of ladies dropped their feather ornamented fans, mouths fell open everywhere, and Angelique heard the telltale chime of crystal breaking—dropped chalices for certain.

The duke's servants, had a very different reaction.

More than one of them slapped a hand over their mouths to keep from laughing. Their eyes bulged, and they—knowing the magic user behind the spell—yanked their gazes from Duke Hubert to Angelique.

Angelique delicately placed a hand on her cheek. "Oh my," she said in false horror, her eyes wide. "I have terribly bungled this!"

The duke finally appeared to realize something was wrong, for he looked down at his chest and his eyes nearly popped out of his head. He made a loud squeaking noise and his face turned red with anger.

Angelique slightly angled herself to the side so Evariste wouldn't be able to view her expression head on. In doing so she was able to meet Duke Hubert's gaze, and she dropped her expression of horror.

Instead she raised an eyebrow and looked from the duke to his undershirt, then mouthed the words "how worthy you are of your station."

Duke Hubert went from bright red to an ashen pallor, perfectly grasping what she was trying to get at.

Her spell had revealed just how worthy he was...and had found him wanting.

With some help from me, of course.

Angelique met his gaze for several moments, until the duke went back to awkwardly staring out at his guests.

Sensing it was time for the moral lesson to end—lest she go *too* far—she turned back to Evariste. She blinked her eyes, giving the appearance of tears of regret—although really they were more tears born from holding back the great guffaws of laughter she wanted to release. "I'm so sorry, Enchanter Evariste—I-I will make amends!"

Angelique snapped her still waiting magic into place, reconstructing the broken illusion in moments.

Clothes reappeared on the startled duke, but he didn't so easily recover his bravado. Instead he brushed his doublet and cleared his throat. "Ahem, yes. Let the celebration begin," he weakly said.

His guests murmured as they finally recovered their air of sophistication. Every eye was on him as he hurried down the stairs.

Thierry coughed several times, covering what suspiciously sounded like a chuckle before he turned to Angelique and Evariste. "If you'll excuse me, Lord Enchanter, Lady Enchantress, I believe His Grace may need my help." He bowed and hurried off.

"I'm not an...enchantress," Angelique finished even though it became apparent Thierry wasn't stopping to hear her correction. She frowned—which transformed into a smile when she watched Duke Hubert cling to Thierry's arm.

Yes, that might not have fixed anything, but with luck it at least planted a thought.

"That was a very smooth—and quick—recovery!" Evariste praised.

Angelique almost jumped in her shoes, having forgotten about his presence. "Thank you, but it was very shameful I dropped it." She made a show of biting her lip and glanced at the duke. "I shall redouble my efforts to keep the spell stable for the rest of the evening!" She then bowed her head to the Lord Enchanter. "I am sorry for failing you," she added in real honesty.

I don't like to let Evariste down, but I don't regret it. This one instance, anyway.

"Accidents happen," Evariste said serenely. He took Angelique's hand and briefly patted it before releasing her and clasping his hands behind his back. "You're an apprentice. It is expected you would make the occasional mistake," he said. "And this was a relatively small one, given how quickly you righted it."

Angelique whipped her head up to gawk at her teacher—for in what continent could this be construed as a *small* error? But Evariste had begun moving away, and only his back was visible.

"Come, apprentice," he called. "We should mingle with the guests—it's a chance for you to meet the most powerful nobles in Loire, after all."

Does he approve *of my "error?"* Angelique wondered as she briefly studied his back. *He doesn't know I did it on purpose, does he? If he did, I think he would at least scold me—not even Evariste can be that even tempered.*

Some of her glee subsided at the thought, and Angelique shook her head. *Yes, he can't know. Evariste would never praise me for purposefully failing at a task. Even if the duke deserved it! ... Would he?*

She pushed the thought from her mind and instead fixed a smile on her lips as she glided after her teacher, winking at the maid she passed who was bearing a tray of drinks.

Regardless, with that illusion snipped, I can consider tonight a true triumph!

EVARISTE HAD to speed walk away from his apprentice to keep her unaware of the laughter he was struggling to hold in.

Duke Hubert is such a pompous, self-centered man. She devastated him and shattered that pride without uttering a single threat or harming a single person.

She is incredible!

When he first agreed to the job for Angelique's sake, Evariste dreaded the party. He had seen Duke Hubert before when visiting the Loire royal family in Noyers. He *hoped* Angelique might attempt to teach the man a lesson...but he never imagined the delivery method she would use to do such a thing!

I thought if I hinted before we arrived, she might make a threat or extract some sort of promise from the duke to treat his land better. Instead, she took him to task herself!

It had been a steep gamble on her part. If she had been a graduated enchantress, there would be repercussions. But she was a mere apprentice, and Evariste's reputation wouldn't even rock from the events of this evening.

She is special. He paused long enough to look over his shoulder and smile as she glided after him with the practiced grace of an elf. *Though she might be afraid of her own magic, she's not afraid to stand for what is right. I hope she can keep that spirit—no, I must see that she remains that way. For the good of the continent.*

His reasoning rang hollow even in the privacy of his own mind. Evariste was not nearly delusional enough to think that perhaps he cared a little too much for the well being of his apprentice only for the sake of the continent.

Still, he couldn't find it in himself to care.

She's worth fighting for, worth protecting...and worth waiting for.

Evariste barely kept himself from cringing—for that last thought was a dangerous one. But he didn't retract it, instead he smiled brightly as he chose a noble at random to greet.

"Ahh, Lord Foix. Please allow me to introduce you to my apprentice, Angelique."

The End

OTHER SERIES BY K. M. SHEA

The Snow Queen

Timeless Fairy Tales

The Fairy Tale Enchantress

The Elves of Lessa

Hall of Blood and Mercy

Court of Midnight and Deception

Pack of Dawn and Destiny

King Arthur and Her Knights

Robyn Hood

The Magical Beings' Rehabilitation Center

Second Age of Retha: Written under pen name A. M. Sohma

ADDITIONAL NOVELS

Life Reader

Princess Ahira

A Goose Girl

ABOUT THE AUTHOR

K. M. Shea is a fantasy-romance author who never quite grew out of adventure books or fairy tales, and still searches closets in hopes of stumbling into Narnia. She is addicted to sweet romances, witty characters, and happy endings. She also writes LitRPG and GameLit under the pen name, A. M. Sohma.

Hang out with the K. M. Shea Community at...
kmshea.com

Printed in Great Britain
by Amazon